The Fall of Gods

A Welcome to the Underworld Novel

Book 2

Con Template

Also by Con Template:

Welcome to the Underworld, Book 1
The Fall of Gods, Book 2 of Welcome to the Underworld
The War of Gods, Book 3 of Welcome to the Underworld

Cover Illustration Design by: Dorothy Duong

Dedicated to my Mom and Dad, and the seekers of "Paris."
Thank you for the once-in-a-lifetime inspiration.

ACKNOWLEDGEMENTS

Firstly, the publishing of this book couldn't have been done without the love and support from my family and friends. Thank you to my parents for being my biggest cheerleaders and my inspiration everyday. Thank you to my wonderful sister for not only being my best friend and advisor, but also the biggest advocate of my story. I count my blessings everyday that I have you as my older sister. Thank you to the close circle of friends who I decided to share in my secret pastime. Your support has meant the world to me and I will forever be grateful. Kevin N., there is not a day that goes by where I don't think of you. I'm overjoyed that you enjoyed the first book and I hope you enjoy this one too. Stay strong, stay safe and come home soon, little cousin.

Secondly, thank you to my beta readers: Anita Law, Anna C., Annie Park, Ghetty Hilaire, Jamie Lee, Kim Tong, My-Trinh Nguyen, and Vivian T. Hoang. None of this would've been possible without your dedication and help. Thank you for giving so much time and love to this story. It was an honor to work with all of you. I also want to thank one of my incredible friends, Jocelyn H., for helping to look over the story despite her busy schedule. It's friends like you that makes me wish I shared in my secret pastime sooner. Thank you for everything.

Thirdly, thank you to my graphic artist, Dorothy Duong. There will never be enough words to summarize the appreciation I have for you. You are a gift to have in my life and I thank you for being my rock during this entire journey. Your talent and creativity is simply awe-inspiring and I thank you for gifting the Welcome to the Underworld novels with your talent.

Last and never least, thank you to all my incredible readers for your outpouring of support. I could've never anticipated the first book to garner such love from all of you. It's been an amazing ride so far and you make it so much more worth it everyday. I hope you enjoy this next level of the journey.

CONTENTS

Acknowledgments

"My Illusionist..."

00: Illusionist

"How is she?"

"We dropped her off at the hospital. Dr. Han treated her. From what he told us, she should be fine. Jun is getting ready to drop her off at your apartment now."

"Good," Tae Hyun said quietly. His eyes skimmed over the bodyguards patrolling the garden as he stood above the balcony of Ju Won's mansion. "You and Jae Won get your rest as well. Thank you for all that you've done today and thank you for helping me take care of her."

"It was my pleasure, boss," Kang Min replied. "Have a good night."

As Tae Hyun tucked the phone in his pocket, a whisper came from behind him.

"What you did tonight...was unwise."

Tae Hyun didn't need to take his focus off the view to discern that it was his Advisor, Shin Dong Min, who spoke those words to him.

"I know," he said without taking his eyes off a particular red rose in the garden.

Dong Min came and stood beside him. His voice grew sterner. "It is unlike you."

"I know."

"There is a whole society waiting for you to be crowned Lord of the Underworld. You are too close to becoming a true God in this world to make mistakes now."

Again, Tae Hyun did not shift his sight from the red rose. "I am aware of that."

"She cannot be your mistake."

Tae Hyun laughed. He finally withdrew his gaze from the world below and settled his full attention on his Advisor. He smiled at Dong Min in amusement. "You think I fought for all these years only to fall from the throne because of a girl?"

"Did you not learn anything from the meeting room?" Dong Min asked firmly. "She is not just a girl. She—"

"I will not fall from grace because of her," Tae Hyun interrupted coolly. His voice did not waver when he stated this. "I have fought for too long to lose my throne now."

"What is your plan with her then?"

He kept his gaze leveled on his Advisor. "She is not leaving my side any time soon if that's what you're asking."

Dong Min shook his head, irritation seeping into his eyes. Despite his bloody appearance from the recent initiation of Choi Yoori, he still exuded nothing short of power as he chastised Tae Hyun. "You really have heard nothing."

"She is not a threat to me."

"Not yet."

Tae Hyun laughed again. It was evident he wasn't taking the concern his Advisor was expressing to heart. "She will not be my downfall."

Dong Min smirked, accepting this reply. "You told me that there was a reason why you brought her into this world—why you chose her. The Underworld is waiting with bated breath. Whatever your plan with her is…make sure to be careful and make sure that it all goes according to plan."

"Of course." Tae Hyun smiled before moving away from the balcony. He gave Dong Min a respectful nod. "Now if you'll excuse me, I have to get back to her."

"Tae Hyun," Dong Min called after him.

Tae Hyun turned just before he stepped off the balcony and back into Ju Won's mansion.

"She is not a threat now," Dong Min ominously forewarned, the icy wind billowing around him. "But what if she becomes a threat in the future? What would be your ingenious plan then?"

"If that's the case, then she will be taken care of," Tae Hyun said without thought, without hesitation. "No one threatens my throne—no one threatens my power over this world. I brought her into this world…I can easily take her out of it."

"Will you take me into a world filled with timeless magic?"

01: The Disappearance of Gods

"Choi Yoori…"

Ignoring the call of the soothing voice, a sleeping Yoori just mumbled incoherently as she nuzzled her left cheek into her pillow.

She was too comfortable.

She didn't want to wake up.

She smacked her lips together. Yoori was ready to drift back into the land of dreams when the warmth of the soothing voice glided over her senses again. This time, it tickled along her right ear, gently pulling her out of her slumber.

"*Choi Yoori…*"

Awakened by the butterflies that had begun to flutter in her stomach, Yoori gradually lifted her eyelids. Although blurry at first, her vision soon cleared once it acclimated with the morning light.

"What time is it?" she whispered sluggishly.

Her eyes snagged on Kwon Tae Hyun, the crime lord boss who was also the notorious King of Serpents, one of the country's most powerful men. She had met him while working as a waitress at Lee's Diner. Through a spell of bad luck, she not only spilled coffee on him, but because of this infraction, he had also blackmailed her into being his personal assistant. Needless to say, she was far from being a respectful assistant with all the constant bickering between them, but the only deal was that she would be his assistant—not necessarily a compliant one.

Tae Hyun was sitting across from her, dressed in a white half-buttoned up shirt topped off with a black jacket and black jeans. With one leg propped up, left hand resting on his knee and his back leaning against the bed frame, Tae Hyun couldn't have appeared more like an enticing aphrodisiac as he sat there with the glory of the morning sun shining down on him.

Did she also mention that her boss, as insufferably hotheaded as he may be, was also one of the most gorgeous men she had ever laid eyes on? Not that she liked him that way or anything.

Though it was early, Yoori surmised that he must've looked a bit more alluring than usual because the rays of the morning sun had touched him at the perfect angle.

It's just the special effects, Yoori reminded herself, wanting to justify why she found Tae Hyun to be so sexy this fine morning. It was the special effects and the simple fact that she was assaulted the night prior during her five-minute initiation with the Advisors, the Underworld's most influential and feared mentors. She probably got hit too hard in the head and was still reeling from the aftereffects of it.

That must be why she was so enthralled by Tae Hyun. It was definitely not because she had a small crush on him, and it was definitely not because she wanted to pounce on him. She was just sleepy and confused.

While she contemplated to herself, Tae Hyun began to smile amusingly at Yoori. He took note that her lethargic eyes were checking him out. Feigning ignorance to that little detail, he chose to merely answer her question instead.

"Time for Sleeping Beauty to wake up." He sounded innocent enough, but Yoori knew better. She knew that Tae Hyun was saying it to taunt her. Who in their right mind would call her a "Sleeping Beauty"?

"Oh God..." Yoori replied in dread.

Sexy Tae Hyun had transformed into teasing Tae Hyun. She rolled her eyes at his mocking statement. The butterflies in her stomach vanished into oblivion. She didn't need a mirror to tell her that she was anything but a "Sleeping Beauty." Her bruised face and swollen eyes were anything but attractive. When taking into account that her hair resembled that of a bird's nest, it was more than enough to convince her that Tae Hyun was purposely trying to make her feel bad about herself.

"*Very funny*," she muttered bitterly, instinctively burying her face a little further into the pillow so Tae Hyun wouldn't be able to get a good look at her swollen eyes. She didn't want him to know that she had been crying after her "initiation" into the Underworld.

Tae Hyun scrunched his brows together. "What? You think I was joking when I said that?"

Yoori continued to roll her eyes, burying herself a little bit deeper into the pillow. "Whatever," she grumbled dismissively.

Tae Hyun shook his head, disapproving of her assumption that he was taunting her. He said no more of the subject and detoured on to another topic—a seemingly more pleasant one that brought playful warmth to his eyes.

"I have a surprise for you," he announced enthusiastically, reaching his hand out to help tuck her loose bangs behind her ear. His smile was uncontainable as he said this. He looked just like a kid who was excited to go to a candy shop.

"What is it?" she mumbled suspiciously. Though she instinctively stilled after his fingers grazed her skin, Yoori's eyes were still on him.

He withdrew his hand. "We're going to go on a company retreat."

Tae Hyun's alluring smile grew just a bit more when he shared this spontaneous information with Yoori.

It was probably because the rays of the morning sun were hitting him at the right angle, but for Yoori, Tae Hyun couldn't look more genuine with his

10

eagerness while he sat there like a damn angel. He was acting especially odd this morning and she couldn't put her finger on why he was acting so strangely. Whatever the case, she was intrigued.

"Company retreat?" Her lips were already lifting away from the pillow in interest. "Like us and the entire gang?"

Tae Hyun gave her a "what-the-hell-have-you-been-smoking" look and shook his head. He inched closer to her. "Just us."

She gaped at him, unable to hide her bewilderment. This was all so sudden. Did he just decide all of this last night or something?

"Why?"

He shrugged indifferently. "I think it'll be good if I took you away from here for a couple of days. It'll be a good distraction." His eyes trailed subtly on to her face when he said this. She knew then that he was staring at the cut and bruise near her lips.

Quickly catching on to his motives for wanting to take her away, Yoori called him out on it. "You know, you don't have to feel guilty about what happened. I mean…it was my own fault for insisting on seeing the Advisors when you told me not to."

Jae Won and Kang Min, the two bodyguards Tae Hyun assigned to her, were held captive by the eldest Advisor, Seo Ju Won. Ju Won had essentially told Tae Hyun that the only way he would release Jae Won and Kang Min was if he met Yoori. Against Tae Hyun's wishes, Yoori insisted on going because she wanted to save them. She had her bruises to show for her decision. The Advisors, being the sadistic people that they were, decided to give her a five-minute initiation to "welcome" her into the Underworld. She was still reeling from their warm welcoming.

"It has nothing to do with that," he assured, though his eyes told a different story. He sighed with dramatic boredom and craned his neck upward. He stared at the ceiling with tired eyes. "I'm just a little bit sick of Seoul right now. I just want to get out of here and go breathe some fresh air."

"Where are we going?"

"I have a lake house. It's about five hours out of the city. It's secluded and very scenic. I haven't been there in a while and I feel like going again. It'll be nice. You'll like it there," he said confidently before quickly adding, "Plus, there's ducks."

Yoori furrowed her brows. "Why would *that* be a deciding factor for me?"

He scoffed defensively, taken aback by her less than graceful reaction to the breadwinner he was using as his persuasion. "I don't know. Don't girls *like* ducks?"

Yoori scoffed at his generalizing assumption. "I like to *eat* them."

He frowned. "Well, there's ducks frolicking around my lake house and I think that should be the final deciding factor to make you jump out of bed. I thought you'd be one of those girls who actually adore the cuteness of ducks. Either way, you can 'ooh and ah' at them or chase after them with my gun. I could care less. All I care is that you go. "

His voice was so decided with bitterness that Yoori couldn't help but laugh in amusement. She shook her head in between laughs. "Um...I don't know," she answered honestly. She was already beginning to feel the aches in her body now that she was awake again. "I'm really tired. I kinda just want to lay in bed all day."

"You don't want to get away from the Underworld for a couple of days?"

She paused when she heard something she liked. Get away from the Underworld for a couple of days? Well, that actually sounded really appealing...

An impatient Tae Hyun took her silence as a response. "You can sleep in the car. Now hurry up and get ready." He pulled the comforter off of her to get her moving faster. "I want to get there by sunset."

Yoori flinched at the bout of cold that encased her once her haven of warmth was ruthlessly taken away. She inwardly groaned. She was still feeling so lazy. She decided to look for an excuse to stay in bed longer.

"But my hands are still filled with—wait a second!" She stopped her sentence midway when she observed that there were no more splinters in her hand.

She gasped, sitting up.

She gaped at her hand and then at Tae Hyun. He was gazing at her expectantly. It was gut instinct on her part, but she knew the disappearance of the splinters and Tae Hyun coincided together.

"Did *you* get rid of the splinters?" She didn't wait for him to answer. She already knew it was him. "How on earth did you do it without me knowing?"

She was impressed, very impressed and simultaneously intrigued.

Anticipating his answer to be a thought-provoking one, Yoori found herself disappointed when all he did was smile slyly and said, "Magic."

She grimaced at his nonsensical answer. "Oh, so you're an illusionist now?"

He shrugged with a smile, his impatience exuding out of him like the warm rays spilling into the bedroom. "Yes and if you keep stalling, the next things I'll make disappear are your clothes. And trust me, if those disappear, you can bet your pretty little butt that I'm not letting you leave this bed. Now go get ready before I decide to bond with you in our bedroom instead."

When all Yoori did was stare at him to challenge his bluff, Tae Hyun suddenly made a move to grab her. Albeit all he did was lower his propped up leg and dropped his hand closer to her, it was enough to scare Yoori off the bed.

"Okay, okay!" she shouted, running into the bathroom. "I'll get ready!"

"Twenty minutes! If you're not ready by then, I'm coming in to help you move along!" he added, suppressing his laughter when he heard Yoori yelp in fear at his threat.

■ ■ ■

"Are we there yet?" Yoori asked for the umpteenth time. She finished the statement with a prolonged yawn.

For the past couple of hours since they had been in the car, much to Tae Hyun's continual insistence, Yoori had been sleeping. At first she combated that proposition, feeling guilty that she would be able to rest while Tae Hyun would be bored while driving alone. But when he hurled a warm, lavender throw blanket in her direction, her guilt was history. With the sound of the wind gliding itself along the surface of Tae Hyun's black Mercedes convertible as her lullaby, Yoori conked out without a moment's notice.

As she tried to readjust her sleeping position against the leather recliner, she felt cool air against her cheeks. The draft of cold wind was a gentle one. It was the kind where you could smell the fresh air and the misty water. The sensation was a pleasant one for Yoori. It felt like she was being pleasantly tickled into waking up. Unable to keep her eyes closed, Yoori lifted her eyelids to see that Tae Hyun had lowered the roof of the car down. It was apparently his subtle way of awakening her.

"We're here, Sleeping Beauty," Tae Hyun announced, smiling at her once she was fully awake.

He laughed when he noticed that Yoori was still blinking her drowsiness away.

Yoori frowned. She knew right away he couldn't be laughing at anyone but her. Was it her fault that she couldn't properly open her sluggish eyes after a long sleep?

Jerk-face, she sourly muttered in her head.

She rubbed her eyes to wake up more fully. Yoori's vision gradually adjusted to the scenic world around her. She wrapped the blanket tighter around her body and gawked at the glory of Mother Nature's handiwork.

She was lost in awe.

The road that they were driving on was a windy and deserted one. Constructed tactically in the heart of the mountains, it did well to blend itself within the sanctity of the nature around it. Gold leaves danced around the car as magnificent trees stood in the acres of green field beside the road.

Yoori suspected then that Tae Hyun had woken her up because he didn't want her to miss the breathtaking view. The curve of a thankful smile took form on her lips. If it was Tae Hyun's mission to bring some warmth into her life by helping her forget about the shadows of the Underworld, then he more than succeeded.

She couldn't be more happy and distracted.

Yoori gasped in amazement when the contours of the road turned into a straight and narrow pathway. Her astonished eyes reflected a majestic lake that glistened in the wake of the late afternoon sun. The sun hovered beautifully above it, the touch of its golden rays gracing over the surface of the water.

Yoori raised her brows in curiosity when she heard soft quacking sounds in the distance. She took her awestruck eyes off the lake and directed her attention to the side of the road.

"Look!" She giggled, moving closer to Tae Hyun's seat. She was unable to hide her enthusiasm. She pointed at a family of five waddling ducks, which consisted of a mother and four ducklings that were trailing along their slow moving car. "Aw! How cute!"

Tae Hyun laughed disbelievingly, thoroughly surprised by her cheerful demeanor.

"I guess we're not shooting ducks this weekend," he observed lightheartedly. He continued to drive down the narrow pathway of the road. A soft smile graced his countenance when he took a quick look around. He, too, was amazed with the world around them.

"Isn't it amazing here?" he said with a sigh of relief. His short black hair ruffled against the wind. He took in a deep breath. "*Ah…*" he exhaled slowly, following it up with a relaxed smile

Yoori nodded, lost in the scenic view of Tae Hyun being enveloped in the light of the sunset instead of the town she was being driven through. She already felt more at peace.

Catching herself before she grew lost in a stupor, she said, "It's hard to believe that winter began last night." She sighed, inhaling another lungful of fresh air. "The weather is so perfect here."

She stared up at the near horizon. Its magnificent gold and orange hues enveloped the vast lake and acres of land beside it.

"You know why the weather is perfect right now?" Tae Hyun asked playfully, the glow of the sunset's rays resting over the exposed area of his chest. He had left a few buttons undone on his white-sleeved shirt, and it seemed to Yoori that the sun was trying to trick her into blatantly staring at it.

She made sure her eyes were firmly glued onto his face instead of the slightly unclothed part of his body when she happily answered, "Because we're here!"

Tae Hyun chuckled, shrugging as he drove. "Well, I was actually going to say because *I'm* here, but sure, I suppose you can include yourself and get the credit too."

She wasn't sure if he was joking, but she decided to play along anyway.

"Oh how considerate of you, my dear crime lord boss," Yoori voiced sweetly, placing a dramatic hand over her heart. She laughed again before taking another survey of the scenery. "Honestly though, it's beautiful here. We should have more company retreats like this."

Tae Hyun laughed. The tentative look in his eyes gave the impression that he wanted to see how this trial basis with Yoori went before promising to come again. "Let's see how this one goes before we get ahead of ourselves."

They soon found themselves driving down a windy path that eventually led them into the depths of a secluded lake house community. All the lake house properties were laid far enough away from each other to give the owners a sense of privacy.

As countless glimpses of magnificent looking lake houses greeted her, Yoori couldn't help but widen her eyes and stare in absolute awe when they finally reached their destination—Tae Hyun's lake house.

It was hidden in the furthest end of the street. The tall trees that lingered around it not only complimented the wooden structure of the house, but also shrouded the house from immediate view. Golden autumn leaves layered its roof and covered its gargantuan lawn. Even the attached glass lamps that hung from the various corners of its exterior made the house appear more whimsical. In this moment, Tae Hyun's two-story lake house couldn't have appeared more picturesque for Yoori. She loved how it just stood out in the presence of the setting sun.

"This. Is. Gorgeous," Yoori emphasized, limping through the dark brown oak doors that led into the spacious lake house. Her body was still sore from her initiation, but the pain was tolerable, most likely due to the fact that she was distracted with the exquisiteness of the lake house.

Unlike the modern affluence that Tae Hyun's apartment contained, the interior decoration within the lake house was simple yet beautiful. It had a large living room and kitchen that were both lined with various black furniture and appliances. There was a section of the house that had glass windows for walls. A flight of glass stairs was present in the furthest right hand corner of the house, leading up to the second floor.

No longer able to hold her excitement in, Yoori gasped and threw her black suitcase to the floor. She rushed over to the massive floor-to-ceiling windows that displayed the view of the gorgeous lake. Outside the window stood a wooden, half moon balcony that had circular lanterns hanging from the wooden railing as decorations.

She smiled absently at the flocks of ducks and geese gliding across the lake. The lake's glistening surface now twinkled with dashes of pink, orange, and gold from the setting sun. The whole atmosphere made her feel like she was luxuriating in the splendor of a picturesque dream.

"How could you ever leave this place?" Yoori asked when Tae Hyun stood beside her.

He was also enjoying the beauty of the tranquil world before him.

"I ask myself that every time I come out here," he replied quietly, returning his gaze to her. "Anyway, let's go get some food." He casually intertwined his fingers with hers, promptly pulling her with him. "There's a park nearby. If we're lucky, we might actually have some fun there."

Yoori nodded, allowing herself to get swept away by Tae Hyun.

The peaceful world around them was probably what set them both at ease, but at that moment, Yoori knew she was going to have an unforgettable weekend with Tae Hyun.

"Are you willing to disappear?"

02: To Find Paris

"So, what made you bring me here?" Yoori asked while they walked side by side.

The peaceful night's sky hung above them, displaying a view of the moon and the twinkling stars. An assortment of statues, water fountains, and rose gardens occupied the park, giving entertainment to Yoori's eyes. She happily feasted on her second corndog and explored the area with Tae Hyun.

The park was livelier than Yoori had anticipated. It was late at night, but there were still people roaming about. Though it was mainly filled with couples walking hand in hand, it was still relatively lively. There was a certain air of peace that came with the companionable silence. All the couples were lost in their own little worlds and Tae Hyun and Yoori were no exception.

"I told you," he said softly. "I figured you could use a break from Seoul." He took one final bite of his corndog and shrugged. "And I guess I figured I could use a break from Seoul too."

Though his voice was casual, Yoori deduced that there was more to his answer – a more specific reason as to why he brought her here. She knew what it was; she'd be a fool if she couldn't figure it out by now.

"You knew I cried last night, huh?" Her voice was low with shame. She was upset with herself for being unable to do a better job of hiding her weakness. Yoori rarely cried. To date, she only remembered crying twice in her life after her amnesia. Once after her family's death and once after she accepted the possibility that she was An Soo Jin, an infamous Underworld crime lord who died three years prior, the exact same time Yoori woke up with amnesia. She always had reservations about crying in front of people, and would only ever allow herself to do it when she was sure no one else was around her. She was fairly certain that she forced herself to stop crying when she fell asleep. She must've continued to involuntarily cry in her sleep. The thought of Tae Hyun walking in and seeing the tears flow down her cheeks made her cringe. She truly hated it when people saw her cry.

Though Tae Hyun didn't verbally answer her question, Yoori intuitively knew that she was right. The way his eyes became gentler when he gazed at hers more than gave away the truth.

"I'm sorry that you had to go through all of that," he finally uttered, his eyes staring at the endless brick pathway ahead. His voice was no longer nonchalant. It teemed with guilt and regret.

"You know it wasn't your fault, right?" She peered up at his profile. "What happened wasn't your fault. I didn't cry because of the violence from the initiation. I was just..." She paused to find the right words. "I was just going through some internal struggles."

Again, he didn't say anything. He seemed lost in his own thoughts.

After a minute or two, as a gust of wind drifted past them, he finally turned to her and proudly said, "I yelled at them for you."

His voice was optimistic. It was clear he hoped that hearing this would make her feel better. He didn't seem to believe that she would cry about anything else other than the violence from the initiation.

Yoori laughed wryly. She didn't feel compelled to keep convincing him that her tears were due to her own issues (like the fact that there was a big possibility she was a monster she didn't want to become). However, she had to admit that she did feel better when a mental image of Tae Hyun screaming at the three Advisors popped into her head. She didn't doubt that he did it. Tae Hyun's temper always had a way of getting the better of him, even under unfavorable circumstances.

"I'm sure you did. What was their reaction?"

"Same political suck up shit," he answered after a sigh. "They congratulated me for picking such a strong and beautiful girlfriend."

Yoori nodded. Of course the Advisors were quick to suck up to Tae Hyun after the initiation.

"They also said that I should watch out for you."

Tires screeched in Yoori's mind.

"Excuse me?" she sputtered, even though she had already heard him clearly.

"They said that I shouldn't trust you," he repeated. His eyes were unreadable when they gazed at her. "They emphasized that if I did, it would be the biggest mistake of my life."

"What?" she practically shouted. Bewilderment blared within her. "Why the hell would they say that?" Soon after she asked, she knew it had everything to do with An Soo Jin. The audacity of them infuriated her. How dare they say such things? The nerve of those old bastards.

"Because they're the Advisors," he voiced jadedly. He wasn't the least bit surprised with how the Advisors operated. "It is in their nature to give advice, no matter how ridiculous it sounds." He smirked. "It is also in Ju Won's nature to pit people against each other. Rival crime lords, siblings, fathers and sons—even boyfriends and girlfriends."

"He *does* like to do that, doesn't he?" Yoori asked resentfully. She recalled the "pearl of wisdom" he gave her about Tae Hyun and Lee Ji Hoon, the reigning King of Skulls, An Soo Jin's boyfriend and Yoori's current suitor. Ju Won shared how ruthless they were and that they would do anything to obtain the Underworld throne. He essentially told her that she shouldn't be afraid of being as ruthless as they were when it came to getting what she wanted. She also recalled the way he always set Tae Hyun and Ji Hoon against each other. Ju Won was truly a master manipulator.

"He enjoys being entertained," Tae Hyun provided, casually grabbing Yoori's hand. He led her off the brick pathway and onto a grassy area.

As the gentle wind rustled the leaves around them, Yoori replayed the events of the prior night in her mind. She wrinkled her brows when she was reminded of something significant

"So what did you and Ji Hoon do during my initiation?" Yoori inquired. She was curious as to what could've taken place on the other side of the door while she was getting her ass whooped in the meeting room.

She heedlessly jumped onto the dock. As they strolled down the wooden structure, the lake around them reflected the moon and the radiant stars.

"Talked about someone whose name rhymes with 'Oogly,'" Tae Hyun answered with a smile.

Yoori stopped in her tracks and glared at Tae Hyun. She was not amused with the unexpected teasing.

Tae Hyun laughed heartily and wrapped his hand around her waist. He easily pulled her along with him when they neared the end of the dock.

"I told him that you're my girlfriend," he shared, his expression smug. "That no matter what he says, what he does, and what he schemes, you'll always be my girlfriend and I'll always have your heart."

Yoori gaped at him owl-eyed. "Why would you say that?" she exclaimed incredulously, "None of that is true!"

"I like to say what's on my mind," Tae Hyun replied, sounding unapologetic. He was distracted after they reached the end of the dock.

He bent his knees and situated himself on the wooden foundation with his legs crossed. He placed his corndog stick beside him. Once he was settled, he gazed expectantly at Yoori. His brown eyes somehow appeared more captivating under the stars.

Following his lead, she took her oversized white purse off her shoulder and bent her knees to sit beside him. Her jeans and the hem of her white faux fur jacket made contact with the wooden structure. She placed her corndog stick down and laid her purse on the floor. Seconds later, she proudly pulled out the lavender blanket Tae Hyun gave her.

"Plus, how do you know it's not true?" Tae Hyun continued to counteract. As he said this, he flicked a small pile of pebbles away from her jeans and into the lake. The pebbles made a soft splash in the water, its ripples causing the reflection of the moon to flicker for a couple of seconds. "I was the one that said it. Not you."

"Because I know you were only saying it to piss Ji Hoon off," Yoori replied swiftly, unfolding the blanket. "You can be deviously competitive like that."

"You'd be surprised," Tae Hyun muttered under his breath. He clapped his hands together to shake the loose dirt off, essentially clouding the vocalization of his answer.

"What was that?" Yoori asked distractedly, not catching the last comment as she offered Tae Hyun half of the blanket.

"I said the moon is huge tonight," Tae Hyun said quickly, drawing his eyes down to meet Yoori's gaze. He then paused and gaped defiantly at the blanket she was offering him. He shook his head, gawking at Yoori's lavender blanket like it was a fabric contaminated with the plague. "No way would I be caught dead covering that over me."

Yoori grimaced at his childish antics. "Stop being so stubborn. I know you're cold. I know I am." Yes, even under the warm confines of her faux fur jacket, Yoori was still shivering.

Tae Hyun snorted, recalling all the times he had to keep her warm. "Nothing new there."

Yoori scowled, her eyes growing wide with the fires of hell inside it. She had lost her patience with him. "Hey! You better take half of it! Who do you think will have to slave around and take care of you if you get sick?"

Tae Hyun continued to shake his head, his eyes set on the quiet lake beneath them. He wasn't listening. "Just keep yourself warm."

Yoori deduced then that Tae Hyun only refused because he didn't want to chance her getting sick. He was looking out for her. She shook her head in awe.

What a thoughtful jerk.

She sighed at his abnormal way of being nice and took it upon herself to scoot closer to him. Sometimes you just have to force things on people and that was what she did. She threw half of the blanket over his back. She smiled proudly and wrapped the other half around herself.

"You're welcome," she said smugly, pulling the end of his half and her half closer together so that they were almost completely covered.

"Okay, smart one," Tae Hyun stated dryly. "Now we both have a fifty-fifty chance of getting sick. Good going. Who the hell is going to take care of who when the plague arrives?"

"Shut up and enjoy the warmth, you cynically considerate person."

"Just so you know, you're sleeping outside with the ducks if you get sick."

"Oh really? I was under the impression that I've been sleeping with a duck already," Yoori said innocently, fluttering her eyelashes at Tae Hyun.

He slowly turned to glare at her when he caught on to what she was insinuating.

Yoori laughed when she saw his appalled face.

Tae Hyun shook his head again and turned away from her with a hidden smile warming his face. "Oh you're lucky I feel like letting you win tonight."

"Whatever," Yoori said happily, satisfied with winning by default.

A brief moment of silence cascaded upon them as they enjoyed the view of the world around them.

"This place is so beautiful," Yoori voiced breathlessly, staring off into the vastness of the glistening lake and twinkling sky.

"It *is* a beautiful sight, isn't it?" Tae Hyun asked, his eyes on Yoori instead of the view before him.

Yoori nodded mindlessly, oblivious to his appreciating stare directed toward her.

She craned her neck upward. Her eyes reflected the moonlit sky. Mumbling to herself, she attempted to count the endless amount of jewels that inhabited the dark canvas above her. She knew her efforts were futile. It seemed like a new star was born every second she spent looking at the sky while attempting a hopeless task. She sighed to herself when an overwhelming realization came upon her. The whole world suddenly appeared so big and vast.

"Doesn't being in the presence of all of this make you feel like you're just a speck in the world?" Yoori asked wondrously, her eyes now reflecting the distant horizon.

"Like your problems can seem so small in light of the greatness that is the world around us," Tae Hyun uttered, understanding what Yoori was talking about. He was also gazing outward at the night's horizon in awe.

Yoori smiled and nodded. She relished in the night's cool breeze, her heart feeling light. It had been so long since she felt this carefree in light of all that had happened.

"I have a question for you," said Tae Hyun intriguingly, focusing his gaze on Yoori.

Yoori turned sideways to face him. She caught the glint in his eyes and eyed him suspiciously. "Shoot," she said cautiously, wondering if he was going to start with his teasing insults again. She was ready to respond accordingly if need be.

"If you could be anywhere right now...where would you be?"

Yoori inspected his question for double meanings. When she concluded that it was a safe and innocent question, she thought about the answer. She smiled shyly. Her eyes returned to the peaceful waters. "You'll laugh at me."

"Yes, I probably will. But what else is new?"

Yoori turned and smacked him on his shoulder disbelievingly. "You're suppose to say, 'I promise I won't!'"

"I don't make promises I don't intend to keep," Tae Hyun stated as though everyone had the same conviction as him. "Now answer the question."

She bequeathed him one final, bitter glare before giving in. "Anywhere?"

"Anywhere."

Yoori smiled to herself. "You better hold on to the dock. I'm about to give you a mind-blowing answer."

Tae Hyun laughed, nodding knowingly. "Oh, I'm sure."

"Okay. I want to go to Pari—"

"Paris," Tae Hyun finished with her.

Tae Hyun's laugh grew warmer as Yoori blushed. "You're right, Choi Yoori. I've definitely *never* heard that mind-blowing answer flow out of a girl's lips before." He shook his head and continued to smile to himself.

Yoori shrugged lightheartedly. She was unapologetic for her generic answer. "Hey, I can't help but be honest—"

"I could take you," Tae Hyun suddenly interjected, his moonlit eyes falling onto her. There was no sign of teasing in his voice. He was serious.

Huh?

Yoori shook her head upon absorbing his words. She didn't hesitate to refuse his offer. "But you can't take me."

The smile on Tae Hyun's lips faded slightly. "Why not?"

"I'm saving the honor of seeking Paris for my future soul mate," she answered with conviction, smiling to herself as she daydreamed about the future when this would occur. Lost in her fantasy world like a hopeless romantic, she was oblivious to any change in Tae Hyun's countenance.

At her enigmatic answer, the faded smile on his lips lit up with amusement. There was newfound curiosity in his voice. "There's an honor that goes along with taking you to Paris?"

Yoori nodded, secretly glad that he asked because she wanted to share her thoughts.

"Paris is the city of love," she began whimsically, a pair of twinkles illuminating her big brown eyes. "You can't go to Paris unless you're madly in love with the person who is taking you. And not just the type of love where you tell one another that you can't live without each other. No...not *that* type of love. But the type of love that is unconditional—the type that is undying. You know...the type that can withstand anything...one of those once—"

"Once-in-a-lifetime love," Tae Hyun instinctively finished for her.

Yoori nodded happily, proud that he read her mind. That was her exact definition.

Tae Hyun's eyes lit up in interest. It was as if he was beginning to see her in a brand new light. "So that's what Paris represents to you? A place where you can only go with a 'once-in-a-lifetime love'?"

Yoori nodded. "That's why you can't take me...because we're not in love. Well, at least not the first trip anyway...because that's like reserved. But you can take me anytime after I go with my soul mate," she added teasingly, playfully pushing Tae Hyun's shoulder with her own. Fulfilling her hopeless romantic desires aside, who would say no to a free trip to Paris?

Tae Hyun nodded, laughing heartily.

"Have you ever been in love, Choi Yoori?" he suddenly asked. His voice did not hide his overwhelming curiosity.

She shook her head, her lips pouting. "That's why I have silly expectations. I've never experienced anything close to it. I just reason that since I haven't found anyone, I might as well just wait for that one perfect guy to come along, you know? So I don't have to deal with bullshit. But then again, waiting for that perfect guy is easier said than done. But a girl can dream, right?"

She paused, looking nowhere in particular as she gathered her thoughts. "I imagine falling in love must be nice though, since the whole world frets about it." She smiled sheepishly at Tae Hyun. "How about yourself?"

He shook his head, almost too quickly. "The concept of love and Paris doesn't exist in the Underworld nor should it be sought. I've never experienced it, never been close to experiencing it, and I personally don't even want to experience it. Essentially, 'seeking Paris' would be a crime lord's worst mistake. The Underworld will eat him alive if he does." He smiled bitterly at himself. "The only thing that exists in the Underworld is the war for power. You can't allow yourself to be distracted with anything else."

Hearing the bitterness in his voice while he explained the rules of the Underworld to her, it seemed as if he was reminding himself of that fact rather than educating Yoori.

Yoori's smile dropped. She couldn't help but feel disappointed with his answer. "So you just plan on being consumed with the shadows of the Underworld?"

"I plan on keeping myself alive and becoming the most powerful figure in the Underworld," he corrected. "Everything else is secondary to that goal."

Yoori nodded weakly, finding it challenging to ignore the discontent in her heart. Tae Hyun always struck her as the type of guy who had always been inherently "good"—it was just that he got caught up in some bad dealings. This was probably why she was always so protective and caring toward him. It was disappointing to hear him be so dismissive to such a normal—and she believed necessary—human desire.

Tae Hyun gave her a small smile. It was his way of trying to lighten the tension forming between them when he caught the disapproving spark in Yoori's eyes.

"You'll tell me what it feels like, right? When you find Paris?" His voice was hopeful—bittersweet even.

Yoori gave him a sad smile. Her heart was still hopeful that Tae Hyun would someday escape from the shadows of the Underworld and find someone who would change him for the better.

"I know you're not seeking Paris…but things might change in the future and you might happen upon it without having to look for it." Her sad smile turned into a genuine one. "How about we both make a pact to let the other know when Paris has been found?"

They were no longer talking about the city itself.

Tae Hyun took a moment to think about the proposition. When it seemed like he would decline, he suddenly agreed and said, "Sounds like a plan."

Yoori nodded in approval. A comfortable silence passed between them. The air had since gotten warmer for her. Satisfied with his concurrence, she pulled up her bent knees, folded her arms over them, and rested her chin on her crisscrossed arms. Her eyelids were starting to feel heavy.

"You're sleepy already?" Tae Hyun asked quietly, watching as her eyelids slowly closed.

"No..." she muttered, shaking her head weakly. "I'm just resting my eyes..."

Though the day wasn't as strenuous for Yoori, she was still recovering from the night prior. It seemed as though the fatigue was catching up with her. Her body was shutting down, needing rest to recuperate. A few minutes later, she was beginning to doze off.

Tae Hyun shook his head while smiling gently at Yoori. His amused eyes took note that Yoori was about to fall into the land of dreams.

An idea suddenly came to him. He knew this was the opportune time to ask Yoori something she would otherwise avoid answering in her conscious state.

"What's your one wish tonight, Yoori?" he whispered softly, purposely keeping his voice low so she didn't wake up entirely.

Yoori was silent for several breaths, and Tae Hyun thought she had already fallen asleep. A few seconds later, she replied in such a low voice that he wouldn't have heard her had he not been paying close attention.

"...I want us to both find Paris," Yoori answered as she slowly drifted into unconsciousness.

"What would be *your* one wish?" she managed to mutter out before she was finally gone to the world.

It was underneath the tranquility of the night's sky and at the warmth of being beside Tae Hyun that Yoori fell asleep before she ever had the chance to hear Tae Hyun's answer.

"Will you disappear with me?"

03: Boomerangs

"I knew I shouldn't have eaten that second corndog you offered me."

"Are we seriously going at this again?" Tae Hyun asked breathlessly as he ran out of the lake house with a furious Yoori trailing right behind him.

Leave it to Tae Hyun and Yoori to spend a perfectly nice day sightseeing around town and ending it with a dinner conversation that erupted in a big argument.

The conversation started out pleasant enough. They were sitting at an Italian restaurant, waiting for their dinner when Tae Hyun informed Yoori that she fell asleep while they were sitting on the dock. She figured that much. He said that since he didn't want to wake her, he took the liberty of carrying her home. At this realization, Yoori nodded, blushed and thanked him for being so chivalrous. The pleasantries ended when their Italian dishes arrived and Tae Hyun made an off-handed comment about how sore his arms were. That was when all hell broke loose.

"You started it when you insinuated that I was fat!" Yoori argued, rushing to catch up after they descended down a slope of grassy hills. "I may have gained about six pounds since I've met you, but that gives you no right to make fun of me, you in-shape person. No one asked you to carry me home. You could've just woken me up!"

"I didn't insinuate that you were fat," Tae Hyun argued back, his voice expressing his aggravation. "All I said was that my arms hurt. It was you who misunderstood and blew things out of proportion."

Turning around, he mindlessly reached his hand out to help Yoori when he saw her struggling to race down the hills. She took his hand without a moment's hesitation.

A teasing grin overtook his face once Yoori was safely balanced on the flat grassland. "And only six pounds? Wow. That definitely means I have to feed you more."

Yoori scoffed at his last comment, thinking it was another one of his insults.

"Nice outdoor shoes by the way," he added, glancing down at her flip-flops before releasing her from his grip and walking away.

"Thanks," Yoori replied automatically. She paused when she registered that his comment was actually sarcastic. Before she had a chance to yell at him for being rude, he had already begun to disappear from her sight.

She ran after him. Her toes clasped on to her white flip-flops while her hands held up her long emerald prairie skirt. She struggled to keep up while her long black hair grazed over the fabric of her white tank top.

"Augh, what a jerk," she muttered to herself, almost tripping over when her flip-flops flew off and landed in a small ditch.

When the day began, Tae Hyun gave her something to look forward to when he mentioned a surprise he had planned for later. Since they spent so much time arguing at the restaurant, he was now in a rush to tend to his surprise. Evidently to Yoori, this surprise was time sensitive, hence the acceleration of their legs and the impending heart attack she was about to be doomed with because she was so exhausted.

"Tae Hyun!" she shouted while panting, her lungs begging for her out of shape self to stop overworking it. "Will you please slow down?"

A frustrated Tae Hyun stopped at the sound of her cry. He whirled around and ran back to her. His short-sleeved white shirt and khaki pants glowed in a modest gold tone in response to the setting sun.

Yoori stared wide-eyed when he came closer. "Eh, eh, eh! What are you doing? Not this again!" she shouted, backing away when she realized that Tae Hyun was running toward her with that look in his eyes. It was a look that said: "Well, if you can't hurry up..."

"No, no, no," she whispered. "I'm just kidding! I can walk fast. I can walk – ahh!"

Without uttering a word of warning, Tae Hyun's arms had already slipped behind Yoori's back and underneath her knees. In an instant, he was carrying her again.

"This is fast becoming an annoying trend," Yoori muttered, her eyes forming into annoyed slits.

He laughed and pulled her closer against his body. The scent of his cologne surrounded her. "Trust me, slowpoke. Before the day is over, you're going to wish I never let you go." He finished that statement with a wink and a laugh that tickled every fiber within Yoori's body.

Ignoring the warm current that electrified her, Yoori rolled her eyes at his words. She suddenly pushed at his chest and made an abrupt jump from his arms. As soon as her feet landed on the grass, she looked back at Tae Hyun, stuck her tongue out at him and ran ahead.

"I don't need you to always come to my rescue, Prince Charming," she voiced playfully, pulling up the long hem of her skirt. She picked up speed. "Now hurry up, slowpoke! Show me the surprise before the sun sets!"

Though there was pain shooting up her legs, Yoori refused to show it. Tae Hyun had good intentions, but she was sick of being babied. The stubborn feminist within her had had it. She could take care of herself; she didn't need him coming to her rescue all the time.

Amused with her dramatic display of independence, Tae Hyun merely smiled and laughed. Placing both of his hands in his pockets, he caught up with her. If the expression on his face gave any indication, he was definitely pleased with her behavior.

"Eh, for what it's worth," he began, nudging her occupied arms. "After holding you for a bit, my arms aren't hurting anymore. I think touching you may have healed my pain."

Yoori snorted disbelievingly. Now she knew he was bullshitting her. "That's surprising, seeing that I ate three big plates of lasagna for dinner."

His smile persevered. "I guess my own three plates offset it."

They smiled warmly at one another, the hatchet on their stupid argument burying instantaneously. Side by side, they continued to walk as they neared the bank of the lake. Tae Hyun had his hands in his pockets and Yoori's hands were still holding up her skirt. In the distance, Yoori could hear the ducks splashing around in the water. She could also hear faint sounds of kids screaming in glee as they chased after one another. It was a euphoric sound to her. Everything was so carefree. She felt at peace.

"Tae Hyun..."

"Hmm?"

"Thanks for a really fun day," she voiced quietly, the warm and appreciative tone in her voice as genuine as the sun shining above them. "I really enjoyed myself."

Tae Hyun sighed at her words. "Don't be in such a rush to say your thanks, Choi Yoori. The day is far from over."

Just when Yoori was about to nod in agreement, a white wooden boat distracted her. It sat peacefully on the field of grass ahead of them, beckoning them to use it as the magnificent sun illuminated the soft shine of its paint.

Yoori smiled disbelievingly at Tae Hyun. He had already approached the boat. He began to pick it up and push it into the lake. In the middle of doing this, he grinned and extended his hand out to a mystified Yoori.

She was in love with his surprise.

She shifted her gaze from the boat to Tae Hyun. To her, he had never appeared more otherworldly. His features glowed under the gold/pink hues of the glorious sun, making it appear like the beauty of this world was created for him to inhabit.

Wonderment suspended over her. She assumed that his surprise would have something to do with eating ice cream at the dock or something crazy like shooting ducks with guns. She never anticipated *this*.

It was much more…romantic.

Not that she was complaining of course! It was a nice change to be treated like a princess—especially when her evil boss typically enjoyed spending his time torturing her.

Man oh man. She was a fan of company retreats now.

"I've never been on a boat," she admitted, trying to hide her cheeky smile. She grabbed his hand and sat in the boat. She took a quick glance at her surroundings. She really regretted not bringing a camera to chronicle this moment. It was all so picturesque.

After she was settled, Tae Hyun pushed the rest of the boat off the sleeping grass and onto the calm lake. He hopped in before it drifted off. He had a smirk on his face when he grabbed a wooden paddle. He penetrated the silky lake with his paddle, alternating between sides and stirring the water.

He gazed up at the sunset colored sky and laughed. "I knew I'd have you sailing off into the sunset with me sooner or later," he commented playfully, raising his brows with interest.

"Hah!" she replied with warm sarcasm. "Oh yeah, your constant courting has finally paid off, my dear friend." She took in a deep breath after she ended her spell of laughter. She glanced around the rose colored lake, admiring everything within her circumference. "This is so nice."

It was probably how the rays of the sunset favored him, but when Yoori returned her focus to Tae Hyun (who was also staring off at the lake) she could've sworn she felt her heart skip a beat. She liked how the light, instead of layering over him, somehow radiated over his smooth skin. Yoori couldn't deny it. Kwon Tae Hyun looked damn sexy paddling the boat as he stared off into the distance, his poignant gaze lost in a world of its own.

Everything was okay for a stare-fest—that was until he broke her trance when he averted his eyes back onto her. Noting her awe-like stare on him, he gave her an awkward look.

"What are you thinking about?"

"*You*," she answered mindlessly.

Her eyes bulged when she pried herself out of her unwarranted stupor. Shit!

"I mean—you—you!" She struggled to find a plausible alternative for her blunt and unfiltered answer. *Ahhhh*, she thought. Her panicked mind ran in circles.

She then caught sight of a duck waddling beside them.

A flickering light bulb turned on.

This was definitely not her best alternative, but it was the only one she could think of in her state of panic. She was going to sound so effen stupid—

"You—You—You stupid duck! Go faster! You're in our way!"

"*Quack...*" was all the duck said as its big eyes gaped at a frenzied Yoori. Allowing a couple more soft quacks to escape its beak, it swam away in a panic, obviously terrified of Yoori. Not that she blamed it.

And a stunned silence was all that Tae Hyun said while he gawked at her in bewilderment. He was probably contemplating throwing her psychotic self off the boat. She didn't blame him. She was contemplating it too. This was what she got for mentally admitting that the guy was sexy.

"What the hell was that?" he finally asked, watching the duck disappear into the distance.

"I—I—I was afraid we were going to hurt it," Yoori lied, shaking in her seat. She could see the flickering light bulb self-destructing in her state of awkwardness.

"This isn't a motorboat, assistant," Tae Hyun deadpanned. "We're going .7 miles per hour right now. I could've stopped the boat if you asked me to."

"I—I know..." Yoori responded dimly, already contemplating suicide. She cursed her stupidity.

When he took inventory of the burning humiliation on her cheeks, a sneaky Tae Hyun hid a knowing smile. He pulled the paddle into the boat and proceeded to lay it beside him. Shortly after, he laid himself across the boat.

Suspended in the center of the lake, where different groups of ducks and geese were playing and swimming in the near distance, he casually said, "I can't believe you made yourself look like an idiot because you didn't want me to know you were staring." He smiled shrewdly at Yoori. "You're a real class act, babe."

Yoori clenched her teeth. All this time, he allowed her to act idiotic when he knew? She tried her best to do damage control.

"I—I was not staring," she combated, her cheeks burning at the embarrassing dilemma she found herself in. She went on clumsily. "I was moving my eyes and I stopped on you for a little bit longer than I should. That's not staring. That was just me being lazy with my eyes and— "

Okay, I should stop now, she thought to herself, feeling like a blubbering fool. Oh how she wanted to crawl into a hole and die right now...

Luckily for her, it didn't even appear as if Tae Hyun was really listening anymore.

Laying his head against the foundation of the boat, he gave a sigh of relief after he fully situated himself across the boat. When he was done, he angled his head toward Yoori.

"You're blocking the view," he noted bluntly.

"I'll block your view with my fists if you don't leave me alone," Yoori muttered threateningly. She was resentful that he allowed her to behave like an idiot. She could feel it in her knuckles. She was ready to punch something—Tae Hyun being the primary candidate. Tae Hyun and maybe a couple of ducks.

"Wow," he responded coolly, nonchalantly patting the empty space beside him, a gesture for her to stop arguing and settle beside him. "My precious little assistant is such a thug. *Scary*."

Yoori rolled her eyes. "I'm glad we can find some humor in the success of my initiation." She threw him a dirty look. "And why should I go to you?"

"'Cause you're not sitting in the right angle to get the best view. Now come here before I ask you what you were thinking about *while* you were staring at me."

No! Under no circumstances was she going to share with him that she thought he looked sexy.

Acknowledging that she had been backed into a corner, Yoori gave in before she accidentally blurted out anything else. Throwing up her white flag, a very bitter Yoori carefully moved to the empty space beside Tae Hyun. With one leg outstretched, she sat beside him, her hair ruffling slightly when a gentle wind flew past them.

"Lay down," he directed, flashing his brown eyes up at her. "We can share an equal view of everything this way." When Yoori hesitated, he added, "The sky is about to become more beautiful and you'll only hurt your neck from craning it for too long. Might as well prevent the trouble. It's not like you don't have enough pain rummaging through your body."

It was probably a psychological thing, but when he mentioned the pain in her body, she began to feel the aches in her neck.

"There she goes..." Tae Hyun stated idly, his eyes reflecting the rays of the sunset.

Excited about the beautiful view and convinced that it was only for the good of her body (even though deep down, she knew it was something else), Yoori settled herself beside Tae Hyun and allowed her head to rest on the smooth base of the boat.

Both resting their hands on their stomachs, Yoori and Tae Hyun smiled in awe at the magic of the nature before them. Her perfume and his cologne mixed together while they watched in serene silence. It seemed at that moment, the whole world stopped to stare up at the heavens above as well.

"Do you know what's crazy?" she found herself asking, her attention becoming lost in the skies above.

"What?"

"Do you realize that our whole lives, every decision we've made, all the roads we've chosen—good, bad, big and small—everything has led us to this very moment in time?" Yoori had a tendency to get philosophical when she was outside long enough. The scenic world had that enlightening power over her.

"What a crazy thought," Tae Hyun murmured, his eyes roaming the picturesque sky.

Yoori nodded, proud of her crazy, simple, but somewhat mind-boggling observation. Another thought invaded her mind.

"Tae Hyun," she launched excitedly, her eager eyes focused on the majestic streaks of color ornamenting the once blue sky.

"Hmm?"

"If you weren't a gang leader, what would you be doing right now?"

He paused to mull over the answer. It threw Yoori off when he said, "What do you mean?"

His slightly bewildered voice said it all: he had never been asked that question before. And based on the tightening of the muscles in his arms, Yoori was sure that he was very uncomfortable with the question.

"Well…you weren't first in line for the Serpents' throne," she began carefully. She was reticent with bringing up his older brother, but she was eager to know his answer since he hadn't dismissed her question yet. "Before you found yourself as the King of Serpents, what were you planning to do with your life?"

When Tae Hyun fell silent, Yoori assumed that he dismissed her question. Just as the silence was about to eat away at them, his voice permeated the fresh, cool air.

"The 1st layer is where I'm supposed to be right now if everything went according to the original plan," Tae Hyun shared unsteadily, his voice more delicate than she had ever heard it.

Yoori nodded, pleased that Tae Hyun contributed to the conversation. It may have been because he felt nostalgic in the lake they were in—the solitude they found themselves in as the only thing keeping them company were the distant ducks, the dancing water, and the glorious sunset. Or it could even be because of her company. Whatever the case, Tae Hyun seemed more at ease when he spoke to her.

"I was raised to take over the 1st layer. The original plan was to have my brother in the 3rd layer, myself in the 1st layer and Hae Jin could choose whichever layer she wanted to be in. I never once thought that I'd spend any real time in the 3rd layer—let alone rule it." He smiled dryly. "I remember being so excited to take over the 1st layer. Going away to business school was one of the best times of my life."

His smiling eyes relived the glory of his college days.

"The world was my oyster and I was excited for the life to come. I wanted to make a name for myself in the corporate world. I wanted to build my own empire and I wanted to bask in the freedom of living the life I created for myself. There's a certain independence you get from the 1st layer. It is different than the 3rd layer in a sense that a lot of your power comes from knowing the right people. It worked to my benefit that I had endless businessmen/politicians who wanted to be my mentors and endless friends who were the soon to be heirs of their own respective empires.

"That's why I had so much power and support when I took the Serpents' throne three years ago. It is unheard of for the younger brother to kill the older brother for the leadership position, even under the confines of the Underworld. There's still a particular code of honor that you should abide by—loyalty being the highest one. But I was 'pardoned' because of my close relations to the Corporate Crime Lords and the mentorship I received from Shin Dong Min. That's how the Underworld works. The 1st and 2nd layers don't have as much power as the 3rd layer, but their influences—especially in large quantities—help to sway the pendulum of power."

He laughed bitterly to himself. "Being crowned the King of Serpents without an uproar was inevitable after that." He turned to Yoori. He smiled when he added, "You would like it in the 1st layer, Yoori. Life is much more carefree in that layer. There's still the struggle for power that involves Underworld business, but the majority of the time, you're allowed to get lost in your own world."

"Do you regret becoming the King of Serpents?" she blurted without filter.

The pause was a short one that felt like an eternity for Yoori. Tae Hyun regarded her silently. She tried to scrutinize his poignant eyes for some emotion with the question she posed. It didn't take her long to deduce that the question may have been unexpected on her part, but it was quite possible that it was a question Tae Hyun may have already asked himself.

His gaze on her remained. He parted his lips. "Would you regret becoming a God, Yoori?"

She paused. "A God?"

When Yoori found herself unable to answer, Tae Hyun went on. "I can't begin to tell you how amazing it felt that first day when I walked into the Serpents estate and everyone in that room got down on one knee and kneeled before me. I also can't tell you how wonderful it felt when I walked into an arena that housed the entire Underworld and everyone bowed their heads down in respect—and fear—of my presence. I am everything that people want to be—"

"—better than human," Yoori finished for him.

Tae Hyun nodded. "There's no point in regretting things that have already happened, things that are beyond your control. I became a crime lord under unusual circumstances, but continued to be a crime lord to quench my thirst for the ultimate power and for my own survival."

"Survival?"

"That's the curse of being a gang leader. You can have as much power as God, but you are never truly God. Regret isn't a luxury that I'm given. The moment I regret anything is the moment I make myself vulnerable to death. People in the Underworld are quick to revere you and they are just as quick to kill you. Regret doesn't transcend in this world, but power does. That's the number one rule, Choi Yoori—you can't regret anything. The moment you do, you might as well kill yourself because someone else will be on your tail and ready to do it for you."

Yoori nodded, her mind venturing on to something else. "You know, you paused when I asked you if you regretted being the King of Serpents."

"Yeah?"

"But you didn't look surprised when I asked. The reaction in your eyes was something of familiarity with the question." She smiled weakly, noting the cautious intrigue in his eyes. "This might not be the case for you, but sometimes, when you ask yourself if you regret something enough, even if you say you don't, sometimes that could be your own subconscious way of telling yourself that you do." She gazed into his eyes. "Do you ask yourself that question enough?"

Tae Hyun immediately shook his head at her question—too immediate for Yoori who felt that she must've hit a nerve within him when she stated that observation. Determined not to allow a tense air to fall upon them, she smiled and nodded, accepting his wordless reply as her answer. She didn't want to push it. He was beginning to open up and she didn't want to scare him away.

Tae Hyun, relieved that she didn't venture further into that topic, turned his head forward, closed his eyes and lounged under the cascades of light that fell upon him. A breath later, he opened his eyes and turned to Yoori again. Curiosity reveled in his gaze. It was his turn to ask the questions.

"What were you planning on doing with your life before I busted in and stole you from your world?"

Yoori smiled. Normally, she'd avoid going into the deep and personal stuff with Tae Hyun because they'd always danced around those types of things, both holding up a wall and only allowing the other in when the trust was built high enough. Much to Yoori's obliviousness, she had already started to take her wall down for Tae Hyun—and him for her. It was a natural progression in their relationship that occurred so subtly that they didn't even notice it was happening.

Because of the serenity they found themselves in (or the fact that Tae Hyun opened up a bit more to her first), Yoori found herself at ease. For the first time, she actually wanted to let him in—but only slightly.

"When I was living in Taecin...I was...really sick," Yoori shared warily, not divulging her amnesia to Tae Hyun. It wasn't the time to tell him—not that she thought there would ever be a time.

Tae Hyun nodded, listening intently as Yoori went on.

"Being sick doesn't really allot you the opportunity to be ambitious, especially not in Taecin because there's nothing there." She smiled to herself. "I had really big dreams. The long-term plan of coming to Seoul was to further my career. Working at the diner was a way to make ends meet so I could pay for my apartment. In all honesty, I wasn't supposed to work there for more than a year. I was only supposed to stay for a couple of months and go find a job elsewhere. But one thing led to another and I became really comfortable there. It was my own little bubble."

She smiled wryly when she remembered Chae Young. She grew despondent when she realized how much she missed her. "I—I don't have a lot of close friends. I was really sick in Taecin so I lacked a lot of friends because of that, you know? But when I started working at the diner, I met this girl who was nice to me. We clicked instantly—just like Hae Jin and I—and became best friends."

She laughed ironically at herself when she was reminded of her relationship with Chae Young. She gently slapped a palm against her forehead. "Oh God, I imagine she must've called me a million times since you 'recruited' me from the diner."

Tae Hyun watched a family of ducks swim beside them when he asked, "Have you spoken to her since?"

Yoori shook her head, her eyes noting that the sunset had begun to disappear behind the trees, the radius of the bright orange lights limited to what was behind the leaves.

"After I ran away from you, I ignored phone calls from her because I didn't want her to get involved. You know, 'gang stuff.' But after that night when you came for me, my phone ran out of battery and I forgot to get the charger when I went back that one time." Yoori shrugged sadly. "I didn't get 'reminders' to call her afterward because my actual phone died. But I suppose it's better this way. I miss her, but I don't want to get her involved in all of this."

When the sun hid deeper behind the trees, Tae Hyun turned his head in her direction. This move caused Yoori to do the same. They were eye-to-eye, nose-to-nose and *almost* lips to lips.

A subtle dash of guilt teemed in Tae Hyun's eyes. She knew what she said touched a sensitive nerve within him. She just didn't know how sensitive that nerve was.

He parted his lips. His voice was soft and unsure, but also hopeful. "We could stop by the diner on our way back to the city tomorrow," Tae Hyun offered, his gaze never leaving Yoori's.

Yoori gave him a strange and quizzical look.

"No, I have a good plan," he continued, heeding her apprehension. The hopeful beam took over his eyes. "I could introduce myself as Kwon Tae Hyun, a young, budding entrepreneur who walked into a local diner after a crappy business meeting with one of his investors. I could tell her that I was having a terrible morning until I saw you—the most beautiful girl that I'd ever laid eyes on. I could tell her that when you accidentally spilled hot coffee all over my hands, I knew then that my life wasn't going to be the same. I'll tell her that after some sweet talk and a lot of courting, I convinced you to run off to Paris with me. I'll apologize to her for stealing you away so abruptly. I'll tell her it was because we fell in love at first sight and it couldn't have worked out any other way. She'll smile and nod at me while giving approving eyes at you. And then I could give you guys some alone time to catch up and then afterward, we'll tell her we're going to jet set around the world, but you'll be able to catch up with her on the phone." He smiled reassuringly at her. "She'll never have to be involved."

"That was a really nice story," said Yoori, unable to hide her bittersweet smile. It would've been nice if she could actually have that fairytale story with someone.

Tae Hyun nodded. A similar, bittersweet gleam was present in his eyes. "Do you want things to happen like that? With some editing of my story, we could make it work."

Yoori shook her head, knowing better than to lie to Chae Young like that. She also knew better than to keep perpetuating that story and bringing it to life. It wasn't true and she didn't need to be reminded every time that it wasn't true.

"It's best if you don't bring me back to Chae Young. I'm honestly not good with keeping secrets and I'll probably end up blabbing everything to her. If I see her, then I see her. But right now, if I can keep her out of it, I'll do that." She smiled appreciatively at Tae Hyun. "Thanks for the offer though. That was very considerate of you."

"Yeah, I do have my days," Tae Hyun concurred, bending his elbow up and resting the side of his chin on the palm of his hand. He forged on with his remaining questions. "Where would you have gone to work after you left the diner?"

Relieved that they were moving on from the somber topic that dealt with Chae Young, Yoori eagerly answered. "A cellphone company. I think I might want to start there first. Plus, there's one with my namesake...I probably would've wound up taking an entry-level job there. It's called Ch—"

"Choi Mobile," Tae Hyun finished for her, a big smile plastered on his face.

Yoori giggled, taking note of the familiarity in his eyes. She was reminded of the 1st layer and Tae Hyun's vast connections. "Don't tell me you know the heir..."

Tae Hyun nodded proudly. "Choi Hyun Woo. He's one of my best friends."

Yoori, somewhat flustered that he had connection to a place she could've wound up, also added, "Well, there's still a chance I wouldn't have met you. I would've applied to work for the competition too! Lee —"

"Lee Quest? Yeah, my other best friend is the heir for that one too. Daniel Lee."

Yoori gaped with rounded eyes. He really was that connected...

When her thoughts traveled back to her philosophical observation earlier in their conversation, Yoori let out a loud laugh. She beamed happily at him. "Y— You...*hehehehe*...you know what this means, right?"

"What?" he asked, staring at her giggling self like she was high on drugs.

"It means that you're like my boomerang."

"It means that I'm like your boom...mer...rang?" he repeated, utterly baffled.

She nodded, very much entertained. "It means that even in an alternative world, you'd always find your way back to me. You can never get away from me."

"No," Tae Hyun suddenly protested.

A confused smile slapped on her face. She stopped laughing. "No?"

"No. It means that you're *my* boomerang because you're the one flying around. Everything that you do, you would always somehow find your way back to me."

Yoori snorted in disbelief. She was surprised that he played along. "So we're both boomerangs now?"

"Yes, we're both boomerangs."

"Augh. Boomerang is such an ugly word though," Yoori admitted, shaking her head. She didn't know how she came up with such weird metaphors.

"I guess you're lucky to have a handsome one."

Yoori made a rude noise at his cocky statement. Even though she agreed with the handsome part, she wasn't sure if she would consider herself lucky.

"Anyway, I really like it here," she added promptly, watching as a couple of geese flew above them. Yoori could become easily distracted, even when her gorgeous boss was staring longingly at her.

"Yeah, I like it here too," Tae Hyun murmured, his eyes resting on a particular pair of pink lips. He found immense interest on the exquisite curves of her pout and the teasing suppleness of her parting lips.

Oblivious to what was happening, Yoori shifted her eyes back to him, ready to ask him a question about what else he did when he came here.

"So do you—" She stopped and gulped uneasily when she realized that he was staring at her lips. One would think that Yoori's awkward self would blurt out something that would scare him out of his longing. But when she found herself lost in his gaze, she couldn't help but stare at him and *his* lips. Her mind went entirely blank. The only thing that existed in her thoughts were Tae Hyun and how inviting his scrumptious lips looked...

Silence hung over Yoori and Tae Hyun. They continued to lay frozen, Tae Hyun staring down at her and Yoori gazing up at him. Their chests heaved up and down in unison – in anticipation. Everything in the world slowed. The lake froze in a trance, the ducks quieted in awe, and the setting sun stopped to stare. The world around them stopped and stared as Tae Hyun and Yoori gazed unblinkingly at one another.

Slow motion...that was how it happened.

The whole world waited and watched as movement began.

Tae Hyun began to descend his lips down to meet her awaiting ones.

The only thing in the breathing world that didn't slow was Yoori's heart.

Beating relentlessly against her chest, it waited in a frantic stupor. Her chest heaved up and down, every nerve in her body tingling in excitement every time Tae Hyun moved closer—every time their lips were closer to meeting.

Closer...

And closer...

And just as their lips were about to meet...

"Huh?"

Feeling something cold and wet entangle itself around the ends of her skirt and legs, Yoori distractedly averted her eyes. Shock rammed into her when she saw lake water seep into the boat.

The boat was leaking!

"Oh my God!" she cried, pushing Tae Hyun off of her just as their lips were about to form a union. She had completely forgotten about the strange stupor they found themselves in. "The boat is leaking!"

"Wh—What?" Tae Hyun stammered, clearly disoriented that his lips never attained the quest they wanted. He looked at her incredulously before turning to see what the hell she was blabbing about. "Wha—no—no. Of course the boat isn't leak—*holy shit*! The boat is leaking!"

With quick instincts, Tae Hyun hastily grabbed the paddle and ran to the area of the boat where water seeped through. He pressed his knees against the leaky area and began to paddle. His obvious goal was getting them back to the foundations of mother earth as quickly as possible.

While he did this, Yoori made herself useful by cupping her hands together and throwing out all the water that made its way into the boat. A swell of indignation gathered over her. It made sense that her life was this rotten that something terrible would happen to ruin her scenic bonding with nature.

"I cannot believe you took me out on a faulty boat!" Yoori complained to Tae Hyun, shivering as she started throwing water out. The water splashed violently onto several ducks when she did this, causing them to quack in terror.

"Who the hell sat here?" Tae Hyun argued, paddling faster. His clothes became moist from sitting across from Yoori and the splashing water.

Yoori flung him a dirty look. "*You* suggested that we lay down. And then! And then you distracted me by invading my space!"

"*You* were the one who started the distraction with that weird boomerang shit!"

"It's not weird shit! It's called being clever with words!"

"'Clever' wouldn't be a word that I'd use!"

She growled, her irritation rising through the roof. "Augh! I can't even look at you right now!"

Tae Hyun scoffed, paddling faster. When it looked like he was about to say a retort, Tae Hyun's eyes grew huge. Something behind Yoori stole his attention.

He stood up slightly and pointed warningly behind her. "Y—Yoori! DUCK!"

Yoori blinked at him. Huh?

Too late.

"Quack! Quack! Quack!"

And at that exact moment three things happened: A duck (that could be arguably viewed as the duck she shouted at earlier) attacked Yoori. Yoori lost her balance and was ready to fall into the lake…but not without Tae Hyun attempting to jump forward to save her. Unfortunately for both of them, the leak in the boat was the least of their problems, especially when both lost their balance and dove in, nearly crushing a couple of ducks as they plunged into the waiting water.

Splash!

Like a vortex, a swarm of ripples and thunders of excess flying water surrounded the area where the lake swallowed them whole. When it appeared as if both would never rise again, a ring of bubbles floated to the surface, a prelude to their masters rising like whales from beneath.

Once they pulled their submerged heads out of the water, both began gasping for air as they coughed out lake water. Blades of cold water attacked Yoori's face while her lips quivered uncontrollably. The lake was amazingly cold and the presence of a cool breeze, no matter how small, caused her lungs to struggle for breath.

Tae Hyun and Yoori glanced at one another to make sure the other was okay. When they were relieved to see that the other was alive and breathing, a dirty glare soon followed the relief. No doubt. They blamed each other for what took place.

Lips shaking relentlessly, they swam toward their leaky boat that now appeared like a chariot from heaven. Yoori found the closest side of the boat to cling onto and Tae Hyun swam a little further out and clung onto the opposite side. They rested their hands over the sides of the boat and gazed at each other in silence. Their dirty glares morphed into lethargic ones.

Yoori took a look around and returned her uneasy gaze back to Tae Hyun. It may have been the cold, or the attack from the stupid duck, or the fact that Tae Hyun was considerate enough to jump after her, but Yoori was suddenly consumed with guilt.

"You know," she began nervously, clearing her throat. Water dripped down her pale face. "I've had a chance to cool down and now that I think about it, I may have overreacted. In the overall scheme of things…a leaky boat is really no big deal."

Tae Hyun blinked lethargically, sighing as his gesture of concurrence.

Yoori nodded apprehensively, more water dripping from her hair and into the lake. Things could've been worse. She mentally nodded to herself. *Yes.* There were definitely worse things than suffering on a leaky boat and falling into a freezing lake.

For instance, she could've been wearing a white tank top as she fell into the water. That in and of itself would've been way worse because the concealment of her bra and skin would've been completely visible to Tae Hyun's naked eye if and when they struggled to get back onto the boat.

Yeah, things could've definitely been worse, especially minutes later when, as Tae Hyun began to stare awkwardly at the ducks, she looked down at her chest to find that she was indeed wearing a white tank top

Oh. My. Fucking. God.

As a downpour of humiliating horror bombarded her, Yoori frantically covered herself with her arms and turned her back to Tae Hyun. He was uncomfortably paddling their leaky boat, purposely looking every which way to avoid staring at her. Though that seemed very chivalrous of him, Yoori was certain that Tae Hyun got a two-second glance at her chest before she had a chance to cover it. It wouldn't make sense that he would look *that* uncomfortable unless he saw something briefly and was mentally restraining himself from taking another quick glance.

Yoori slammed the palm of her hand against her forehead in misery. She contemplated jumping into the lake to purposely drown herself.

Could this day get any worse for her?

Little did Yoori know, the answer to her question would be subjective.

In the bigger scheme of things, the whole "falling in the lake" fiasco was going to do little to imprint itself in her memories. There were bigger and more eventful things awaiting both her and her handsome "boomerang."

"Let's disappear, Princess."

04: Never Have I Ever

Yoori squeezed the last drips of water off of her newly showered hair and expelled a tired sigh after she threw her purple towel onto a nearby chair.

Picking up her blue and white plaid pajama pants so the hem wouldn't get in her way, she descended out of her bedroom and down the glass stairs. Yoori smiled wryly when she spotted Tae Hyun. With the recollection of the "almost kiss" purposely hidden in the depths of her memories, she inverted her brows in curiosity when she approached him, wondering what he was doing. Normally, Yoori would be more adamant about having a talk with Tae Hyun about what happened, but a big part of her was too scared. She was afraid he would simply laugh at her for being a silly girl.

Yeah, Yoori thought decidedly. *It's no big deal. Don't think too much of it.*

Her decision set, she drew closer to Tae Hyun.

Her wry smile graduated into a cheery one when she saw that Tae Hyun stood behind the bar. He took several bottles of alcohol out of four brown bags.

Her spirits lifted like a hot air balloon.

The awkwardness of wanting to forget the "almost" event aside, it was also no secret that she was left feeling pretty shitty after the unannounced wet t-shirt incident. As her cheeks turned red at the reminder, Yoori was grateful that Tae Hyun held the ticket to her sanity in his hand.

The brands of the alcohol ranged from the likes of Hypnotic, Jack Daniels and her two personal favorites: Grey Goose and Southern Comfort—two much-needed friends to help alleviate the pang of embarrassment and shame she was being tunneled through.

"Is this our late night snack?" she asked cheerily, approaching the bar after Tae Hyun pulled out two shot glasses. He looked just as excited about their newfound alcohol "buddies."

Nodding proudly, Tae Hyun smiled at Yoori. His hair, face, and entire body were still misty from his shower. A bout of perverse daydreaming overtook Yoori. She found herself ready to float in another staring stupor. Luckily, having learned her lesson from earlier, she quickly snapped herself out of her unwarranted reverie. She kept her eyes firmly on the curves of the alcohol bottles. It was a tough show of restraint on her part because her eyes were swayed by the wonders his black muscle shirt was performing for his body. She hated that it accentuated the curves of his sculpted chest and did little to cover the scintillating muscle on his arms.

She inwardly shook her head in disapproval. Damn this Kwon Tae Hyun! He was so promiscuously dressed. If she didn't know better, she'd think he was trying to seduce her.

"I figured we could make good use of this with the day we've had," he shared casually, oblivious to the fact that Yoori was ready to gauge her eyes out because they were getting ready to succumb to perverse temptation.

He picked up the Grey Goose and poured the drink into two shot glasses. Once the vodka filled to the rims, Tae Hyun handed one to Yoori. She took it without hesitation.

Ah yes, she definitely needed this. She was feeling too tense and too awkward (more so than usual). She needed something to loosen her up and this little glass of holy water was going to do the trick.

Tae Hyun raised his shot glass in preparation for a toast. His face was beaming with a virtuous quality. It was an expression so righteous that Yoori couldn't imagine anything offensive coming out of those innocent lips.

Unable to keep her cheeky smile contained, Yoori happily raised her shot glass. Man, she was excited to drink!

"Here's to Choi Yoori," Tae Hyun began exuberantly, his smile growing wider as he held his shot glass toward her.

Yoori smiled prematurely at his prepared toast.

"—the only girl I know who got attacked by a duck and lived to tell the tale." What the—

Yoori's smile melted under the scorching fire of her cheeks. Her eyes narrowed into slits and she shot Tae Hyun the dirtiest glare she could muster. She was beside herself. How dare he tease her about something that horrible? Just like that, her memory of their awkward "almost kiss" was erased. She was too distracted with his teasing nature.

Tae Hyun smirked proudly and took a swift gulp, emptying the alcohol contents into his stomach without a second's notice.

Yoori, although very bitter with his stupid little speech, made herself feel better by taking a swig as well. The results were instant. She could feel the warmth of the vodka bubble in her stomach. It felt good!

Tae Hyun placed his shot glass down in satisfaction and emerged from behind the bar. He didn't make it out two strides before they gaped at one another in shock.

Up and down their eyes went, the similarities of their pajama clothes freaking both of them out—Yoori more so than Tae Hyun.

Yoori wore a black tank top and Tae Hyun wore a black muscle shirt. In addition to the similarities of their upper garments, they both sported nearly identical looking bottoms. Both wore a mixture of blue and white plaid pajama pants.

Soon after, an uninterested Tae Hyun dismissed the gaping fest.

"What are we...modeling for a Macy's catalog?" Tae Hyun asked curtly, taking the words right out of Yoori's mouth.

Paying no more mind to the unusual likeness of their nightwear, he marched out, holding a Grey Goose bottle in one hand and his shot glass in the other.

Though she scoffed along in agreement, Yoori secretly admitted the obvious: they looked like a very cute couple when they matched. She laughed for a second before she ran over to the bar counter and grabbed her alcohol of choice, Southern Comfort. All the necessities in hand, Yoori followed Tae Hyun into the living room, boredom already holding her prisoner.

Because of their eventful day and the fact that they were leaving in the morning, Tae Hyun had informed her that he didn't have anything planned for them to do that night. Recalling this, Yoori knew the only thing that would help entertain her and her bored self was the alcohol and more "getting to know each other" activities.

"Hey, we should play a game," Yoori suggested, sitting down on the silver tiles just as Tae Hyun was about to take a seat on the couch. She was very excited for an excuse to drink and frankly, the lake house ambiance was so tranquil that she really wanted to hang out with Tae Hyun a little more before they left for Seoul in the morning. She doubted he would be as easy going and open once they returned to the confines of the Underworld. She might as well take advantage of the undisturbed time they had and pry some more information out of him.

When she saw the uncooperative look in his eyes, she hastened to add, "You know...so we don't seem like alcoholics..."

Tae Hyun chuckled at her excuse. "You're not considered an alcoholic if you drink with someone else, assistant," he reasoned. "You're only an alcoholic if you drink alone. If you drink with someone else, then you're a 'social drinker.'"

Yoori laughed at his witty reasoning. "Okay, social drinker. Get your ass down here and socialize with me by playing a drinking game. Let's have some fun before I die of boredom."

"I know a couple of vengeful ducks willing to help get you out of your boredom," Tae Hyun teased, hiding back a playful smile.

Yoori's eyes sizzled with unrelenting fire. She held back a chain of curses. Instead, she grouchily held up three fingers (her index finger and two middle fingers on her right hand) in a sequential line toward him.

Tae Hyun regarded her, puzzled as to what she was doing. Unable to hide his curiosity, he said, "What are you—?"

"Read *between* the lines, buddy," Yoori enlightened tersely, holding her three fingers higher in view.

Tae Hyun's eyes lit in amazement. He laughed in astonishment when he realized that she was subtly flipping him off.

He nodded, giving credit where credit was due. "Nice."

"I'm glad we understand each other," Yoori said proudly. She was pleased that she got her point across in not wanting to be reminded of her arch nemesis—the stupid ducks. "Now hurry up and play!"

Tae Hyun expelled a sigh and drew himself over to Yoori. As he walked, a swell of inspiration glazed over his eyes. Almost instantly, his bored demeanor transformed into an excited one.

"I call the name of the game," he announced, rushing to sit down when he realized he could get something out of it. His eyes were already twinkling with sneakiness.

Yoori regarded him with open suspicion. "What's the game?" she cautiously asked before allowing herself to concur.

"'Never Have I Ever.'" He smiled innocently at her before adding, "By the way, it's this game or no game at all. So please choose between your many options wisely."

Yoori twiddled her fingers uncertainly. She took a second to think things over and then nodded slowly. Whatever. She wanted to have some fun. The game sounded harmless enough.

"Okay, okay. Let's play it," Yoori conceded, wanting to spice up their night. They each began to pour alcohol into each other's shot glasses. Still feeling a bit bitter from his teases about her and the ducks, Yoori found herself absentmindedly adding, "Mine would've been more fun though."

"What would've been your game of choice?" Tae Hyun asked uninterestedly, clearly expecting a mundane answer from her.

"Body Shots."

The smug smile that adorned Tae Hyun's lips disappeared when he heard this. He gazed at her. His eyes were ready to form tears of regret. His visage was reminiscent of a child who got his favorite toy taken away. He held his confused eyes on her while he poured the vodka into her glass. His shocked expression asked her if she was serious.

When all she did was shrug with a crooked smile that could easily be seen as a tease, she could've sworn she saw a downpour of regret crawl in his eyes when he thought about the alternative game that would've brought the biggest smile to his face.

She scoffed inwardly, highly amused and not surprised with Tae Hyun's show of regret. As the old saying goes, boys will be boys.

He emerged out of his daze when he realized that the drink he was pouring her had spilled onto the tiles. Lost in a state of mystification, Tae Hyun lowered the bottle slowly and parted his lips, ready to suggest a flexible alternative. "W—We could—"

It took all of Yoori's willpower to suppress her giggles. It was comical to see him so confused and sad.

"No, Kwon Tae Hyunnie..." she started in a mocking and teasing tone. "You said it yourself. It's your game or *no* game."

Tae Hyun scoffed when he finally, amid his confusion and regret, caught on to the fact that Yoori was just messing with him.

"Ohhh," he voiced, shaking his head at her. His eyes rippled with the need for vengeance. "This is war."

Yoori giggled proudly, ready to have some fun.

"Okay, let's get some rules straight," she began, not wanting "sex" to be the main topic of their game. "We can't ask any personal questions pertaining to sex-"

"—Never have I ever *not* had sex," Tae Hyun interrupted promptly, a challenging smile apparent on his face.

Yoori gawked at him disbelievingly. The first question and he was already going personal?

"Uh..." She stared cautiously at their shot glasses. As she had anticipated, he didn't hold his shot glass up to drink.

His challenging gaze on her grew stronger when he noted her hesitation to play. "New rule. You can't lie and you only have five seconds to answer. If you lie or you surpass your five seconds, you have to take an article of clothing off."

Yoori's eyes nearly fell out of her sockets. "*What*?"

What the hell was this?

"Starting...now!"

"Ahhh!" She hastily grabbed her shot glass and drank from it, inadvertently agreeing to the rules of the game in her state of panic.

Tae Hyun raised his brow in interest. He happily poured her another round of vodka. He was very pleased that he got back at her for teasing him about the "Body Shots" game.

"Oh goodness, there's a virgin being dangled in front of me. This is terrible...just terrible..." he muttered to himself. He placed the Grey Goose bottle down and looked at her. "Great. Now I've lost interest in the game. The only thing going on in my mind is that I want to teach you."

Teach?

Yoori shook her head wildly, knowing very well that he was messing with her now. "I don't need *you* to teach me," she combated sternly.

She didn't need anyone to teach her!

Tae Hyun laughed, very much amused. His eyes became sinfully sultry. "Babe, if I teach you, you won't ever want to learn from anyone else. Remember that."

Yoori dropped her mouth in shock. Anger rose through her. Her patience was kicked out the door. "Oh God, you *love* making things awkward, huh? You and your stupid sexual innuendos. This is seriously sexual harassment. Watch out next time, or I'll sue you."

"Haven't we already established that only 'unwanted sexual advances' counts as sexual harassment?" he replied calmly, unfazed by her outburst.

"Are you saying you're not making sexual advances when you, even under joking pretenses, clearly are?" she retorted, unwilling to lose this battle of wits.

She had to be wittier.

She couldn't keep losing to this guy.

"No, I'm saying that the sexual advances, even under joking pretenses, are not *un*wanted." He finished that statement with a sly wink that left Yoori with her mouth agape.

Her mind spluttered with blankness. Whatever the reason, she actually took that statement to heart. Feeling rushes of anxiety rummage through her, her eyes widened in shock. Did she want him to make advances on her? No. No, of course not! She may have thought he was cute and all, but she didn't want to have sex with him. She accidentally bit her tongue when she thought this. Damn him for tricking her into thinking that she wanted him to hit on her!

Tae Hyun shook his head and moved the topic along. "Plus, *you* were the one who started it with the 'Body Shots' comment. Do you know how awkward that made me feel? I could sue *you* for sexual harassment."

Yoori was outraged. "It was a joke because you had such a one-track mind with this game," she said angrily. She waved her hand at him as if she was swatting a fly away. She was done with this senseless argument. She would never win anyway. Damn thug was too witty for her.

"Anyway," she dismissed. "Continue! *My* turn!"

"Okay, okay," Tae Hyun uttered, clapping his hands in anticipation. He was ready to continue with the game.

Yoori started out slowly, unsure of what to say. She mustered out the first thing she could think of. "Never have I ever...had more than one girlfriend at once!"

"Crap..." he mumbled sourly, reaching out for his shot glass. He drank out of it.

A knowing smirk tugged at her lips. Why wasn't she surprised? "When and how many?"

"*College and four*," he muttered, staring awkwardly at the ceiling while he uneasily scratched the back of his head.

"What was that?" Yoori asked, not hearing it the first time since he said it under his breath. Why was he acting all shy now?

"Hurry up and fill up my shot glass!" he shouted, obviously trying to move the game along.

"You didn't answer my question!"

"I did and it's not my fault you didn't listen. Anyway, my turn," he said without giving her a chance to answer.

"Wait, no—"

"Never have I ever...fallen for someone I shouldn't have fallen for."

Without thinking, both Yoori and Tae Hyun took a swig from their respective shot glasses. In that instant, Tae Hyun was the person that popped into her mind. She shook the image away. She surmised it was only because he was sitting right in front of her. She immediately dismissed it as nothing.

"Who?" Tae Hyun asked when they poured another round into each other's glasses.

Uncomfortable and not keen on telling him that *he* popped into her disordered mind, she kept her mouth sealed. She was ready to move the game along. She felt beads of sweat form on her forehead. This game was getting intense.

"Eh, eh! Who?" he asked when he saw that she wasn't planning on answering.

"My turn!" she shouted decidedly.

"No, wait—"

"Never have I ever...had my heart broken by someone."

Both of their drinks remained as they stared at each other. It was palpable that they had never fallen in love—much less had their hearts broken. Yoori frowned at herself. It was the first statement that popped into her mind in her state of panic and it couldn't have been a more boring question for the game.

She sighed, allowing her harsh gaze to fall on Tae Hyun.

"Your day will come, Kwon Tae Hyun," she voiced decidedly, referring to getting his heart broken. She tried to sound dangerous and scary as she gave him a dirty look. She was extremely disgruntled that he turned this into such an uncomfortable game.

"As will yours, Choi Yoori," Tae Hyun countered, his voice feigning equal sternness. His glare was just as dirty.

They took another second to glare evilly at each other, their eyes unblinking. Soon after, sounds of snickering evaded their lips. It was probably the alcohol or because they were so comfortable around each other, but they couldn't take each other seriously at all.

Finishing her last bout of laughter, Yoori stared down at the shot glasses uneasily. Playing "Never Have I Ever" was definitely more intense when played with Tae Hyun.

"This game is making me slightly uncomfortable."

Finishing his last bout of laughter as well, Tae Hyun said, "I would think that the alcohol would've started loosening you up already."

He was clearly amazed that Yoori was still sober.

46

Yoori quickly caught on to the fact that he probably assumed she was a lightweight because she was vertically challenged (compared to his tall self).

"For your information, I can handle large consumptions of alcohol," Yoori shared, her voice proud. It was a random and true fact. She got a kick out of showing people how "talented" she was.

Tae Hyun gazed at her suspiciously. He didn't believe her. "Really?"

"Yeah."

"How large?"

"Large," she answered confidently. She knew her next statement would get a rise out of Tae Hyun. "Probably more than you."

Tae Hyun tilted his head at her answer. The look he gave her was pure male challenge. "I'll take you up on that challenge later."

Yoori nodded, ready to accept any future challenges. A light bulb went off in her head when she realized they could sit there and share random tidbits of information without playing dangerous time sensitive, stripping-games.

"What about you?" she began sternly. "Random fact."

"I hate band-aids," Tae Hyun said at once, taking a swift drink out of his shot glass. He appeared to still be thinking about Yoori and her so-called high alcohol tolerance.

"You...hate...band-aids?"

Tae Hyun nodded unabashedly. His expression scrunched in distaste at the reminder. "Yeah, I can't stand them. They look disgusting and I hate seeing people take them off after using them. There's always little pieces of lint and hair and blood and goo stuck to the—"

"Thank you for the mental image," Yoori promptly dismissed, shuddering as she held up her hand to stop him from continuing. Great. Now she was a hater of band-aids too. She downed another shot to clear the disgusting band-aid thought from her head.

"I have another question for you," she went on after drinking from her shot glass. She held it up and waited as Tae Hyun poured her another round. "What is the one thing you haven't done in your life that everyone else has done—that you want to try?"

Tae Hyun deliberated while he poured her drink. Judging by his countenance, he was impressed with her good question. After a couple minutes of awkward thinking, he finally answered.

"Go on a date with a girl," he muttered quietly, his cheeks turning a bit red.

Yoori nearly choked on the vodka when she heard Tae Hyun's innocent answer. Dramatically spitting the vodka out to the side, Yoori slammed her hand against her chest to get the excess liquid out from her throat. She didn't know what she expected Tae Hyun's answer to be, but she would never in her life think that Tae Hyun had never gone on a date with a girl.

Clearing her throat, she smiled apologetically and returned her gaze to him. He took another swig from his shot glass and he did not look amused.

"Sorry about that," she said clumsily, picking up the Southern Comfort to pour into his shot glass. "My throat clogged up."

"Uh huh," Tae Hyun replied blithely. He held up his shot glass while she poured the drink in. The expression on his disapproving face said it all: he didn't believe her lie about why she choked.

"Anyway, wow. Never been on a date, huh?" she started casually, filling up her own shot glass. "I would've thought you'd have dozens of girls hanging off of you."

Hearing this, Tae Hyun gave her a defensive look. "I do."

Yoori bunched her brows in confusion. "But you said—"

"You've got it all wrong, Choi Yoori. I don't need to take girls on dates to successfully court them."

Yoori gave him a strange look. "Well, what do you do to successfully court them?"

He thought about it and shrugged.

"I don't know," he stated, looking askance. It was as if he was trying to figure out why earth was created. "I walk into a room and girls stare. I choose the one I like, talk to her for a bit, turn on the charm and next thing I know...I've made a new friend."

Yoori clenched her teeth at Tae Hyun's sinful misuse of the term "friend." She felt a tinge of jealousy bubble within her when a mental image of Tae Hyun hitting on a girl appeared in her head. She had never seen him interested in other girls, let alone hit on them. The thought of him sweet-talking some random girl made her mad.

Unable to contain her outrage, she demanded, "What charm?"

Was it his constant teasing? What charm was he talking about?

"You have to be there to experience it. I can't explain it."

"Show me."

"What?"

"Show me. I'm curious what your charm is like. Since you know...you have been anything but charming since we've met."

Tae Hyun grimaced at her statement and shook his head. "I'm not going to turn it on for you. If I do, you'd be ready to pounce me. We're going to move on from this topic. It's your turn to answer that question."

Yoori was about to keep pushing the "magic charm" that Tae Hyun insisted he had, but decided against it. What if he actually used it on her and it worked? She shook her head mentally at the thought.

She shifted her attention back to the question. She took another gulp of alcohol and played with the brim of the shot glass with her teeth. She didn't want to share, but she knew she was going to have to since Tae Hyun shared the innocence of his "never gone on a date with a girl" bit.

"Dance," she muttered, purposely keeping her eyes firmly set on the tiles.

Tae Hyun frowned from not being able to understand her answer. "Are you speaking in duck language or something? Speak louder."

"Dance," Yoori repeated, grimacing slightly.

"Oh." Unable to restrain himself, Tae Hyun chuckled at her reply. He smiled gently at her. "Wow. You are definitely a deprived little boomerang."

"I haven't had a lot of time for that stuff," she admitted inaudibly.

Tae Hyun nodded, suddenly standing up and catching Yoori by surprise. Smiling slyly, he extended a hand out to her.

"What?" she asked, her heart racing in nervousness. She hated it whenever he stood up with no warning. Such acts preceded him going off to a warehouse to beat up people or molesting her from behind with an embrace.

"Tonight," he declared, "I'll get what I want: my first date with a girl. And in return, I'll give you two things you want: your dance and my charms."

"Oh God, you want my dancing virginity?" Though she sounded unsure, Yoori was secretly excited. She had never been on a date either.

He nodded and waited for her to grab his hand. When she did take his hand with much nervousness and excitement, he helped pull her up.

"Are you ready for the night of your life?" Tae Hyun asked charmingly, intertwining his fingers with hers and pulling her through the door.

She laughed and nodded her head, happy that she wasn't bored anymore and that she was about to be entertained.

Without another word, Yoori and Tae Hyun ran out of the lake house, their young hearts pounding in excitement. The moonlit sky and stars welcomed them as they sped into the night.

"I found Paris."

05: Finding Paris

Little pricks of cold chills ran up Yoori's leg as they walked barefoot onto the grass beside Tae Hyun's lake house. Though Yoori didn't typically fare well in cold weather, this night was different. It was probably the alcohol pulsating in her body (or the fact that she was with Tae Hyun), but she had never found herself more nervous or more excited for something.

A slew of magnificent stars smiled upon them when they descended further from the dim illumination of Tae Hyun's lake house. While walking, they drew past a family of sleeping ducks. A bitter Yoori entertained the idea of kicking one that reminded her of the duck that attacked her. This idea was quickly vetoed when she decided it was best to not mess with nature's "friendly" animals—especially when a whole group of them could go psycho and attack her all at once.

As though anticipating Yoori's violent need, Tae Hyun pulled her away from the sleeping ducks. He didn't want to deal with getting attacked by vengeful ducks either.

They continued onward, the soothing silence swallowing them whole. Yoori was once again lost in the beauty of all that surrounded her. She didn't mind that Tae Hyun didn't share where they were headed. She liked the anticipation leading up to the surprise. If anything, she trusted that wherever they were headed, it would be beautiful. To date, the surprises that Tae Hyun threw her way were breathtaking (leaking boats, vengeful ducks, and unplanned wet t-shirts aside of course). She trusted that this one would be up to par. It wouldn't be like Tae Hyun not to top his last surprise.

Yoori smiled eagerly with this reasoning in mind. She continued to walk with Tae Hyun across the field, further and further away from the lake house properties, and closer and closer to their own little world. Soon, all that was left was the nearby lake, the swaying grass, the gentle wind, and the moonlit sky. Then out of the night, a flicker of light winked in Yoori's direction. The faint light did little to illume over the shadows, but did much to radiate over her and leave her in awe.

Amid the spell of darkness stood a magnificent white gazebo that sparkled in the calm silence. The structure was enclosed with a circle of eight tall pillars that reached up to its octagonal glass roof. A series of smaller railings inhabited the space between each pillar. With its cupola pointed toward the starry skies, the gazebo was majestic. Yoori's eyes glistened in admiration when she spotted the white icicle lights that elegantly twirled themselves around each pillar and open space within the gazebo. Garlands of pink and white flowers adorned with green leaves intertwined the icicle lights, making the gazebo appear as if it was sent from the heavens.

Oh my goodness...

The sight of such splendor took Yoori's breath away.

Without saying anything, Tae Hyun merely smiled and watched her admire the structure before them. His eyes gleamed of satisfaction with her reaction. He sighed with content and then, as soft pricks of wind caressed their skins, he pulled her with him.

They approached the gazebo, their bare feet touching the cold surface of three small stairs that led up to the white stone foundation. Leaving Yoori to stand in the center of the gazebo, her eyes lost in wonder, Tae Hyun took a seat on one of the railings and placed his iPod beside him. He folded his arms and rested his back against the pillar.

"Do you see that mansion over there?" he finally spoke, his voice waltzing around the serene silence. He subtly lifted his chin in the direction of the mansion.

Yoori turned. Her eyes were greeted with a view of the white mansion in the distance. Little flickers of light emitted from it, indicating to her that someone currently resided in it. She nodded and returned her curious gaze to Tae Hyun. He unfolded his arms and reached for his iPod.

"The man who owns that mansion is one of the older residents in this lake house area." He turned on his iPod, scrolled through the screen and made his selection. He placed the iPod back on the railing.

He stood up and approached Yoori with a soft gaze in his eyes. Naturally and skillfully, his hands found a comfortable hold around her waist. The charm he boasted about in the lake house came out, successfully enrapturing her.

There goes being doubtful about his charms, Yoori thought breathlessly.

As he pulled her closer, Yoori, lost in the lure of Tae Hyun's mesmerizing presence, wrapped her arms around his neck. A bashful smile embellished her lips. She met his gaze, this time feeling comfortable enough to keep her eyes firmly set on him.

Yoori surmised that it must be because she was excited to have her first dance under this beautiful gazebo (or because the setting was especially romantic). Still, she couldn't help but blush as she tightened her hold around his neck. Her heartbeat became unsteady when she drew herself closer to him.

They took a quick second to smile warily at each other as they waited for the music to begin. The gentle glint in Tae Hyun's eyes grew more potent while his gaze remained on her. Before Yoori could attempt to decipher his thoughts, the music streamed out of the iPod's speaker.

It all happened so naturally.

Like wind chimes in the wind, their synchronized bodies glided peacefully under the embrace of the majestic gazebo. The music was soft and slow, perfect for Yoori and Tae Hyun, both lost in their own world.

To Yoori, everything felt right.

Magical even.

Over the peaceful music, Tae Hyun continued his story, his soft brown eyes never leaving Yoori's. His voice somehow became the appropriate lyrics for the beautiful melody. It sounded perfect to Yoori, who felt breathless while she listened to him. She didn't understand what was going on with her. She had never been this...enthralled.

"He was a very successful businessman," Tae Hyun went on, his hold around Yoori's waist growing a bit tighter with care. "When I bought the lake house three years ago, I was doing a little sight-seeing and I stumbled upon this gazebo." He spared a glimpse at the railing where his iPod rested. "I saw him sitting at that very spot. He was alone. Curiosity got the best of me and I asked him if he was waiting for someone. I didn't want to intrude if they wanted their time alone. Smiling, he nodded at me and said, 'Yes, but she doesn't know that she's coming yet.'"

Even under her trance, Yoori gave Tae Hyun a perplexed expression.

Tae Hyun smiled warmly at her confused reaction.

"That was my reaction too," he assured her. "I grew more curious and asked him what he meant. He told me that he and his wife had this big fight. A huge fight in the city and she was furious at him. She told him she wanted a divorce because they were growing apart and she couldn't hold on to their relationship anymore."

Yoori smiled sadly at this.

Tae Hyun continued. "He explained to me that he bought that mansion and built this gazebo for her. It was in this very gazebo where he proposed to her. They're a very argumentative couple so at first, he told me she was hesitant with accepting his proposal. But he promised her that this gazebo would change their lives. They made a deal that should life ever get in the way of their love, they'd come to this lake house and dance in this very spot. It would remind them of all that they'd been through and why their love would continue to endure all the troubles that life threw at them."

"Did she ever come?"

"As I waited with him, seconds became minutes, minutes became hours and I realized that she wasn't going to make it. It was getting late and I had to leave, so I bid him goodbye and wished him luck with everything. He laughed at me and told me he didn't need luck. He had faith that she'd appear soon. I didn't have the heart to tell him that if she hadn't arrived already, then she'd never come. Feeling sorry for him, I just nodded and walked off."

Tae Hyun smiled to himself.

"As I was about to disappear out of sight, I realized that the air had gotten a *bit* warmer—like there was more happiness to it. I turned around and sure enough, there they were dancing together, all the problems the world hurled at them set aside as they basked in the magic of being around one another. After that, I shrugged and said, 'Fine, I'll buy it.'"

"That was a really sweet story," Yoori remarked gently, her feet gliding in sync with Tae Hyun's. She really enjoyed hearing it. It brought immeasurable warmth to her soul.

"I thought you'd be the ideal audience for it," he replied proudly.

Yoori nodded again, her heart racing against her chest.

"You're a natural at this, by the way," Tae Hyun commented as they continued to glide with the music. The gentle wind accompanied their dance. "I figured you'd be stepping all over me by now."

"It's hard not to be a natural when you have a setting like this bestowed to you," Yoori commented with a shy smile.

For reasons she couldn't explain, she found it harder to make eye contact with Tae Hyun. There was something different in her eyes that she didn't want him to see—something she had never let out before: her fragility.

She gazed at Tae Hyun and felt the walls around her lift. She finally understood why she was overwhelmed with all these foreign feelings. For months now, she had been holding back on her feelings for him. She could feel the warm endorphins seep through her while she held her arms around his neck, never feeling safer in someone's arms. She could feel the clouds lifting her up as their legs continued to dance, completely oblivious to the unblinking stares their masters were giving to one another.

More than once, as the cool wind whispered across their skins, Yoori parted her lips to say something to break the silence that ensued because it was in her nature to break the tension. But every time her lips would part, she found herself unable to utter any words.

When it appeared as though Tae Hyun was about to say something, he instead lifted up a hand and slowly rested it on her flushed cheek.

Every part of her body—every fiber, every atom—her very essence, they were all waiting in anticipation as if they all knew what was to come. She couldn't deny it and she knew then that Tae Hyun felt everything she was feeling. The emotions...the desire...the tension they had built up from being around each other...all of it exploded. All it took was one magical night to unleash everything they had hidden from one another.

And just like that, the wind dissolved into oblivion, the moon and stars disappeared, the lake evaporated, and the dancing grass slept. All that was left in Yoori's presence was the majestic gazebo and the feel of Tae Hyun's fingers on her cheek—stroking her, caressing her skin as he gazed at her with the same spellbound look. He was unyieldingly mesmerized with the breathing temptation before him.

For the very first time in their lives, both Yoori and Tae Hyun were left without witty words. The very tactical weapon they used against one another was rendered useless as the walls to their fragility cracked. It was all gone now; the walls were crumbling. Their fragility and irrefutable desire were now, slowly but surely, being unleashed.

His soft fingers glided down the frame of her warm cheek. After they landed under the contour of her chin, he ever so gracefully moved his thumb up and rested it on the tip of her lips. His touch was hesitant. It was as if her lips were a fragile treasure he was afraid of even remotely hurting. His touch, though hesitant, was powerful enough by nature to take her breath away. If she could, she would've closed her eyes and enjoyed every whisper of his touch.

She gulped awkwardly and continued to stare up at Tae Hyun. His eyes were vulnerable, genuine, and mesmerizing. He, himself, had never appeared more alluring for Yoori than that very moment in time.

There was so much desire in the air. So much desire as the silence of their anticipation hung in the cool night's air. So much desire as they each bit their own lips with anticipation, each yearning to quench that captivating attraction they had for one another.

It was intense.

Yoori's blood boiled, her heart raced, and her lips went mad with yearning while their breaths mingled in eagerness.

Soon after, just as the world around them waited with bated breaths... something occurred.

Yoori, no longer able to suppress her desire, instinctively lifted her short frame up using the tips of her toes...

At the very same instant, Tae Hyun, no longer able to hold back on his own desire, bent his head down. With his hand lifting up her chin, they moved in, their lips attracting one another like magnets.

A kiss.

A simple kiss.

That was all that happened when their lips met: a simple, *scintillating* kiss.

They touched and an explosion occurred.

Suddenly the sounds of the twinkling stars were heard again as they frolicked in the night's sky, the gasp of the moon permeated into the ripples of the tranquil lake, the once sleeping grass danced in unison as a stream of delighted wind grazed upon it.

The world breathed into life as if whispering, "*Finally*."

It started out as a simple kiss. Yet as their lips crushed upon one another, they found themselves eager for more. With each deepened kiss, their bodies surged with more energy. With each deepened kiss, they tilted their heads, Tae

Hyun's fingers stroking Yoori's long black hair and her fingers stroking his short black hair. Their lips grew greedy for more attention and care. Each time they withdrew their lips thinking it was enough, a second later, their lips would meet for more—each meeting lasting longer than the last.

They were so overwhelmed, so overwhelmed with primal emotions.

They wanted each other.

They needed each other.

As they prolonged their kiss, their hearts beating as though doused with ecstasy, streaks of a frenzied blur began to take form as the world spun at lightning speed.

The only thing suspended in this space and time was Yoori and Tae Hyun.

Oblivious to everything, their lips continued to find one another, their grasp on each other tightening with the utmost care.

From the crown of her head to the tip of her toes, Yoori felt her whole body grow weak. She was lost in the enchantment of Tae Hyun's hold. She tightened her hold around his neck, feeling the weight of her body faltering as it fought to stay balanced on her weakened toes.

She was struggling and slowly losing the fight with gravity...

Even when Tae Hyun fought to hang on to her before her heels crashed to the ground, it was too late. Akin to falling off the clouds, the heels of Yoori's bare feet collided with the hard surface of the floor, ending her daze.

Crash.

That was what occurred.

An assault of reality flooded over her, overwhelming her senses. She tried to acclimate her distracted mind with reason.

She was...kissing...Tae Hyun?

Her eyes widened.

She was kissing...*Kwon Tae Hyun?*

She gasped for breath and immediately untangled her arms from Tae Hyun's neck.

No, no, no! This wasn't supposed to happen.

Tae Hyun, who had the same look of disbelief on his face upon returning to reality, breathed heavily and untangled his arms from around her waist.

Identical, *"Oh crap..."* expressions were plastered over each of their faces.

Panting in shock, they began to back away from one another, their eyes lost in an unblinking stupor.

The kiss with Tae Hyun was mind-blowing for Yoori. It was amazing beyond all words. But much like the spinning of the world around them, Yoori found herself dizzy with uneasiness when she realized the repercussions of what just occurred.

They weren't supposed to go this far.

How did she let herself come this far with Tae Hyun? How could she actually believe that something would work out between them? It couldn't. It wouldn't. It was impossible. Tae Hyun and her…they could never be. Kwon Tae Hyun doesn't fall in love—he refused to. He told her himself.

She scolded herself for her stupidity. How could an innocent night turn into this?

Yoori looked at him uneasily.

Tae Hyun's shock-filled eyes told the same story. She could tell he was asking himself the same questions. How did he let it go this far? How did he allow himself to be this tempted? How did he lose his composure?

Inhaling the last breath of air, Yoori found her lips stuttering when she spoke. She still had a chance to make this right.

"I'm sorry," Yoori uttered, her lips quivering. "I had too much to drink tonight."

It was a lie.

She was drunk, but not on alcohol. She was drunk on her desire for Tae Hyun. But they couldn't go there. She couldn't allow herself to go there. She'd only get hurt. It was one thing to crush on him from time to time, but it was another to get lost completely. She couldn't allow herself to get lost completely.

As the vulnerability pulsating in her heart yearned for him, Yoori gulped fearfully, already beginning to build back the crumbled walls around her heart.

*Please don't fall for Tae Hyun. Anyone but Tae Hyun…*the core of her mind—her very instincts—begged as she backed away from him.

Tae Hyun nodded, his eyes lost in a trance of confusion. "I had too much to drink too," was all he said as he ran his fingers through his hair, a gesture to slap himself back to reality.

Yoori nodded slowly, vaguely relieved that they were on the same page. Yet as relieved as she was, she could no longer handle being outside with him. She cleared her throat. While doing this, she felt her heart drop to her stomach. She didn't want to leave, but she had to. It was for her own good.

"I'm really tired. I'm going to go to bed."

Before giving him a chance to answer, Yoori's bare feet took off in an unmatched frenzy. She stepped onto the dancing grass, the toes of her feet *aching* to revert back to Tae Hyun as she ran further and further out of sight.

Yoori sprinted straight to the lake house without looking back. She was too preoccupied with trying to shake off her desire for Tae Hyun. As she disappeared into the shelter of her weekend home, her breathless heart was very afraid of accepting the fact that someone almost took possession of it.

She never looked back that night.

She never looked back to see Tae Hyun sitting on the railing of the gazebo, his head sunk low while he ran his fingers through his hair. Unleashing his face from the captivity of his hands, Tae Hyun's eyes were wide from shock while he touched his lips and recounted what occurred.

He shook his head, not wanting to believe that the impossible happened. Yet as a gleam of comprehension penetrated his bewildered eyes, the next words out of Tae Hyun's lips were a telltale sign of what he realized as the inexplicable truth.

"Holy fucking shit," he groaned out loud.

With his jaw tightening in anxiety, a look of doom clouded over Tae Hyun's pale face. He desperately returned to burying his face within the confines of his hands.

It was official; the impossible had occurred...

The King of Serpents had stumbled into a foreign country—a foreign emotion—that he once promised himself that he would never venture into.

"No world can be unjust for so long."

06: Friends and Lovers

A grim winter dawned over the city of Seoul and the menacing weather proved that fact. The presence of the sun had been overshadowed by dark, gray clouds that hung over the city like poisonous spiders.

There was a sense of urgency as people walked the streets, each desperately clinging on to their coats and umbrellas as the relentless rain showered them with spiteful chills—chills that left them shivering to no end. No one wanted to be outside with the unforgiving weather. No one wanted to be outside as sounds of roaring thunder resonated over the dark sky. No one wanted to be outside when the tornado-like winds arrived.

The only ones unaffected by the treacherous weather were those who found themselves warm havens within the confines of homes, offices, and stores littered across the rain-infested city.

Inside a grocery store, where bright lights and warm heat shrouded over its customers, two gang members and a personal assistant walked side by side, unaware of the callous weather taking form outside. They were too preoccupied with catching up on the happenings of each other's weekends—and confronting a certain someone about a cloud of awkwardness that hung over her and a significant other.

Walking at the further left hand side of the aisle, with the arms of his brown hooded jacket folded across his chest, Jae Won darted his curious eyes over to Yoori.

"What the hell happened on your little getaway trip with the King of Serpents?" he confronted, taking a sideway glance at a cookie box that caught his eye. Only momentarily distracted, he returned his focus to Yoori and continued. "The tension was so damn thick that I was surprised Kang Min and I didn't suffocate from being in the same room with the two of you."

Yoori scowled in response to Jae Won's straightforward observation.

Blunt much?

Yoori couldn't deny that Jae Won's statement was accurate.

Since returning from the lake house, it was no secret that there was awkwardness between herself and Tae Hyun. They hadn't spoken that night after the "unfortunate incident" took place. To further lengthen the tension, on the drive back to Seoul, both shared that they were too hung over from the alcohol to talk. This equated to a long car ride that resulted in Yoori pretending to sleep and Tae Hyun pretending not to know she was actually awake.

If that wasn't enough, after returning to the apartment, both announced that they were too tired from the car ride to talk. This led to a whole day of "catching up on work" and completely ignoring one another. The trend of pretending to not notice each other was also carried out in the days that followed. Tae Hyun immersed himself with his Underworld duties and Yoori occupied herself with her assistant activities. Both parties threw out forced conversations concerning official Underworld business to alleviate some of the anxiety, but both Yoori and Tae Hyun adhered to total avoidance of other matters as the days went on.

Despite the evasion of a certain topic, Yoori knew that although they didn't speak of it, both were consumed with the one issue that started all of this awkwardness.

Yoori had no doubt that Tae Hyun was still trying to wrap his mind around what occurred under the gazebo. She, too, hadn't been able to think of anything else but the kiss they shared. It was one of those kisses that was too mind-blowing and monumental. You couldn't forget it—no matter how hard you tried.

In any case, it certainly came as no surprise to her that Jae Won and Kang Min must've felt the unbearable tension when they came to pick her up for grocery shopping. Normally, Tae Hyun would insist on going with her. On this day, however, he stated that he was too busy with "Underworld duties" and immediately called for the brothers to come and accompany her instead.

Though Yoori admitted to herself that such actions hurt her feelings, she knew it was best if they kept their distance for the time being. Hurt feelings aside, she couldn't imagine having a conversation with Tae Hyun that wouldn't tempt them into talking about "the kiss." It was a topic that Yoori wanted to avoid talking about for as long as possible.

She blew out a dejected sigh.

Still, it bummed her out that it had been more than a little while since she and Tae Hyun had a proper conversation. Though he drove her crazy half the time, Yoori couldn't deny that she missed him a lot. Not that she liked him or anything! She just missed him…as a friend.

Yoori pursed her lips at the predicament she found herself in.

All because of a stupid kiss, she thought bitterly.

She returned to reality and quickly thought up an answer to give the brothers (one of which wouldn't go into the specifics as to what happened).

She clumsily fiddled with the teal crocheted beret that sat on her hair. Pushing her non-prescribed, stylish black-rimmed glasses higher up the bridge of her nose, Yoori feigned distraction and kept her inattentive gaze on the vast aisle of junk food that lined the shelves.

"We had a little misunderstanding," she provided vaguely, thinking the white lie was appropriate.

Indeed the kiss was a big misunderstanding between both of them.

She tucked her hands in the pockets of her black jacket and cleared her throat uneasily. Her black Uggs, which she had tucked the hems of her dark blue jeans into, thumped while she walked down the store aisle. It was as though her own shoes were scolding her for being such a terrible liar.

Jae Won narrowed his eyes at Yoori. A frown of disapproval shadowed his countenance. It was clear that he knew there was more going on than what she shared. When it looked like he was about to say what was on his doubtful mind, another voice swam through the aisle.

"I'm sure whatever it is, Yoori and Tae Hyun can work it out themselves," Kang Min provided understandably, walking in between Jae Won and Yoori.

The back of his black leather jacket straightened when he hunched himself forward. He rested his arms on the metal railing of the shopping cart and continued to push the half full cart. He smiled reassuringly at Yoori, who gave him a small smile in return. She appreciated his non-probing ways.

She hated that she was being secretive around the brothers. However, despite how much she trusted them, the event that took place with Tae Hyun was an uncomfortable conversation for her to have with them. It was more of a "girl talk" that she needed. She couldn't imagine the brothers being a good outlet to help "analyze" her feelings and confusion. If anything, she was certain they would scold her for kissing Tae Hyun. After all, they did warn her that they weren't sure if Tae Hyun was trustworthy.

"Have you thought further about what we talked about in the limo?" Jae Won asked suddenly. His eyes still displayed curiosity about what happened between Tae Hyun and Yoori during their weekend away. In spite of this, he was ready to move on to more important topics.

Jae Won's gaze on her was cautious and attentive. It mirrored that of Kang Min's, whose own curiosity dwelled in his unblinking gaze on Yoori. Yoori sensed then that the brothers had been meaning to ask her this question since they picked her up from Tae Hyun's apartment.

"I haven't really," she answered, instantly feeling a rush of uncomfortable emotions surge through her.

It was a half-truth and half-lie. She hadn't given much thought about the "untrustworthiness" of Tae Hyun and Ji Hoon because she trusted them wholly. In the same token, she had given much thought to the terrifying possibility that she was the notorious Queen of the Underworld. The reminder continued to send chills up her spine.

"Anyway, can we not talk about this stuff?" she asked, already feeling the prelude of a migraine form in her head. The last thing Yoori wanted to talk about was Soo Jin. "I haven't been feeling too well and I want to leave that stuff alone."

Yoori expected the brothers to counteract her request with a rebuttal. What occurred next was a pleasant surprise for her. Instead of insisting on having the conversation, the brothers acknowledged the immense discomfort on her part and smiled reassuringly at her. Saying no more, they continued to walk down the aisle. Their white sneakers tapped on the tiles while the shopping cart creaked along with them.

Relieved with their understanding, she blew out a relaxing breath. She followed them down the aisle.

"How was your weekend?" Yoori chirped out merrily, wanting to shift the spotlight to someone else. She grabbed several boxes of cookies that she knew Tae Hyun liked and threw them into the moving cart.

"Kang Min and I hung out together...with our girlfriends," Jae Won shared blissfully. A happy grin livened his bruised face.

Such a pleasant reaction was not shared by Yoori – who was stupefied with his response – or by his little brother.

Hung out with their girlfriends?

"What?" Yoori squawked out, not believing her ears.

"She's not my girlfriend!" Kang Min shouted at the same instance.

All three had stopped walking. They wore three different expressions on their faces. Jae Won smiled, Kang Min frowned, and Yoori was confused.

"Wait. Time out, time out, time out!" Yoori shouted, bouncing both her hands together to make a capital "T" shape.

Her curiosity spiked to its apex. She had always viewed Jae Won and Kang Min as her dorky little brothers. The thought of them having girlfriends was enough to bring a great big smile on to her face. For a moment, she placed her frustrations concerning the unexpected kiss with Tae Hyun (and the strong possibility she was An Soo Jin) aside.

In between the glare on Kang Min's face and Jae Won's smug expression, they turned to her and gaped at her strange hand motions.

Yoori ceased with the "time-out" hand gestures when she registered how silly she must've looked. "You guys have girlfriends?" she asked, bringing her hands down.

"She's not my girlfriend!" Kang Min blurted out again. His cheeks flushed in the tone of a tomato.

"She's his on-and-off girlfriend," Jae Won corrected, rolling his eyes at his brother's sudden bashfulness. "And yes, boss. There *are* other girls in our lives besides you."

Yoori growled quietly. She wasn't trying to be territorial. She quickly relinquished the bitterness and got right back on topic. "You guys had a double date this past weekend?"

"Something like that," confirmed a happy Jae Won.

"We've been off for a while, which means she's *not* my girlfriend," Kang Min clarified, still trying to clear the misunderstanding about him and his "girl." "We're just friends."

Yoori grimaced. Uh oh, where had she heard that before?

"Uh huh, 'friends,'" Jae Won repeated skeptically. He turned to face Yoori. "My girlfriend and I are having another dinner date with him and his 'friend' tonight."

Feeling naughty, Yoori giggled and teasingly said, "Oooh, what a good *friend* you are, Kang Min." She playfully nudged his arm.

Kang Min, who was blushing immensely, sighed in disbelief. "Not you too, Yoori." He brought a frustrated palm to his forehead. "Can we move along from this conversation?"

"Yes, one last thing," Jae Won said in an understanding voice. It would've been genuine if there weren't mischief in his eyes when he turned to Yoori and revealed, "His 'friend' is Kwon Hae Jin!"

At that moment, three things happened: Yoori's mouth formed into the shape of a capital "O", Jae Won, as if being pulled away from an oncoming semi-truck, dodged out of the aisle as Kang Min's angry fist buried a hole into a nearby cereal box—the exact position Jae Won's head would've been had he not moved in time.

Streams of Cheerios flowed out of the listless box after Kang Min withdrew his irate fist. He scowled at his older brother like an angry lion.

"You just had to tell Yoori, didn't you?" Kang Min asked indignantly, resting his hands back on the railing of the shopping cart.

When he saw that the coast was clear (polluted Cheerios aside), Jae Won returned to the aisle with a satisfied grin on his face.

"Oh come on, baby brother," Jae Won said thoughtfully, standing beside a shocked Yoori. Her eyes and mouth were still agape from bewilderment. "This is Boss Choi we're talking about. She's not going to tell anyone." Jae Won turned to Yoori to confirm. "Right, Boss Choi?"

"You—You're Hae Jin's boyfriend?!" Yoori finally asked, her voice so high-pitched that it would've cracked glass. Her mind was spinning. Before giving Kang Min a chance to answer, she posed another highly anticipated question. "Does Boss Kwon Tae Hyun know?"

Her question was answered when Kang Min started to worryingly scratch the back of his head. He avoided eye contact.

"If the almighty King of Serpents knew, do you think our Kang Min would be standing there with all his bones intact?" Jae Won answered for his brother. He pointed at the crumpled cereal box that still had Cheerios falling out of it. "His head would be like that Cheerios box."

Yoori briefly blinked in agreement. Punching a hole in Kang Min's head *did* sound like something Tae Hyun would do for his baby sister.

"Good point," she breathed out.

Kang Min groaned in agreement before eyeing the Cheerios box.

"Great," he complained regrettably. He pouted and grabbed the Cheerios box he assaulted. He bitterly placed it into the cart. "Now we have to buy this."

Jae Won continued to speak. "But boss, they've been 'on-and-off' for three years now. Don't you think it's time for Kang Min and Hae Jin to officially be 'on' for longer than two weeks?"

As he said that, Jae Won's phone began to ring. He looked at the screen.

"Okay, this is Underworld business. I'm going to take it outside." Before leaving, he turned to Yoori and whispered, "Boss, Kang Min needs some sense knocked into him about his relationship. I think he'll listen to you. Will you talk to him?"

Jae Won stalked off with his phone pressed against his ear before allowing Yoori the opportunity to answer with an, "*I don't even know what the hell is going on*" response.

"I hate you," Kang Min said indignantly, glowering at Jae Won when he walked past him.

"Love you too, baby brother," Jae Won replied with warm mockery. He purposely ignored the death glare Kang Min bequeathed unto him.

Pushed over the edge, Kang Min said the one thing he knew would push his older brother over the edge.

"Your ass is fat!"

A self-conscious Jae Won stopped grinning. Fire ignited in his eyes. He bestowed Kang Min with a death glare of his own. His voice rose to that of a roaring lion's. "Why you little — !"

"Love you too, big bro!" Kang Min mocked in a high-pitched voice, satisfied with the reaction he pulled out of his brother.

"I'm going to fucking kill — "

"Jae Won, shut up and go take your call!" Yoori shouted irritably. She was getting a headache from all their arguing. You know you've gotten too comfortable around certain people when you could yell at them with no fear. Though Yoori felt bad when she saw Jae Won fall silent, she didn't regret yelling. How the hell was she supposed to talk to Kang Min and find out what was going on when Jae Won was arguing with him?

Jae Won made a disgruntled noise and bitterly obeyed Yoori's commands. As he was getting ready to disappear out of the aisle, he reminded Kang Min, "Don't forget that you have to go to Hae Jin's place to help prepare dinner!"

That message delivered, he flew completely out of sight.

"Oh yeah..." Kang Min recalled slowly. His anger subsiding, he appreciatively shouted, "Thanks!"

Yoori gawked in deranged awe. It was amazing how quickly they could get into fights and how quickly they could make up. These two brothers would drive her crazy one day. She knew it.

She inhaled with anticipation when an air of peace fell over them. Satisfied that Jae Won was finally out of sight, Yoori smiled warmly and purposely approached Kang Min.

"So you and Hae Jin…" Yoori casually launched with a cheeky smile on her face. "As shocked as I am, I must say that you two make a very cute couple."

"It's not like that, Yoori," Kang Min corrected, his expression firm.

"So I hear," Yoori commented with equal sternness. The nosy bug within her was unwilling to back down. "Is Tae Hyun the reason why things between the two of you are complicated?"

"We shouldn't be together," Kang Min answered at once.

Yoori crinkled her nose at his brisk answer. "That wasn't my question."

"That's my answer," Kang Min replied stubbornly. He was determined to look unyielding. Though he was anything but intimidating for Yoori, she had to give the kid credit. He was one hardheaded cookie.

"Okay, you stubborn person," she compromised, slapping a palm to her forehead. She placed a surrendering hand to her chin. "Can I at least get a little background info on you guys?"

Kang Min's eyes turned into suspicious slits. He attempted to decipher what Yoori was up to. When he surmised that there was nothing wrong with a little bit of a history lesson, he obliged with her request. "Okay, fine."

Yoori hid a sneaky smile when he gave in.

All I need is for you to let your guard down and then I'll have you singing like a bird, she thought mischievously.

"You two met when you joined the Serpents, right?"

Kang Min nodded. "I was fifteen when I joined the Serpents. Since we were the same age, Tae Hyun placed me in school with Hae Jin to watch over her. I basically started off as her bodyguard."

Yoori smiled pleasantly at the reminder of Tae Hyun and his nice little deed.

"The 'on-and-off' started then?" she asked, getting back on topic.

Kang Min shook his head, his eyes lost in a reminiscing daze. "Hae Jin was cold to me in the beginning. She'd avoid me during class, ditch me after school, and yell at me a lot. I thought Tae Hyun was going to have someone kill me because I kept losing track of her whereabouts. I was convinced that she hated me and wanted me decapitated."

"That doesn't sound like Hae Jin," Yoori observed out loud.

"I thought she was a spoiled brat. It wasn't until Tae Hyun had 'the talk' with me that she started to come around."

"'The talk?'"

Kang Min elaborated. "You see, when you're assigned to be someone's bodyguard, you have to have a certain bond with them – the type where trust is heavily involved. With my first boss, I grew up with her, so we had that bond. With Tae Hyun, we have that bond—that trust. But with Hae Jin, she was very distant and Tae Hyun could tell. He told me that I needed to fix it. I needed to make it right *or else*."

Yoori empathized by pursing her lips up in distaste. Those "or else" threats were the worst.

"After that, I thought for sure I was going to die a slow and certain death. But I guess after Tae Hyun spoke to me about it, he spoke to Hae Jin too."

Yoori smiled. "Was that when Hae Jin started opening up?"

Kang Min confirmed with a relieved exhalation. "It started out slow, you know, like it always does. But she was making the effort because I guess she didn't want it on her conscience that someone died because of her. Anyway, we got along really well. We understood each other and that bond began. One day, she shared with me the reason why she was so distant in the beginning and why she found it hard to trust me—or any other guy for that matter. Well...any guy with the exception of Tae Hyun of course."

Clearly not wanting to get into the specifics, Kang Min merely spoke a sentence that provided her with all the information she needed. He, too, knew that Yoori had been enlightened with this important fact. "I joined right around the same time Tae Hyun took over the Serpents' throne. It was right after their eldest brother died."

Yoori understood the situation when she was reminded of their bastard eldest brother and how he raped Hae Jin when she was younger. Tae Hyun came home in time to catch his older brother committing that unforgivable act. They got into a fight and Tae Hyun ended up killing his older brother and thereby assumed the position as the King of Serpents. Yoori brushed off this memory and gave Kang Min a stiff nod to acknowledge her comprehension. She wordlessly gestured for him to continue. They didn't need to go into that part of the story.

His jaw tightening upon being reminded of what happened to Hae Jin when she was fifteen, Kang Min continued with his story. "After she opened up, we started to become close. Not in the boyfriend and girlfriend sense, but as friends— best friends. But as the months went by, one thing led to another...there was this awkward tension between us because I realized that I might actually like her as *more* than a friend. I imagine she went through the same phase." He sighed. "Long story short, we tried it and it didn't work. It became this repetitive cycle of working and not working. It didn't work when we were together and it *definitely* didn't work when we weren't together. So right now, we're in limbo."

"Hence your 'on-and-off' relationship," Yoori supplied, understanding more and more. After a moment's pause, she said, "Why didn't it work? Was it because she and Ji—?" The words escaped her lips before she had a chance to filter them. Clamping her lips shut, Yoori blinked regrettably. What the heck was she doing bringing up Ji Hoon? The reminder of Hae Jin and Ji Hoon sleeping together would bring up bad blood—for Kang Min and her combined.

Though her efforts to move away from this topic were commendable, it wasn't enough. Kang Min had the look on his face that said he wanted to address this topic.

His eyes darkened when he spoke. "You have no idea how pissed I was when I heard about that. I was livid at Hae Jin for being that naïve as to get drunk with someone like Ji Hoon. Her better judgment gets obliterated when she drinks because she can't handle her alcohol." He scoffed to himself. "But you know what pisses me off more? She was drinking because it was *I* who dumped her that night. We went through that phase where the secret of being together was killing us so I gave up—*again*. I broke up with her and left with another girl. So essentially, *I* was the one who threw her all that alcohol and *I* was responsible for causing her to get into bed with Ji Hoon."

Kang Min raked his fingers through his hair in frustration. He took a moment to stare at the railing of the shopping cart before returning his gaze to Yoori.

"Do you see how fucked up we are, Yoori? When Hae Jin and I are together, there's so much shit in our way because it has to be a secret that we're in a relationship. And it wasn't only because we had to keep it a secret. There were just too many obstacles. They kept appearing and wouldn't stop. When it gets too hard, we leave each other, get wasted and sleep with the first scumbag or ho that comes near us. Then the next morning, we get back together. It's a fucked up cycle that seems never-ending." Kang Min laughed dryly to himself. "And you know what else is funny? The fact that I *know* this relationship isn't going to work out, but I keep hanging on to it because I can't let her go. I—"

He exhaled depressingly, realizing an inexplicable truth that he couldn't escape from. "I'm in a doomed relationship with Kwon Hae Jin. That's where I am. That's why we're 'on-and-off,' because we both know that we're never going to end up together. I'm one of the sub-leaders of a *gang* for fuck's sake. It's almost guaranteed that I'll die before I reach my nineteenth birthday. I—I don't know why I bother to torture myself with this."

"You're in a doomed relationship if you give up. So it's all the same," Yoori said bluntly, her eyes scrutinizing Kang Min.

Kang Min gaped at Yoori, thunderstruck by her words. "What?"

She folded her arms and stared at Kang Min unsympathetically. The sternness in her voice remained. "I said that you're in a doomed relationship all the same if you're with her or not. Make the most of everything now. Be 'on' with her and be happy. The ending will come when it comes. If you die, you die. You can't help what happens in the future. In the meantime, steal borrowed time and be happy with her. Why not, right? Like you said, you're in a doomed relationship. You'll end up with the same outcome no matter which path you choose, but at least you'll be able to give yourself some happiness before you reach the end."

"Wouldn't the ending hurt more if I allowed myself to fall even harder for her?" Kang Min asked, absorbing what she was saying.

"Wouldn't the ending hurt more if you realized that you purposely gave up? The world can fuck you over and you'd be fine with it, but the ending would be worse if you realized that *you* were the one who fucked yourself over."

Kang Min blinked dubiously at her. A stagnant silence hung over them before Kang Min parted his lips and said in amazement, "That crock of shit actually makes sense."

Though she was glad that she got through to him, Yoori frowned at Kang Min's atypical compliment.

"I think there's a stronger effect because you're wearing glasses today," Kang Min observed distractedly. He assessed her glasses. "I didn't realize you had bad vision."

"I don't," Yoori answered at once, adjusting her glasses. "These lenses are clear."

Kang Min blinked dubiously again. "You're weird," he stated before also adding, "And you cuss a lot."

Yoori bounced her head sagely. "Guys listen more when you cuss."

In response to Yoori's pearls of wisdom, Kang Min was about to say something else when his Blackberry alarm went off. Breaking from his train of thoughts, Kang Min took out his Blackberry and turned off the alarm.

"Okay, I gotta head over to Hae Jin's to help make dinner," he announced, placing the Blackberry back in his pocket. He looked at her. "You'll be fine alone for a little bit, right?"

Yoori smiled. "Yeah, of course! Go have fun making dinner," she urged, elated that Kang Min seemed to be feeling better. "Give Hae Jin my greeting and make sure to keep that 'crock of shit' in the back of your mind."

"I will," Kang Min said after a laugh. "Thanks for listening. I never thought I'd come out being so enlightened."

"It's the glasses," Yoori supplied with an approving nod. "Now hurry up and go. Don't keep her waiting."

"I'll see you later," he said, taking his hands off the shopping cart. He started to walk off before he stopped in his tracks. He whipped around to face her. "And Yoori?"

"Hmm?"

"For what it's worth...I trust Tae Hyun too."

Yoori stilled and Kang Min addressed her confusion. "I wasn't sure that night. But that was before I saw how awkward he was at the apartment."

Now Yoori was more perplexed. "What does that have to do with anything?"

Kang Min shrugged, clearly not wanting to get into any specifics. "I guess it's a guy thing. You might want to share that crock of shit with Tae Hyun. I think he needs to be enlightened too." He shrugged again before venturing out of the aisle. "Just a thought. Anyway, see you later, Yoori."

Seconds later, Yoori was left alone in the deserted aisle. Her mind reeled. Yoori didn't know how long she stood there, lost in a stupor while she pondered what Kang Min said.

Was Kang Min insinuating that Tae Hyun was going through the same internal conflicts as him? The only difference being that the girl on Tae Hyun's mind was—

All of a sudden, like a cat being spooked at night, a rush of uneasiness surged through Yoori, causing her to instinctively whip her head to the side. Her eyes landed on the gap between the shelves that gave view to the other aisle beside her. She focused her gaze on a particular spot where she was positive she felt a pair of eyes stare at her. Yoori was spooked to find that there was nothing there, just a view of the coffee beans on the other aisle.

Huh... she thought uneasily, her breathing growing shallow. She surveyed the aisle around her. Was it her imagination? After staring at the vacant aisle around her for a couple more seconds, Yoori shook her head at her active imagination. Being in the Underworld for too long made her paranoid.

Yoori was in the process of dismissing her uneasiness as nothing when she felt her gut churn in worry—again. At the call of her second wave of instincts, an alerted Yoori twisted her neck to the side, expecting to see someone standing behind her. She was greeted with an empty aisle that had a view of other customers shopping in the far distance. Though she couldn't see anyone near her at her vantage point, the worry in her gut told Yoori otherwise.

A swarm of chills crawled up her body. Her heart thumped in worry. She was really starting to freak out. It could be Jae Won who came back from taking his call, or Kang Min, or another nice customer, right?

Wanting desperately to rid herself of the uncertainty that plagued her, Yoori mentally nodded at her consoling theory. She forced a smile on to her face and concluded that she was indeed being paranoid. Yoori placed her hand on the railing of the shopping cart and began to push, ready to get out of this aisle.

Sounds of the distant thunder rumbling outside could be heard as she uneasily pushed her creaking shopping cart down the aisle. She shuddered from anxiety. The weather outside was definitely not helping her overexcited nerves. Despite her fears, she continued to mentally console herself. *It's okay. It's just your imagination. It's just your—*

Before she was able to stop it, Yoori twisted herself backward to finally catch sight of whatever was behind her. After so many false alarms, Yoori was almost sure that she would end up seeing nothing.

The blooming fear in her eyes told a different story.

It happened for a split second when she turned, but Yoori was sure that she saw a jet of black hair disappear behind the further end of the aisle beside hers.

OHHHH SHIT! Yoori thought fearfully, sounds of the roaring thunder somehow taking possession of her heart. She pulled her non-prescribed glasses down for a second to observe the area again.

There was nothing there.

The aisle was as she saw it seconds prior: completely void of anyone else. The only difference now was that she knew better. That jet of black hair wasn't a figment of her imagination. Some might argue that it was since she was wearing glasses, but what she saw wasn't her eyes playing tricks on her. The lenses of her non-prescribed, stylish glasses were clear for goodness sake!

Lifting her glasses back up to the bridge of her nose, Yoori began to shake when she detected the anticipatory breathing of another. Surely this wasn't another figment of her imagination—Yoori knew that much.

Shit, she thought worryingly, retreating backward.

Her eyes were fully fixated on the area in which she saw the jet of black hair disappear.

Where the hell were her bodyguards when she needed them?

Her pace quickened with each retreating step she took, her unblinking eyes firmly set on the aisle walkway ahead of her. Yoori felt the rate of her heartbeat escalate when she realized the breathing was somehow drawing closer to her.

Closer…

And closer…

And closer…

And finally…

"Yoo—Ahh!"

"Get the fuck away from me!" Yoori shouted, interrupting the flow of the stalker's voice. Whipping around, she grabbed the assaulted Cheerios box out from her shopping cart. With unmatched strength, she slammed the Cheerios box against the stalker's forehead. Not done with her assault, Yoori followed that attack with an unforgiving fist to the chest, a move that had the stalker yelping in pain.

Sounds of a loud thud, coupled with the splattering of the Cheerios, could be heard as the stalker fell down with a scream that shook Yoori out of her defensive state.

Yoori's bewilderment escalated when she observed that the stalker, who was now twitching on the floor, looked much weaker than she originally assumed. Yoori gulped anxiously. She kept her eyes trained on the stalker, whose long bangs fell forward to cover her face. All that Yoori could hear was a distinctive moan of pain. The sound of the voice shocked her.

Her stalker was a girl?

"Boss!" A voice sprinted through the aisle, garnering Yoori's attention. She took her eyes off the faceless stalker and watched as Jae Won ran toward her. He panted relentlessly after stopping beside her.

"I heard you scream! Are you okay?" he panted, taking a moment to glance at the stalker, whose face was still covered by her bangs. "What the hell happened?" Jae Won asked distractedly, trying to get a good view of the girl's face.

Yoori beamed proudly, happy that she was able to take care of herself without Jae Won's help. "That stalker was following me and was getting ready to attack me. Luckily, I was able to—"

"Honey?" Jae Won squeaked, his eyes nearly popping out of his sockets once he recognized the stalker's face. A look of panic flooded over his countenance. He hastily ran past Yoori to help the "stalker" up. Sounds of the "stalker" rubbing her chest and heaving for air could be heard as Yoori stood there, baffled.

"Honey?" Yoori parroted. The confusion within Yoori intensified when she turned to see Jae Won helping the stalker girl up.

Astonishment slammed into Yoori after the full features of the girl's face were revealed.

"Damn it, Yoori! I haven't seen you in forever and the first thing you do is fucking attack me?!"

A mixture of bewilderment and recognition cascaded over Yoori's shocked face. Almost disbelievingly, she said, "Chae Young?"

"For every lie. . .there is a truth."

07: Denial

"Chae Young? Oh my God, Chae Young?" Yoori squeaked out.

She squinted her frantic eyes to make sure it was actually her friend.

Lee Chae Young was dressed in a pair of faded blue jeans with white sneakers and a white jacket that had remnants of Cheerios stuck to it. Yoori knew the impossibly terrible had occurred: she assaulted her best friend.

Feeling every ounce of regret a human could bear, Yoori ran over to the Cheerios infested tiles where her friend stood. Chae Young heaved and coughed for air while Jae Won helped to flick the residual Cheerios off of her shoulder length hair.

"Chae Young, I'm so sorry!" Yoori cried when she reached her friend.

Chae Young moaned in pain. She rubbed a hand over her assaulted chest. Jae Won helped rub her back while he continued to gaze at her worriedly.

Yoori went on, guilt clawing at her. "I didn't know it was you."

Chae Young gaped at Yoori with incredulity. She eyed Yoori's glasses. "How could you not know it was me when you're wearing glasses?"

Yoori opened her mouth to explain. She was cut off by Jae Won.

"See?" Jae Won shouted, clearly annoyed with Yoori for hurting his girlfriend. "I told you these non-prescribed vanity glasses would ruin your vision one day!" With his anger intact, he suddenly reached for her glasses and proceeded to rip them off of her ears.

Yoori flinched, thrown for a loop when he did this.

"Don't touch my stuff!" she snapped when the shock passed, startling Jae Won. He stared at her and her glasses. A pang of grief infiltrated his eyes when he realized that he overreacted.

Unfortunately for Jae Won, his pang of grief was about to multiply.

"Yeah, don't rip her glasses off like that!" Chae Young abruptly screamed, glaring at Jae Won, who jumped in fear at the sound of her roaring voice. "You could've hurt her!"

Jae Won's frenzied eyes began to water. His expression mirrored that of an ant dying underneath the contempt of a magnifying glass on a sunny afternoon. At that moment, it became clear to Jae Won who the real bosses in his life were.

"I'm sorry," he squeaked out. A fleeting moment passed before he was able to speak again. He turned to Yoori. Muttering a string of scolding curses to himself, he respectfully bowed his head down. "I'm really sorry, Boss Choi."

Under normal circumstances, Yoori would've smacked Jae Won silly before she accepted his apology. Violence aside, her main priority was making sure her best friend was alright and figuring out why the hell she stalked her in the first place.

Yoori turned her attention back to Chae Young. "And you. Why the hell were you sneaking around? Do you know how much you scared me?"

Chae Young made a disgruntled noise. "Oh yeah, apparently I felt *all* your fear."

Chae Young continued to rub her chest in pain. The sight of this caused Yoori to soften her stern expression. She had never felt more horrible. Who in their right mind would assault their own friend—especially a friend they hadn't seen in forever?

After she steadied her breathing, Chae Young explained her side of the story. "You were wearing your hat and I was thrown off by your stupid glasses. I wasn't sure if it was you. I didn't want to scare you and have you run off before I got a good look at you. That's why I was being sneaky. You kept on turning around, being all ninja and shit and scaring me. Finally, I had to just run to you and get a close up view. When I got closer, I knew for sure it was you. I was getting ready to call out your name...but then I got attacked before I ever got a chance to say anything."

The rubbing on her chest grew more intense.

"You, of all people, should know that I have the worst reflexes," reprimanded Yoori.

She folded her arms in defense. She felt guilty, but Chae Young should've known better! She recalled the countless times in the past where Chae Young would sneak up from behind her and playfully poke her waist. Long story short, it took more than a dozen broken trinkets of dishes and cups for Chae Young to stop sneaking around in the diner—or anywhere for that matter.

At Yoori's response and reminder, Chae Young receded with her bitterness, blinked to surrender, and nodded in concurrence. She also clearly recalled the same incidents.

A momentary air of silence perused through the aisle before Yoori and Chae Young both looked at the glasses Jae Won held. In the same instance, Jae Won's eyes darted from Yoori to Chae Young. Yoori was reminded of a crucial fact. Chae Young and Jae Won also realized a crucial fact.

A long overdue, light of realization dawned in each of their eyes. Their words synchronized like the chorus of a symphony when they all asked: "You two know each other?"

This question acted as the catalyst that jumpstarted a slew of other questions.

"Boss, how do you know my girlfriend?"

"Honey, how do you know Yoori?"

"How the hell did you two become a couple?"

Leaving Yoori to hang on her own question, the couple turned to one another and began to answer each other's questions instead.

"Yoori's my boss, the one I told you about," Jae Won answered swiftly. "How do *you* know her?"

"Yoori's the best friend I told you about. She used to work with me at the diner." Chae Young turned and gaped at Yoori when she processed the term "boss." "What the hell have you been up to, Yoori?"

Yoori smiled wryly, her eyes slithering to Jae Won and then back to Chae Young. "I should ask you the same question. But before we do that…" With absolutely no warning, Yoori lunged herself forward. Her arms were stretched out toward Chae Young. Happiness heaved inside her when she wrapped Chae Young in a warm embrace.

First things first, a long awaited embrace between them was needed.

"I've missed you so much," Yoori whispered, her voice breaking slightly. She tightened her embrace around Chae Young. It had been too long since they'd seen each other. What a twist of fate to meet again like this.

"I've missed you too," Chae Young whispered, tightening her embrace on Yoori.

Yoori's smile remained. She sighed, her throat ready to erupt with all the gossip in the world. "I have so much to tell you."

■ ■ ■

"You guys kissed?" Chae Young squeaked out in amazement.

Yoori bashfully nodded to Chae Young as Jae Won gave her a blank stare.

Granted, having Jae Won sit with Chae Young and Yoori, legs crossed and all, on the floor in the corner of the vacant area of the grocery store wasn't the ideal "girl talk" for Yoori, she, herself, knew that she couldn't be too picky. She had to catch Chae Young up on everything and she couldn't be mean and kick Jae Won out of the conversation. It would be rude to kick Jae Won out of the mix just because he's a boy. Though she nodded inwardly at that belief, the stream of words from Jae Won's mouth tempted Yoori to retract that thought.

"That's why you two were acting so damn awkward," Jae Won commented. He shook his head reprovingly. It was clear that Jae Won recalled informing her that he wasn't sure if Tae Hyun should be trusted. However, affected by Chae Young's presence, he kept his opinions to himself. No doubt he didn't want to get yelled at again.

"Shh!" Yoori scolded, putting a finger in front of her lips to emphasize her point.

She didn't have time for interruptions. For the past hour, Yoori had caught Chae Young up with everything. From the happenings of the diner incident (being blackmailed), living with Tae Hyun as his assistant (handcuffs and sleeping in the same bed included), being chased by Ji Hoon, and getting initiated by the Advisors. Yoori shared everything. Well, almost everything.

Since Jae Won was sitting there, Yoori filtered out the information about her amnesia, the fact that there were snipers involved during her initiation (and that she instinctively fought back), and that there was a strong possibility that she was An Soo Jin. Anything up to date, apart from those pieces of information that she felt she should keep to herself, Yoori shared with Chae Young and Jae Won.

"We kissed before so it's not that big of a deal," said Yoori, replying to Chae Young's earlier reaction about their kiss under the gazebo.

"Yeah, but that was a 'start talking to me' kiss," Chae Young contended. "That didn't count. You guys didn't even know each other. But this one…this was an *actual* kiss. I mean, I thought you said there was tongue involved. There was tongue, right?"

Feeling shy that Jae Won was listening to everything, Yoori merely blinked as her wordless confirmation.

A squeal of approval emitted from Chae Young's mouth.

Everything was nice and dandy until Jae Won's voice came bouncing in to ruin the nice girl talk. "Did he say you were salty again?"

The girls' eyes grew agape at his thoughtless question.

Having no more patience with Jae Won, and embarrassed that he could bring up the "salty" observation from Tae Hyun, Yoori retaliated by stating, "Your ass is fat."

A shocked gasp ran out of Chae Young's mouth while Jae Won's eyes enlarged.

"Yoori!" Chae Young shouted. She intertwined her hand with Jae Won's as her means of comforting him. "Was that really necessary?"

"Why are you checking out my ass, boss?" Jae Won retaliated, hurt that everyone was criticizing his behind.

"I wasn't, you little brat!" Yoori argued, suddenly feeling like she was arguing with her younger brother. "You're sitting down for God's sake! I'm just trying to shut you up!"

It was a low blow, but Yoori was unwilling to offer any apologies for what she said. It was never a good idea to provoke her when she was at her wit's end and Jae Won did just that when he kept teasing her. She could only handle one person teasing her and it sure as hell wasn't Jae Won.

"Okay, you two," Chae Young appeased, patting both of their stiff shoulders. "Let's make peace."

Yoori nodded, taking in a deep breath. Maybe she overreacted a little bit. "Okay, I'm calm. I'm cal—"

"No wonder he said you were salty," Jae Won mumbled under his breath.

And that was what pushed Yoori over the edge.

"You know what?" Yoori began steadily.

A dramatic silence took hold of them when Yoori held up three fingers that were lined up in a sequential line. She mentally smirked. This comeback always had the "shut up" effect on people.

As expected, Jae Won furrowed his brows in confusion. Walking into the trap, he asked, "What are you—?"

"*Don't* read between the lines, honey," Chae Young instructed, grabbing Yoori's wrist and pulling it down with a frown.

Yoori blinked bitterly. She forgot that Chae Young was there with her whenever she used that move on patrons who pissed her off.

"Anyway," Chae Young began soothingly, bringing a bitter Yoori and a confused Jae Won back on topic. "What happened afterward? Did you guys start confessing your love to one another under the moonlight?"

Yoori ogled Chae Young.

The thought of her and Tae Hyun having a confession under the cloak of the moonlight was too strange. It didn't fit their personalities. This belief was shared by Jae Won, who snickered at his girlfriend's question.

Ignoring the strange alternative universe where Tae Hyun and herself would ever end up confessing their love for one another, Yoori continued on with the story. "Well, after the kiss, I was slapped back to reality. I imagine he was too. We started panicking when we realized we were kissing each other. Next thing I knew, we pulled ourselves away from one another, proceeded to tell each other that we had too much to drink, and after that, my ass fled back to the lake house. It's been more than a couple of days since we've been back in Seoul and the awkwardness has been unbearable." Yoori felt a disappointed tug in her heart. "We speak when we have to, but the majority of the time, we don't speak at all."

"Oh God, the morning after effect," Chae Young groaned out loud. She sighed and shook her head at Yoori. "Why can't you tell him that you like him?"

"Whoa, stop right there," Yoori interjected with a raised hand. Her eyes bloomed at Chae Young's incorrect observation. "Let's get a couple of things straight. I don't like him like that. I have a small crush on him because he's cute."

Maybe hot is the better word, Yoori supplied in her mind.

She could see Jae Won smirk in her peripheral vision. It was as though he heard what she was thinking. Doing her best to ignore him, she shifted her full attention to Chae Young. "But being superficially attracted to him aside, I don't like him like that." A rush of discontent loomed in her heart when she was reminded of something else. "Plus, Tae Hyun would be a nightmare of a guy to fall for. He told me himself that he refuses to fall in love. He said that it would distract him from more important things. What girl in her right mind would fall for a guy when he says that?"

"Wow," Jae Won replied with a raised eyebrow. "That was a long answer when, 'I don't like him' could've sufficed."

Chae Young smiled coyly, sharing the same sentiments as her boyfriend. "It sounds like you're trying to convince yourself rather than trying to convince us."

Unnerved, Yoori self-consciously played with the crochet of her beret. "We're just friends," she proclaimed feebly, already knowing that it was a weak argument.

"Is being 'friends' the new term for liking someone?" Chae Young asked, turning to Jae Won. She was genuinely curious. No doubt, she was also reminded of the term Kang Min and Hae Jin used so freely.

"Yeah, apparently the saying, 'we're friends' and 'your ass is fat' is popular in this damn grocery store," Jae Won answered indignantly, pissed that anyone would dare to insult him.

Yoori rolled her eyes at Jae Won's bitter comment while holding back another insult.

Chae Young nodded to appease the second round of argument that was ready to commence if someone didn't put out the flames right away. "Well, anyway," she started, turning back to Yoori. "Only you would know how you truly feel about him."

"Yes. Thank you," Yoori stated appreciatively, unable to hide her smile. Oh how she missed her friend. "God, Chae Young, I wish you were there with me in the beginning. I mean, I feel like I lifted this big boulder off my chest. For once, I feel like I can breathe again."

Chae Young pursed her lips. "Yeah, I'm glad someone's chest is feeling better," she replied with warm sarcasm. She took a moment to rub her chest before saying, "Why did you send me that shifty text message about having a family emergency? All we had was the surveillance tape of you talking to some guy in a red cap and you following him after he left seconds later. Do you know how mad I was? I thought you lied about the emergency, got wooed by a stranger and left to go marry him or something. I can't believe you got blackmailed by the King of Serpents. We were just talking about the Underworld that day too!"

Yoori nodded. *Oh the webs of life*, she thought.

"I didn't want you to get involved in the Underworld stuff. I figured if we were supposed to meet again…then we would. And here you are." Her eyes swung toward Jae Won. His hand was intertwined with Chae Young's. "Apparently you got involved in the Underworld stuff without me having to pull you in."

Yoori smiled at the unexpected couple before her: her best friend who was like a sister to her and her bodyguard who was like a brother to her. "This is the part where you guys tell me how you became a couple," she prompted happily.

Chae Young obliged, a huge grin radiating on her face. "Do you remember that idiot short-term 'boyfriend' I had?" Chae Young began. Though her voice was filled with distaste, her smile remained. "You know…the one who cheated on me at the nightclub with the hostess?"

Yoori nodded, recalling the last conversation they had before she met Tae Hyun.

"Jae Won was at that nightclub too. I remember seeing him from across the room and thinking he was really cute…"

Jae Won hid a cheeky grin when he heard this.

"But I got distracted with the cheating asshole. After I kicked that dumbass in the shins, I caught Jae Won's eyes and he started to pursue me. You know, wooing me at clubs, staying late to pick me up when I closed the diner, taking me out..." Chae Young beamed, leaning in closer to Yoori to whisper, "I like him a lot. At first, I wasn't sure. I thought I was just infatuated because I have a thing for bad boys."

"Don't we all," Yoori empathized warmly. She spared a look at Jae Won, who smiled nonstop, and said, "Has Jae Won told you everything about himself? Who he's affiliated with? What he does when he's not with you? Everything?"

Chae Young nodded, her smile hiding the small frown on her face. Chae Young, despite realizing the hardships that came with being with someone who was affiliated with the Underworld, wanted to be with Jae Won regardless.

"Aside from him never calling you anything but 'boss' and myself never calling you anything but my 'best friend,' we tell each other everything." She smiled wryly, turning to Yoori. There was a dim light in her eyes when she realized something. "Um, just because I know all this Underworld stuff...I don't have to be initiated…do I?

Yoori and Jae Won exchanged sneaky grins.

"Normally no one cares when a few outsiders find out the inner workings of the Underworld," Jae Won explained, tightening his grip on Chae Young's hand. He jutted a chin at Yoori. "Boss, here, was the exception because the Advisors wanted their time alone with her. They would've made up any excuse to have her initiated."

Yoori nodded. It was true. The Advisors would've gotten their five minutes with her no matter what. The excuse of her being privy to the inner workings of the Underworld was convenient for them.

"That's terrible," said Chae Young. Reserved horror swam in her voice when she turned back to Yoori. "Just because you resemble that girl..."

"Well, let's not worry about that," Yoori dismissed casually. She didn't want to talk about Soo Jin. "Things are going well between the two of you? You don't need me to give you guys a pep talk, right? I can't really threaten to break anyone's bones because I know both of you."

It was unfortunately true.

How was Yoori supposed to threaten both Chae Young and Jae Won, and keep them from breaking each other's hearts? It wouldn't work. They wouldn't take her seriously anyway. She was sure of it. Yoori was determined to save herself from the embarrassment of even attempting to look intimidating.

Chae Young and Jae Won shook their heads at her and laughed.

"It's been going really well," Chae Young provided. Her face was genuinely mirthful when she turned to Jae Won. "I've never been happier with someone."

Jae Won returned her smile, his dorky face beaming. "I love you too, honey," he cooed before leaning in to give Chae Young a quick kiss.

"Oh man," Yoori complained, sending her gaze upward. As much as she adored them as a couple, it was another thing to have them kiss in front of her. Yuck.

"I still cannot believe that you two are together," she muttered to herself. Her eyes widened when another realization hit her. She looked at Chae Young. "You've met Kang Min and Hae Jin too?"

Chae Young bounced her head to confirm. Her eyes twinkled with adoration. "Yeah! Hae Jin and Kang Min are great. They're so adorable together. There's such an awkward tension between them because you know that they want each other. I don't know...I guess they're still working all of that out."

She looked over to Jae Won to see if he wanted to add anything.

Jae Won heeded the opportunity and said, "Hae Jin and Chae Young really hit it off. For the first hour of dinner, Kang Min and I couldn't even get a word in edgewise because they were too busy bonding."

Yoori laughed. She wasn't sure if Jae Won was complaining, but the information was, nonetheless, heartwarming. It made sense that Chae Young and Hae Jin would hit it off since they both hit it off with her in the beginning as well.

Chae Young suddenly pouted, interrupting Yoori's reverie. "I feel bad though. Hae Jin is left out on many of the secrets." She looked at Jae Won. "She doesn't know that you and Kang Min are brothers and she doesn't know that Yoori's not actually her brother's girlfriend—" Chae Young interrupted herself and turned to Yoori. "Hae Jin adores you by the way. When we had dinner, she wouldn't stop singing praises about her brother's new girlfriend. I was getting a bit annoyed because I didn't know who the hell she was talking about since you have so many alternative names. 'My best friend', 'my boss', 'my boss's girlfriend', 'my brother's girlfriend...'"

Though the listing of her alternative names made her feel awkward, Yoori forced a smile to stay on her face. She continued to listen as Chae Young went on. "But now that I know she was talking about you, it makes sense."

Yoori blushed, her love for Hae Jin growing with the passing seconds.

Having more on her mind, Yoori cleared her throat and asked, "The four of you are doing another double date tonight?"

They nodded.

"Do you want to come?" asked Jae Won. It was a genuine invitation.

Chae Young wordlessly asked the same question. She nodded frantically, gesturing for Yoori to agree.

Almost too quickly, Yoori shook her head. She had prior engagements in mind. "No, I want to stay in tonight."

And maybe hang out with Tae Hyun.

Chae Young and Jae Won raised a suspicious eyebrow, but said nothing more.

"Anyway," Yoori began, taking a quick look around. "Do you guys need to leave soon? Is it almost dinner time?"

Chae Young and Jae Won stared at the watch on Jae Won's wrist. They nodded when they realized it was time for them to leave.

"Yeah, I should take boss home so we can make it to dinner on time," Jae Won said to Chae Young. The three of them got up on their feet. Jae Won reached a hand out to Chae Young. "What did you come here to buy?"

"Wine for the dinner," Chae Young answered, taking his hand and fully straightening herself out. "I'm not sure what to get though."

"I'll help you decide," Jae Won offered. He looked at Yoori, who had gotten to her feet and started dusting dirt off her pants. "Why don't you and boss finish talking? You can come find me in the alcohol aisle when you're done."

Chae Young nodded. "I'll see you in a bit."

The girls waited for him to disappear into an aisle before turning to face one another. Like a kid waiting to throw a party after her parents had left, Chae Young flew toward Yoori and gave her another hug.

"Damn it, I've missed you, you bum," she squealed in delight. "I can't gossip with anyone at the diner now."

"I've missed you too," Yoori complained back. A pout took hold of her lips. "This damn Underworld is filled with boys. The only girls I know are Hae Jin and Jin Ae. And one of them would like nothing more than to rip my eyes out so I don't have the numbers on my side."

Chae Young laughed, pulling out of the embrace. "At least you got some nice gang members looking after you." At her own statement, Chae Young couldn't help but scoff in disbelief. "I still can't believe that the last thing we talked about at the diner was the story about the 'Queen of the Underworld' and now look at you…people actually say you resemble her. How crazy is that?" She was seemingly ready to end her speech until she added, "And you have *two* crime lords chasing after you. How ironic is that?"

"I know. It's crazy and – wait a second," Yoori thought out loud. "There's only one that's chasing and that's Lee Ji Hoon. Kwon Tae Hyun isn't chasing me. He's just…" She struggled to find the right term to use. "He—He's just pushing me."

Chae Young blinked slowly. "He—He's *pushing* you?"

"Yeah, you know. Teasing me, torturing me…" She thought about the kiss and became bitter again. "Pushing me toward the effen brink of insanity."

A quiet laugh emitted from Chae Young. "Oh gosh, you're always so dramatic. For what it's worth, I'm rooting for you and the King of Serpents."

Yoori eyed her friend strangely, thrown by the cheerleader mode in her. "I thought you would be a rooter of the King of Skulls."

Chae Young shrugged. "That was before the King of Serpents came into the picture and swept my best friend off her feet."

Yoori groaned in annoyance. "For the last time, I do not like him like that. There's nothing to root for."

"Choi Yoori, listen up," Chae Young began seriously. "Here's what I'm going to do. I'm going to leave you with parting words that will change your outlook on things. I didn't want to talk about this when Jae Won was sitting here because it's more of a girl thing, but do you want to know if you really like a guy? Even if you, yourself, are in denial?"

No, Yoori replied in her mind.

"Sure, of course I want to know," Yoori said half-heartedly, wanting to humor Chae Young.

Chae Young gave Yoori a suspicious gaze. When Yoori's bluff seemed real enough to her, she blinked seriously and began. "First off, the world doesn't revolve around you and only you—or anyone in particular for that matter. At least not in the physical sense. However, you have power over your own world, which means that psychologically, you can have your world revolve around someone. Are you following me?"

"Okay…"

"Kisses are typically the deciding factor on whether or not you like someone. But how those kisses play out usually entail how much you like that person—how much you, even subconsciously, are willing to allow them to affect your world."

"Okay…" Yoori said again, this time listening carefully.

"When you kissed him…what happened to your world?"

"Weird things happening in the environment around me doesn't mean that we should be together," Yoori protested, refusing to answer.

Chae Young's features hardened. "Yes I know, but it does mean that you like him. We just have to figure out how much."

Yoori sighed, not wanting to answer. She blinked in frustration and then made a thoughtless comment. "The easy part should be figuring out if you like someone…"

"And the hard part should be figuring out if you belong with them," Chae Young finished for her.

Lost in her thoughts, Yoori asked, "In your opinion, how would you know if you belong with someone?"

Chae Young paused to deliberate. "If you keep coming back to each other—even if you don't want to." Chae Young bit her lips, trying to recall something. "What are those things called where you throw them and they keep coming back to you?"

"Boomerangs," Yoori provided. Sudden warmth illuminated over her when she was reminded of her conversation with Tae Hyun on that leaky boat.

"Ah yes…boomerangs…" Chae Young said nodding again. "But we're getting ahead of ourselves. My only objective right now is to help you figure out the easy part. You're on your own with the hard part. Stop wasting time and tell me what happened while you kissed him."

"It will never work out between us," Yoori resisted, unwilling to answer.

"Uh-uh," Chae Young said dismissively. "That wasn't my question. You're always so stubborn. Just answer it, will you? I'll tell you what it means. "

Though she didn't want to answer, Yoori knew that she would have to share. It was in Chae Young's nature to be persistent. There was no use in prolonging the inevitable.

Yoori blinked in dread and indulged her friend. "My world stopped, then came to life, and spun for him."

Chae Young grinned expectantly. "That means you like him."

Something pulled at Yoori's heart. The answer was too obvious.

"That was because I was caught up in the moment. After we were done, my world came crashing down," Yoori stated ominously, thinking this would deter Chae Young from her first statement. "Doesn't that mean something stronger?"

Yoori was surprised when she saw that Chae Young was still smiling.

"That means you like him…a lot."

Yoori laughed at Chae Young's reply. Feigning an understanding nod, she smiled at her friend. It was palpable to her that she wasn't going to get an objective answer here.

"Did the world send you back to me to try and push me into falling for Kwon Tae Hyun?" she asked suspiciously.

Chae Young shook her head, her face sympathetic. "No, I'm here to shine some light on a couple of things you refuse to acknowledge. You've always been amazingly stubborn, my dear friend. Always in denial about anything and everything that may have the power to make you vulnerable to getting hurt." Chae Young then smiled reassuringly. "But that's okay. You'll come around. You always do."

When it looked like Chae Young was about to bid goodbye and leave, she suddenly turned around and faced a skeptical Yoori again.

"Oh and by the way," she began whimsically. "I can't push someone who has already fallen."

"For every injustice..."

08: The Epiphany of a God

A swarm of ice-cold wind filtered into Yoori's skin once she stepped outside the grocery store. Yoori folded her arms across her shivering chest in an attempt to keep herself warm.

Cooped up within the confines of the store, Yoori had no idea that the weather had become this bad. The sky was darker and much angrier than her last meeting with it. Resounding screams of thunders could be heard as Yoori did her best to stand outside, fighting the unforgiving cold.

After bidding goodbye to Chae Young, Yoori knew that the couple must've wanted their alone time before Jae Won took her home. At first, Yoori insisted that she wait in line to pay for all the grocery items she picked out. She wanted to give them the opportunity to go off somewhere on their own and spend time with each other. Much to the resistance of Chae Young and Jae Won, Yoori had to back down when they insisted that they wait in line with her.

Determined to give the couple some time alone—and to avoid Chae Young after that enlightening speech that Yoori was skeptical about—Yoori manufactured a lie about wanting some fresh air and ran out of the line before they could stop her. She was ready to give herself a pat on the back for being so considerate until she stepped foot outside.

As her teeth clattered like cans against one another, Yoori regretted her decision. She knew it was going to be cold, yes, but she had no idea it was going to be this cold. Even her Uggs were shivering.

She tried to think of warm, happy thoughts. It was truly a cursed attempt because Yoori's first inclination was to stare longingly into the windows of the grocery store. Her eyes caught sight of Jae Won and Chae Young. They were waiting in line, hugging and laughing while they flipped through the various magazines next to the cashier line. Every now and then, they would give quick kisses to one another before hugging again.

Unnerved by the ripple of envy that inundated her, she turned away, no longer able to stare without feeling a downpour of despondence wash over her. Uncrossing her arms, her hands found the respective pockets of her jacket. While her left hand found an empty haven to take solace in, her right hand found an unexpected object that occupied the space of her pocket.

Yoori grabbed the object and took it out.

It was her non-prescribed glasses that Jae Won returned to her.

It sat steadily on the foundation of her right palm; the glass surface of the dark-rimmed glasses showed a modest reflection of Yoori.

Chae Young's voice accompanied her as she fell through a state of contemplation. *"I can't push someone who has already fallen."*

Yoori knew very well how silly she looked wearing these non-prescribed glasses. She also knew, regardless of the fact that it was her favorite accessory, how peculiarly eye catching her bright teal crochet beret was. To top it off, her black Uggs made her look more like a vertically challenged elf than a tall fashionista.

Yes.

Yoori was terribly ashamed to admit that she not only knew all of this, but she also purposely chose all these accessories *because* she knew all this. It was a show of desperation on her part. She wanted to make herself a walking target so Tae Hyun would be tempted to talk to her again. She wanted him to make fun of her so that they could squash the awkwardness they were plagued with. She wanted to go back to the days before that stupid kiss made things terribly tense between them.

Yoori never thought she'd be the one to admit it, but she missed Tae Hyun and his teasing nature. She missed talking to him. Who knew an unexpected kiss could be the cause of this headache for Yoori?

She exhaled sadly and placed the glasses back in her pocket. She allowed her eyes to rest on the pavement of the sidewalk, its shiny exterior marked with remnants of rainwater. Her mind began to wade through all the possible ways she could go back to the apartment and start talking to Tae Hyun again. Who knew Tae Hyun would be so good with the silent treatment? What was going through this guy's mind? All Yoori could do was wonder.

As she stole another glimpse at the status of Chae Young and Jae Won's queue in line, a thrash of wind stole her unyielding attention. The wind brought a cloud of scattered mist and swam right through her. Before a scream could escape her lips, the gust of wind stole something from her. Her teal crochet beret.

Yoori's eyes exploded in urgency. She watched her beret fly upward with the powerful draft. The unforgiving force of mist and wind thrashed violently against her long black hair, leaving her frozen with shock. The shock lasted momentarily. Unfeeling of the merciless cold, her eyes locked on her beret as it flew further and further out of sight. Adrenaline pumping through her, Yoori felt her legs take off, matching in pace with the velocity of the wintry wind. She had to get it back!

The soles of her Uggs impaled themselves within the core of rain puddles that sat scattered throughout the sidewalk. Splashes of cold water flew into the air as she ran, her breathing growing steady with her running. She had to get it back. She had to get her beret back. Her day was already bad enough. She couldn't let it end so terribly.

The unexpected chase took Yoori down two vacant blocks. The howling wind began to die down when she reached the second block, the force of its power lowering the beret down to earth. Yoori smiled at the sight. She thought the beret would fall straight to the ground. Instead, the residual air blew it into the opening of an alleyway.

"Oh shit," Yoori muttered under her breath, ceasing with her running.

Of all the rotten luck...

It had to be her luck that her beret would tumble into an alley of all places.

Yoori considered running back to the grocery store and forgetting her beret. She reconsidered that immediately. Wouldn't all that running be a waste if she didn't at least try to get it back? She entertained the idea of going back to get Jae Won and having him accompany her to get the beret. But wouldn't that be a waste of *his* time? She bit her lips, her mind venturing on. Who was to say there were gang members in the alley? Who would be out in this terrible weather?

I'll take a peek and if someone is there, I'll make a run for it, she assured herself. Inwardly nodding at the precaution she was taking, Yoori tiptoed to the right corner of the building wall that stood as a guard for the pathway into the alley. Once her hands reached the brick wall, she carefully tilted her head out to determine what was in the alley.

To her heart's content, all Yoori saw was an empty alley that housed her teal beret. The beret sat motionless in the center of the long alleyway.

Run in, grab it, and leave, Yoori instructed herself. Plan set, Yoori threw herself out from behind the wall and raced into the alley. The resounding trot of her shoes and her heavily shrilled breathing could be heard as it echoed off the high alley walls.

Her sprinting was quick.

Too quick.

Too quick and too careless.

"Ahh!" Oblivious to the crack in the pavement that impeded her running, Yoori took a nosedive when she reached her beret. However, thanks to her quick reflexes, Yoori was able to avoid the collision between her face and the concrete.

Instinctively extending both hands forward and laying them flat on the wet pavement, Yoori swiftly repositioned herself so the landing was done on her kneecaps instead of her chin.

Her heart breathed faintly, its beats thankful that Yoori avoided another bone shattering accident. As she steadied her breathing, her brown eyes landed on the beret that rested on the concrete.

"This is because you're my favorite accessory," Yoori voiced, shaking her head at the teal beret.

Her kneecaps resting on the pavement, Yoori grabbed the beret. Her first inclination was to grab it and run out. Yet, when her fingers enclosed around the soft fabric, an urge to take a look around the alley clamped over her.

It was an odd urge that became the catalyst for what occurred seconds later.

Sprinkles of rain cascaded down on her, its damp touch accompanying her eyes as they bloomed with a sudden bout of realization.

There was something very familiar about this alley.

Why does this place feel like déjà vu? she asked herself, the sprinkles of the rain picking up. She continued to kneel on the concrete.

The answer to her question came in a roar of thunder that infiltrated the world beneath it. At the same moment, a string of voices and familiar images filtered through Yoori's mind when she looked upward at the dark sky. The reflection of lightning coursed in her eyes.

Slowly, purposefully and intentionally...the reminder as to why this alley felt so familiar came to her in a string of dream sequences that had been plaguing her since she arrived in Seoul.

"If I..." he began in a quiet voice. *"If I do this, then I would lose you. I would never see you again."* He averted his gaze away from her as bolts of lightning spilled into the sky. *"There has to be another way. You don't want to do this."*

This alleyway...*this* was the place.

This was the place in her dreams.

"There's no other option for me but this. If I don't die, then I have to live with what I did." She paused, taking a moment to exhale sharply. Distant sounds of thunder bellowed overhead while she spoke. *"And I can't do that."*

The siblings...

Then, like the cascading of the rain, the puzzle pieces began to fall right in front of Yoori.

He turned away from her and dug his hand into the pocket of his black jacket. He withdrew a small liquid vial. From there, everything seemed to play out in slow motion. He removed the cap and inserted the needle into the vial. Together, they watched with bated breaths as the clear liquid swam into the needle. Their breaths only returned when the needle was filled to the core.

He narrowed his solemn eyes onto her.

An Young Jae...Yoori thought mindlessly.

At this point, she had finally stopped shaking. Unable to hold his gaze and knowing what was to come, she broke eye contact. She merely lifted her right wrist to him. Things would be a lot easier if they minimized eye contact as much as possible.

An Soo Jin...

"Are you completely sure about this?" he asked one last time.

"I can no longer lead life as your right-hand soldier," she replied, ready to finalize it all. "It's time to end this."

The string of images in Yoori's mind journeyed on to another dream.

"You don't understand what I'm going through!" Pain, indignation, guilt, and shame were all present in her elevated voice. "I can barely breathe without getting sick to my stomach. I can't eat. I can't sleep...I can barely even look at my brother! All I can do is think about it...what happened...what should've happened and what I can do to make things right. I can't go on pretending that everything is fine. I can't. I can't live like this anymore."

She began to retreat again, her pace quickening by the second. She knew he would have a hard time accepting what she had to do, but she didn't think he'd put up such a fight.

Her pace was matched by her significant other's pace.

Lee Ji Hoon...Yoori thought, closing her eyes in dismay.

"Do you realize how selfish you're being right now? Do I really have no say in this matter?"

"If you're not going to support me, then that's fine," she uttered, stopping abruptly. She gazed at him unblinkingly, her determination never faltering on what she had to do. "But do not think for one second that you can change my mind!"

The puzzle pieces began to click together for Yoori.

An Soo Jin was *never* murdered, Yoori concluded with bewilderment.

She was never murdered.

Soo Jin had planned her death all along.

"Tonight is the night where he helps me make things right," she continued, her voice breaking. She held back the tears ready to stream out of her eyes. "Tonight is the night where I make things right. If you love me, then you'll help me make things right as well."

"No," Yoori whispered when the conversation she had with Chae Young, pertaining to the Queen of the Underworld, poured into her mind.

"What happened to her?"

Disappointment teemed in Chae Young's brown eyes.

"That's the sad part. She went missing for a couple of days and her body was eventually found in the back of a known gang alley. Someone had shot her point blank in the head and disfigured her face. The ones who found her said she was not even close to being recognizable. She was only later identified when her brother confirmed a birthmark on her neck or something. After her body was discovered, fingers were pointed as to who was to be blamed for her death. Some people say that she got into a fight, got her face disfigured and ended her own life

because of it. I, personally, think it's someone from the Serpents gang who didn't want the Skulls and the Scorpions to merge. But it's all speculation..."

"Oh God," Yoori uttered breathlessly. She slowly stood up. Her knees were weak as they threatened to succumb to gravity. She ran her shaking fingers through her hair. Her mind was swirling.

An Soo Jin was never murdered.

She wanted to kill herself and she wanted her brother to help her do it...

Young Jae's final words to his sister haunted Yoori's psyche.

"Goodbye, little one," she heard her brother utter before she lost all consciousness. "I'm sorry for not doing what you asked me to do."

Young Jae never killed Soo Jin. Whatever it was he injected her with, it never killed her. It never killed her and he did something to her. He did something to her and turned her into—

Finally...it all clicked together.

Yoori covered her mouth in horror. Losing strength in her legs, she fell backward. The wall of the building behind her caught her fall.

Her.

An Young Jae turned An Soo Jin, into...her.

He turned Soo Jin into...Choi Yoori.

It was then and only then that Yoori realized how silly she had been, how silly she had been to keep denying her relation to Soo Jin.

Drops of crystal clear raindrops fell harder from the sky as Yoori stood there, her face pale from bewilderment, disbelief, and horror.

Her breathing grew rapid...violent.

No longer able to stand in the very alley where Soo Jin tried to kill herself, Yoori made a run for it. Her lungs gasped for breath as the inevitable truth tugged at her heart.

All these months...

Her legs took off like the wind.

These months of countless denial...

Her arms swung like a pendulum.

These months of purposely keeping herself from piecing the obvious together...

Her long black hair danced in the wind as rain poured over her.

These months of trying to separate herself from the guilt of being An Soo Jin...

She bit her lips, fighting the urge to scream out in the purest of aggravation.

These months of constant hatred for Soo Jin when deep down, she knew the inexplicable truth...

There was no more possibility—no more denial.

I'm An Soo Jin, Yoori declared in her mind.

Her shoulders shook and she fought to keep the tears from escaping her eyes.

"I'm An Soo Jin," Yoori repeated out loud, her voice breaking at every syllable.

The truth shouldn't hurt this much.

As she continued to run, a train of inevitable questions materialized in her mind. Nothing made sense. What happened to her? What did An Young Jae do to her? Why couldn't she remember anything?

Why can't I remember anything? she repeated in her mind. *Why can't I remember? Why can't I—?*

"Boss!" Jae Won called, running out of the corner and catching Yoori after she sprung out of the alley.

"Huh?" Yoori uttered, slapped out of her trance.

"Where have you been? I've been looking for you. I—" Jae Won halted with his words when his eyes wandered into the alleyway. She knew when his eyes enlarged in shock that Jae Won recognized that this was the alleyway where Soo Jin's "dead" body was found. Unwilling to say anything pertaining to that matter though, he composed himself, turned back to her and asked, "Boss, what were you doing in there?"

The irony of Jae Won calling her "boss" tortured Yoori. All this time, he called her "boss" with the belief that she was merely a lookalike, when in truth, she really was An Soo Jin. She had been An Soo Jin all along...

Resolved on maintaining composure, Yoori lifted up the beret. This newfound revelation wasn't something she wanted to talk to Jae Won about.

"The wind blew this into the alley," she answered easily. "I ran after it and went in to grab it."

Though there was so much cycling through her mind, there was only one thing she wanted to do at that particular moment.

"I want to go back to the apartment," she added at once. "I want to go back to Tae Hyun."

Jae Won took note of the color that drained from Yoori's face and nodded. "Let's go," he said, asking no more questions.

The rain picked up when they powerwalked through the sidewalk. Yoori shook while she walked—not from the cold, but from the tsunami of revelations that rained over her.

She couldn't deny it anymore.

She couldn't deny anything anymore.

The fracture in Yoori's dam had cracked and Yoori knew that the inevitable was taking place...

She could feel the guilt of being Soo Jin taking form in her mind – her heart. She could feel the disgust for herself...She could feel the hatred for herself for merely breathing...

88

For Yoori, it had already begun.

The unbearable had already begun to plague her.

Despite being besieged with these unforgiving thoughts, there was one thing that overshadowed everything else: Yoori knew she had to tell someone about this.

She couldn't hold it in anymore. Not something as big as this.

She couldn't handle this by herself.

Her mind was resolved.

She needed to tell the one person she trusted most.

She had to tell Tae Hyun.

She had to tell Tae Hyun everything.

"There is revenge."

09: The Thing About Boomerangs

"Are you sure you're alright?" Jae Won asked when he placed the last of the grocery bags on the counter. His face was coated with concern.

Yoori feigned a smile and easily lied by saying, "Yeah. I think running in the rain wore me out. I'm feeling better now though. Thanks for asking."

She finished that sentence with an even bigger smile of appreciation.

Jae Won took a moment to gauge her expression. When it didn't appear to him that she was lying, he gave a relieved smile. "That's good. Do you need help with anything else?"

Yoori shook her head, her fake smile remaining. "No, go have dinner!" she urged excitedly. She pushed him to the door. "Give everyone my greetings."

"I will," Jae Won said with a nod. "Give the King of Serpents my greetings as well, alright?"

Apprehension coursed through her when she was reminded of Tae Hyun and the talk she needed to have with him. "I will."

"Alright then, boss. I'll see you later." Turning the doorknob, Jae Won gave one last wave and walked out the door.

Yoori's tentative smile faded when the door closed. Her mind ran in circles, replaying what occurred earlier. She was nervous about what she had to tell Tae Hyun. She needed time to think.

Washed with an overwhelming urge to organize the groceries (along with her frantic thoughts), Yoori kneeled on the kitchen tiles. She pulled a grocery bag filled with fruits toward her and opened the refrigerator door. A warm glow illumed from the appliance while a breeze hovered around Yoori's body.

The grocery bag elicited a small cackle sound every time Yoori reached in. Every grocery item she pulled out acted as a mirrored twin to all the thoughts she singlehandedly pulled out of her head.

It had only been twenty-five minutes since she acknowledged that her life had been a lie. It had only been twenty-five minutes since she rid herself of denials and accepted the fact that she was the one person she hated most: An Soo Jin.

She knew there was something wrong with the "family" that she woke up with because she never felt any connection to them. With her denial gone, it made sense that they had no relation to her at all. This begged the question: how did they end up with her? Yoori sighed and placed those thoughts in the back of her mind. She would deal with that later. Right now, she had more pressing matters to tend to.

I'm An Soo Jin, she dreadfully declared in her mind.

It had only been twenty-five minutes and the truth hurt more and more.

It all felt like a terrible nightmare that she couldn't wake up from. No matter how hard she tried, no matter how hard she bit her lips and held her breath, she couldn't wake up from it. The painful truth was that *this* was her reality. Her life prior to this particular moment *was* the dream. Yoori had woken up and now, she hated her reality.

The icy, concentrated air continued to murmur around her. She made room for more fruits in the fridge.

Yoori didn't know if it was normal. She didn't know if it was normal to tremble relentlessly as she grabbed the last of the fruits. Her stomach rippled with agony. She didn't know if it was normal to struggle to breathe evenly—not from the lack of air, but from the lack of wanting air. She didn't know if it was normal to hold back her tears, not because she didn't want to cry, but because she *hated* crying and she hated that she couldn't control herself. Though her eyes began to water, Yoori refused to allow any tears to escape from her eyes. Taking a deep inhalation, she allowed the natural air to dry her eyes. Her shaking hands reached for the bag that held all the vegetables.

Yoori sniffled to herself, her lips trembling when she was reminded of Tae Hyun and the truth she would have to tell him.

In the course of the past twenty-five minutes, Yoori changed her mind more than a million times when it came to telling Tae Hyun the truth.

How would he look at her after this? Would he even believe her? Should she keep this to herself and continue to live in her dream world?

These questions lingered in her mind when she rode in the car with Jae Won.

She grabbed the last of the vegetables, wrapped the grocery bag into a ball and threw it into the corner. Her quivering hands then reached for the bag that held the drinks.

Though Yoori had changed her mind more than a million times, she also made up her mind more than a million times. This secret was too big to keep to herself; she couldn't handle this herself. She had to tell someone and she knew it had to be Tae Hyun. Not only because she trusted him the most, but also because he deserved to know the most. Apart from an argumentative relationship, Tae Hyun had truly become her best friend in this unforgiving society. After all these months of him taking care of her, he deserved to know. If anything, he deserved to know whom he kissed—even if the kiss itself was a mistake.

Yoori drew in a sharp breath. The vital questions now were: how would she tell him and more importantly, how would he react?

It wouldn't be a pleasant reaction. Regardless, she hoped that he'd be able to look past everything and realize that she was still the same girl. She hoped that Tae Hyun would not disappoint her expectations of him as her friend—her best friend. She hoped that he wouldn't let her down.

After placing the last of the drinks into the fridge, Yoori stood up and closed the refrigerator door. She approached the counter and reached for the grocery bag filled with cookie boxes and canned food.

These would be her last bags.

Although there were three more grocery bags on the kitchen counter, Yoori decided she would deal with all of that later. She had already stolen too much time to herself. Though she was confused and worried, she shouldn't prolong the inevitable anymore. She had to tell Tae Hyun everything and she had to tell him tonight.

That goal in mind, Yoori placed the last cookie box into the cupboards.

Her tentative brown eyes, which still had remnants of tears glazed over them, wandered across the living room. Though Tae Hyun was nowhere in sight, he was somewhere in the apartment.

Closing the cupboards, she took off her shoes and made her way down the hall. She pushed the bedroom door open. She poked her head into the room, thinking that she would find Tae Hyun sitting on the bed doing his usual paperwork for his Underworld stuff. When all she found was an empty room, Yoori's brows bunched in confusion. She could *feel* Tae Hyun's presence. Why was he nowhere in sight? How odd.

Yoori returned to the living room more befuddled than ever. He wasn't in the apartment, but she knew he was close to her. Slowly, her eyes landed on the glass sliding door that separated the living room and the balcony outside.

He couldn't be outside when the weather was so crazy cold, right?

Eager to find out for herself, her legs took off in the direction of the sliding door. Her hand landed on the lever and she slid it open. She poked her head outside. The winter breeze billowed through her hair like curtains dancing in the wind. It didn't take her long to spot the one she was looking for.

Her heart soared when she saw him.

Sure enough, Tae Hyun sat on a long, rectangular table that was pulled off to the corner. He wore a white jacket and dark blue jeans. He sat with his legs folded, his messy spiked hair rustling in the calm wind and his back resting comfortably against the wall. The rain had ceased for the time being, leaving Tae Hyun to enjoy the relaxed ambiance with closed eyes. The tranquility was probably the reason why he braved this gloomy weather.

The scene looked utterly picturesque. If they weren't suspended in midair, she would've thought he was performing a photo-shoot with his attractive self as the main model.

She wasted no more time to greet Tae Hyun.

"Hey Snob," Yoori greeted warmly.

She did her best to hide the big smile fighting to bloom unto her lips. If the outpouring of butterflies that flew in her stomach gave any indication, then Yoori had no doubt that she was excited to finally see him. Suddenly all her troubles, although they still existed powerfully in her mind, appeared far away when in the presence of Tae Hyun...

Yoori waved happily when Tae Hyun lifted his eyelids and turned to her. His eyes held a glimmer of joy that made her feel warm all over.

"Hey Brat," he greeted back, his face mirroring Yoori's. He tried to hide that he was excited to see her as well.

"Why are you sitting out here?" Yoori went on, secretly happy that they were communicating again. Name calling aside of course.

Tae Hyun shrugged. "I had a lot on my mind and I wanted some fresh air." He drew his eyes away from her to appreciate his surroundings. "Plus, I like sitting out here when the weather is unfriendly like this. No one else is outside...it makes me feel like I have the entire world to myself."

Yoori nodded, immediately understanding his reasoning. As crazy as the weather was, there was a sense of peacefulness that came with all the chaos.

She stepped onto the wet surface of the balcony, casually sliding the glass door closed. The cold stung her bare feet, but Yoori kept the unpleasant reaction off her face. She didn't want Tae Hyun to kick her back in for not being able to handle the cold.

The concern of being kicked back inside was warranted with Tae Hyun's next set of actions.

"Eh!" Tae Hyun reprimanded once he saw her approaching him. "You're not allowed out here!"

Yoori pretended to be ignorant. "Why not?"

While approaching him, she spotted a red towel on the floor. Tae Hyun had wiped the table clean of water before sitting on it himself. Further comforted by the fact that she was going to be sitting on a dry table, Yoori strode past him, happily got on, sat right across from him, and eyed him pleasantly. She presented him with a sheepish smile. It was her subtle way of telling him that she wasn't planning on going back inside anytime soon.

Though he scoffed, there was a curve of a smile on his face that told Yoori he wasn't that upset. Nevertheless, Tae Hyun didn't falter with his objective of kicking her back inside.

"Do you not recall having a bad track record when it comes to handling the cold? Where's the blanket I bought you?"

Yoori shrugged. "Somewhere," she said briskly, honestly not knowing where the blanket was.

Tae Hyun frowned in disapproval.

"Go back inside, Choi Yoori," he said tiredly, taking his eyes off her. "I don't want to deal with you getting sick."

Yoori shook her head, stubbornness embedded inside her. Though the goal of telling him she was An Soo Jin continued to linger in her mind, Yoori wanted to casually catch up with him before they went into earthshattering realities. She wanted to prolong the innocence of her dream for a couple more minutes.

Just a couple more minutes…and then she'd wake herself up.

Tae Hyun wearily closed his eyes at her defiance. "Assistant, listen to me. You need to go back inside—"

"I miss you," she interjected swiftly. There was no filtering of her answer. It was the cold, hard truth.

The sternness in his face softened when he opened his eyes. He didn't believe his ears. "What?"

Under different circumstances, Yoori would be quick to retract that statement so she wouldn't appear too vulnerable. However, in this moment, she had too much on her mind. She wanted to be with Tae Hyun and talk to him again. She no longer cared about looking vulnerable.

"We haven't talked in a while…and I just…miss you," she finished quietly, this time finding it a bit more difficult to keep eye contact. She felt incredibly exposed.

Tae Hyun sighed again after hearing her unfiltered reply. It didn't seem as if he liked her answer too much. Shaking his head at her, he gave her one last look before unfolding his legs and jumping off the table. Without another word, he drew away from the table and disappeared into the living room, leaving Yoori to sit on the table alone, her face dejected from being snubbed.

Guess we're still not talking, she thought despondently, regretting that she was being so honest with her feelings.

She continued to sit there, allowing a couple more minutes to pass. Her eyes lingered on the sliding door. Her gaze was hopeful that Tae Hyun would feel bad and come back outside. When all she was left with was the howling of the wind, the blinking city lights, and the waves of cars swimming underneath her, the hope flickered out of her eyes. Disheartened that he wanted to further extend their awkwardness, Yoori was ready to jump off the table when she heard the door slide open.

A smile tugged at her lips when Yoori watched Tae Hyun approach her. He was holding a teacup in one hand and her lavender blanket in the other. When he reached her, Tae Hyun placed the jade colored teacup on the table and unfolded the blanket. He promptly wrapped it around Yoori like a cape. Yoori couldn't take her eyes off him. She was lost in an awe of gratitude. He carefully made sure every part of her, from the chin down, was covered with the blanket before he got back on the table.

"Thanks for ignoring me a couple of minutes ago, *Snob*," Yoori confronted warmly. "I thought you left for good."

She contemplated thanking him for the blanket before he laughed and said, "You're welcome for the blanket, *Brat*."

Yoori wrapped the blanket closer around her. A small, appreciative smile graced her countenance. She watched Tae Hyun situate himself on the table.

He only went back inside to bring me my blanket, she thought happily.

Catching the sparkle of appreciation in her eyes, Tae Hyun quickly added, "By the way, I'm not being nice. I just don't want to deal with you getting sick."

"You're such a thoughtful jerk," Yoori commented affectionately, unable to conceal her widening smile.

"I'd like to think so," he answered, smiling back. His eyes rested on the teacup he brought out for her. He enclosed his hands around it and handed it to her.

"That's for me too?" Yoori asked uncertainly. She gawked at the steam flowing out of the teacup. She thought she was only getting the blanket.

"Take it before it gets cold," he advised, extending the teacup further out to her.

Yoori grabbed it at once. The heat from the cup did a wonderful job of thawing her cold hands. She brought the cup to her nose. She loved to get a whiff of her tea before she drank from it. The heavenly aroma filled her nostrils and Yoori was surprised to find that she had been introduced to this tea before.

"It'll be the best thing you've ever tasted," Tae Hyun urged warmly, thinking that Yoori's bout of recognition with the tea was hesitation on her part to drink it.

However, before she could even grace the taste with her lips, miniature ripples within the tea began to take form. Instinctively, both Yoori and Tae Hyun lifted their eyes to meet the dark sky above. Trickles of mist tickled their faces.

It started sprinkling, an obvious prelude to the shower of rain to follow.

"Is this the part where we go back inside?" Yoori asked, crestfallen that her time with Tae Hyun might end earlier than she anticipated. She didn't want to go back inside and Yoori had a good feeling that Tae Hyun didn't want to either. Nonetheless, it wasn't ideal for them to sit outside when the rain was about to deluge upon them.

"Do you want to go back inside?" Tae Hyun asked coolly. There was something in his question that told her he had another alternative to sitting outside.

Yoori shook her head. She was curious as to what he had up his sleeves.

Tae Hyun lowered his eyes unto the table they were sitting on. Though he didn't say anything, an amused Yoori knew what he was thinking. Leave it up to her crime lord boss to come up with the most interesting of alternatives...

"You're suggesting that we sit underneath the table?" Yoori thought out loud. Her amused smile never left her lips.

"All we need is something to prevent us from getting wet," said Tae Hyun with one of his charming smirks.

Yoori nodded, open to this suggestion. She was secretly pleased that he suggested this. To a small degree, it meant he wanted to hang out with her too. It also meant that their awkwardness since the lake house was fading fast.

Yeah! she thought happily. *Friendship conquers all!*

Presenting each other with one final blink of confirmation, Yoori and Tae Hyun, just as the rain was about to pick up, unfolded their legs and jumped off the table. With her blanket draped over her and her teacup in hand, Yoori followed as Tae Hyun bent his knees and moved in underneath the table. He extended out his hand to help hold her teacup. Her hands firmly clenched around her blanket, Yoori bent her knees and slid underneath the table.

Due to her small frame, Yoori wasn't worried about her comfort level underneath the table. Nevertheless, she was worried about its conduciveness for Tae Hyun, whose tall frame would get him in trouble anywhere. To her pleasant surprise, the height of the table was high enough for Tae Hyun to sit comfortably underneath.

Yoori looked around.

Despite the unconventional shelter, Yoori profoundly enjoyed sitting underneath that table with Tae Hyun. She felt safe. It was mere assumption on her part, but she had an inkling that Tae Hyun shared in the same contentment.

Like ten-year-olds, they sat with their legs crossed, their backs against the wall, and their eyes fully fixated on the view of the horizon. Her perfume and his cologne breathed together as rain pelted around them.

Yoori was grateful that the barriers around Tae Hyun's balcony were glass, which meant that even under the table, they could get a breathtaking view of the world before them. Trickles of rain cascaded onto the glass railing of the balcony. The liquid droplets blocked the full view of the blinking city—but only slightly.

"Here," said Tae Hyun, pulling her out of her staring state. He handed her the warm teacup.

"Thanks," Yoori whispered, grabbing the cup at once.

Tae Hyun watched with anticipation.

The warmth from the glass comforted her. Going back to where she left off before it started sprinkling, she brought the teacup up toward her. Yoori lowered the tip of the cup to her lips and began to sip from it. Sure enough, as she felt little drops of heaven fill her mouth, the big tread of coldness that once ran over her body left instantaneously. As a cold wind accompanied them underneath the table, she was certain now that she had this tea before. It was undoubtedly the same tea Ji Hoon shared with her when she saw him the other night.

"Is this…" she started, trying to recall the name Ji Hoon shared with her. "Is this queen of Babylon white tea with a mix of rooibos rose garden tea and a tou–"

"—touch of German rock cane sugar," Tae Hyun finished for her. He was surprised that she knew the name. "How did you know?"

"Uh…is this not a popular drink?" she asked apprehensively, not wanting to bring up Ji Hoon.

Tae Hyun took a moment to deliberate the answer. Seconds later, he laughed. "I guess the trend caught on," he replied before adding, "You know that I mixed this tea together, right?" There was pride in his voice. It mirrored that of a proud kid showing off his straight A's report card.

"Yeah…I know because I sure didn't," Yoori replied, misunderstanding what Tae Hyun was trying to share with her.

He gave her an odd look. "No. I mean I invented it."

Yoori's eyes rounded like baseballs. "You *started* this drink trend?"

Tae Hyun nodded. A prideful smile illumed his face. The heavy, yet peaceful, splattering of the rain could be heard as Tae Hyun went on, his eyes lingering on an undetectable space of the city.

"Well, I don't know. It's a pretty easy drink to mix together so other people probably thought of it too. But when I was younger—a lot younger—I was bored so I started mixing drinks together. I mixed the queen of Babylon white tea and the rooibos rose garden tea together. Then, I threw a bit of German rock cane sugar and after that…I created heaven in a cup." He laughed as he reminisced. "It was a thoughtless mix, but the Underworld is filled with tea enthusiasts…so I guess whoever tried my drink got hooked."

What a small world that Lee Ji Hoon's favorite tea was the one that Kwon Tae Hyun created, Yoori mused. The irony was incredible.

Tae Hyun turned to her. "How did you know about this drink?"

Yoori smiled timidly. She was determined not to bring up Ji Hoon. "I guess the Underworld sets the trends and the rest of the world follows," she replied, bluffing quite easily. To avert his attention from calling her bluff, she offered the tea to him.

Distracted, and unable to refuse his favorite drink, Tae Hyun took the cup, inhaled a bit of the aroma and promptly took a couple of sips from it. He sighed as if he was in heaven and handed the teacup back to Yoori. He made sure there was enough left for her.

The torrent of the rain picked up when Yoori grabbed the teacup. Remnants of water streamed off the outer sides of the table. Though they were getting partially wet from the residual water that slithered beneath them, it wasn't enough to knock Yoori or Tae Hyun from their peaceful state. A companionable silence settled between them when they took in the panoramic view. The city lights blinked under the canvas of the murky sky. All that could be heard was the rhythmic drumming of the rain and the howling of the wind. It was peaceful, almost hypnotizing. It somehow acted as a reminder to Yoori as to what she had to talk to Tae Hyun about.

Seemingly anticipating the train of her apprehensive thoughts, Tae Hyun's voice swam through the wave of the serene silence. "Something seems to be bothering you. Did you want to talk to me about something?"

It occurred to Yoori that even under the façade of her smile, Tae Hyun knew her enough to discern when she was troubled. It showed how close they'd become when, even under the greatest of her bluffs, he could see right through her.

She heaved a breath. Her eyes focused on the view of the city before she nodded. She wasn't even sure where to begin. Surely a conversation that began with, "I'm An Soo Jin" would throw anyone off the balcony. Even though she was determined to tell him everything, she wanted to take things slowly. She didn't know how Tae Hyun would react and she wanted to prolong the inevitable for just a couple more minutes.

Recalling the one silver lining of this entire day, Yoori parted her lips and said, "I met Jae Won's girlfriend today."

She took a sip of the tea before handing the cup over to Tae Hyun.

One of the bigger things she would have to filter out of this conversation was that she also knew who Kang Min's girlfriend was. God knows how the King of Serpents would react if and when he finds out that his baby sister is dating one of his gang members. Yoori sure as hell didn't want to be the one to tell him.

"Did you like her?" Tae Hyun asked casually, stealing Yoori away from her thoughts. He grabbed the teacup from her and lifted it up to his lips.

Yoori bounced her head to confirm. He would enjoy this news with her. "Yeah, apparently his girlfriend is Chae Young."

Tae Hyun's face lit up. A smile touched his lips when he handed the teacup back to her. "Your friend from the diner?"

Yoori beamed and nodded again.

Tae Hyun laughed, sharing in the same happy reaction. "Wow, what a small world."

"I know, right?"

"That's amazing actually," Tae Hyun remarked, thrilled that Yoori had her friend back. "Congrats, Choi Yoori. Everything seems to be working out for you."

Yoori smiled wryly. Her heart dropped. If only he knew.

Tae Hyun instinctively pulled her closer to him when a stream of water edged closer to her pants. "Why aren't you hanging out with her right now?"

Yoori took a moment to suppress the tingling sensations that surged through her when she felt the warmth of his body. It felt nice to be closer to him.

"Oh, she and Jae Won had dinner plans," Yoori provided, blushing uncontrollably. She hated that the slight grazing of his fingers reminded her of their dance—their kiss. She struggled to answer, her mind venturing back to their night under the gazebo. "I—I didn't want to intervene…you know? 'Cause…you know…couples need their time alone…"

Yoori wasn't certain if Tae Hyun was aware of the awkwardness she exuded. If he wasn't aware then he was really oblivious and if he knew, he did a good job of hiding it.

"Yeah, I just spoke to Hae Jin. She has dinner plans too." He smiled to himself. "Apparently everyone has dinner plans tonight." His eyes momentarily roamed around the balcony before they landed on the teacup Yoori held. After that, the charismatic lure of his brown eyes fell on hers. "This is some dinner we're having, huh?"

There was a magnetic smile on his face, one that was so playful and innocent that Yoori couldn't help but adore it.

"I like it out here," she assured him with sparkles in her eyes. She continued to sip from the teacup. The heavenly drops of the tea continued to warm her body.

"I've been thinking," Tae Hyun shared steadily, garnering Yoori's undivided attention. Like magnets their eyes were locked. "I've been thinking that…aside from that Italian dinner we had a while back…I've never really done anything special with you for dinner…"

A mental gasp vocalized in Yoori's befuddled mind. She was thankful for the drumming of the rain. It did a wonderful job of overshadowing the drumming of her own heart. Was Tae Hyun talking about taking her out on an actual date? She listened intently as he went on, his eyes tentative while he spoke to her. To Yoori, Tae Hyun had never seemed so nervous about something in his life. Now that she thought about it, she, too, had never been so nervous (and strangely excited) when it came to listening to someone.

He uncomfortably scratched the back of his head. "I mean…I think it might be nice if I took you out and treated you to a nice dinner or something. Or…I don't know, I guess I can cook for you as well and just eat here. I could probably take out some candles to give a nice ambiance or somethin—"

He stopped talking.

He stared quietly at a confused Yoori. His eyes dimmed of warmness and brimmed with a flood of guilt. It looked as though a thrash of reality had hurdled itself in his face. It was then that Yoori, in the midst of still trying to figure out what was happening with her heart, realized that there was something Tae Hyun wanted to tell her as well—something he had been dreading to do.

It was at that precise moment where Yoori hated her instincts the most. She hated the feel of her gut heaving in agony. She hated that she could anticipate something terrible before it happened. She hated that this terrible moment was the *one* moment where she had to tell Tae Hyun everything. She started to panic. She couldn't let Tae Hyun continue to speak without telling him everything first. She couldn't let this dream go on anymore. She couldn't let herself, or Tae Hyun for that matter, plunge any deeper without knowing what they were getting themselves into.

The same stream of reasoning was also visible in Tae Hyun's reeling mind. He wore the same countenance as hers. It was a countenance that spoke of guilt. It was a countenance that spoke of the extreme desire to let out a burning secret that had been consuming him.

"Yoori…"

"Tae Hyun…"

They spoke at the same time. Their voices throbbed with pure angst.

"There's something I want to talk to you about," they finished together, their breathing synchronized in apprehension.

Thrown by the identical statement they posed, Tae Hyun nodded at Yoori. "Go first."

The rain started to pour aggressively unto the world beneath it. There was no more peace around them.

Yoori shook her head. She was not ready. The dread in her stomach began to boil at this point. It was like her insides were begging her to not tell him anything.

"No, you go ahead," she insisted, wanting to give herself more time to think.

Though Yoori was in the midst of her own internal conflicts, she was also aware of how torn Tae Hyun seemed to be with himself.

"I…." he started unsteadily, staring into her big brown eyes. There was remorse in the King of Serpent's voice. It was unlike any tone she'd ever heard from him. "I've been keeping something from you."

Yoori instantly froze.

The earthshattering roar of the monstrous thunder could be heard in the near distance. The rain grew more violent with thrashes of wind accompanying the worsening storm.

"Wh – What have you been keeping from me?" Yoori stammered, blinking fearfully. Her worried gaze never left his. Wariness plagued all her senses. What had he been keeping from her? Why did he look so troubled—so guilty?

Upon seeing the fear in her curious eyes, Tae Hyun shook his head, regretting bringing all this up.

"Never mind," his quiet voice muttered out. He shifted his eyes onto an undetected area of the balcony.

Tae Hyun's cryptic words spun in her mind, stealing every ounce of warmth from her body. As her heartbeat slowed in fear, Yoori forgot about her obligations to tell him what she needed to tell him. She only cared about him and the secret he had kept from her.

"Tae Hyun," Yoori said without delay. She gently shook him to get him to look at her.

At her touch, Tae Hyun relinquished his gaze from the balcony and returned his eyes to hers. Though guilt was present in his eyes, there was a different light of conviction to it.

"You can't start off with, 'I've been keeping something from you' and end it right there. You have to tell me—"

"I know that you look like An Soo Jin."

A paralyzing dread appeared inside Yoori. Her pale eyes were wide from shock and dismay. Through her uneasiness, Yoori's lungs struggled for breath. She used all the strength she had to further question Tae Hyun.

"What?" she gasped.

Noting the distraught state he left her in, he turned away from her. The light of conviction in his eyes grew dimmer. "I—"

"I thought you never met An Soo Jin," Yoori interjected, the light of fire igniting in her eyes.

Did he lie about never meeting Soo Jin? Did he—?

"I haven't," he assured before her train of thoughts trekked any further. He turned back to face her. His eyes were unyielding with truth. He paused for another moment before adding, "But I do know that you look like her."

Before Yoori's distressed self could even begin to question what he meant, Tae Hyun elaborated. A distant grumbling of thunder accompanied his voice.

"The night of your initiation, after you left, the Advisors met with Ji Hoon and me. They told me of your resemblance—your *uncanny* resemblance to An Soo Jin to be exact. A resemblance that is so uncanny…that they are completely sure that you *are* her. They went on to say that Soo Jin was a trained killer and a ruthlessly trained one at that. They said she—*you*—could never be trusted—"

"That it would be the biggest mistake of your life if you did," Yoori provided brokenly, the truth stabbing into her like daggers.

They told him?

They actually told him?

Her heart raced in relentless fear. She could feel her heart beg her to not tell him anything. She could feel it beg her to keep quiet so that she wouldn't push Tae Hyun away.

Tae Hyun nodded. He was unaware of the internal war taking form within Yoori. He turned away from her. His eyes fixated on the rain-infested city before him. Streaks of lighting embalmed the dark sky. The bright white lights reflected upon their pale faces while the wind continued to ravage the world.

Wasps of a sickening horror multiplied within Yoori. She struggled for breath underneath the storm that took place in her body.

She knew it.

This was the moment to tell him. It was a terrible moment, but the moment nonetheless. She couldn't steal anymore borrowed time. The inevitable had come…

Tae Hyun continued to speak over the raging storm. "It sounds ridiculous when I think about what they said. I mean, even Ji Hoon said that they were out of their minds." He scoffed to himself. "I told them that I couldn't give two shits who you look like—that it doesn't matter who you resemble. The only thing that matters is that I know you and I know that I can trust you. I know that you're not her. You could never be her."

The last of his words swam in Yoori's mind.

It drowned her...

"I know that you're not her. You could never be her."

It acted as the last tug for Yoori. It was the last tug that Yoori needed to tell Tae Hyun everything.

The silence became her hellish cue.

"Tae Hyun," she said quietly, struggling to steady her trembling voice.

Her body shook harder. Despite all the perseverance of her instincts commanding her not to say anything, she struggled to find her voice. Then, when she felt her voice brim at the upper height of her throat, Yoori knew this was it. Once she shared these words with Tae Hyun, there was no going back. She could no longer live in her dream world. She had to wake up and face her horrific reality. She knew all of this, yet she was ready.

Feeling the weight of the entire world on her chest, she finally spoke those excruciating words...

"I'm An Soo Jin."

Tae Hyun froze like a statue.

Like the darkness of the night's sky, the residual warmness in his eyes grew faint as dimness took its place.

The rumbling world, though loud by nature, wasn't powerful enough to steal their undivided attention from one another.

To both their ears, the whole world had collapsed into silence.

To them, the whole world no longer existed.

Slowly, purposely, and hesitantly, Tae Hyun returned his gaze to a distressed Yoori. The only emotions decipherable in his eyes were shock and disbelief.

It was then, as her heart pounded against her chest, that Yoori knew that this was going to be one of the most terrible conversations she would have in her life.

"What did you just say?" he asked slowly. His wary, yet stern eyes bore into hers. There was a glint within his gaze that told her he was silently praying that he heard wrong.

Yoori had the chance to stop there. She had the chance to lie to him and tell him she was joking. She had the chance but, no matter how painful it was for her, she couldn't back out now. She trusted Tae Hyun too much to keep this from him.

"I have amnesia," she provided, her voice breaking at every syllable.

Yoori took in a sharp breath as she watched the warmness vacate Tae Hyun's body.

"You – You have amnesia…" he repeated disbelievingly. He inhaled sharply before asking, "How long?"

"Three years," Yoori breathed out.

Though she didn't give Tae Hyun much to go on, he was a very smart individual. She didn't give him much information, but he would figure out everything regardless.

Tae Hyun took in another sharp breath. If the light of realization in his eyes gave any indication, it was clear to Yoori that he understood that Soo Jin's "death" was a fraud and something occurred to turn her into…Yoori.

Yoori watched him painfully. He sat beside her physically, but she could see that he was drifting further and further away from her emotionally. The way he looked at her made her feel like there were knives being carved at her skin. He stared at her like she was a complete stranger to him.

A tense silence loomed between them. The only buffers of sounds shared in their environment were the sobs and screams of the night's sky. As a flood of rain deluged more violently from above, Tae Hyun, without any warning, turned away from her and tore himself out from beneath the table. With unmatched speed, he began toward the door.

"Tae Hyun!" Yoori called after him, throwing her blanket aside. The teacup spilled onto the surface of the balcony when she got up after him. The contents of the tea Tae Hyun made for her mixed fiercely with the spiteful rain.

Though she had thrown herself from underneath the table, Yoori found herself unable to run after Tae Hyun. She was too overwhelmed to run after him. It took only seconds for her entire body to become drenched under the merciless rain.

She watched his hand make contact with the lever of the sliding door. However awful it was for her to stand there like that, her body freezing from the cold, the spiteful weather was nothing compared to the coldness of how Tae Hyun treated her.

He had never treated her like this.

"Tae Hyun, please wait," she finally whispered when he was about to pull the door open.

Her voice barely made a sound above the thunderous storm. It was hardly audible to the world around them. It was hardly audible, yet it was enough to cause Tae Hyun to stop in his tracks. She knew then Tae Hyun didn't hear her voice, but her pain.

He stood in place, his back turned to her. His chest heaved up and down.

Yoori didn't know how long they stood there, completely soaked in the storm. It must've been a while because her body grew so numb that she stopped shaking. It must've been a while because even her heart grew numb as it waited nervously for Tae Hyun.

Tae Hyun, she begged in her mind, her eyes never leaving him. *Please talk to me*.

As though hearing her unspoken plea, he finally spoke.

"You're An Soo Jin..." He whipped around to face her. His face was completely drenched from water and pale from disbelief. "You were An Soo Jin all along."

"I—I didn't know I was her," Yoori uttered, her voice fighting to keep steady. She felt the pent up emotions simmer within her...waiting...just waiting to erupt.

Tae Hyun scoffed doubtfully. "You were plagued with amnesia three years ago, the *exact* same time as when An Soo Jin 'died,' and you didn't think for one moment that you were her?" His voice was shrouded with skepticism.

Another growl of thunder echoed in the abyss sky.

Awakened by the thunderous judgment in his own voice, Tae Hyun closed his eyes in dread, regretting using that tone with her.

However regretful he looked, the tone of his voice was the straw that broke the camel's back.

Her lips quivering uncontrollably, Yoori snapped.

"Do you think I want this?" she shouted. Remnants of rain dripped off her. Her body shook in anger. "Do you think I want you to look at me like this? Do you think I want to be *her*?" Her eyes bubbled with tears. "You have no idea how much I've tried to avoid this moment. Deep down, even though I knew all along, I kept on denying everything because it pained me to even try and remember anything. For months, I ignored the fucking obvious, all the clues because I *didn't* want to be her!"

Yoori paused to rub her hands against her eyes, making sure that no tears escaped. Her chest heaved violently. Once she was done, Yoori took a second to avert her red-shot eyes to the horizon. Her breathing grew steady. She calmed down. She placed her right hand over her left arm and began to rub it up and down. It was her own way of further calming herself down.

When she was ready to face him again, she returned her gaze to Tae Hyun

He remained as she had seen him seconds ago. He was rooted in the same position, his legs frozen to the same space and his hand still glued to the lever of the sliding door. The difference was that he wore a pained expression on his face. Yoori wasn't sure if it was pain from finding out that she was Soo Jin or pain from seeing her in such a volatile state. However much it looked like Tae Hyun wanted to approach her and comfort her, the better part of him—his rationale—kept him rooted in his stance.

Through her pained sniffling, Yoori continued to speak. "Every time I try to remember anything, I get headaches—migraines. I don't remember anything from her life...what she did or who she really was." Yoori paused to rub her red-shot eyes before continuing. "I can't remember anything...yet I can *feel* everything. I can feel the guilt...all her guilt." She swallowed convulsively. "All *my* guilt. I hate An Soo Jin with all my heart because, at the core of my mind, *I know that I'm her*." Her voice broke. "I hate that I can't breathe without feeling the guilt rip my soul up. I hate that even when my hands are dry, I can feel blood on them. I hate An Soo Jin with all that I am because I knew that it would only be a matter of time before she poisoned my world. It would only be a matter of time before she killed me — just like she tried to kill herself."

More than once, in the course of Yoori's words, Tae Hyun ran his fingers through his hair with an aching expression on his face. There was so much pain and frustration in his stance. Yoori didn't know what was running through his mind. All that she knew was that he was troubled. He was troubled and he didn't know what to do. She blinked and waited for his reply in the rain. Never once in her life did she feel as fragile as she did at that particular moment.

"Tae Hyun," she called softly, wanting desperately to hear his voice again.

"Why did you tell me all of this?" he finally asked, his poignant eyes locking with hers through the pouring rain. His voice, though throbbing with disbelief, was soft when he spoke to her. He swallowed tightly. "Choi Yoori, don't you know who I am?"

A flash of pain rippled in his eyes when he said her full name. She knew from the shaking of his head that he no longer knew if it was even appropriate for him to keep calling her that.

Not allowing this to beset what he wanted to say, Tae Hyun continued to speak, a tornado of wind accompanying his stern voice. "I'm the leader of the Serpents. The one gang that An Soo Jin..." He stopped for a second. He gazed desolately at her before, much to Yoori's dismay, correcting what he said. "The one gang that *you* despise the most."

He scoffed to himself, his voice suddenly elevating with the purest of frustration. "Why would you tell me all of this? Don't you know that I could fucking kill you right now?"

"Would you?" Yoori asked at once, challenging his spoken words. The cold wind blew through her as she shouted this.

As Yoori anticipated, Tae Hyun stilled at her question.

Yoori struggled to find her breath as she went on, her eyes never leaving Tae Hyun's. "You are the epitome of everything I shouldn't trust. You keep secrets from me, you never tell me how you feel, and you never show any type of weakness or vulnerability. You try to keep anything and everything from me." She thought about the moments where he took care of her, the moments they shared when they were alone, and the moments they shared at the lake house — all the memories that were dearest to her heart.

"Yet, despite you not wanting to tell me anything, I see you for who you really are. I see you as Kwon Tae Hyun, the person you've been hiding under your façade as a gang leader. I told you that night, Tae Hyun, that there was more to you than what meets the eye and I don't regret saying that. You've proven to me that I was right."

She continued to speak, struggling to maintain eye contact with Tae Hyun. "I told you who I really am because I trust you…*wholeheartedly*. I trust that, even though you feel the need to follow your obligations as the King of Serpents, you'll override that with your instincts of being Kwon Tae Hyun. I trust that you'll take care of me—that you'll always have my best interest at heart. I trust that you would never hurt me, let alone kill me. I trust you because you *deserve* that trust."

As if the last sentence was too much for him to bear, Tae Hyun exhaled sharply. There were so many internal conflicts bubbling within him that it was taking a toll on him. He took a moment to close his eyes and lift his head toward the skies above. Tae Hyun allowed the streaming rain to wash over his face. It trickled like crystals along his jawline, flowed down the skin of his neck and filtered into the various contours of his body. When it appeared as if the cleansing helped him to gather his frantic thoughts, Tae Hyun lowered his chin and opened his eyes.

He breathed quietly, staring intently at Yoori, who was as rain-soaked as him. "Why are you no longer in denial?"

Yoori paused, thrown by his unexpected question. When she was about to answer him, he spoke for her.

"Things are coming back to you, aren't they?" he asked carefully. "Your memories…your past. You're beginning to remember everything…"

"I—I don't want too," Yoori struggled to reply. She didn't want to remember anything. She wanted to go back as they were. She wanted to go back into her dream world.

He posed another question. "Have you told anyone else about this?"

Yoori shook her head, her body relieved that his tone had changed. "No, just you."

Something in him, a guilt of sorts, was present when he heard her say this. Perhaps he felt that he shouldn't have the honor of being the one person she trusted because he didn't seem happy that she chose to tell him and only him.

The guilt embroidered on his face, Tae Hyun nodded before saying, "You can't tell anyone else about this. We'll keep playing off the fact that you resemble her and *only* resemble her. It'll be safer for you if we do this. You have to remember, you can't tell anyone else. If anyone else in this world knows…"

He blinked, never finishing his sentence. It was too much for him. Too much for him to even think about.

The thunder roared louder as another fleeting moment of silence fell through them. For the first time since they'd met, Yoori had absolutely no idea what was going on in his mind.

As a violent gust of wind attacked them, Tae Hyun parted his lips and spoke again. His voice was low. It was mixed with the harshness of the wind, yet it thrashed against her all the same.

"I'm sorry for everything," he said, staring at her with regret in his eyes.

Yoori's own eyes blossomed at his unexpected apology. When she was ready to tell him that it wasn't his fault, he continued to speak.

"If I had known you were An Soo Jin, I would've never pulled you into this world." His voice agonized with remorse. It was one that pained Yoori to hear.

She immediately shook her head. "It wasn't your fault. You didn't even know her or what she looked like—"

"You wouldn't have to come this far, you wouldn't have to be exposed to all of this," he continued, the rain dripping off of him, "and you wouldn't be hurting right now." He paused, allowing the rain to continue to cloak them. And then, he painfully added, "And *we* wouldn't be in this situation."

At his own words, Tae Hyun blinked in dread. It was as if, for the very first time in his life, Tae Hyun couldn't deny all of this anymore. With a light of epiphany that dawned in his eyes, Tae Hyun took one last look at Yoori before he took in a harsh breath.

"Tae—" Before Yoori could even get a word in, Tae Hyun shook his head, his eyes set with resolution.

"I can't be here anymore."

The sliding door flew open, the ends of the side making a crashing sound as he flew into the living room.

"Tae Hyun!" Yoori shouted, nearly slipping over the river of rain on the balcony as she found herself running after him.

She ran into the bright lights of the living room. Her eyes immediately caught sight of Tae Hyun. He emerged from the bedroom. His wet clothes were off. He wore new jeans and was pulling a dry black shirt over himself. He headed for the door.

"Did she do something to you?" Yoori asked with urgency, her voice much smaller than she had ever heard it.

Questions poured into her mind.

Did Soo Jin do something to him? Why was he being like this?

She followed Tae Hyun like a desperate shadow as he walked past her and went for his shoes. He never answered her and he never looked at her.

"Are you that disgusted with her that you can't even look at me?" she asked again, trailing after Tae Hyun. Residual rainwater dripped unto the carpet from her hair and clothes while she followed him.

He approached the closet and again, he never answered her or looked at her. He pulled the closet door open and reached in for his black raincoat.

Yoori's mind swirled with agony. Why was he treating her like this?

She struggled to ask the right questions. "Are you thinking about what the Advisors warned you? That you couldn't trust me and it would be the biggest mistake of your life if you did?"

"I *trust* you," he answered at once, breaking his silence and locking his eyes with hers. There was desperation in his voice. It was the only thing he was sure of.

Yoori shook her head at Tae Hyun, her lips quivering uncontrollably. "Then why are you being like this?"

Apparently the question was too much for Tae Hyun to handle. He turned on his heels and headed for the kitchen counter where the key to his Mercedes sat. He walked past her, one arm running through the sleeve of his rain jacket.

"Stop ignoring me," Yoori voiced, wishing terribly that she could use a stronger tone with him. "Don't do this to me."

He didn't listen.

With his keys in his hand, and his other arm running through the other sleeve of his jacket, Tae Hyun was ready to leave. He sped to the door, turned the knob and pulled the door open. He was ready to step out when Yoori's voice swam into his ears.

"I need you right now," she whispered. She was cemented beside the kitchen counter, her vision blurred with tears that had been waiting to come out since she found out she was An Soo Jin.

One hand on the door, Tae Hyun stopped when he heard Yoori's voice. Though he kept his back to her, Yoori knew by the stiffening of his stance that he knew she was crying.

Yoori hated herself...not for being An Soo Jin, but for being weak.

She hated herself for having the overwhelming urge to grab his hand so that he wouldn't leave her. She hated that her voice broke at every syllable when she spoke to him. She hated herself for not being able to control her weakness and she hated herself more for needing Tae Hyun. She hated herself for being weak...yet she couldn't stop herself from saying the string of words she never thought she'd be pathetic enough to say to anyone. "*Please*...don't leave me."

Tae Hyun didn't say anything nor did he turn around to face her. He just stood there.

It was only seconds, but it felt like an eternity for Yoori, who wanted him to turn around and talk to her again. When he finally made a move, Yoori was almost sure that he was going to turn around and come back to her.

Instead of facing her, all that Tae Hyun quietly said was, "I'm sorry."

And without saying anything else, he was out the door, leaving an utterly distraught Yoori in his wake.

Disbelief rained over her as Yoori stared at the door in shock.

No...he didn't leave. He'll come back, she assured herself. *He'll come back.*

Slowly, very slowly, Yoori approached the closed door.

Her throat went dry and her vision grew blurrier with tears. Regardless of such maladies taking form in her body, Yoori continued to approach the door. When she was a half-foot away from it, she stood off to the side and waited beside it.

Though Tae Hyun had left, a big part of Yoori hoped that he'd come back to her.

Tae Hyun has to come back, Yoori reassured herself, her tears drying slightly from the small hope. He was her friend—her very best friend. He had always been there for her and he couldn't leave her like that.

She was convinced he would come back—that was why she stood there for eighteen minutes, her eyes never leaving the door.

Tae Hyun's coming back, I just know he is....

Eighteen minutes then became twenty-three minutes.

Twenty-three minutes became twenty-nine minutes.

Twenty-nine minutes then became thirty-six minutes and fifty seconds.

It was after thirty-seven minutes that Yoori stopped counting.

It was after thirty-seven minutes and nine seconds that Yoori's eyes became blurred beyond recognition with red-hot tears.

It was after thirty-seven minutes and twenty seconds that Yoori leaned against the wall beside the door, covered her mouth with her hands, and slid down the wall in anguish.

It was after thirty-seven minutes and twenty-eight seconds that tear after tear escaped from her eyes as she sobbed quietly to herself.

It was after thirty-seven minutes and fifty-nine seconds, while she continued to sob alone, that Yoori finally admitted to herself that Tae Hyun wasn't coming back.

He wasn't coming back for her.

Whatever his reason for leaving, she wasn't enough for him to come back.

Yoori's heart ripped as the seconds flew by. She felt her heart, very slowly and painfully, rip itself apart as the cold wind from the balcony escaped from the sliding door they left open.

She was no longer dreaming.

She had finally woken up.

This was her reality.

She was really An Soo Jin...

And Tae Hyun left her *because* she was An Soo Jin.

Yoori shook her head at the ironic and pathetic state of her life.

One would think that after so many weeks of denial, it would hurt more for Yoori to find out that she was Soo Jin. Yoori didn't blame anyone who might've thought that because that was what she thought too.

She could've never imagined anything else that could tear her apart—more so than when she found out that she was Soo Jin. Yoori could've never imagined she'd be sitting against the wall, crying like the girls she had pitied because a guy left her when she begged him not to. She could've never imagined that out of everyone, it would be Tae Hyun who left her.

Tae Hyun...the one she counted on the most...the one she trusted the most...the one who had always been there for her until now.

Biting her lips, Yoori shook her head and wiped the tears away from her eyes. She couldn't be in this apartment. She couldn't stand to be in this apartment anymore. Her mind suddenly set, Yoori used the back of the wall as her prop, threw herself to her feet, and took off like the wind.

That's the thing about boomerangs... Yoori thought as she violently rubbed her tears away with the palms of her hands. She sped through the hall and burst into the bedroom.

It is guaranteed that it will make its way back to you...

Sniffling quietly, she threw her damp clothes on the floor and quickly re-dressed into dry clothes.

The only thing that isn't guaranteed is that there isn't an obstacle in its path to prevent it from returning to you.

Zipping up her raincoat, fresh tears began to dwell in Yoori's eyes. She ran out of the bedroom and sped toward the door.

The only thing that isn't guaranteed is that the cruelties of life won't deter him from making his way back to you – from coming back to you.

It was then, at 10:47, as Yoori walked out of the door—completely absent of Tae Hyun's presence, her heart never hurting more—that one thing made sense to her. The only thing she understood as the rain poured over her was that he left her.

He left her without ever turning back.

He left her when she needed him most.

He left her and he didn't come back to her.

"For every empire..."

10: The Morning After

"Why are you up so early?" Chae Young asked the next morning, picking up the freshly brewed tea and pouring the liquid contents into a nearby cup. Once the tea filled to the rim, she placed the teapot down. "Go back to sleep. You got in late last night."

Ever so carefully, Chae Young picked up the white teacup and began toward Yoori, who was finishing up with folding her beige comforter. Chae Young's white puffer jacket rustled as her body stiffened to balance the tea.

"I'm not sleepy," Yoori replied wearily. Her voice was completely hoarse.

She placed the folded comforter on the leather couch where she slept the night prior and threw her white pillow over it.

After leaving Tae Hyun's apartment, Yoori, not wanting to be alone, found solace in being with her best friend. How appropriate was it that she found Chae Young on the same day she needed someone the most?

Chae Young returned from dinner to find Yoori sitting in the hall of her apartment. Yoori had her face buried within her knees and she was drenched from head to toe. To say that Yoori looked miserable was an understatement.

Shortly after an exchange of embraces, Chae Young ushered Yoori into the apartment. Her first priorities were to find Yoori some warm clothes, turn up the heat, and ask her what happened. Though Yoori had stopped crying, her swollen eyes were a telltale sign of a terrible night. She suspected that Chae Young could tell it dealt with Tae Hyun.

After changing into some of Chae Young's warm clothes, Yoori sat down with Chae Young and talked about what happened—or tried her best to. In the interest of keeping the fact that she was An Soo Jin to herself (and to keep her trembling heart from struggling to breathe at the terrible reminder), Yoori was very vague when explaining to Chae Young what took place.

She essentially told Chae Young that they got into a huge fight and Tae Hyun left even when she asked him not to. Though Chae Young was confused due to the lack of details, she didn't ask for details. She nodded at the vague information Yoori gave and more importantly, she was there for Yoori when she needed her, which was all Yoori wanted that night.

When they were done talking, Chae Young insisted that Yoori take the bed while she took the couch. However Yoori, feeling quite terrible for imposing on Chae Young, was stubborn and threw herself on the couch before Chae Young could even combat her resolution. Chae Young, being the good friend that she was to Yoori, threw herself on the nearby sofa and slept in the living room with Yoori. It wasn't expected, but it was much appreciated on Yoori's part. Having Chae Young keep her company in the living room was exactly what she needed to get some much-needed rest. Granted she didn't get much sleep because she spent the entire night thinking about Tae Hyun, it was still a better rest than she would've gotten if she returned to her apartment alone.

Using her fingers to tuck the loose bangs behind her ears, Yoori smiled appreciatively and grabbed the teacup Chae Young handed her.

"Thank you," she said meekly, grateful that Chae Young took the time to take care of her before she went off to work at the diner.

A reminiscent thought overcame her when she thought about the diner. What Yoori wouldn't give to go back to those carefree days where she was a clueless diner girl...

"You're welcome," Chae Young said sympathetically, noticing Yoori's forlorn state.

The couch squeaked in response as Yoori's black jeans and white top made contact with it. The radiant glow of the morning sun tickled her skin when she sat against the leather fabric. It was amazing how beautiful the morning was when just hours prior, there was a terrible storm that nearly drowned the city beneath it.

Allowing the aroma of the tea to fill her senses, Yoori brought the cup to her lips and took a couple of sips from it.

"Good?" asked Chae Young.

Yoori nodded, taking another sip before she placed it on a coaster on the coffee table. It was good, but definitely nothing compared to the heavenly tea she had been introduced to.

"How are you doing right now?" Chae Young tentatively inquired, sitting down on the sofa. She pushed her unmade comforter to the side to make room for herself.

"Better," Yoori said honestly. Her heart was numb and she felt somewhat dazed. All that took place felt like a surreal dream.

She was upset, but it wasn't anything she couldn't handle. That was the thing with waking up after a horrible night...you're too exhausted to continue to be disappointed. If anything, it was the time to be bitter.

She grabbed an apple from one of the decorative bowls and bit out a big chunk of it. Her face was marked with resentment.

"That asshole," she grumbled in between bites, feeling a bit of her spunky personality return. It was the first time since the event took place that she called Tae Hyun a bad name. Though her heart trembled at the reminder of him, she felt vaguely better that she was able to let off some steam. Disappointment aside, she was beyond pissed at the guy.

"I can't believe he left me," she continued. "What a fucking good friend he is."

Chae Young curbed the urge to roll her eyes over the term Yoori used for Tae Hyun. She merely shook her head and gazed hopefully at Yoori. "Have you checked your phone? What if he tried to call you?"

"He doesn't care enough to call," Yoori grumbled. She bit into the apple again while thinking: *He's too disgusted with Soo Jin to want anything to do with me.* She sighed while glancing at Chae Young, who was waiting for a sufficient answer. Yoori cleared her throat. "And I didn't bring my phone."

"You didn't bring your phone?" Chae Young cried with eyes wide open. "But what if he's calling for you right now?"

Yoori snorted. "Oh I'm sure that's happening," she voiced with a sarcastic eye roll. "If Kwon Tae Hyun wants to find someone, then he'll find them. He doesn't need to call."

Chae Young sighed at the bitterness brewing out of Yoori. "Do you think it's over between you guys?"

"I don't know," Yoori answered honestly, feeling her gut wrench in knots. "All I know is that I'll never forgive him for leaving me when I asked him not to." She shrugged and took another bite out of her apple. "Not that my forgiveness matters. He made it quite obvious last night that he wanted nothing to do with me."

Chae Young tried to hide her pout. "What are you going to do now?"

"I don't know. I need some time to clear my head and forget about last night. I'll probably be bumming around." She eyed Chae Young when an alternative illumed in her mind. "Or do you want me to help out at the diner? I could use continued company and I wouldn't mind keeping myself busy."

Chae Young laughed, shaking her head. Yoori's offer reminded Chae Young that she had to get to work. Grabbing the black handbag that rested beside the sofa, she picked it up and began toward the door.

"I don't think so, missy. You get some much-needed rest. I wouldn't want you pouring anymore coffee on our customers."

Yoori frowned at Chae Young's bad joke.

Chae Young laughed warmly at her expression while happily stating, "I love you!" She opened the door. "Use this day to relax. You definitely need it. You know where to find me if you need anything."

"Thanks again!" Yoori shouted as the door was about to slam closed.

"Try not to attract any trouble today!" Chae Young warned jokingly before the door clicked shut.

Yoori smiled as she stood up and grabbed her black jacket from the ground. Her mind was all over the place, but she definitely didn't want to sit around in the apartment all day. She suddenly had the urge to take a brisk walk around town before settling at her favorite hangout spot. After putting on her jacket, she bent down and grabbed her white handbag. Throwing the apple away before she walked out the door, Yoori had no idea how much that last warning from Chae Young would be appropriate for the day she was about to embark on.

■ ■ ■

The business district in the late afternoon was a busy one. A sea of people swam through the streets as businessmen and women flocked from one building to the other, their phones attached to their ears like leeches and their hands gripped over their briefcases like spiders.

Though everyone was seemingly stressed out with their days, there was one who sat on a bench nearby that appeared completely at peace with herself. Some people enjoy sitting outside as a means to clear their minds. For Yoori, her means of clearing her mind revolved around sitting on a bench in the business district and staring at people who were too busy to notice her.

It had been nearly three hours since she sat her butt on the wooden bench and she enjoyed it immensely. She spent the majority of the morning walking around town to get a change in scenery and to calm her senses. She eventually came to her favorite hangout spot: the benches in the business district. There was a certain tranquility that came with sitting in the business district for Yoori. All she needed was a book in hand, a sea of people to calm her, and she was mild like still water.

Yoori squinted her eyes at the looming sunset. It hid behind the towering skyscrapers before it. The orange shade gave a calming ambiance as it ignited like fire over the busy world beneath it.

So pretty...Yoori mused, her eyes reflecting the natural fire from the sky. She was ready to return her gaze to the contents of her paperback book until she saw someone who caught her unyielding attention.

The guy looked deathly familiar as he held his Blackberry to his ear.

Yoori smirked to herself. The coincidences of her life would never cease to amaze her.

It was indeed Lee Ji Hoon.

He wore a gray dress shirt with dark gray slacks. He looked like he had just gotten out of a meeting with one of his 1st layer associates. He was so immersed in the call he was on that he didn't even notice that she was staring at him.

Yoori debated about whether or not she should call out his name. In light of all that had taken place, it would've been a bad idea to talk to him. She knew this, but a stubborn Yoori also wanted to be in his company. She needed another friend to talk to and she wanted Ji Hoon to be that friend.

As he drew closer to her, utterly oblivious to her presence, Yoori opened her mouth with the intention of calling his name. She was ready until she heard what he said to the person on the other line…

"Are you wearing that lingerie I bought you?" he crooned with such seduction that she had no doubt he was talking to another one of his playmates.

Of course, Yoori thought mildly, not very surprised with this little fact. It made sense that Ji Hoon would have a playmate on the other line while he casually strolled through the business district. Though the thought of him having a phone foreplay with some girl made her cringe, it wasn't enough to put her off from wanting to talk to him. She would feel bad if she allowed him to pass her by without greeting him.

"Ji Hoon," she greeted, her head tilting up toward him.

The look on his face when he saw her sitting on that bench was priceless. He was completely and utterly surprised. She would even dare say that he was thunderstruck to see her sitting there, waving at him.

"Yoori," he croaked, hastily hanging up on his playmate on the other line.

A nervous smile tugged at his lips. Albeit he seemed excited to see her, there was a light of worry in his eyes when he sat down beside her on the bench. She didn't doubt that he was wondering if she heard his conversation on the phone.

"Did I interrupt your call?" Yoori asked innocently, playing coy and pretending she didn't overhear anything.

"Just a call with a business associate," Ji Hoon lied easily, flashing Yoori an innocent smile that would throw any suspicious girl off track.

Yoori nodded, wearing a grin that hid the true knowledge that she knew he was lying to her.

Yoori briefly wondered about Ji Hoon and his lying skills. She thought about the fact that if she hadn't personally overheard his conversation on the phone, then she would've easily believed the lie he told her. She would've believed him because Ji Hoon was that good of a liar. He was able to look at her straight in the eye, with no bluff whatsoever, and he was able to lie to her. Undoubtedly, she was also reminded of the fact that she was An Soo Jin and the fact that Ji Hoon had been lying to her since she met him. Out of everyone, he alone had been telling her that she bore absolutely no resemblance to Soo Jin, when in fact he was actually the first one to call her Soo Jin.

Yoori mentally scoffed at herself. Now that her denial had vacated, all the little things that didn't make sense in the past were adding up perfectly.

"What are you doing here?" Ji Hoon asked, his warm eyes marked on her.

"Relaxing," Yoori said blithely. She closed her book and placed it back into her purse. She'd rather talk to Ji Hoon than read anyway.

"How have you been since I last saw you?" There were treads of concern in his voice. He stared at the remnants of bruises around her lips.

"I'm doing a lot better," Yoori reassured, flashing him an even bigger smile to prove her point. "How have you been?"

"A lot better now that I've seen you," he said warmly. His eyes grew a bit more affectionate.

It took all of Yoori's strength to keep that smile on her face. In the past, Ji Hoon's charms managed to make her heart skip a beat. But for whatever reason, as she sat there with him, it didn't offer the same effect. If anything, the only effect from being around him was despondence—which was no fault of his own.

Guilt clawed at her while she gazed at the one who used to be Soo Jin's boyfriend—*her boyfriend*. Yoori suddenly regretted calling out his name. Her mind started swirling with endless questions. Yoori wondered why there was only guilt pelting over her and nothing else when she gazed at him.

She should be jealous that he was talking to another girl on the phone. She should be telling him that she knew without a shadow of doubt that she was An Soo Jin. She should be telling him that she wanted to be with him again. She should be saying that, but none of those urges existed within her. She cared about him a lot, but not to a romantic degree.

It may be that she dreaded being around him because he reminded her of a past that she had been fortunate enough to be made oblivious of. The answer could be that...or it could easily be because she couldn't get her mind off a certain someone who would never fail to command her unyielding attention—

"Where's Tae Hyun?"

Yoori froze at the verbal reminder of the one person who affected her most in this world. The insistent quivering of her heart commenced and she fought for composure. She didn't want Ji Hoon to know about Tae Hyun leaving her and the reason *why* he left her.

"Something came up..." She shrugged vaguely, her bluff going strong. The brightness of her smile overshadowed any doubt. "He had to leave for a while."

Ji Hoon nodded, satisfied with the answer. It didn't seem that he truly cared about Tae Hyun's whereabouts. He only cared that Tae Hyun was out of the picture—if only for the time being.

"You know, I was thinking about you the other day." He smiled to himself. "But then again, I think about you all the time so that really doesn't merit much of your attention. But I was thinking of you and something specific the other day."

Yoori raised a curious brow.

"I was thinking about that date you promised me."

"Date?" She was thoroughly confounded. What was he talking about?

He nodded at her with amusement. "That night in my car," he reminded good-naturedly. "You said you'd make it up to me by giving me another date."

"Oh!" Yoori cried, the contents of the night where she probed him for information about An Soo Jin flashing through her memories. "Oh yes," Yoori said, smiling at him nervously. "I remember."

Though it had only been about a week since she made that promise, it felt like it had been months ago. Yoori supposed that was the shelf life of events that occurred in the Underworld. Even if it had only been a few days, it still felt like it had been months.

"Are you proposing that we hang out today?" A part of her secretly hoped that they could do it another day. She wasn't ready to face him in such an intimate setting. She wasn't ready to be reminded of the fact that he was her boyfriend in another life.

"Are you busy?" His eyes were hopeful that she would say no.

Yoori shook her head, not wanting to lie to him. "No, but are you? This is so last minute."

Ji Hoon's smile remained. "I'm never too busy for you."

"But what about your business associate?" she continued to ask, hoping that she could find an excuse on his part to not hang out. She knew his lingerie-clad playmate was probably waiting for him.

"What business associate?"

Holding in a laugh, and knowing he had already forgotten about his lie, Yoori lifted her chin and indicated to the Blackberry in his hands.

Memory flew through his eyes. "Oh, *that* associate." He chuckled, tenseness present in his laughter. He put his phone on silent before putting it back into his pocket and standing up. "I'm sure they'll be able to take care of themselves. It's not a big deal. Anyway, have you had dinner yet?"

There were no more excuses she could plead out. He was determined to have his date with her and he was determined to have it at that very moment.

Yoori shook her head at his question. She threw her handbag over her shoulder and reluctantly stood up as well.

"I know a good place where we can eat," shared Ji Hoon. "It's a couple of blocks down. I think you'll really like it there."

"I'll take your word for it."

Deep down, for very obvious reasons, Yoori knew that it was a bad idea to continue to be in Ji Hoon's company. Despite this, she also couldn't deny that it was such an uplifting feeling when she was around him. Whether he saw her as Soo Jin or not, he cared about her immensely and there was no lie about that. Perhaps it wouldn't be so terrible if she kept her word and went on this one date with him…

Side by side, they began to walk as the winking sunset hid behind the gargantuan skyscrapers.

"Was there a reason why you chose to relax in this particular area?" Ji Hoon asked, shifting his eyes down to her.

Yoori smiled to herself and looked around. "I like to people watch in this area. I felt really lost when I first moved here. The only time I don't feel so lost is when I'm sitting here, reminding myself of the future I want." She pointed to the tallest building in the area. "For instance, it would be my dream to own that building." She pointed at the second highest building beside it. "And that one." She pointed at several others in the area. "And that, and that, and that, and I want that group of people leaving to work for me in the future." She laughed to herself. "My problems seem smaller when I can sit around and bask in a world I want to turn into my future."

He laughed warmly at her actions. Curiosity then creased over his brows. He backtracked. "Wait a second, when you *first* moved here? Where did you move from?"

An uneasy sensation rolled over her now that he was asking about her questionable past.

"Taecin," she shared carefully.

"I didn't know that you weren't from Seoul." Amazement was embedded within his voice. "It seems that there are quite a few things I don't know about you."

"Same to you," replied Yoori.

Ji Hoon nodded with a determined look in his eyes. "We definitely need to fix that, don't we? Let's start getting to know each other."

"Alright then," said Yoori, though she was wary of talking about herself. It wasn't like she knew too much about herself either. She would have to wing it as best as she could on parts where she wasn't sure if the answer was accurate.

"You can move the topic along," she suggested politely.

"How about we talk about what we were like growing up? Do you think we can start there?"

Yoori took a moment to deliberate as they walked down the sidewalk. She knew that this conversation would entail her lying about what her adoptive parents told her, but Yoori was ready to do what was needed to keep her secret intact. It would only have to be tonight where she'd have to lie to him about her questionable past...

Yoori nodded, knowing that this was going to be a long night since it was about to start off with such a big lie. "That sounds good. We'll start there."

"There is a downfall."

11: Training of Royals

Several blocks later, Yoori and Ji Hoon arrived at Vertical VII, one of the most prestigious and glamorous hotels in Seoul.

Their arrival brought a cautious impulse out of Yoori. When she bestowed him with a suspicious glare, Ji Hoon merely placed his hands up to mark his innocent intentions. He explained to her that his favorite pastime was having dinner on the rooftop of this hotel. Though there was a twinkle of mischief in his eyes, Ji Hoon assured her he didn't bring her here with the intention of taking her anywhere *but* the rooftop.

Her wariness dissipating, Yoori nodded in understanding and followed as Ji Hoon led her inside the affluent hotel. It was an understatement to say that Yoori was impressed when she walked onto the rooftop of Vertical VII.

Glass walls that were at least five foot high embroidered the three sides of the rectangular shaped rooftop. Streams of running water pulsated through the three-inch glass. The little flickers of lights within it made it appear as if you were staring at captive stars. The only side of the building that lacked the embrace of the glass décor was the fourth corner of the infrastructure. Long and spread out, the empty space glowed with pride as it held the beauty of the busy city in its hands.

The entirety of the rooftop was bare but marked with style as the décor of the streaming glass wall embraced them. The only object that inhabited the base of the rooftop was a table under the touch of the sun. Placed strategically on the center of the rooftop, a mahogany table long enough to seat at least ten people awaited Ji Hoon and Yoori. On it laid various dinner dishes that made Yoori's mouth water.

They ate while the sun descended and the moon rose. It would've been an ideal dinner date if Yoori weren't consumed with thoughts of both Soo Jin and Tae Hyun. Both parties haunted her as the hours passed, their conversation never straying from getting to know one another. It was hard not to be reminded of all the things she wanted to escape from when she was sitting across from Ji Hoon. She was constantly reminded of her pain as they tried to continue along with their conversation. Yoori was transparent though. It was evident that Ji Hoon knew something was bothering her. He just chose not to point it out.

The contents of the conversation sailed smoothly until they travelled on to a touchy topic.

"You don't have any siblings, right?" Ji Hoon asked, sipping his red wine. They had finished dinner and the last of the dessert.

Yoori shook her head, picking up her glass before the servers picked up her plates. "It was just my parents and I."

"Was?" Though he attempted to hide his interest, Yoori could tell by the creasing of his brows that her answer caught him off guard.

Yoori wanted to slap herself for not being more careful with her words. Why the hell was she letting him know that her adoptive parents died? A lump formed in her throat and she nodded quietly. "A year and a half ago…"

She didn't feel the need to finish her sentence. Ji Hoon was smart enough to pick up on her reluctance. Yoori knew by the apprehension in his eyes that Ji Hoon regretted speaking out so fast.

He looked at her understandably. "I'm sorry."

Yoori smiled uneasily, not wanting to stray on to that topic. She speedily moved it along. "Do you have any siblings?"

"A younger brother," Ji Hoon answered, before also adding, "He's in China right now, being trained for the 1st layer."

"Trained?" There was no filtering of her attention. Her eyes blossomed in interest. "Wait a second, how old is he?"

Ji Hoon smiled. Perhaps it was because he wanted to help take her mind off whatever it was that was bothering her, but he didn't seem to mind elaborating on the topic he threw them in.

"He's twelve," he answered as if that would be a big difference. "And ten is the standard age for all Underworld heirs to get trained." He raised a brow at her, noting the extreme interest in her curious eyes. "Tae Hyun never spoke to you about this?"

"We never got on to this topic," Yoori said quietly. Tae Hyun rarely spoke about the Underworld if he could help it.

"Do you want me to get into that topic?" he asked delicately. His eyes were gentle on her, as they always were.

Yoori didn't even take a moment to consider his proposal. She bobbed her head, excited to learn more.

He grinned at her excitement and commenced with the enlightening. "Every heir's training varies according to their individual abilities and skills. The standard age to start any type of training is ten—it gives you more time to develop your skills before you make your debut in the Underworld." He took a sip from his wine. "I started off my basic training in China, moved across all of Asia to garner different skills that best suited my needs, and returned to Seoul to be specifically trained by Shin Jung Min. That's the typical life cycle of an heir's training. You go all over the place before you come home and make your official introduction in the Underworld."

"All heirs to the respective thrones go through that?"

"More or less," said Ji Hoon. "The Skulls family has close ties to the Chinese Underworld, hence the reason why I went to China for basic training. The Serpents family also has close ties to the Chinese Underworld. This was the reason why Kwon Ho Young started his basic training in China as well. After several years, he returned to Korea for more specific training."

The next question was an easy one for Yoori. Since they were talking about the heirs of the Underworld and the specific gangs, there was one she was dying to learn more about.

"What about An Young Jae?" Yoori asked at once. She hadn't forgotten about his relation to her. He was not only her older brother, but he was also the reason why she became the person she had become. It was astonishing that even her own sibling was a mystery to her.

There was brief caution on Ji Hoon's countenance before he casually answered her question. He seemed stiff, but tried to play it off as being uncomfortable from the cold.

"The Scorpions family has very close ties to the Japanese Underworld. Young Jae's mother was the daughter of one of the more respected Underworld Elders in Tokyo."

Yoori froze at the mention of Young Jae's mother—*her mother*. How strange it was for her to listen to this when she couldn't even put a face to her brother or mother. She kept her inner turmoil at bay and listened as Ji Hoon went on. She'd deal with that later...

"Typically heirs get their basic training in a neighboring country and they come home for the final honing of their skills. Young Jae was the only heir who received basic training in Japan and stayed in Japan for the entire cycle of his training. It had something to do with his mother's death that he spent so much time in Japan, but he formed very close connections to that country."

"Where is he now?" she asked, her curiosity getting the best of her. "You don't think he's in Japan, do you?"

A subtle shrug danced on Ji Hoon's shoulders. "After Young Jae disappeared from our world, there were whispers that he returned to Japan. No one knows for sure though. He's been doing a great job at keeping a low profile."

"Is it that easy for an Underworld Royal to disappear?" asked Yoori. She was frustrated that no one seemed to know what happened to Young Jae.

"It's easy for an Underworld Royal to do a lot of things," Ji Hoon said easily. He tilted his head. "You have quite the curiosity when it comes to the Scorpions family, don't you?"

"Oh...heh, heh..." Yoori laughed tensely. She tried to downplay her extreme interest. "I heard about the Underworld and its gang leaders when I worked at the diner. There's such a mystery concerning this world and I sometimes can't help but want to learn more when I have a good source in front of me."

Ji Hoon nodded before going on to another topic. "Why doesn't Tae Hyun talk to you about any of this?" His voice was gentle, but it had a touch of craftiness. She suspected he was trying to figure out the relationship between her and Tae Hyun with her next answer.

"We usually talk about other stuff," she answered candidly.

Like ducks and arguing about nonsensical things, she corrected in her mind.

Her curiosity about Tae Hyun heightened. Since she was already talking to Ji Hoon about this, she might as well take it a *bit* further.

"Tae—" Yoori began unsteadily, her carelessness when it came to learning more about the Underworld tempting her again. "Tae Hyun wasn't the first heir of the Serpents' throne. You said that your younger brother is getting trained for the specific task of leading the 1st layer. Surely Tae Hyun was trained in a similar way. He was only trained for the 3rd layer later on in life, right?"

Ji Hoon gazed at her thoughtfully, his eyes noting that she knew little to nothing about Tae Hyun's background in the Underworld. Resolution reveled in his eyes and he began to enlighten her.

"Tae Hyun was *only* supposed to be trained to be in the 1st layer. That's typically the training cycle of the second born heirs. They go through the basic training for fighting and then the majority of the time, they spend their time shadowing other business leaders. However, Tae Hyun's training was different solely because Shin Dong Min adopted him to be his advisee. This was something an Advisor in the 2nd layer had never done, which was to personally train an heir who was only meant for the 1st layer."

Though Ji Hoon tried to hide it, Yoori caught the resentment in his voice when he continued.

"In addition to Dong Min, Tae Hyun caught the support of all the business tycoons and revered politicians in the 1st layer. They not only mentored him in the ways of corporate politics...but also instilled within him all their knowledge when it came to fighting and weaponry. He was the adopted protégée of some of the most well revered crime lords in Asia—hence his bigger standing in our world when he killed his brother and stole the Serpents' throne three years ago."

There was disgust in his voice. It was a tone that Yoori caught and a tone she was bothered with. She knew exactly why Tae Hyun had to kill his brother and she didn't like that Ji Hoon was trying to subtly instill within her that Tae Hyun only killed with the mere hopes of taking over the throne.

Ji Hoon straightened in his seat when he realized he might have been a bit too unfiltered with his distaste toward Tae Hyun. He didn't miss the frown on Yoori's face. He cleared his throat and changed the pace of the conversation by waving his hand in the air. The gesture brought two servers out.

Yoori loosened the tenseness in her body when new company joined them. She breathed in relief when she saw that they were each holding a jade, cast iron teapot. She definitely needed some tea to calm her nerves and warm her up.

Though the winter breeze was a mild one, it was cold enough to give her goose bumps every now and then.

The waiter and waitress approached them and placed two jade teacups in front of them. They steadily poured the contents of the tea into their cups. Once the tea filled to the rim, Yoori and Ji Hoon imparted their thanks to the servers and they were once again left alone on the rooftop.

It didn't take long for Yoori to realize that the tea they were drinking was the heavenly tea she liked so much.

"Did you create this tea mix yourself? I've never tasted anything like it. It's delicious."

It was a leading question; she wanted to know if Ji Hoon knew it was Tae Hyun who created it.

A sad smile tugged on his lips when he took a sip out of the teacup.

"Soo Jin introduced me to this drink," he shared slowly, his demeanor showing that he walked on to a territory he had been trying to avoid all night. "It was her favorite."

His answer took Yoori by surprise. She cursed to herself. Fuck. She just had to remind him of Soo Jin.

Unease tugging at her heart, Yoori nodded and drank from the teacup. Who would've thought it was Soo Jin who got hooked with Tae Hyun's drink and introduced it to Ji Hoon? This world was evidently too small if its crime lords were connected, even under the concealment of a well-loved drink.

Yoori wondered what Soo Jin would've thought if she had known that her favorite drink was created by a Serpent, the one gang Soo Jin hated the most because her father died under the hands of its previous King—Kwon Ho Young. Yoori knew without a shadow of a doubt that Soo Jin would've hated that fact. She would've hated it—just as she would've hated Tae Hyun because he was a Serpent.

The heat from the tea seared her tongue, pulling Yoori out of her impromptu daze. She had lost concentration and drank too much of the hot tea at once.

Though her tongue burned, it was a pain she was willing to endure to remind herself that she shouldn't allow her thoughts to venture this far. It would only cause more headaches (and heartaches) for her. She wished she could be stronger and stop herself from thinking about Soo Jin and Tae Hyun. She had to be stronger because her new life wasn't going to involve either of them. It couldn't involve Soo Jin because Yoori was determined to keep her out of her life and it couldn't involve Tae Hyun because he didn't want to be in her life.

Resolution teemed inside her. The objective tonight was to keep her promise to Ji Hoon and to keep the fact that she was Soo Jin to herself. She didn't want anyone else to know, especially Ji Hoon.

Oblivious to what was pooling in Yoori's mind, Ji Hoon regarded her. There seemed to be a million things running through his mind. There was a soft glaze in his eyes. It was a glaze for someone who was reminiscing. There was only one woman commanding his attention at that moment and it definitely wasn't her.

He gave a quiet sigh and stood up. He slowly approached the aisle of the rooftop that wasn't confined within the glass walls. There was no verbal invitation for her to accompany him, but Yoori somehow knew he was waiting for her to join him. She pushed her chair back and approached the end of the rooftop. She stopped right beside Ji Hoon. They stood side by side as the city blinked under the cloak of darkness. Yoori folded her arms, feeling the billowing of the evening wind surge through her. A long moment of silence waltzed between them before Ji Hoon finally spoke.

"This was the very roof where Soo Jin first opened her heart up to me."

Yoori stilled. She hadn't expected to hear that. She stared at him questionably.

The coolness of his voice remained while he continued to speak, his eyes absently focused on the city vista. "In the car the other night, when I told you how I met her…you asked me what I did to woo Soo Jin and finally get her to become my girlfriend." He smiled to himself. "People have this grand assumption that I pulled out all the stops to court her, to make her mine. The truth was…I did pull out all the stops. I gave her all the charms I was able to give out. But regardless of giving her everything I was able to muster out, she was never too impressed with anything. That's the thing with Soo Jin. She wasn't easily impressed…not with my charms, my affection, or even my determination. I thought my chance with her was over until the assassination of her father took place a couple of months after I met her."

Yoori recalled that it was Ho Young who killed Soo Jin's father—her father. She shifted uneasily, knowing that this was probably the main reason why Tae Hyun left her.

Ji Hoon was still lost in his own world. "Around this time five years ago, I brought Soo Jin up to this very roof after her father's death. I realized that night the difference between Soo Jin and other girls I've been with. Soo Jin wasn't moved by innate charms or anything of the like." The cold wind blew harder against their bodies. "She was moved by power, a power that goes beyond being human. I realized that fact when I stood beside her in silence—in her time of need. I told her that no matter what happened…I'd always be by her side. I told her that I would be able to give her anything and everything she wanted and I told her I knew what she wanted most." His eyes hardened. "I promised her that I'd make sure to punish every living Serpent for what they did to her father. *That* was how I wooed her. I offered her vengeance and that was what she was impressed with—what she was infatuated with. I offered all of that and the rest was history…she became mine."

He was quiet for a while before he spoke again. "You know," he murmured, his eyes shifting from the city and then onto her. "You remind me of her…"

Yoori turned back to him. Tension overwhelmed her senses. How was she supposed to react to that? Luckily for Yoori, she didn't have to say anything. Ji Hoon had already continued, an expression of guilt outlining his countenance. The contents of his words created more anxiety for her.

"I lied to you when I told you that you didn't resemble her in the least bit."

Yoori began to shake like a leaf. It wasn't because of the cold wind. Swallowing thickly, she was quiet as he went on.

"You *do* look like her. In every way possible, you resemble her." He laughed to himself, his eyes becoming more vulnerable. "It gets harder every time, you know? When I see you… Every time I see you, my heart skips a beat…like it did when I was around her. Every time I see you, it gets harder and harder to let you go back to Tae Hyun."

Ji Hoon allowed himself to fall silent while he waited for her reply.

Fighting off the urge to tell him the truth, Yoori blinked in frustration. "Why did you lie to me?" was all that she uttered out, her eyes focused on the city before them.

She couldn't look at him—not when he was beginning to tell the truth and not when she was adamant on not telling him who she really was. She didn't want to be Soo Jin and she couldn't tell Ji Hoon because he'd want her back *as* Soo Jin.

She could tell by this point that his soft eyes were on her. They were waiting, almost begging, for her to look at him.

"There was no point in telling you the truth," he whispered. "I doubt girls are flattered when they're told they resemble someone's ex-girlfriend."

"Then why is there a point to tell me the truth now?" She tried to hide the accusatory tone in her voice. She didn't mean it; she didn't mean to use such a strong tone with him. She just wanted to continue to act shocked so she didn't compromise her cover.

"Because I can't stand seeing you with Tae Hyun any longer."

Though she had anticipated this answer, the vocalization of it did little to ease the growing tension in her heart. She finally turned to him and held his poignant gaze. Her lips trembled to speak, but nothing came out.

Her silence didn't matter for Ji Hoon had more he wanted to vocally share.

"I don't think it's a secret that I've wanted you since I saw you in that warehouse. It's also not a secret that I've been fighting off the temptation to steal you away from him."

He drew closer to her, an action that caused her to stiffen up. She wanted to retreat, but found herself cemented in her stance.

"I honestly never thought you'd last with Tae Hyun for that long. I was convinced if I laid low, stood back and allowed you to become attached to me every time we met again, then you'd start to fade from him and come to me." A frown tugged at his expression. "But every time I see you, it seems that you grow closer and closer to Tae Hyun. It's like you're falling harder for him everyday."

His voice grew severe, almost possessive. "I don't like knowing that he gets to touch you when I can't. I don't like knowing that he gets to take care of you when I can't. I don't like knowing that everyday, it seems like you're falling harder for him while I fade away in the background. It's a sickening feeling and I want to end it right now."

"Ji—"

"There's another reason why I'm telling you the truth right now," Ji Hoon interrupted, saving Yoori from uttering words she had yet to garner.

She was still speechless as to what to say to him.

Yoori was quiet while she listened, her heart and soul scorching with dread. In her mind, she tried to find the best way to vocalize the dreaded answer she wanted to give to him.

"Soo Jin didn't die being on Ju Won's good side," Ji Hoon stated, acquiring Yoori's undivided attention.

Her eyes bloomed in fear.

Noting the panic in her eyes, Ji Hoon went on. "He isn't showing it, but he's angry—*really* angry. He's convinced that you're her and the thought of you being her pisses him off with the passing seconds. He told Tae Hyun that you resemble her and warned Tae Hyun against trusting you and having you around."

It felt like he was drilling nails into her. It was hard to listen, but she fought through it because she wanted to know what was going on.

"I told Tae Hyun what Ju Won insinuated was absurd. I told him that you didn't resemble Soo Jin at all. I think that helped to throw Tae Hyun off for a bit, but he might have taken what Ju Won said into consideration."

He did, Yoori thought to herself, the final drilling of the nail having more impact on her than anything else she heard.

Her train of thoughts was short-lived when she felt Ji Hoon grab her hands.

"Be with me," Ji Hoon said tenderly, pulling her toward him. His voice was strained with desperation and determination. He was agonized as he stared at her. "I can protect you from all of this."

She shook her head. Thoughtlessly, she said, "Tae Hyun can protect me."

As soon as it came out of her mouth, she knew it sounded absurd. Why was it that even under the direst of circumstances, she still had so much faith in Tae Hyun? He walked out on her when she needed him most. He didn't deserve that faith.

Ji Hoon was angry at her answer. She could see it in his eyes. Despite this, he kept his composure. "Do you know why Ju Won favors Tae Hyun more than me?"

Yoori shook her head, almost afraid of finding out the answer.

"Because Ju Won has seen me at my weakest. Anything that deals with Soo Jin hits a nerve within me. He knows this—everyone knows this. They all know this and they will never forget it." He held her closer, making sure she knew how serious he was being. "Tae Hyun has the upper hand right now because he had always been ambitious. He keeps one goal in mind and he sacrifices *everything* else for it."

The reminder of Tae Hyun seared into his mind, causing his eyes to burn with hatred. He was angry, bitter and jealous.

"Do you think that he would care about you if the Advisors told him to get rid of you? Do you think he gives a damn about you? He'll leave you. The first chance he gets where he senses you're about to get in his way, he'll leave you. He won't stand by you like I will. He'll leave you and he won't come back to you."

Yoori was quiet, her mind wandering off to the nightmare of the night before. Tae Hyun really did leave her. It wasn't a possibility; it was her reality.

It was a mistake on Yoori's part to allow the disappointed shadow to take over her pale face. It was a mistake on her part to not shrug off Ji Hoon's words. Because, even if it was only for a brief second, she had forgotten that Ji Hoon was inspecting the reaction on her face. It was a brief moment, but he caught her bluff. He caught on to what she was feeling.

His eyes enlarged with realization.

"He's already left you, hasn't he?" Ji Hoon asked knowingly. "He already allowed what the Advisors told him to get to his head."

Silence claimed Yoori's lips. She didn't say anything, but her inability to speak was enough for Ji Hoon. It gave him fuel to continue on with his quest to make Yoori give up on Tae Hyun and come to him.

"That's the thing with Tae Hyun. All the girls he's ever been with came flocking to me because he doesn't care enough to keep them," he probed, feeding on the worsening dread on her face. "Tae Hyun is incapable of caring about anyone but himself."

She didn't want to listen anymore.

"Yoori," Ji Hoon called, staring her straight in the eyes. "Be with me. I can give you anything and everything you want. I'll give you the world and I'll never leave you."

"No, I can't!" Yoori combated at once. She pulled herself from Ji Hoon. It was true that Tae Hyun didn't care about her, but it didn't automatically mean she didn't care for him. She didn't know what was going on with her; she just knew she wanted to get away from Ji Hoon. She couldn't stand to be around him anymore.

This was when Ji Hoon lost it.

"Why are you so fucking hung up on Tae Hyun?" Ji Hoon shouted in disbelief. It was the first time he had ever raised his voice at her. Jealousy swarmed the now smothering rooftop. His voice elevated. "You haven't even known him for that long and you've fallen *that hard* for him already?"

"I don't know!" Yoori cried, frustration rippling within her.

She was livid with Tae Hyun, but she was even angrier that Ji Hoon spoke so horribly about him. She couldn't stand Ji Hoon talking about him with such negativity; she couldn't stand him trying to pull her away from Tae Hyun. If she hated Tae Hyun, then she'd hate him herself. She didn't need anyone to add fuel to the fire.

"I don't know how I feel about him! All I know is that you need to stop, Ji Hoon! I won't stand here and listen to you as you throw him under the bus. I don't know how I truly feel about him, but I know how I feel about you."

She drew in a sharp breath, the dreaded words coming out of her quivering lips.

"I'm sorry." Her voice broke. "You've been nothing but kind to me since we've met. I know that you care a lot about me, I really do. And I care about you too...but I don't have *those* feelings for you. I just don't."

His hands fell from hers.

He stared at her in silence, his chest heaving up and down. Then, when Yoori was ready to voice another apology, his eyes grew dark. He scoffed to himself, his face angrier than she had ever seen it. He didn't take the news lightly and he wasn't too intent on hiding it.

"All because of Kwon Tae Hyun, right?" Ji Hoon accused, the last of his composure diminishing into the darkness of the night. "You're only like this because of Kwon Tae Hyun—*fucking* Kwon Tae Hyun!" He raked his fingers through his hair in fury. His angry hands drew up in the air as he spoke to her, as he yelled at her. "You're blinded by whatever spell he placed on you. Everyone in this *fucking* world seems to be!"

"Ji Hoon, stop it," Yoori ordered firmly. Though her voice was severe, she was actually scared stiff. Ji Hoon was a different person when he was angry. He looked terrifying.

He scoffed to himself again, his eyes leaving hers and landing onto the city below him. "The great Kwon Tae Hyun...the crime lord who was raised to take over the 1st layer, but garnered control over the 3rd layer instead..." Ji Hoon shook his head, lost in his own bitterness. "There's nothing great about Tae Hyun yet everyone in this goddamn world reveres him like he's God's gift to our world. The two Advisors, the majority of the 1st layer and *you*." He turned back to her. "You're all blinded. *I* was the one who rightfully claimed my Skulls' throne. *I* was the youngest crime lord in the 3rd layer. *I* was the one with the most revered Queen in my arms. *I* was the one and *the only one* who was supposed to be the contender for the Underworld throne. Yet when that fucking bastard came into the picture, this entire world fell on their knees and kneeled before him instead!"

She began to back away while he spoke. She didn't get far when he caught her by the hands and pulled her closer to him. His expression softened upon seeing the fear in her eyes.

"I'm sorry," he said tenderly. "I didn't mean to scare you." His hold on her tightened. "But don't you see how much it's hurting me that you're with him? It's killing me. It's ripping me apart. He doesn't deserve you. He's too selfish and he will never be able to love you like I would be able to. Come back to me and be with me again."

"Come...Come back?" Yoori asked incredulously, shaking in her stance.

He wasn't speaking to her like she was Choi Yoori.

He was speaking to her like she was An Soo—

A voice interrupted her thoughts, pulling her and Ji Hoon from their conversation.

"Get your fucking hands off my girlfriend, Ji Hoon."

"For every temptation. . ."

12: Fallen Kings

Her once shaking body froze like ice upon hearing the familiar voice.

Her heart revved to life and jumped in anticipation.

Could it be?

She breathed sharply, an electrifying surge of energy pulsating within her body

Was that really *his* voice?

Slowly, *very slowly*, as if afraid it would only be her imagination, she turned her head to the side. Sure enough, she caught sight of the one person she was so angry with and the one person she couldn't deny that she missed terribly.

Kwon Tae Hyun...

He came back.

Standing a couple of feet away from them, dressed in a blue dress shirt with his sleeves rolled up to his elbows and black slacks, Tae Hyun looked intimidating as he stood there with an angry countenance. He looked tired, *definitely* annoyed, and as handsome as ever. It wasn't healthy to have so much anger and so much attraction toward this guy and Yoori knew that. She knew it, but she couldn't control it. It was a weakness she hated and a weakness she reveled in.

"Who are you to tell me what to do?" Ji Hoon combated at once, breaking Yoori from her daze. His hold on Yoori tightened.

Tae Hyun stiffened in annoyance when his eyes fell on the hands of Ji Hoon's that still held Yoori's.

"Lee Ji Hoon," he began warningly, his voice low and dangerous. "I am going to bash your skull against that glass wall if you don't take your filthy hands off of her."

Though Tae Hyun was calm, the fire that brimmed in his eyes was enough to burn anyone alive. He didn't like Ji Hoon touching Yoori and he was goddamn ready to do something about it.

"Ji Hoon, let go of me," Yoori commanded, knowing that Ji Hoon would listen to her as opposed to Tae Hyun.

She didn't want Ji Hoon to get hurt.

She didn't want either of them to get hurt.

130

"Yoori, he'll hurt you the first chance he's able," Ji Hoon warned gently, refusing to let go. There was care in his voice when he went on. "Remember what I told you. He only cares about himself. He—"

"Yoori…" Tae Hyun interrupted quietly, his soft eyes finally landing onto hers.

It had only been a day since they'd been apart and to Yoori, it felt like she hadn't seen Tae Hyun in centuries. How odd was it that just this particular interaction was enough to lift Yoori's heart? How odd was it that he was speaking to her again, despite the severity of how he treated her? Recalling the pain he caused her, Yoori found herself unable to say anything to him. Though every fiber on her body wanted to run up to him and hug him, she kept still. She was still hurt. Why was he here? Why—?

"Chae Young said that you were at her apartment," Tae Hyun continued, his eyes never leaving hers.

Yoori paused at this information. He went to see Chae Young at the diner? He had been looking for her?

"I went to her apartment and you weren't there."

Yoori's stomach wrenched when he confirmed her unspoken question. She thought to earlier in the morning. She left moments after Chae Young left to go work at the diner. If she hadn't left, then Tae Hyun would've came and—

"I've been looking for you all day," he shared. His voice was apprehensive yet firm. He knew she wasn't happy with him. Regardless of such knowledge, his gaze on her remained gentle and very much determined. "I'm sorry it took so long for me to find you, but I'm here now and I want to take you home." He sighed. "Let's go home, Yoori."

There was so much running through her mind. She didn't know how to react to what Tae Hyun was sharing with her. She felt relieved, happy, and resentful. Happy that Tae Hyun had been looking for her, happy that he came back for her. Yet she was resentful because of the way he treated her last night, how he left her when she begged him not to.

There wasn't much time to deliberate what she wanted to do, but whatever it was that she needed to resolve, it had to be resolved with Tae Hyun. She had to leave Ji Hoon and go back with Tae Hyun.

"Ji Hoon, let go," Yoori said firmly, turning her gaze back over to him. Her mind was set.

"Yoo—"

"*Now.*"

With much reluctance, Ji Hoon released his hold on her hand.

Without another word, Yoori approached Tae Hyun, her face stern with anger. It didn't matter that he had been looking for her all day. She hadn't forgotten what he did to her. She hadn't forgotten how much he hurt her. It would be terrible to give him the cold shoulder, but he surely deserved it.

"I haven't forgotten what you did last night," Yoori warned when she reached him. Her voice was low enough where it was only audible to Tae Hyun.

The wind blew past them and he nodded.

His small smile remained. Noticing that her bangs had gotten into her eyes from the wind, Tae Hyun lifted both his hands and tucked her windswept bangs behind each of her ears. His touch was light, but powerful enough to cause Yoori to hold her breath. For a distracted second, she almost forgot that she was angry with him.

"I haven't forgotten either," he whispered back, his voice and expression packed with regret. She noticed that there was a peculiar look in his eyes. If she didn't know better, she would've thought he missed her too.

He had more to say. He had more to say and she was dying to hear everything he wanted to say to her. Unfortunately, such as the situation they were in, the forgotten third party wasn't happy with the scene that was taking place before him. He was damn well ready to end it.

"Do you think I'll let you take her away from me that easily?"

Reminded of his rival's presence, Tae Hyun withdrew his hands from Yoori and turned to Ji Hoon with a lethargic, but very annoyed, expression on his face.

"Don't test me, Ji Hoon," he said sternly, fighting hard to keep his composure. "You have no idea how tempted I am to teach you a lesson right now. In the past, I didn't care when you went after any other girls I'd been with, but Choi Yoori is different."

Yoori breathed faintly after hearing this.

Tae Hyun went on. "You're not taking her away from me and I'm not even going to let you try."

Tae Hyun placed his hand over her shoulder and was ready to walk out with Yoori when Ji Hoon's next words froze their stance.

"You're only doing this because you know how much she means to me!"

That was the last straw for Tae Hyun.

He had enough.

His eyes burned when he whipped around to face Ji Hoon, who was breathing heavily in anger.

"Don't you *fucking* tell me why I do the things that I do!" Tae Hyun shouted back, shocking Yoori with his quaking fury. "I told you that night that she's not An Soo Jin!" He was furious. Not because of what Ji Hoon said, but because Ji Hoon reminded him that she was An Soo Jin. "I told the Advisors and I told you…Choi Yoori is *not* An Soo Jin. She's her own person and I'll be damned if I let you force her to become someone she doesn't want to be."

There was a double meaning to his statement. It was one that Yoori could understand and one that she could appreciate.

Ji Hoon laughed mockingly. "You're a fucking wonderful actor, you know that? If I didn't know you well enough, I would've thought you cared about someone other than yourself."

"I'm not the one playing the heartbroken prince charming," Tae Hyun snarled back.

It looked like Tae Hyun had a couple more choice words for Ji Hoon, but he resisted the temptation to say more insulting things. His main priority was to leave with Yoori. Everything else was secondary.

Intertwining his fingers with hers, Tae Hyun pulled Yoori, who was taken aback by what had taken place, along with him. They were ready to leave until…

"Let's break the pact," Ji Hoon declared, stopping Tae Hyun and Yoori in their tracks.

Ji Hoon went on, knowing he had Tae Hyun's undivided attention. His voice erupted with fury.

"We're the Kings of this layer, Tae Hyun. That old bastard has no right to 'request' anything of us," he continued, referring to Ju Won. "It's been too long since we've had our last rumble and I'm sure you're yearning for my blood as much as I'm yearning for yours."

"No," Yoori stated tightly, interrupting Tae Hyun before he could reply.

She had had enough of this heated exchange between them.

She glared at Ji Hoon. "*You* asked me for a date and I gave it to you." She flickered her glare to Tae Hyun. "*You* came here for me and I'm leaving with you." She glanced from one to the other. "You two aren't fighting. The night is over and we're leaving."

"What do you say, Tae Hyun?" Ji Hoon incited, ignoring Yoori's wishes. His eyes rested solely on Tae Hyun. Yoori's blood boiled at the dismissal.

Tae Hyun looked tempted. He looked downright tempted at the invitation to rip Ji Hoon to shreds. Yet, when he felt Yoori tighten her hold on him in silent disapproval, he curbed his violent desire. "I'm not wasting my time with you, Ji Hoon." He glanced at Yoori. "I have more important matters to tend to."

Ji Hoon smirked when Tae Hyun was about to turn away from him.

"I've never taken you for a coward, Tae Hyun," Ji Hoon goaded. "Aren't you the almighty King of Serpents? I thought there had to be something special about you since everyone seems to revere you like you're a God. But I see you for who you are…who you've *always* been. You're nothing but a coward who got lucky with a title that supersedes him." He laughed dryly to himself. "You're a piece of cowering shit without your title—just like your fucking father."

Tae Hyun's jaw clenched at the reference to his father.

Ji Hoon, reveling in the reaction he wanted to get out of Tae Hyun, went on mercilessly.

"He kneeled before me, you know…" Ji Hoon continued to taunt, already rolling his sleeves up to his elbows. "Begged me to spare his life." He chuckled.

"But then I guess your family is a family of kneelers..." His eyes darkened with malice. "*Especially* that slut sister of yours who got down on her knees and gave me the best fucking blowjob I've ever had in my life."

And that was it.

At that moment two things happened: Yoori, shocked and disgusted with Ji Hoon's behavior, released her hold on Tae Hyun's hand. There was no point of restraining Tae Hyun. He was livid and he was going to make Ji Hoon eat his words.

With a scorch of vindictive fire in his eyes, Tae Hyun charged for Ji Hoon with his fist flying like a bullet in the air. In no time, Tae Hyun's iron fist collided onto the cheek of Ji Hoon. The resounding impact of a bone shattering collision shook Yoori to her core. She could've sworn she saw the blinking of a white tooth dance in the sky as Ji Hoon spat out coagulated blood into the air.

The fight was on.

Ji Hoon staggered to the ground. Before he fell, Tae Hyun caught him by the collar and delivered another punch to the right side of his cheek. The echo of the blow sang through the night as another spurt of blood escaped from Ji Hoon's lips.

When it appeared as if Ji Hoon was about to fall to the ground, he instead crouched down and swiftly rammed himself into Tae Hyun's stomach, catching Tae Hyun off guard.

A loud rumbling reverberated across the rooftop after Ji Hoon pummeled Tae Hyun against the glass wall that sat between them and the world beneath.

Tae Hyun winced in pain at the impact.

Using his elbow, Ji Hoon threw another blow against Tae Hyun's cheek, causing him to slam one side of his face against the trembling glass. Ji Hoon was ready to throw a punch when Tae Hyun retaliated by embedding his knee against Ji Hoon's stomach, causing him to gasp for air.

Cursing and nearly losing his balance, Ji Hoon countered that attack by throwing an uppercut against Tae Hyun's jaw. The blow left Tae Hyun to inadvertently lift his head up and smash it against the wall behind him.

The next few moves happened so quickly that a stunned Yoori was only able to watch in shock. Ji Hoon, with fire burning in his own eyes, clenched his right fist and threw it toward Tae Hyun's head. With lightning speed, Tae Hyun was able to duck his head down. The sounds of glass cracking could be heard as little roots of destruction sprouted unto the once solid glass. Ji Hoon's fist had hit the glass instead. The water inside the glass seeped out, the lights within it flickering in terror.

"Fuck!" Ji Hoon cussed when he withdrew his fist. However much damage he made unto the glass structure, the damage surely didn't match the pain he inflicted upon himself.

Seizing the opportunity of distraction, Tae Hyun grabbed Ji Hoon by the collar and threw him head first against the glass wall. Three gargantuan cracks of disturbance appeared on the glass. Water streamed out of the wall like a waterfall. Tae Hyun's hands found the back of Ji Hoon's neck. Keeping true to his original threat, an enraged Tae Hyun started to bash Ji Hoon's skull against the glass structure.

Once.

Twice.

It wasn't until the third collision that Ji Hoon strategically steadied his neck, used all of his energy to push it backward and slammed the back of his head against Tae Hyun's face.

The tactic to get Tae Hyun off of him worked.

Tae Hyun stumbled a couple of steps back. He was undoubtedly seeing stars as blood seeped from his nose. Staggering briefly to the floor, he managed to pull himself up. Like an angry bull, he charged for Ji Hoon and sent another flying fist in his direction. It went straight for Ji Hoon's nose.

The back of Ji Hoon's head collided into the unstable glass wall once more. The unsteady glass trembled when the harsh wind blew against it. Water poured over Tae Hyun and Ji Hoon as they continued to exchange blows beside the deteriorating glass wall.

Seconds later, in the process of exchanging merciless blows, both crashed into the glass wall and created the final impact that shattered the once solid glass into a million flickering pieces.

"Noooooooo!" was all that could be heard from Yoori's horrorstruck voice as she watched them teeter off the foundation of the rooftop.

They flew through a typhoon of tinkling glass and disappeared into the abyss of the world beneath them.

"Shit! Shit! Shit!" Yoori shouted, her legs taking off in the direction of where Tae Hyun and Ji Hoon fell. Vertical VII was one of the tallest buildings in the district and Yoori could only imagine that their bodies were splattered all across the busy streets below.

What a horrible way to end the night if they died on her, she thought morbidly, a strong gust of wind accompanying her rising fears. Once she was an inch away from the edge, she peered down with eyes wide open.

Needless to say, at the sounds of shuffling and obvious signs of life from below, Yoori was surprised at the deliriously amazing sight before her.

Relief swam over her like a wave.

They were still alive!

"Oh, thank God!" Yoori cried in joy once she saw that the balcony to one of the VIP suites caught them mid-flight. The platform of the balcony twinkled with broken glass as Tae Hyun and Ji Hoon continued to exchange merciless blows.

Tae Hyun had thrown another punch in Ji Hoon's direction, an attack to which Ji Hoon retaliated with a knee to the stomach.

Yoori breathed a sigh of relief once she observed that the fall did little to screw up their bodies. If anything, it seemed as if they were more energized to fight after the unexpected fall.

Enough was enough. She had to stop them.

She threw herself backward and ran toward the stairway. She ran down every step, the resounding echoes of her boots bounced off the once empty stairs.

Stupid, stupid! Why didn't you stop them, she scolded herself, increasing her pace.

She didn't understand what was wrong with her, why she stood there and watched them fight. She didn't understand what came over her when the fight took place. It felt like a rain of cement poured over her legs and her rationale. She was mesmerized while watching them fight. Every move they threw, she *analyzed*. Every move they threw, she *studied*. It was an odd daze that was only slapped out of her when she realized they were about to fall off the rooftop.

Thank God. Thank God, they're still alive, she thought to herself, wondering how she could stand there and watch them pummel each other to death.

And what were they fighting for?

Their pride?

Her?

She held on to the railing as she rounded the curvilinear landing of the staircase. Idiotic. This entire ordeal was idiotic.

With seven steps remaining, Yoori, being very impatient as to the well-being of the two Underworld Kings, chose to gallop onto the next level's landing as opposed to merely running onto it. Crouching down once her legs landed on the platform, her hands reached out for the door that led into the floor of the VIP suites.

Warm lights shined over her skin when she burst into the affluent hotel hall. She stopped to breathe heavily. She gazed at her surroundings. The hall appeared endless. Her eyes followed the myriad of doors that graced the hall. Where the hell were they?

The answer to her question came in the form of a loud collision that rocketed the once peaceful hall. Her eyes narrowed onto the door to the room where the sound originated. She took off in the direction of the fifth room to the right. Her hand scarcely stroked the doorknob when out of nowhere, a fist speared through the wooden door.

"Oh shit!" Yoori cried.

She jumped back before the fist inadvertently rammed into her nose. Yoori's extremities shuddered at the thought of getting a broken nose from the fist that had splinters of wood piercing out of its knuckle. The owner of the fist gave a disgruntled growl (one to which Yoori was sure was Tae Hyun's) and withdrew his bloody fist from the door. The heavy door shook violently.

The sound of fighting commenced. Sounds of glass shattering and walls rumbling could be heard while Yoori tried to open the door from the outside but to no avail. She cursed a string of expletives and used the puncture in the door to reach in and pull the knob down from the inside. The door promptly opened for an irritated Yoori who wanted to end the fight right then and there—

"Fuck!"

Unfortunately for Yoori, she didn't get to put one foot in before a body slammed into the door, slamming the wooden structure onto her unsuspecting face.

Pain.

Insufferable pain electrocuted through every corner of her face, leaving her to collapse onto the carpeted floor. She groaned, opening her eyes to see darkness and various shades of bright stars. With her throbbing head resting on the floor, Yoori lifted a trembling hand over to her nose. Blood slithered out of it when her hand touched the little nub.

Fury rammed into her. They gave her a bloody nose!

"Bastards!" she cursed heatedly, wiping the blood away from her nose. "Fucking bastards!"

Wrath possessed her and overrode the pain prominent on her face. She lurched to her feet with a growl and pushed the assaulted door open. She knew it wasn't logical to be mad at Tae Hyun and Ji Hoon for giving her a bloody nose, especially when they didn't even know that they were the cause of it. She knew this, but Yoori wasn't the most logical person when she was in pain. She wanted someone to pay for her bloody nose.

The VIP suite she stormed into was a mess.

The suite looked like it had been hit by a ferocious tornado. Everything in the room was broken. Her eyes flickered around the room and she finally spotted Tae Hyun and Ji Hoon. They were still going after one another. Tae Hyun had just kicked his foot into the wall and Ji Hoon had pierced his fist into the adjacent wall. Both had successfully evaded each other's attacks.

"Eh! Stop!" she hollered at the top of her lungs. Her anger was sky high. "Stop fighting already!"

The Underworld Kings didn't hear (or refused to listen). They each threw a kick toward each other's stomachs and sent one another flying across opposite sides of the room.

A synchronized collision thundered all throughout the room as each slammed into the walls behind them.

Knowing that standing in between them was going to be ineffective, and thoroughly pissed at them for injuring her nose, Yoori muttered a string of indignant curse words and reached for the two plump oranges that laid in a ceramic bowl on a nearby dresser.

After making sure that her nails dug their way into the skin of each orange and making sure that juices were flowing out of them, Yoori lifted her arms and aimed it when Tae Hyun and Ji Hoon rose to their feet. There was bloodlust in their eyes.

Right when they were about to charge at one another, undoubtedly with the sole purpose of ripping the limbs out of the opponent, Yoori, with all the strength that she had, threw the plump oranges in each of their directions.

"Fuck!" they both shouted after the heavily plump oranges ate away at their noses and squirted stinging juices into their eyes.

Blood seeping out of their nostrils, Ji Hoon fell to the floor and knocked his head against a nearby table while Tae Hyun staggered to the ground and accidentally slammed the back of his head against the wooden post of the bed behind him.

A tense silence waltzed into the assaulted room. Sounds of heavy breathing accompanied its presence. The silence danced against the shards of shattered glass that flickered from the balcony, slid in and out of the countless fist/foot made puncture holes on the walls, staggered heedlessly around the blood stained carpet, hovered over the groans of both Tae Hyun and Ji Hoon, and dispersed around Yoori who was glaring unblinkingly.

"I told you two to stop fighting," she said simply, unwilling to apologize for throwing the oranges at them. She would've chosen to throw her heeled boots if she had not caught sight of the oranges. Bloody noses aside, they should've counted their blessings that she didn't throw something more lethal.

Yoori swabbed the blood away from her own assaulted nose and watched Tae Hyun and Ji Hoon do the same thing with their noses. After long seconds of heaving their chests up and down, they opened their orange stained eyes. Their hands resting on their respective battered heads, their surprised gazes landed on Yoori.

She could tell they were fighting the urge to further groan in pain. Whether it was to appear strong in front of her or appear strong in front of each other, she wasn't sure. All she knew was that it was due time to leave Vertical VII before they caused more damages. God knows the next time they fall out of the building, there won't be another extended balcony to catch them.

Careful not to give them another second to gather their strengths, she commenced with the evacuation plan.

"Tae Hyun! Hurry and take me home!" she commanded roughly. She had things to resolve with him. She knew Tae Hyun was not used to getting spoken to so brusquely, but she could hardly care. She was livid with him.

She had anticipated him to scream at her in contention but instead, Tae Hyun merely took a second to bitterly glare at her before obeying her wishes.

Wow, that was easy, she thought when he stood up from his position.

She cleared her throat when he approached her. He looked like he emerged from a battlefield. He was soaked with water and was gleaming with broken glass, debris, and blood. Somehow the guy still looked good though. *Blessed genetic freak*, Yoori thought when he reached her.

"Could you wait outside for me?" she asked tentatively, her tone gentler this time.

She had one final issue to finalize with Ji Hoon before she left him. She knew this wasn't going to be a request that Tae Hyun would be fond of, which was why she used the softer voice. She didn't want to push her luck by continuously being rude to him—at least not when she wanted to leave the hotel as soon as possible.

As anticipated, his face flared with irritation. He didn't like the idea of her being alone with Ji Hoon. Tae Hyun spared a second to lower his eyes onto Ji Hoon, who had risen to his feet as well. There was a moment where warning glares were exchanged between them before Tae Hyun wiped away the remaining blood from his lips. However disgruntled he was that Yoori wanted him to leave the room, he didn't vocalize his displeasures and instead stalked off toward the door.

Yoori exhaled in relief. Tae Hyun was being unusually receptive to her wishes. She thought about it further. It was probably because he wanted to get on her good side before they had the inevitable conversation about him leaving her. The thought made her stomach coil in anger. As obedient as he was being, she sure as hell wasn't going to make it a pleasant conversation for him.

"Yoori," Ji Hoon whispered hoarsely, pulling her out of her thoughts. He clutched on to a nearby table and straightened himself up. The fight with Tae Hyun took an extreme toll on his body. He could hardly stand. He was definitely worse off than Tae Hyun.

The sight made her heart grow heavy with guilt.

"Ji Hoon..." Yoori started delicately, fighting the urge to run over to him to help him.

She wanted to help him, but she shouldn't. If she helped him, then the misunderstanding between them would continue to fester. She had to cut it off with him and she had to cut it off entirely. God knows Tae Hyun and Ji Hoon would never survive in the same room and it was only a matter of time before she had to choose between them.

It was a puzzling predicament for Yoori because she was technically An Soo Jin, which meant that Soo Jin had more attachment toward Ji Hoon. On the other hand (the more important hand), Yoori had more attachment toward Tae Hyun. And being technically Soo Jin aside, Yoori couldn't force herself to have romantic feelings for someone she didn't feel *that* way about. She just didn't feel anything more for Ji Hoon. And as far as Tae Hyun went, no matter how angry she was with him, it was clear that she cared about him more than she cared about Ji Hoon. No matter how heart wrenching that reality may be, it was the cold hard truth that she couldn't deny.

Yoori swallowed tightly when resolution prevailed over her. Though her decision had been set long ago, tonight was where she had to formally vocalize it.

For her, it would always be Tae Hyun.

Her heart grew heavier as she whispered words that told Ji Hoon of her decision. "I'm sorry for everything."

She began to back away from him. Her face was veiled with grief. It was hard, *so hard* to see the disappointment devour his face. She wanted to say that she hoped that they could be friends, but she wasn't that naïve. Their relationship, as complicated as it was, would merit them being anything *but* friends.

His gaze momentarily landed on the doorway where Tae Hyun stood in the hall and then reverted back to her.

"All because of Tae Hyun, right?" Ji Hoon said hoarsely, his eyes darkening with anger and pain.

"I'll let your men downstairs know that you're up here and that you need them," she went on, not wanting to answer his question. Why answer something they both knew the answer to? "Goodbye, Ji Hoon."

Without waiting for his reply or stealing a final glimpse at him, Yoori turned on her heels and rushed to the door. Though the guilt was prominent within her, she was confident that she did the right thing. She cared about Ji Hoon too much to dangle him about. She cared about him, but not in *that* way. Never in that way...

The hall was quiet when Yoori walked out, her face paled with fatigue. There was no one in sight, but Yoori had the innate feeling that there were patrons pressed against their doors, their eyes straining through the peephole to get a sense of what was happening. The thunderous rumble inside the VIP suite from hell was anything but quiet and Yoori was certain that the entire hall heard the sound of glass shattering from above. You'd have to have bad hearing if you didn't think something was happening.

Noting that they should leave before the authorities arrived and further complicated things, Yoori rushed over to Tae Hyun who stood next to the elevator. His hands were in his pockets and his back was pressed against the adjacent wall. His eyes were closed as he stood there, looking quite at peace.

Yoori furrowed her brows at the sight. She resisted the temptation to gawk at his wickedly beautiful state. For a split second, she forgot that she was livid with him.

Why the hell was he standing there like that?

Who was he modeling for?

Weirdo.

She thought about speaking to him about what happened the night prior, but quickly decided the time and place wasn't right. They'd talk when they returned to the apartment. For now, they had to leave.

"We have to let Ji Hoon's men know that he's up here…" Yoori said clearly, interrupting the serenity hovering around him. "So they can come help him."

Tae Hyun's brooding gaze fell on her. His gaze was so intense that it mesmerized her momentarily. He was quiet. His compelling eyes held her gaze with inquiry pooling within them. She knew then by the expression on his face that he was probably wondering why he should go down and inform Ji Hoon's men that he needed their help. Tae Hyun looked unhappy and she assumed it was because he also didn't like that she was showing so much care for Ji Hoon.

When Tae Hyun finally parted his lips, all of her assumptions dissolved.

"How the hell did you get a bloody nose?"

She was mentally tossed against a wall from his unexpected question, which had absolutely nothing to do with her showing concern toward Ji Hoon. Apparently, she wasn't very good at reading him after all. And as the night lingered on, Yoori would come to realize that her lack of knowledge to the inner workings of Kwon Tae Hyun's mind would extend further than the non-verbal misunderstanding beside the elevator.

"There is a God who falls."

13: 10:48 P.M.

Once Yoori found Ji Hoon's men, the same ones she saw when they walked into the hotel, she promptly told them that Ji Hoon was up in the VIP suite and that he needed them. They were initially confused until they saw Tae Hyun waiting for Yoori by the revolving doors. A dawning bout of knowledge illuminated in their eyes and they immediately understood what occurred in the VIP suite. With unmatched speed, the five men ran into an elevator and went to their boss's aid.

Grabbing a couple of tissues from the coffee table in the lobby, Yoori stuffed some in her pocket. She started to wipe her bloody nose with the tissue while approaching Tae Hyun and the revolving door.

The cold air swallowed them when they walked out into the wintriness of the night. Yoori was cold, but much to her own sadistic delight, Tae Hyun was colder since he was drenched from head to toe.

It was a childish thought, but she was still extremely resentful toward the guy.

"Give me your keys," she ordered, turning to Tae Hyun once they reached the curb where his black Mercedes sat. "I'm driving."

She fought the inclination to be uncivil with him. Though she had the urge to give him the biggest piece of her livid mind, she maintained self-control. She had all the opportunity in the world once they got home.

He gaped at her like she was crazy.

"Why are you driving? I can drive," Tae Hyun combated, shivering in the cold. It was the first time she had seen him shudder from any breeze.

Yoori snorted at the dried splatters of blood on his face and clothes. Who was this guy kidding? He was so fucked up that Yoori was sure they'd get into an accident if he were the one behind the wheel.

"Give me the keys," Yoori repeated. Her voice bore of impatience.

Under standard situations, it would be expected that Tae Hyun would continue to combat her wishes. Despite this, Yoori knew that Tae Hyun, being as perceptive as he was, knew it was best to give her what she wanted, *especially* if he wanted even a remote chance of getting on her good side. And judging by his demeanor, he knew he needed all the points he could get to be on her good side.

Tae Hyun sighed while digging his right hand into his pocket. He pulled out the key to his Mercedes and handed it to her. He didn't look too happy when the key exchanged hands but he kept his dissatisfaction to himself.

The lights to Tae Hyun's Mercedes blinked in response when Yoori and Tae Hyun pulled the respective car doors open. The soft beeping of the car hummed melodically until Yoori shut her side of the door. Being vertically challenged in comparison to the vertically triumphant Tae Hyun, Yoori readjusted her seat and fixed the mirror in the car to best suit her needs. She was ready to drive off when she saw that Tae Hyun winced in pain when he clicked his seatbelt shut. However, when she turned to look, Tae Hyun, as expected, was cool and collected while showing no signs of pain.

Poser, she wanted to say to him, but curbed the inclination for another urge overwhelmed her senses.

His face was veiled with faint blotches of dried blood and remnants of water. This sight bothered her.

Distracted by this, she reached into the depths of her pocket and pulled out the clean tissue she took from the hotel. Rolling them into a little ball, she readjusted in her seat and faced a confused looking Tae Hyun.

He was surprised by what she was getting ready to do.

It was pure instincts on her part.

Her hands reached out and she started to clean his face of the blood that stained it. She didn't like that the blood sullied his face. She didn't like that there were remnants of water marked on him, making him more receptive to the cold weather. She didn't like that he was obviously hurt and she didn't like that the only thing she could do was clean the surface of the maladies.

Tae Hyun remained unusually quiet. His dazed eyes focused on her as she continued to free his face from blood and water. There was a light of tenderness and apprehension in them. He was dying to talk to her, but didn't know where to begin. The longing in his eyes made her believe that he actually missed her. She wasn't sure if she was right, but the thought did lift her spirits slightly.

His light breathing warmed her hands when she finished wiping away the last droplet of blood near his lips, revealing remnants of bruising and small cuts on various corners of his skin.

Before she could catch herself, her fingers rested on either side of his cheeks, the smoothness caressing her own fingertips. She could feel his attentive gaze on her and it caused her cheeks to flush.

Her heart pounded.

Was it hot in here or was it just her?

Her apprehensive eyes met his and almost immediately, Yoori was reminded of how much she cared for him and how much she missed him. Equally as prevalent, she was also reminded of how disappointed she was with him and how much she hated him for not being there for her when she needed him the most. She hadn't forgotten what he did and she wasn't sure if she ever would. The acidic anger in her stomach began to form as she relived the events of the night before...

Unknowing of these thoughts and now ready to break the tense silence, Tae Hyun parted his lips, "Yoori..."

Animosity streamed through her after he said her name. Being civil was now out of the question. She was ready to blow Tae Hyun out of the water with her unfiltered feelings.

"Yoori...I...*Holy Fuck*!" He flinched once Yoori grabbed a handful of his cheeks and started to ruthlessly pinch him. "Ow—OW. Damn it! Choi! Choi Yoori!" he shouted in agony. He tried to pry himself from the claws of life that Yoori had imparted unto him.

Yoori scrunched up her face in resentment and applied more pressure to his cheeks.

"Did you think I was just going to go back home with you and everything would be okay?!" she berated at the top of her lungs. "How could you leave me last night, you asshole? What kind of friend are you?!"

She continued to pinch him. He was hurting like hell, but she didn't care. Surely his pain was no match to what she felt last night.

By now, Tae Hyun was trying to pull himself away from her hold. He had his head pulled back, but unfortunately for Tae Hyun, the seatbelt he wore didn't give him much leeway. Yoori knew that the only reason why he was still in her grasp was because he didn't want to push her away. She knew that Tae Hyun would never push her or do anything to hurt her. She damn well used this piece of knowledge to her advantage.

"Yoori! Ow, ow, ow!" he groaned, slamming his temple against his seat in anguish.

She started to shake. Her fingers were starting to hurt now.

"Yoori! Ow! Damn it, assistant! You're killing me!"

Noting the violent shade of red coursing over his face, Yoori alleviated the pressure of her pinch and tore her shaking fingers away from his cheeks.

"Who the fuck do you think you are coming back and taking me home like nothing happened?!" she roared loudly, the anger multiplying within her as she watched him rub his cheeks in agony.

His piercing eyes laid on her. He looked like he couldn't believe what she was asking him. "Would you rather I not come to get you?" He sat up straight, the same fury dancing through him. "Do you know how long I've looked for you? I ran around the whole fucking city for you. And *this* is what I get?"

"What took you so damn long?"

He gaped at the absurdity of her second question.

"Choi Yoori..." he began slowly, lowering his hands from his burning cheeks. "Does it look like I have some radar or some spider sense that makes it easy for me to find you? You weren't at your apartment, you weren't at Chae

Young's, you weren't at the mall, and worst of all, you didn't even have your damn cellphone on you. I couldn't have a bunch of Serpents looking for you because I didn't want to make it public that you were outside alone. I couldn't call and I didn't even know where to *begin* to look for you. So yes, I'm sorry that it took a while, but I did the best I could."

She made a rude noise at his reply. The idiot would've never had to run around if he didn't leave her in the first place. Unable to hold back her emotions, Yoori poured it all out to Tae Hyun.

"You're sorry it took so long?" The resentment sizzled inside her. "How can you sit there and apologize for taking forever to find me when it was *your* fault I left in the first place?" A stream of pain slithered up her throat. She was beyond reason. She was consumed with emotions—raw emotions.

"You *left* me!" she shouted. "I *begged* you not to leave that night! I told you that I needed you! I opened my heart to you and you left! You left and you never came back—"

"I can't come back to someone who doesn't wait for me!" he suddenly argued. His voice and gaze were filled with the same frustration and anguish.

"You—" She froze. "*What?*"

He leveled his eyes with hers. "Where were you when I came back?"

Yoori was flabbergasted. "What...what are you talking about? Did you expect me to wait for hours on end? You only started looking for me today! I didn't see you until tonight—"

"10:48," he replied calmly, his eyes never leaving hers.

Yoori paused, her breathing heavy. She swallowed past the uncomfortable thickness in her throat.

Her voice was low, confused. "10:48?"

"I came back at 10:48 last night," he said again. "I came running back for you and you weren't there. Where were you?"

His voice splashed on to her pale face like a bucket of cold water.

Where was she?

Where was she at 10:48 last night?

She was in the streets hailing a cab. She was in the streets crying her eyes out as she hailed a cab to escape to Chae Young's. She was in the streets crying and wondering how he could leave her and not come back for her.

"I—I left at 10:47," Yoori stammered, feeling her heart lift at the fact that he returned just moments after she left the apartment.

Though her bitterness faltered slightly, it didn't falter enough to diminish the anger that had built up within her. It didn't matter if he came back that night, she reasoned. It didn't matter because he shouldn't have left in the first place.

"Well, you shouldn't have walked out the door and left in the first place!" she shouted again, unwilling to submit the white flag and forgive Tae Hyun for what he did. She shook her head at him. "How could you?"

"I walked out the door...but I didn't leave."

Yoori froze.

She stared at him, utterly dumbfounded. "You...you...you didn't...you didn't leave?"

"You asked me how I could leave you," he elaborated, his compelling eyes growing more poignant. "I walked out, but I *didn't* leave."

Her mind was reeling. "Y—You—"

She stopped.

It was then that she understood.

"You were in the hall the *entire* time?" She didn't give him a chance to answer. "What were you doing out there? I thought you left!"

"I couldn't leave you," he replied, his eyes filling up with something he rarely showed: emotions. Raw emotions; raw emotions that mirrored Yoori's. "I kept hearing your voice in my head, begging me to stay, and I couldn't leave."

"Why...why didn't you come back inside?" Her voice was strained and nearly broke.

She could feel the anger seeping out of her and a sense of relief taking its place.

Kwon Tae Hyun...

Kwon Tae Hyun...why was he doing this to her?

Why didn't he leave and why didn't he come back inside?

"What do you want me to say, Yoori?" he shouted with the same frustration. His eyes brimmed with impatience. He wasn't impatient or irritated with her. He was frustrated with himself. "I'm not perfect. You threw a bomb at me and I needed time to clear my head. I couldn't leave you, but I couldn't go back inside either. So I just stood there and stared at the door while I tried to process everything."

"How long were you standing out there?" she asked thoughtlessly, her voice faltering while her thoughts became scrambled. She couldn't even think.

"I stood in front of that door for thirty-seven minutes," he said quietly, frustration brewing, not only out of his voice, but from his posture as well. He was so confused that he didn't know what to do with himself. "I thought if I could steal a few moments alone, then I'd be able to quickly process everything and figure out what was happening to me." He inhaled deeply and closed his eyes, recalling what occurred. "I stood there and I couldn't even think. All I could hear was the sound of your voice before I closed that door. All I could hear was the sound of your voice breaking..."

He opened his eyes and ran a frustrated hand through the strands of his wet hair. He looked agonized as he stared at the dashboard.

"I didn't know what the hell I was doing...standing out there. It should've been so easy to leave, but I couldn't. It should've been easy, but I couldn't take a step away from that door. I stood there until I couldn't stand anymore. After thirty-seven minutes, I fell by the wall beside the door and I kept thinking that I should leave. I didn't understand why it was so hard for me to leave so I just sat there. Everything inside me felt like it was being ripped apart and all I could hear, all I could see, and all I could think about was you."

His distressed eyes flickered to meet her thoroughly shocked ones.

"I had no idea what was happening. It was the first time...the first time in my life where I wasn't being rational. The realization ripped through me and ate at me as I tried to gather my thoughts. Nothing was coming together for me though. It got so bad that I rose to my feet and ran off toward the stairs. I figured it would've been easier to leave you if I physically distanced myself from you."

He shook his head to himself, a self-deprecating laugh whispering from his lips.

"But the further I ran down, the harder it became. I ran until I couldn't run anymore. I ran until my mind contained one thought, one realization: I couldn't leave you even if I tried. I turned around and I came back. I came running back for you. I came back and—"

"I wasn't there," Yoori finished for him, regret vibrating in her voice. She felt fragmented, possessed with disappointment. She stared at him quietly, the anger dispersing out of her eyes as quickly as it penetrated them.

They were silent, their panting chests breathing together.

Tae Hyun was quiet while he stared at Yoori, his eyes urging her to say something else. Yoori was quiet as she stared regretfully at Tae Hyun, her frantic mind running through the events of last night like a movie.

She could see it so clearly now...

She could see herself waiting in front of that doorway while Tae Hyun was outside...staring at that same door. She could see herself crying against the wall when she realized she wasn't good enough for him to come back for when in actuality, she was enough for him to sit outside against the very same wall, agonized that he couldn't leave her in the first place. She could see it so clearly as she walked out that door and stepped into the elevator with tears brimming her eyes... She could see Tae Hyun sprinting up from the stairs and back into the hall as she descended down the elevator.

It was all so clear now, but one thought grew prominent in her mind.

She could see herself giving up on Tae Hyun when he didn't give up on her—when he *couldn't* give up on her.

How terrible was that?

Her heart ached as this realization rooted itself within the core of her emotions. She could see it so clearly and she could feel all the disappointment bear down on her. She was no longer disappointed in Tae Hyun, but disappointed in herself, disappointed in herself when she gave up on him.

Dazed with regret and guilt, Yoori lowered her weakened eyes and quietly readjusted herself in her seat. She didn't even know what else to do.

"Can...Can you drive? I don't think I'm up for it anymore," was all that she voiced out.

She didn't wait for his answer. She was already opening the door to her side of the car. Her mind was too blurred with thoughts. It was blurred with so many emotions that she couldn't distinguish them from each other.

With no contention, and understanding her frazzled state, Tae Hyun unbuckled his seatbelt, got out of the car, and promptly got into the driver's seat.

After Yoori situated herself in the passenger seat, Tae Hyun helped her by buckling the seatbelt for her. His visage was overcome with concern when he placed a gentle hand on her cheek, holding her eyes with his.

"Yoori—"

"Let's go home," Yoori interrupted.

It was her subtle way of telling him that she needed time to herself—that she needed time to think.

She needed time to think about all of this.

"Just because you're more powerful than human. . ."

14: The Story of Boomerangs

Yoori was surprised when Tae Hyun agreed to her needs, withdrew his hand from her cheek, and began to drive home. She was surprised because Tae Hyun wasn't normally this compliant. He typically had a lot to say and would be fighting with her, forcing her to talk to him.

It could be that he was being understanding, it could be that he was doing all that he could to get her forgiveness or it could be both, but Tae Hyun was quiet as he drove. He was quiet when they finally made it home. He was quiet when they took the elevator back up to the apartment. He was even quiet when Yoori, wanting a distraction, motioned for him to unbutton his shirt so that she could help wipe away the blood from his body. It bothered her that the blood had seeped through his shirt.

He was quiet while they stood in the bathroom for fifteen minutes. He stood still while Yoori quietly wiped the dried blood away from his bare upper body.

He was quiet until he couldn't stand the silence anymore.

"Yoori, can't you say something?" he urged tiredly, looking over his shoulder. Yoori wiped the damp, warm towel over a cut on his shoulder blade. "Are you still upset with me?" His voice was apprehensive. He sounded like a kid. It perturbed her to hear him like this. He sounded so fragile even though he was anything but.

She sighed, circling from behind his back. She stopped right in front of him, the towel whispering over the last dried blood on his hard chest.

"I'm no longer disappointed with you, but I'm still bothered by how you treated me after I told you the truth," she responded bluntly, narrowing her eyes on the ice pack that rested in the sink.

Though it was difficult to stay mad at him, Yoori tried her best to keep the anger flowing. If she were angry, then she wouldn't have to deal with other tempting emotions that were waiting to consume her. It was a lame and cowardly way out of dealing with her feelings, but she didn't care.

She picked up the ice pack and pressed it against one of the bigger bruises forming around his right torso.

"Does this hurt?" she asked, hoping the unexpected cold would distract him from trying to get her to talk about her feelings.

Tae Hyun sucked in a sharp breath once the cold ice pack made contact with his skin. His steel-like abs contracted in response.

"No," he lied, his wincing face saying otherwise.

She inwardly snorted at his obvious lie.

Standing there, pressing the ice pack against the area around his torso, Yoori used all the strength she had not to gawk at the sinfully eye catching aphrodisiac before her. She was so frazzled with her thoughts that she had less self-control than she would normally possess. She couldn't stop the hitch in her breath whenever she caught sight of the contours of his biceps, the ripples of his washboard abs, and his muscled chest. Even the stupid cuts on his body were adding some special effects to his overall sexual appeal. It also didn't help that wiping the dried blood away with the damp cloth left an angelic glow on his upper body.

Kwon Tae Hyun was a walking enticement and she hated him for that.

Distracting bastard, she thought bitterly, training her eyes on the ice pack instead of on anything else.

"Hey, Choi Yoori," he said firmly, pulling her out of her semi-perverted thoughts. He was unwilling to let the silence prevail. He grabbed the ice pack and threw it into the sink. He turned back and lowered his determined eyes on her. "Stop giving me the silent treatment and tell me what's on your mind."

She frowned, peering up at him. Weakness of the female heart aside, she was ready to address all that had been running through her mind. Only one dreadful thought prevailed in her busy mind anyway.

"Did you think telling me that you never left me would make everything okay?" she asked blithely, fighting to keep her voice from breaking. She had to bring up the one topic that led to this whole nightmare. "You walked out because you were disgusted with the fact that I'm An Soo Jin. That fact hasn't changed—"

"Wait a second," he interrupted, his eyes enlarged in disbelief. He looked flabbergasted. "You thought I left because I was *disgusted*?"

She bounced her head as if it was the obvious answer. "I could tell by how you were looking at me last night." Her tone was colder and more resentful as she instinctively backed away from him.

Her actions were stalled when she felt Tae Hyun rest his hands on her hips.

He shook his head and effortlessly pulled her closer to him. "There were a million things running through my head that night..." His eyes held hers. "But being disgusted with you for being An Soo Jin was never one of them." He furrowed his brows as if he couldn't believe her reasoning. "I mean...why would I be disgusted? I didn't even know the girl!"

"Then you should've told me that when I was trying to talk to you last night, you mute!" she shouted impatiently. It wasn't like he gave her much to go on last night. Regardless of the relief that he didn't leave her because he was disgusted with her, it still wasn't a sufficient answer for her. She glared at him furiously. "What made you leave then?"

He awkwardly looked away, visibly hesitant with divulging in that information.

"See?" she pointed out. "You're a mute again!"

Having had it with his silence, she struggled to pull herself away from him. She was getting so angry that she didn't even want to be around him anymore.

Despite her objection to his presence, Tae Hyun's grip on her moved to her waist and tightened. It wasn't strong enough to hurt her, but it was strong enough to hold her in place.

"Let go!" she shouted at the top of her lungs. "Let g—"

"You weren't the only one who opened your heart last night, Yoori!" he finally blurted out.

She stopped her fighting when his words froze over her.

A light of vulnerability plagued his eyes. He continued to speak, his arms encircled around her waist. Emotions poured out of his once reserved persona.

"Before things got worse last night, I opened my heart up to you as well."

She distinctly recalled him getting ready to ask her out on a dinner date...

"You asked me why I acted the way I did. I acted that way *because* I found out you were An Soo Jin."

Yoori looked away, but not before Tae Hyun reached out, gently placed his fingers under her chin and guided her gaze back to him.

"It was never because she was in the opposing gang and it was never because I felt threatened by her," he explained to her, lowering his hand and returning it to her waist after he claimed her undivided attention.

"Why then?" she asked, her patience soaring away with the emptiness of the night. "Why would you leave me if it wasn't because you were disgusted with her or because she was in the opposing gang?"

"Because I care about you!" he shouted, effectively silencing her. He stared deep into her eyes. "Isn't it obvious? I—"

A bout of silence consumed him when the vocalization of his own words hung over him like rain clouds.

"Holy fucking shit," he breathed faintly, so faint that Yoori could scarcely hear him.

His hands loosened from around her waist. He turned away from her. His fingers ran through his hair in shock. He looked disoriented, like he couldn't believe he allowed those words out of his mouth. His distressed eyes flickered to his reflection in the mirror. Yoori wasn't sure what he was thinking about, and what he realized, but Tae Hyun seemed at peace with himself when he returned his gaze to her. There was no more reservation in his eyes, only genuine sincerity. He swallowed tightly, stepping closer to her. His visage was flushed with more vulnerability than she had ever seen.

He went on, his voice gentle yet throbbing with resolution. "I care about you…so much more than I ever should. I have no idea what happened to me, but I can't shake the fact that you mean something to me."

He smiled dryly to himself. He, too, did not believe the predicament he found himself in. He looked tempted to reach out and hold her again, but he restrained himself.

"I was never like this, you know? I'm always rational...but whenever I'm around you, I'm the most irrational idiot there is. I could have ten guys pointing rifles at my head and none of that would ever equate to the fear I felt when you told me you were An Soo Jin."

"It shouldn't matter," Yoori vocalized quietly, killing the inclination to melt under Tae Hyun's previous words.

Be strong, Yoori, she urged herself, her eyes sterner than ever—even when her heart was melting all the anger away.

"No, it did," he interjected. "It did because Choi Yoori wouldn't leave me…but An Soo Jin would." Tae Hyun elaborated when he saw the quizzical look on her face. "It was the coward's way out and I'll be the first to admit it," he started remorsefully. "What I did was wrong. I wanted to save myself the risk of caring about someone who would end up leaving me. I wanted to save myself before I dug myself in too deep. That was why I asked you why you're no longer in denial—that was why I walked out on you when you told me you were remembering everything again. If I wanted to save myself from the pain of dealing with you leaving me after you get your memories, then I would have to leave you as soon as possible. *That* was why I took off."

Yoori's emotional eyes held his gaze as Tae Hyun went on.

"When I was going down those stairs…all I could think about was you. I underestimated how much I've grown to care for you. All I could think about was that I should be in there with you—I should be there for you. So I came back for you and here I am now." He swallowed roughly, uncomfortable but still allowing the next string of words to escape his lips. "It was never because I didn't care about you. It was because I realized then that...I may care too much."

He exhaled deeply. The muscles of his jaw clenched, indicating to her that sharing all of this was one of the most difficult things he ever had to do. He was reeling from it.

Yoori, on the other hand, was a bit more demure with her reaction.

She gazed up at Tae Hyun, completely speechless. She had never felt so overwhelmed. It was the first time in their relationship that Tae Hyun had been so truthful with her. It was the first time he told her how he felt about her. There was a myriad of conflicting emotions rioting inside her, but the one emotion that seemed to easily prevail was the one that compelled her to let go of her inhibitions, run into his arms and melt into his hold.

She realized how ridiculous it was that she could easily go from hating Tae Hyun, to being disappointed with him, and to wanting to be in his arms. And why? Because, after months of being around each other, he had finally uttered the words she had hoped for? Was it even a big deal? So what if he cared? She had always known that. The only thing that was still unknown was how deep that care went.

Yoori bit her lips at the host of thoughts and emotions lingering within her.

It would've been the perfect moment to express her own feelings to Tae Hyun, but Yoori chose not to. She was broken from the night prior and she wasn't willing to put herself in that same vulnerable situation again. For the time being, she'd prefer to remain oblivious to the obvious signs and sexual tensions in life. She wanted to go back to the way things were with Tae Hyun. She wanted to be carefree and aloof with him again.

Yeah, she confirmed in her mind. Yeah, she'd do that. It would be less of a headache and it would prevent any further disappointment in her mending heart.

Hopefully Tae Hyun would play along...

"I'm still mad at you," she finally whispered, holding back a smile. She folded her arms across her chest. She didn't mean it though. It was just something to say.

If the relaxed nerves within his body were any indication, then it seemed that Tae Hyun was relieved that they didn't dig deeper into the wave of truth that he showered over her. Clearing his throat, he nodded, very much relieved. She knew that Tae Hyun could detect the playful sparkle in her eyes and that she had forgiven him. With a hidden smile on his own face, he reverted back to being his usual self.

"And you should be," Tae Hyun agreed, the playful glint of his own eyes reappearing once he saw that the carefree and spunky personality of Yoori had returned. "You have every right to be."

She smirked at the grin that washed across his face. He seemed so relieved that they were fine again. She wanted to be evil and wipe that smile off his face.

"So you agree that you deserve to be punished?"

As expected, and much to Yoori's secret delight, his smile faded. Though his eyes pooled with worry, he nodded apprehensively. His arms casually wrapped around her waist again.

"Just don't give me the cold shoulder."

Yoori feigned a scoff when she pulled away from Tae Hyun. How dare he subtly try to seduce her so that she wouldn't punish him severely?

But damn...

She stared at him longingly, still feeling the warmth of his hold, even though he wasn't even touching her. The speed at which her heart raced was becoming unbearable for her. Tae Hyun made her weak in the knees, the mind, and in the heart. Even his smallest gestures of touching her and speaking softly to her were making her crazy with attraction for him.

Was this the charm he stated would make her pounce on him if he should ever throw it her way? Yoori wasn't sure, but she had a distinct feeling that it was merely the tip of what he could do to make her melt in his arms.

"I'll figure out what to do with you," she said sternly. It was hard to keep her voice firm with him when he was staring at her with his puppy dog eyes.

Fucking Tae Hyun, she thought bitterly, her anger subsiding. Whether he was making fun of her or throwing his reserved charms at her, he was a damn tease all the same. A damn tease who would never fail to take her breath (and sanity) away.

"Well, I guess this is all over and done with then," she concluded tiredly. She walked past Tae Hyun, whose gaze followed her like a shadow. She turned off the lights to the bathroom. "Just don't piss me off for the time being or you're in for a world of hell. You got it, Snob?"

"Got it, Brat," he pleasantly complied when she stepped into the dim hallway.

Yoori was happy, relieved. She was happy they were able to put these troublesome matters to rest and move on. She thought everything was done and over with for the night until Tae Hyun decided there was another matter he wanted to resolve.

She was in the process of marching into the bedroom when she felt a pair of strong arms wrap themselves from behind her. With the scent of his cologne enrapturing her, he wrapped his arms faintly over her arms and rested his hold just above her chest. Gently, *very gently*, he pulled her closer to where no space remained between them. She could feel the faint, synchronized motion of his breathing chest. His breathing chest caressed her senses and caused difficulties for her own breathing. There was no reservation in his hold.

Though Yoori froze in her stance, there was nothing paralyzing in terms of all the other effects Tae Hyun's unexpected touch had on her body.

A multitude of heated emotions coursed through her like delighted electricity. Her heartbeat tripled in speed. Her eyes were widened with passion and desire. Her breathing grew shallow, the air around her somehow not being enough to sustain her weakened knees. The heat of Tae Hyun's embrace warmed and excited her immensely.

All these side effects grew worse when Tae Hyun lowered his head and rested his chin on her left shoulder. It grew more unbearable when he nuzzled himself into the nook of her neck, his strong arms veiling her, holding on to her as she struggled to keep herself from teetering between dream and reality.

Am I dreaming again? she asked herself.

He breathed gently into her neck, answering her unspoken question and telling her it was indeed real.

The feel of him, however much shock it placed through her small frame, felt peaceful to her too. It felt…wonderful being embraced by him like that. The seconds he held her felt like blissful eternities. It was the same feeling she had when she danced with him under the gazebo. It was the same feeling she had when they kissed. It was one of those moments where everything stood still and all that existed in the world was them. It all felt magical and it all felt right.

He said nothing as he held her, but she somehow heard his words all the same.

I'm sorry. She could hear him apologizing to her for walking out last night. *I'm sorry.* His hold on her grew stronger with care and she could hear him saying how sorry he was that he wasn't there for her when he should've been. *I'm sorry.* She could hear him assuring her that he'd do everything in his power to make it up to her, to overshadow his shortcomings of that night.

As her means of nodding in understanding, she lifted her hands and crossed it over his arms, locking him there with her. A smile touched her lips when she rested her cheek against the foundation of his arm.

Would it be selfish and naïve of her to want this moment to last forever?

The apartment dimmed while they stood there. The only being that accompanied them was the radiance of the moonlight on the tiles surrounding them. A certain stillness of life veiled over them, the only sound being the harmonic breathing rooted between Yoori and Tae Hyun.

Such serenity dispersed when Tae Hyun moved his lips near her ear and allowed his warm breath to tickle her senses.

"I'm not too sure what's going on with me and why I'm acting the way that I am…" he whispered slowly, uncertainly. "The only thing I know is that I can't leave you. Even when I tried, I came back. Against all rationale, I came back."

He fell silent. She wasn't sure if it was to gather his thoughts or his nerves, but he only took a moment before his enthralling voice drew closer to her ear. She could feel a reassuring smile—one that stole every ounce of her breath—ignite unto his lips as he said words that would forever ingrain themselves in her heart.

"I just wanted you to know that no matter where life takes me, no matter the distance, no matter the length of time, no matter the obstacles…I'll always come back to you. Even if I, myself, am not sure if I'll come back…in the end, I'll *always* come back. 'Cause that's the thing about boomerangs, right? They come back even if they feel they shouldn't, they come back even if the world tries to stop them, they come back because they ultimately know where they belong…and *who* they belong to."

If he wasn't holding her with such care, then Yoori would've slid to the floor and melted into a puddle of goo. To say that her breath was taken away was an understatement. What he said touched her…more than he'd ever know, more than she'd ever know.

Breathe in…

Breathe out...
Breathe in...
Breathe out...

Awkwardness began to take over and Yoori was speechless. She didn't know how to respond to his incredible words. Her heart warmed in elatedness. It urged her to respond with something that told him of how she felt. Equally as pressing as her eager heart was her rational mind, which had already started to build the defenses around her. As sweet as it was, she wasn't ready to give her genuine response to it. She wasn't ready to get hurt again. She wasn't ready...which meant that the next words out of her mouth were as awkward and unromantic as a drunken slob's.

"Heh...oh you...hehe...you...you're a real sweet talker tonight, aren't you?" Yoori asked, simulating a joking tone.

She concealed both a frown and a pout. She nuzzled her cheek over his arm. Her chest ached at the absurdity of her words. Her face was flushing immensely and she was confused with herself. She was scared...not of Tae Hyun, but at her reaction to what he said. She couldn't explain the multitude of emotions running through her. If he continued to speak as he did, then she was going to die from a weakened heart.

Though it was quite obvious that Tae Hyun caught on to how stiff she became, he didn't react awkwardly to her remark. To her relief, he merely laughed warmly. The resounding tone vibrated from her shoulder and then to her head where he laid his chin. She thought she felt him give her a quick peck behind her head, but she wasn't sure.

"This won't last," he assured her, distracting her from her brief curiosity.

She could feel him smiling playfully, the wickedness in his voice reminding her of Tae Hyun and his teasing personality. It was one that she hated and adored with a passion. She already felt less awkward and she had a hunch that was Tae Hyun's objective when he decided to return to his old ways.

"I didn't sleep well last night so I'm feeling a bit disoriented right now, but I'll return to my old self tomorrow."

Thank God, Yoori thought to herself. She could handle the playful and teasing Tae Hyun, but she wasn't sure if she could handle sweet-talking and seductive Tae Hyun. The latter would have her weak in the heart (not to mention knees) for sure. If he didn't turn off the charms in time, then his smoldering upper body wasn't going to be the only thing that would be bare for the remainder of the night.

She nodded inwardly. God bless ignoring obvious sexual tensions and going back to silly bantering. It was all that Yoori could handle for the time being.

"Augh...thanks for reminding me of your old ways," she muttered, pretending to be bitter. Realization sprinted across her gaze. "This reminds me," she started slowly, craftiness sparkling in her naughty eyes. "Since we're arch-enemies, I'm definitely still punishing you."

"I wouldn't expect anything less from you." Though his voice was confident, she could detect the thread of fear within it. Surely he knew she wasn't planning on going easy when it came to punishing him.

Speaking of which, she knew just the right punishment to give him.

"Hey Tae Hyun," Yoori launched excitedly, her chin resting on his arms.

"Hmm?"

"I decided on your punishment..."

There was a long silence before he said, "What is it?"

His weary eyes anticipated something horrifying.

She held back an evil giggle and said, "I need a personal assistant."

She could feel his heart freeze up. A grimace of despair devoured his face.

Yoori smiled. Her own heart pumped in excitement.

Making herself comfortable under the warmth of his stiffening hold, Yoori's sheepish smile grew wider as Tae Hyun groaned in misery behind her.

"Damn, you evil little minx, are you serious?"

"What'd you call me?" she confronted, pulling herself out of the embrace. She turned around and faced him with a stern expression. Her eyes challenged him to combat what she wanted.

"You're serious?" he asked again, ignoring her question. He gazed at her with incredulity. The heaving of his bare chest was profound with worry now.

Yoori crossed her arms and gave him a condescending stare. "Do you not agree?"

Though he looked inflexible to a compromise, his words sang a different tune. "I'm sure we can think of something else—"

"Don't talk to me anymore," she interrupted dramatically, turning on her heels with the quickest of ease.

As she anticipated, a hand caught her wrist.

"No, wait!" Tae Hyun shouted, pulling her back to him.

Yoori held in a knowing smirk when he turned her around to face him.

"I'll do it, damn it. I'll do it, okay?" he complied. His face was marked with bitterness. "How...how long?"

"A month."

"A *month*?" He snorted. Even under the confines of stress and trying to get back on her good side, the proposed timeframe was ludicrous to him.

"Eh, Choi Yoori," he began severely, making her stiffen in her once confident stance. Why did he have so much power when he used that tone of voice? "Did you get attacked by another duck today or something? Be reasonable."

Yoori grimaced at the reminder of the stupid duck. She knew a month sounded absurd, but she wanted a good negotiation to start off on.

"Fine! Three weeks!" she bargained.

"Three hours," he countered curtly, folding his arms across his chest.

Trying to ignore the scintillating contours of his defined arms, Yoori mouthed a muted curse at him and then said, "Two weeks."

"Two hours." His voice was calm and collected. He looked unyielding and Yoori was beside herself.

"What the hell, Tae Hyun?" she sputtered out. "What kind of negotiation is this?"

"You're not being rational, so why should I?"

"Fine!" Yoori shouted irately, extremely bitter that she couldn't even get two weeks out of him. "A week! *A week!* Was that what you wanted to hear?"

He nodded calmly, clearly hiding a satisfied smile on his face.

"Yes, I'll be your personal assistant for a week," he agreed blithely. He didn't take it very seriously. "Now can we go to bed? I'm exhausted from chasing after you all day."

She stared at him blankly, the resentment for losing at the negotiation having yet to leave her. "Who says you're sleeping on the bed?"

His eyes rounded in horror. "But I—"

"Uh, uh…" Yoori warned authoritatively, holding up an index finger to stop him from speaking. "Be careful with raising your voice with me."

"*You* raise your voice with me all the time," he accused, noticeably lowering his voice.

"Well, that's because I'm special!" she answered irrationally. Her eyes turned into slits. She gazed at him up and down with judgment. "But you're not, so you better watch your mouth."

"My entire body is tearing up with pain," he argued desperately. He deliberately made his eyes look weak as they tried to reason with her.

She shrugged, giving him a careless smile. She wasn't going to fall for the sad puppy dog act.

"Well then…you definitely shouldn't have fought Ji Hoon, you definitely shouldn't have brought up the duck attack and you definitely shouldn't have been so good with the negotiation, right Tae Hyunnie?" she responded mockingly, making her way to the bedroom.

He was ready to close his eyes in misery when she suddenly stopped. With one hand holding her steady, she hung listlessly from the doorway, smiling at Tae Hyun who was entranced with the sudden glow of the moon that veiled over her.

Was that adoration in his eyes that she saw?

Yoori wasn't sure and chose to ignore it. She continued to smile at him. As much as she was planning on making his life miserable for the week to follow, Yoori acknowledged that she was elated that Tae Hyun was back with her. It was the way it should be.

"It's nice to have you back, boomerang," she whispered delicately, her voice borderline teasing. Taking a step backward, she also added, "But get some sleep, will you? You have a long week ahead of you...and you'll need all your energy."

She imparted a devious wink and disappeared into the bedroom, leaving a completely devastated and miserable Tae Hyun to wallow in self-pity for the fact that he was now her assistant—or at least that was what she thought he was doing.

The curve of a small smile appeared on his face as his eyes flickered with desire after her departure. There was genuine warmness within his gaze while he stared longingly at the doorway where she stood seconds before. Yoori didn't know it then, but that was actually the moment where Tae Hyun realized something that was unquestionably detrimental to his entire livelihood. He realized that against all his resistance, *somehow*, she had stolen every inch of his stubborn heart. She had stolen every inch of it and she had him in the palm of her hands.

It was a terrifying yet exhilarating realization for Tae Hyun. And if that charming smirk was any indication, then Yoori had better save up all her energy for Kwon Tae Hyun had decided he was going to steal her stubborn heart as well.

"Just because the world kneels before you..."

15: Human Again

"Did you have to kill him?"

She shook her head. Her face was drained of color. She sat still on the steps of the quiet alley. When she spoke, her eyes were frazzled, distracted. "I just wanted to see if the guilt will eat me up alive."

"Is it?"

His question was barely audible over the booming thunder. The sky was getting darker. A storm threatened to befall them. Yet, even though the threat of rain was present, they continued as they were. She was still sitting passively on the steps and he was still standing across from her, his hands buried deep in his pockets while he watched her with pity in his eyes.

She smiled dejectedly to herself. Her eyes were trained on an undetectable area of the alley. Misery glazed over her gaze. She may have heard his question, but she didn't feel the need to answer it. She was too lost in other thoughts.

"When they trained us...they told us we'd be better than human." Her voice was soft, remorseful even. "They told us that killing would be an easily acquired taste. All we had to do was keep killing and our souls would disintegrate. All we had to do was keep killing and we'd lose our souls and become better than human. We'd become Gods..."

She cast her attention to the pavement where blotches of blood continued to linger upon it. Tears brimmed her eyes.

"No one ever told us about that excruciating moment when our soul is returned to us—that moment where our tortured soul is decaying with pain. No one ever told us that once our soul comes back...then so do the faces of those we've killed. No one ever told us that this life would be worse than death...that we'd no longer be better than human, but *less* than human..."

"This is only momentary," he interrupted, his voice strong yet anguished. "It happens to the best of us. Your time will pass."

"This won't," she declared with confidence.

"Lil sis—"

"Did you know those kids were begging me not to kill them?" Her lips quivered. "They didn't even blink when I pulled the trigger. They never stopped crying and they never closed their eyes when I shot them. I killed them..." Her voice broke at the last of her words. She shook her head with disgust. "And all for what? For this? To be sitting here...like this?"

His brows creased into a deep frown at his sister's logic. "And you think killing yourself will make things right?"

She nodded freely, the tears finally escaping her eyes. Her broken and weak voice spoke again. "I just can't live like this anymore. It hurts..." She bit her quivering lips. "It hurts to breathe."

Her brother shook his head. He stared down at her, the needle she had given him firmly held between his fingers. "Do you realize the risks involved with that formula you gave me? If I inject it into you, there's no guarantee that you'll die. You'll be paralyzed, thrown into a coma, or even lose your mind—all of which would be worse than death. Will you be able to handle those type of lives if this doesn't kill you?"

"The amount I gave you will ensure death. A quick and easy one at that."

Her stubbornness began to aggravate his patience. "I can't believe you called me over here to listen to all of this."

"Please," she continued, holding on to her older brother just as he was about to leave. Her hold on him was strong. It was just as strong as her desperate eyes, which was beckoning him to consider her request. "You know I can't break my ties from this world unless you do it."

He was quiet for a long while, lost in his own contemplation. It was clear he was considering all the options available. When he spoke, she had anticipated him to ask her why she had to do this, why she had to kill herself to make things right. She had anticipated him to ask her how she became so weak. The next words out of his mouth took her by surprise.

"What life would be better than this one, baby sister?" He was attentive when he awaited her answer. The content of his own question surprised him too.

She deliberated his question. Tears stroked her lips. What a dangerous question to ask someone who wanted to kill herself... Would it hurt to answer? No, it would be nice to answer. It would be nice to hear the answer even if she'd never truly get to live it.

"If I had it my way, I'd start over. I'd want a life far away from here...away from all of this...one where I can just breathe...one where I can just be human again..."

■ ■ ■

It was a dreary Saturday morning in Mint Park, an affluent park area known for its well-groomed scenery, spacious surroundings, and tranquil ambiance. Saturday mornings at Mint Park were always calm, especially in the winter when the light of the gray morning loomed overhead. The wind was cool, but not so cold where people needed bundles of layers to go out. The park, though filled with people, was a serene one.

It was peaceful until a happy squeal illuminated the once quiet ambiance. "Ahhhhh! Hahahahaha!"

Park goers, those of whom consisted primarily of joggers, sight see-ers, and scenic photographers instinctively whipped their heads in the direction of the voice. A crooked smile crept onto each of their faces once they saw the heart-warming scene before them.

A couple had just raced down the jogging track of the park. The boyfriend, who was panting relentlessly, was shirtless as he only wore a pair of black basketball shorts and black running shoes. His girlfriend, who had her black hair tied up in a ponytail that bounced every which way as she came down the track, was dressed in black shorts, black running shoes, and a sky blue workout tank top.

The park goers smiled, not because they had never seen couples workout together before, but because this particular couple had an interesting approach to working out together. The boyfriend, as striking as he was, looked forlorn as he heaved violently, his jogging pace decreasing when they neared a park bench that was no doubt his preferred resting spot. On the flip side, the girlfriend looked utterly at ease with herself. A gorgeous smile remained bloomed across her lips. Her arms were encircled around his neck while he was giving her a piggyback ride. It seemed that she enjoyed the "ride" and the "workout" immensely. Even as her boyfriend jogged unenthusiastically down the pathway, her smile never faltered.

"Faster, assistant! Faster!" Yoori urged happily.

She giggled beside Tae Hyun's ear.

At her command, Tae Hyun, who was still heaving for air—quite bitterly at that—increased the acceleration of his jog for the final haul.

"Yaaay!" she cheered merrily, tightening her arms around his neck. She closed her eyes. Her smile widened with ecstasy. The morning wind whispered past her face and into the locks of her ponytail, leaving her to bask in the glory of being Tae Hyun's "boss" for the past glorious week.

Oh yes, time definitely flies by fast when you're having fun, Yoori thought when she opened her eyes and leaned her chin on Tae Hyun's bouncing shoulder. And, boy, did she have fun.

For the past six days, Yoori had a blast with being Tae Hyun's boss. To say that she had taken revenge on Tae Hyun for being such a demanding boss over the past couple of months would be an understatement. She had completely tortured the poor guy over the course of the past six days and she damn well loved it.

Yoori had Tae Hyun, who at first still seemed quite assured that she was too chicken to torture him, perform the usual chores that consisted of cleaning up the apartment, doing all the laundry, washing all the dishes, and driving her anywhere she wanted to go. Easy stuff and she knew that. Her wicked fun, and the ultimate demise of his confidence that she didn't have the nerve to be such a demanding boss, came in the form of unreasonable demands that killed any energy Tae Hyun had.

In the middle of the night, where she still wouldn't allow Tae Hyun to sleep on the bed, she would wake up more than once and unabashedly shake Tae Hyun awake. After pulling the poor guy out of his much-needed sleep, she proceeded to tell him that she needed a bedtime story so that she could fall back to sleep. Feeling quite lazy to read her romance novels, she threw a chunky paperback book at him and instructed him to read her the story until she fell asleep.

Whenever it looked like he was about to combat her wishes, Yoori always made sure he saw the crease of a frown form on her face. Evidently hell-bent on not upsetting her too much, as he was still trying to get back on her good side, he pouted as he dejectedly opened the book and started reading from it. The poor guy, who looked like he was so miserable and was ready to fall asleep before her, kept on reading for a good two hours until Yoori finally fell back asleep. Once that time passed, much to his own horror, he realized that even though Yoori was able to sleep through the morning, he had to wake up soon after to go to the local grocery store to buy breakfast food that she demanded he make for her every morning.

She actually felt pretty guilty about all that…especially when she saw him hiding in the corner, sleeping soundly when she sought him out to make her the heavenly tea. Not that she blamed him for sleeping in corners—or hiding for that matter.

Essentially any moment where Tae Hyun was beside her, she'd make him do the most horrendous things that any sane guy would commit suicide over.

Craving special ice anyone? Yoori made Tae Hyun sit on the kitchen counter for hours on end, carving her stars out of ice cubes. The labors of his hard work dissipated before his eyes when Yoori unknowingly turned on the heat in the apartment and melted everything in plain sight. Poor Tae Hyun's pale hands wouldn't stop shaking after that horrible ordeal.

Shopping anyone? Yoori had never been much of a shopper, but for the past week, she had the biggest urge to shop. This ultimately meant countless hours of Tae Hyun trotting around with her in stores, waiting in line for the fitting rooms for her, and waiting in line to help pay for everything. It got so horrible for him that he even offered to buy the whole mall for her so he wouldn't have to deal with shopping with her. She still didn't know if he was serious about that or not. If all of that wasn't terrible enough, the girl started having cravings for working out. And in working out, she meant him giving her piggyback rides while jogging all around the neighborhood while she just screamed, "Faster, assistant! Faster!"

"You're an effen horrible person," Tae Hyun scathingly spat out after he sat a very happy Yoori down on the bench. He was clearly pushed over the edge for that was the third time in the recent week that he called her a bad name.

"Evil, that's what you are," he panted after he collapsed onto the bench. His abdomen rose and fell dramatically while he tried to coordinate his state of breathing.

"I should punish you for calling me names, but I'll forgive you since you just ran a couple of miles for me," she replied sympathetically.

She cast her eyes onto the bench instead of on his tantalizing abs. *My, my, my...how sexy those things look though...* She sighed, taking stock of his fatigued countenance. She felt guilty for wearing him out so much, but not guilty enough to wipe the pretty little smile off her face. She moved closer to him with the intention of making him feel better. What fun would all of this be if Tae Hyun wasn't at least civil with her?

"Come on," she began, nudging him. She pouted when he kept his eyes closed, refusing to make eye contact with her. "Fine, if you can't handle this, then you can quit," she suggested almost mockingly. She knew what to say to get him to talk to her again. "You've actually been a pretty good assistant this week. If you're too weak to continue on, then you can quit."

"Quit?" His eyes flew open. He sat up straight and narrowed his eyes onto her. "I nearly killed myself this week being your assistant and you're telling me I can quit?" He laughed dryly. "Thanks for the offer, *boss*, but I agreed to take this punishment like a man and I'll come out like one." He then snorted. "And 'pretty good' assistant? I've been nothing short of amazing."

"You talk back though. That's a no-no in my Master handbook—err—" She stopped when she realized she said something unfiltered and offensive. "Sorry I meant 'Boss' handbook, not 'Master' handbook. Heh...I don't know why that came out..."

He shook his head at her. "That's because I'm your *assistant*, not your *slave*." He stopped to glare at her in bitterness. "The difference of those terms may have gotten lost on some people, but I reserve the right to be able to at least talk back. It's the only thing keeping me sane."

"Fine," Yoori said quietly, crossing her arms and casting her eyes over to the scene of two parents teaching their son how to ride a bike. She was still secretly happy that Tae Hyun was willing to be her assistant until his term ended, but she wanted to fake being sad and forlorn with him so he wouldn't be too bitter with her. She was sneaky like that.

They were quiet for long seconds before Tae Hyun, who had since calmed down, turned to her. "And were you having a dream this morning? I heard you murmuring something when I woke up to shower. You seemed pretty bothered."

However hostile their previous topic of conversation was, he seemed genuinely concerned when he asked this. That was the thing about Tae Hyun and Yoori—they were that versatile as a conversational couple that they could go from bickering, to having a heart to heart within a moment's distraction. This change in mood was no exception.

Yoori shrugged, recalling having a dream. She just couldn't recall what it was she dreamt about.

"I don't know, maybe? I don't really remember the dreams I have anymore."

It was an honest reply. After finding out that she was An Soo Jin, Yoori had been consciously, and subconsciously, freaked out about having dreams. She wouldn't be surprised if she was having dreams, but was too subconsciously afraid to recall them. Not that she cared too much. Her dreams were never good dreams anyway.

"It's funny because I remember mine clearly," Tae Hyun shared whimsically.

Yet again, the mood was switched up as quickly as it was switched down.

She eyed him. Naughtiness was in his eyes when he stated this. It really made Yoori curious. "What'd you dream about?"

His eyes grew strangely sultry when he smiled at her. She almost regretted asking that question. Before she could even rescind her words, he had answered.

"I dreamt that my little assistant has been *very* bad as of late." Yoori held back a knowing smirk as he went on. "I also dreamt that today would be the seventh and final day of my punishment. In the dream, I remember telling her, 'You should definitely watch how you treat me today because I've been keeping track of everything you've been doing and rest assured that I'm ready to return the favor.'"

She laughed fretfully when she was reminded that payback was just around the corner. Of course Tae Hyun wouldn't go down without a good fight.

"Aww, that's true, right? Our roles switch tomorrow..."

Tae Hyun nodded smugly, unable to smother the grin off his face. He was deviously happy.

Yoori smiled back, not afraid of Tae Hyun and what his payback may be. "Are you going to make me give you piggyback rides too? Or make me carve stars out of ice? Or perhaps burn the romance novels I made you read?"

She faked a pout when she said all this. She wasn't worried. This week had been too good of a week and nothing could bring her down—not even the threat of retaliation.

A muscle worked in his jaw when he was reminded of the romance novels. The subtle fire in his eyes said it all: he was going to burn it all.

But then, something occurred that threw Yoori off course.

He kept his grin and said, "Don't you worry about what happens tomorrow, babe. Let's just say if everything goes well tonight, you won't have to worry about anything."

Yoori furrowed her brows. It sounded straightforward enough, but she could've sworn she saw a suspicious crafty light in his eyes. Not to mention the usage of his smooth and silky voice raised a red flag for her. She was actually a bit intimidated at that moment.

Since their last "questionably romantic" encounter, Tae Hyun had reverted to his "normal" self. But every now and then, he'd use that silky smooth voice on her and she'd feel the nerves of her legs weaken as his voice stroked over her. He never went too far with it, but every single day, he'd use just a bit more charm on her. It was like he was preparing her for something... But, of course, she wasn't too sure if it was preparation for anything or if he was just teasing her because he secretly enjoyed watching her become socially awkward.

It was probably the second possibility, she thought, eyeing him suspiciously.

"What are you up to?" she accused shrewdly. Surely the guy was up to something. She knew him too well.

He manufactured a look of confusion. "I'm just trying to remind you that I've done nothing but complied with your wishes this week." He gave her one of those breathtaking smiles of his. "Just make sure you free up our night. I have a surprise for you."

She was very interested. "A surprise?"

He nodded, his firmly sealed lips hinting to her that he wasn't going to give anything away.

"What are you planning?"

He gave her a chiding look. "If I told you, it wouldn't be a surprise anymore, would it?"

"Fine." She knew when to back down from Tae Hyun and when to set up a fort and fight. As for the defenses for this little battle, it wasn't worth the energy — at least not at that moment.

Unable to pinpoint what it was he was up to, Yoori reprised a smile unto her face. She knew that Tae Hyun must've had some master revenge plan up his sleeves, but it didn't scare her. The only thing that mattered was that she had one last punishment to seal the deal and she would be done for the week. Well, it wasn't necessarily a punishment per se...just something she had always wanted to do with him.

"I know that you've probably concocted some big revenge plan, but I have one thing I wanted you to do with me anyway. After that, I'm pretty much done with your 'punishments.'"

The smile Tae Hyun had faded once he saw the crafty look in Yoori's eyes. The muscles throughout his body stiffened. He stared at her with caution. Fortunately for Tae Hyun, he was smart enough to know that Yoori was going to save the punishment of all punishments for the last night. Unfortunately for him, there wasn't anything he could do about it.

"Oh God, what are you going to make me do with you?"

"We're going to the movies."

A look of doom came over his face. He already knew what movie she would be dying to see and knew what movie he would die *from* seeing. "Are you kidding me?"

Though her smile remained, she gave him a look of warning. "Kwon Tae Hyun, be good. If you ruin this experience for me, I'll hate you forever." She made sure to smile sweetly as she drew closer to him. "Come on, I think you'll have fun. You can hold my hand if you get scared."

He glared at her attempt of a joke and then shook his head at her. Misery and resolution poured into his stubborn eyes. "No...no I'm not going. You've gone too far this time, Choi Yoori. I won't sit by and have you put me through a world of misery. I won't...I won't let you do that to me..."

Yoori rolled her eyes at his stubbornness. "Stop being such a baby. I really think you'll like it and we could—"

Quack! Quack!

She stopped talking when she heard the voice of an old enemy. Tae Hyun's eyes grew concerned when he spotted the source of the sound before her. Like a lioness spotting her nemesis, she whipped her head around and caught sight of it: the stupid duck.

Her eyes morphed into bitter slits. "There's ducks here too?" she inquired gravely.

"There's a pond around here," Tae Hyun answered hesitantly.

"Eh, Tae Hyun, Tae Hyun," she said urgently, nudging his bicep. "Doesn't that duck next to that cute fat kid look like the stupid white duck who attacked me at the lake house?"

"No," Tae Hyun replied at once. He was clearly lying.

"Don't lie to me!"

He gazed at her uncertainly. The muscles on his body tensed up like he was ready to hold on to her just in case she decided to do anything violent to the duck.

"Why the hell are you looking at it like that?"

She wasn't paying attention to his question.

"Go kick it," she commanded instead, her eyes still on the duck and the little boy.

"*What?*"

"Hurry, hurry! It's coming closer!" she informed urgently, still nudging Tae Hyun, who had an expression of horror on his face.

The cute fat kid was throwing a trail of bread on the ground and the duck was following the trail. It was a picturesque sight for everyone else in the park, but a horrific sight for Yoori and Tae Hyun. The direness worsened when the duck and the cute fat kid inched closer and closer to them. Yoori felt her blood boil at the sight of the duck being so carefree.

"I'm not kicking a fucking duck that's playing with a cute fat kid in a park that I exercise in everyday," Tae Hyun clenched through his teeth, folding his arms in defiance.

Yoori scowled. She knew she was being unreasonable, but she was too angry at the memory of what the stupid duck at the lake did to her to care. Because of the damned duck, she had been the constant butt of jokes for Tae Hyun. He was always teasing her about the duck attack and it was killing her. Someone—or something—had to pay for this misery and it was going to be the animal of the same species.

"Aren't you a gang leader?" she tried to instigate, feeling the urge to pinch him to do as she commanded. She wanted to tell him it was his fault that she harbored so much hatred for ducks. Despite the urge, she kept this information to herself. Tae Hyun didn't need more reason to feel proud of himself because of how much he affected her.

"*That's* your way of trying to convince me to assault a duck?" he asked incredulously. He was clearly unimpressed with the mechanics of her persuasion.

"You're such a bad assistant!" she finally shouted impatiently, anger searing through her. "I would totally do it for you."

That was a lie. She totally wouldn't.

"Don't try to apply peer pressure on me. I won't do it."

"Ugh! Okay, get ready to run then."

"WHAT?" Tae Hyun bellowed, stiffening up in his seat and unfolding his arms in disbelief.

"On the count of three," Yoori instructed like she was a sergeant on a mission.

"Wait—"

"One."

"Choi—"

"Two"

"—Yoori!"

"THREE!"

Tae Hyun tried to reach out to grab her but it was too late. Yoori had escaped his hold by mere whispers of a millimeter and was now charging at full speed toward the duck and the cute fat kid.

At that moment, several things happened:

KICK!

"QUACCCCCCCCCCCKK!"

"WAAAH! MOMMMMY! MOMMMY!"

Yoori had kicked the duck with full force, the duck was sent flying like a squawking soccer ball into a nearby pond, and the cute fat kid was crying mercilessly at the unforgiving violence shed before him. As the duck flew into the pond, people were gaping in dismay as Yoori, like a little blue cheetah, vacated the scene of the crime, leaving a horrorstruck Tae Hyun to stand in the middle of the park with his eyes and mouth gaping open.

"HAUL ASS, TAE HYUN!" Yoori commanded in the distance, snapping Tae Hyun out of his dumbfounded state.

Smiling nervously when all eyes of the park rested on him after Yoori called out to him, Tae Hyun bowed uncomfortably. He began to retreat backward in the direction in which Yoori made her dramatic exit. No longer able to withstand the stares of disgust and horror bestowed upon him, Tae Hyun turned on his heels and sped out of the park with lightning speed. His neck twisting about, he muttered a muted curse as he searched for his partner in crime—or partner who performed a crime.

"Tae Hyun!" a dim voice called out from the corner just as he was about to run across the street.

He turned and saw Yoori standing nervously behind a big oak tree. The only part of her that was visible behind the big trunk was her head and her beckoning hand.

Panting with a shake of a head, he walked over to her beckoning hand.

"You just kicked a duck," Tae Hyun voiced appallingly when he reached her.

Though guilt was displayed on her face, Yoori couldn't help but scrunch up her face in defense.

"Don't judge me," she said weakly. She was already judging herself for her moment of unprecedented weakness and anger.

"You just kicked a defenseless duck that was standing next to a cute fat kid," he elaborated again with disapproval. "You made a cute fat kid *cry*."

"He was a casualty of war," she combated dimly, already feeling the flood of guilt rise through her.

"He's a cute fat kid that's crying," Tae Hyun countered swiftly.

Leave it to Tae Hyun to not only continually jab her with relentless guilt, but also to be the only one who could affect her enough to knock some guilty sense into her. Despite the fact that she knew she was wrong to give into her violent temptations, she couldn't help but further defend herself.

"I had to get my revenge! Do you know how angry I am that the stupid duck attacked me?"

"So you go crazy and attack a lookalike duck instead?"

"I—I—I..."

Shit, he had such a good point.

She was flabbergasted on what her next witty comeback should be.

"I—I—Shut up, assistant," she replied desperately, knowing her only way out of this argument was to take advantage of her "power" over him.

Tae Hyun scoffed knowingly. "I knew you were going to pull out the 'boss' card."

"Can we just go home now?" she asked tiredly, wanting to get as far away from the scene of the crime as possible.

She emerged from behind the tree and stood beside Tae Hyun. She could still hear that cute fat kid cry in the distance. Or was it the duck? Someone or something was crying in the distance and she was sure it was one of her victims.

"Yeah," Tae Hyun voiced lethargically, casually grabbing her hand and intertwining his fingers with hers. "Let's go before your ass gets hauled in for animal abuse."

"Har har, you got jokes, huh?" Yoori voiced bitterly at his statement. She was so fragmented with guilt that she didn't even realize that they were actually holding hands.

With locked hands and bitter faces on, they began to head back to the apartment. Feeling the cool morning breeze murmur over their skins, Yoori began to feel a bit at ease with herself until her "assistant's" voice brought cryptic words of wisdom into her mind.

"You know that this means that more ducks are going to attack you, right?" Tae Hyun prompted gravely. He was hiding back a smile. Clearly he was trying to freak her out.

Though she knew what he was trying to do, Yoori's eyes expanded in horror nonetheless. "Don't jinx me!"

Freaking jerk shouldn't give ideas to the universe!

"It's how nature works," he continued unperturbed. "You got your revenge so the ducks will get theirs soon enough."

"You're just trying to get back at me because I'm making you watch that movie with me," Yoori bit back bitterly.

A frown enveloped his once smiling face at the reminder of a movie he didn't want to see for the life of him. "I'm not going and you're not going to make me. I told you, I'm not going to watch it."

Yoori snorted. "We'll see about that."

"I swear to God, Yoori. If you make me watch it with you, I'm punishing you tonight."

"Punish me?" Yoori inquired skeptically. "What are you going to do? *Spank me?*"

She laughed at her own question until she caught a certain naughty sparkle in Tae Hyun's once frowning eyes. It was as if she had just suggested something to him and he was considering it...

"What?" she asked nervously, her eyes suddenly glancing at his bare chest and tight abs. Was it natural that as soon as she saw some naughtiness in his eyes, she felt naughty too? Yoori shook her head inwardly at this question.

"You *have* been a bad girl," Tae Hyun murmured more to himself than to her.

As Yoori stared at him in horror, Tae Hyun just smiled sheepishly, tightening his hold on her hand once they swept closer to the entrance of his apartment building.

"My offer still stands in terms of conserving water...boss," Tae Hyun reminded sultrily when they neared the revolving door. His voice was filled with sensual promise and joking humor.

170

"We are *not* showering together!" Yoori shouted in blushing dismay.

As a joke, Tae Hyun had been offering to give her sponge baths ever since he became her assistant. Though Yoori knew he was only teasing her because he knew what a prude she was, she couldn't help but blush and be tempted with the offer. She couldn't deny that she wanted to give Tae Hyun a sponge bath too.

She restrained her eyes from venturing on to the tight abs she loved so much and ripped her hand from his grasp. She made a run through the revolving door by herself—or so she planned.

Tae Hyun was quick on her heels. His hands encircling around her stomach, he pulled her into a quick embrace as they walked through the revolving door together. Holding her closer, he delicately pushed her through the door and dipped his lips beside her ear.

"One of these days, you'll give in and I'll be more than happy to run soap over that pretty little back of yours...among other things..."

As if anticipating it, Tae Hyun untangled himself from behind her and ran off to the elevators just as Yoori was about to turn around to smack him.

"Stop whispering stuff into my ear!" she shouted after him, blushing uncontrollably. "It's annoying!"

It was annoying because it gave her butterflies every time he did it. It seemed to be something he was doing a lot of and it was annoying the hell out of her. It was like he was purposely "flirting" with her just to tease her.

That jerk.

Yoori muttered a curse for her "assistant" and his inability to respect her authoritative role once she heard him laugh in amusement. The elevator doors dinged open. Chasing after Tae Hyun, who was waiting for her while he smugly held the elevator door open, Yoori knew that her final "punishment" would have to stand.

Oh yeah, the fool was *definitely* going to watch that movie with her now.

"Does not mean that you're exempt from the cruelties of life. "

16: Paris Pact

"I can't believe I just let you do that to me," Tae Hyun gritted through his teeth several hours later, his smooth skin glowing under the illumination of the street lamps beside the movie theater.

He tucked his hands into his black jacket and stood still. His black pants swayed under the gust of wind blowing in their direction. They had just finished watching the movie that Tae Hyun deemed as "the movie from hell" and it became clear early on that Tae Hyun wasn't the only one bitter about a horrible movie experience.

"I can't believe you just ruined that for me," Yoori griped sourly. She wore a white faux fur jacket with dark jeans and black boots. Though she looked as innocent as could be, there was nothing but anger spewing out of her.

She had been dying to see this movie with Tae Hyun for ages and when it took place, the experience couldn't have been more terrible for her. This night was supposed to be the pinnacle of her wonderful week. Now, all that she had to show for it was a surprise that ended in shambles because Tae Hyun always had a way of fucking things up even when he wasn't directly doing it.

Surprised with the toxicity spearing through her voice, he turned to her in disbelief. He was flabbergasted as to why she was acting the way that she was.

"Why are *you* bitter? You got to watch your movie."

"I got to watch the movie?" She narrowed her eyes. Her anger escalated at his obliviousness. "What did I get to watch? All that I could remember was *you* complaining, *you* getting up and leaving every so often, *you* whining, and *you* being fawned over by girls whose high-pitched voices were so loud that I couldn't even hear what was happening in the movie."

It was an unfortunately accurate statement.

Since Yoori chose the chick flick of all chick flicks, from the beginning to the end of the movie, all the eyes of the rabid fan girls were on Tae Hyun as opposed to the movie screen. It was so terrible. There were constant whispers of girls who had yet to hit puberty, giggling about how sexy Tae Hyun was and that he was going to be their future "hubby."

"He's so hot!" they exclaimed, completely forgetting about the male heartthrob that was supposed to be in the movie. Instead, they focused their undivided attention on Tae Hyun, who was cringing while he watched the movie. She was even sure one of those fan girls called her a bad name, but she couldn't make out what it was they were calling her. All that she knew was that she hated that they were looking at him like he was a piece of meat. Not that she was jealous or anything.

"It's not my fault they were staring at me," he argued. It was evident that he was more than uncomfortable with the sleazy winks the fan girls were throwing his way.

Though it wasn't his fault, she directed her anger toward him nonetheless. He should've done something to keep himself from being in that position.

"Well, you should've worn a hat or something!" It was a completely illogical argument, but she had to say something. She didn't know why she cared so much, but she just did. She was so excited to watch the movie with him and now everything was shot to hell. What a horrible movie date...

"Well then maybe we shouldn't watch a movie like that next time because I *hate* wearing hats."

"I should've brought Kang Min and Jae Won instead. I'm sure they would've appreciated this movie more," Yoori said bitterly, though she didn't mean it.

Well, she was almost sure they'd enjoy the movie, but she didn't mean it when she said she should've brought the brothers instead. Tae Hyun would always be her first choice.

Tae Hyun scoffed at her statement. "Oh yeah, I'm sure those two would be the ideal candidates to appreciate a guy who *sparkles* in the sunlight."

She frowned. "Stop being so insensitive," she chastised, even though she thought the sparkling part was strange too.

"Whatever," he dismissed tiredly, his eyes giving way to the fact that he wanted to forget about the terrible movie altogether. "Are you ready to end a hellish movie experience with a good night?"

Her ears perked up. Anything that could end her final night as his boss with a positive bang was music to her ears. "What do you have in mind?"

There was mischief in his eyes when he said, "Do you remember at the lake house when you told me that you can handle a lot of alcohol...probably more than me?"

"Yeah?"

"I want to take you up on that challenge," he said with a wicked smirk.

Yoori rose a challenging brow. "You want to get your boss drunk?"

Tae Hyun shook his head, fabricating innocence. "I just want to see if my boss can really handle her alcohol as she led on." His brow rose up challengingly as well. "But of course if you're afraid of losing..."

"Where are we going?" Yoori interrupted immediately.

She refused to be seen as a wimp. She could take Tae Hyun. Of course there was a bigger chance he'd be able to withstand more alcohol than her, but that didn't intimidate her. She was up for any challenge, especially ones that could involve Tae Hyun losing his sense of control before she lost hers.

"Are we going to a bar?"

Tae Hyun shook his head again, amusement filling his eyes at her acceptance of his challenge. "We're going to be drinking outside."

Outside?

Yoori apprehensively cast her gaze at the dark sky. Judging by the looming black clouds and the wintry wind, she knew it was only a matter of time before snow accompanied them. At least that was what the weatherman said awaited the citizens of Seoul tonight.

"Where would we go to drink outside in the snow?"

He didn't answer her right away. He merely allowed the silence to peruse between them as his amusement filled eyes stared at her with excitement. His emotions were blatant yet his intentions weren't and she hated that. She hated that he made things so obvious yet he was also so good at hiding things.

"It's a surprise," he stated with allure embroidering his voice.

She had anticipated that this would be his answer and she wasn't content in merely accepting it as such. Determined to at least get some knowledge of the surprise, Yoori decided to be stubborn and dig deeper for an answer.

"Give me a hint or I'm not going anywhere with you."

"You're just a little Brat, aren't you?" he asked in disbelief, his first sign that he was already giving in.

"I think that's already been established, Snob," she replied plainly, trying to remain tough and stubborn while keeping her eyes locked with his.

Tae Hyun had a thing with staring people down, measuring them and their bluffs before he gave anything away. Unfortunately for her, he knew her too well and knew that she was bluffing. She was dying to go with him and he damn well knew that. Fortunately for Yoori though, Tae Hyun also had a habit of giving her what she wanted, even if it was in the form of the smallest of hints.

"I have one word for you," he shared with a knowing smile. It was one that already hinted to her that she was going to love this surprise. "Swings."

Sounds of car doors slamming at full force was heard once Yoori received Tae Hyun's answer. She didn't even need time to think about where he was taking her.

The park.

The park they went to the night of her initiation.

The park that had the playground in which Tae Hyun said he'd take her to again...

Excitement pulsed in her veins as a myriad of streetlights streamed through her eyes. They were driving at full speed to hit a local alcohol shop and it didn't seem like they were going fast enough for her excited nerves. The alcohol buying experience was so short that she felt like she just inhaled the experience rather than walking within it. Not that it mattered because the only thing she cared about was finally having her fun in that park.

Alcohol and a playground in a secluded park?

What more could a girl ask for?

The car ride to the park was long in length, but short in occurrence in terms of Yoori's awareness. Amidst the happy chattering of Yoori and Tae Hyun, the sounds of alcohol bottles clinking together, and the happy green lights of all the traffic lights, they were there before Yoori could even blink twice.

Once Tae Hyun parked his Mercedes, both got out of the car and happily stood with bags of bottles in each of their hands. Big smiles spread across their faces. The silence that embalmed them was shrouded with anticipation. It was one of those companionable silences where you could feel it in the air: something special was definitely going to go down tonight...

"Come on, boss," said Tae Hyun, breaking the wintery silence. He casually intertwined his hand with hers, pulling her in the direction of the swings. "The night is young and we still need to get you drunk."

"You're going down, buddy!" she squealed, tightening her hold on Tae Hyun's hand. They jumped onto the playground sand. Her competitive side sparked to life. "There's no way in hell you're getting me drunk before you."

"We'll see about that." He then gazed at her warily just as they separated to their own swings. Something possibly alarming crossed his mind. "Uh, you're not an emo drunk, are you?"

"No, of course not." Though even as she said it, Yoori was almost sure she was going to have to eat her words later on.

A good two hours later on in fact...

"Ugh...I think I drank too much," Yoori complained, her head resting against the metal chain holding up the swing.

They sat facing each other, Tae Hyun in one direction and Yoori in the other direction. The pace of the swings they were sitting on had since slowed as the alcohol began to resonate through their bodies. Allowing one leg to draw a line in the sand, Yoori brought up another big bottle of vodka to her lips even though she had just complained about drinking too much. Guzzling the contents like she was drinking water, she drank until she was fully quenched. The air was cold, but it wasn't cold enough to penetrate through the warm fort her alcohols of choice had formed over her body.

Her swing creaked when she cast a gaze over to Tae Hyun. He was still swinging back and forth slowly. He had just finished guzzling his fifth bottle of vodka and was already starting on his sixth.

For the past two hours or so, they had been drinking stubbornly with the sole intention of getting the other drunk. The first hour started off with rowdy jeering that consisted of Tae Hyun calling Yoori a "genetic freak" and Yoori calling Tae Hyun a "closet light weight". Unfortunately, the rowdiness died down when they realized that both didn't seem to even be remotely close to getting drunk. If anything, it appeared that both were closer to becoming "tipsy emos" —or Yoori anyway.

"What's on your mind, assistant?" Tae Hyun asked, taking inventory of the fact that she had grown unusually quiet and despondent. "Are you still upset about the movie thing? If you're that upset with it, I'll take you to watch it again..."

"No, it's not that," she appeased slowly, finding it hard to keep her eyes opened. The cold wind continued to swim around them. She wished she was still hung up over that, but she had since moved on to something a bit more depressing—something she had been trying to avoid talking about for quite some time now.

Yoori's eyes turned into quick slits when she realized that he had just addressed her by the wrong name. Her week as his boss was ending, but it hadn't ended yet.

"Sorry, I meant, 'boss,'" he amended, hiding back a smirk when he saw her playful glare. "Come on," he urged her with that warm, encouraging voice of his. "You're unusually quiet and I know you have a lot on your drunk mind right now. Whatever we talk about on this playground stays here."

Now what girl with some emotionally pent up issues and more than enough to drink could say no to that offer? If it were anyone else, then she would've kept her mouth shut. But because it was Tae Hyun, the words that flowed out of her lips came as easily as water from rain clouds.

"I'm not drunk," she quickly corrected before going further into any conversation with him. She just wanted to put up that disclaimer because she hadn't lost to him yet.

He rolled his eyes at her perseverance and gave her a bitter nod as confirmation that she wasn't drunk.

Satisfied with this, her eyes roamed around the creaking merry-go-round, the monkey bars, and the slide beside them. After gathering up her nerves to open up to him, she gave a sigh and began.

"I get jealous, you know?"

Her eyes were firmly solidified on the slide while she spoke. Her voice pulsed with raw emotions that she had kept pent up for the whole week, only to be released when she drank too much and was no longer able to control her inhibitions.

"When people talk about what they were like when they were kids, I get really jealous because I want to do the same."

She momentarily closed her eyes. Another gust of wind blew past them. "In the past, I've often wondered what I was like when I was a kid. I always imagined that I pretty much just ran around the playground, swung on swings, slid down slides, and hung on to monkey bars when I was younger. But the past week, since everything became confirmed that I was Soo Jin in my past life, I've been thinking about all of this more and more." Her eyes moved onto the merry-go-round. "I wonder if I played with dolls after they trained me to kill someone. I wonder if I had ice cream as I watched people die. I wonder what they did to me to turn me into the person I hated the most. I wonder what they did to me to make my life so horrible that I ended up committing 'suicide' three years ago."

Her words were met with a haunting silence that bothered her.

She flickered her gaze onto Tae Hyun, whose eyes were still gentle on her.

"What was your childhood like?"

"It was…busy," he answered slowly.

She recalled what Ji Hoon shared with her in regards to the typical training of an Underworld Royal. "When did you start your training?"

"Ten."

"What was that like?"

He sighed, taking a moment to stare up at the sky. His expression was stoic when he said, "It was agonizing."

Yoori gazed at him surprisingly. She did not expect such a blunt answer.

He went on, his reminiscent eyes still on the sky. "My training was different from the rest of the Royals. Whereas many others were sent to a specific country to train, my father decided that he wanted his second born son to have a more well-rounded education. While Royals like Ji Hoon were getting comfortable in neighbor countries like China, I was never allowed to get comfortable. Once I was done learning the things I needed to learn from a specific mentor, I was to leave as soon as possible to become trained by another mentor. It was a cycle that seemed never ending." He swallowed roughly. "I still remember my first night of training like it was yesterday. I was sent to a rural area in Laos and as my first initiation, my mentor decided that it was best to introduce me to the sight of death as soon as possible. As soon as I stepped on his estate, he threw me into a ditch filled with corpses and ordered me to sleep there for the night."

As Yoori covered her mouth in horror, he went on. "Needless to say, that scared the shit out of me. After that, I trained endlessly. I was pitted against other kids, fully grown men and murderers alike. I can't tell you how many times I was a breath away from death and how many lives I took during my training. There were some nights where I was tempted to put a bullet in my own mouth because I was so miserable."

Yoori could scarcely voice her next words. "What kept you going?"

"My father," he stated simply. "He assured me that it would all get easier. He told me that this agonizing moment would pass. He said that this was a debt all Royals must pay if they wanted to be free of human weaknesses. He said that one day, when all of my weaknesses are gone, I would become better than human." He smiled desolately. "He was right. Slowly but surely, as the years passed, this violent life became easier. Every time I killed, I felt more and more powerful. Every time anyone kneeled before me, I felt more and more like a God. Yet, no matter my current state in life, it doesn't change the fact that my childhood wasn't a pleasant one." He finally turned to her. "You said you wondered what your childhood was like, but you should know that Soo Jin wasn't just any other Royal. She was different. She was the protégé of the three most powerful Advisors in the Underworld. She was trained at Ju Won's mansion her entire childhood. At least I got to see different parts of the world growing up—she did not have the same freedom." He smiled. "It is an excruciating road to become a God in this world. Perhaps it is your blessing that you do not remember your childhood. It is a rarity for Underworld Royals to have good childhoods—we are too busy losing our souls."

Yoori smiled sadly at Tae Hyun. Only her crime lord boss would recollect unpleasant memories of his past to make her feel better.

"You know, you never asked me anything about being Soo Jin," she stated wearily. She looked at him as she continued to swing listlessly. "You're not curious about how much I remember? You're not curious about my inner turmoil?"

He knew enough, which was that Soo Jin wanted to commit suicide and she had asked her brother to help her. He also knew that Soo Jin somehow became Yoori. He knew all the important stuff she shared with him, but he never once asked to know more about what was going on in her mind. She had always wondered if he was ever curious or if he was just being considerate.

"Of course, I'm curious," he admitted, his eyes never straying from her attentive ones. "Who wouldn't be?" He shrugged. "But I figured if you wanted me to know more, when you're ready, you'd tell me."

She liked his answer. He always gave good ones and he was always genuine about them. That was his charm: he was straightforward. Whether it be in-your-face straightforward or subtly straightforward, he always gave the answer he truly felt and she appreciated him for that.

"I have two questions for you," she continued, knowing that Tae Hyun would be the best person to go to for advice. "There are a couple of things I can't seem to figure out myself and I think you may be able to help me figure them out."

His attentive silence prompted her to continue.

"I can understand that something occurred in that club massacre that shook her to her core. There was a trigger and she snapped. What I don't understand is why she tried to kill herself. I mean…Soo Jin was a trained killer…surely killing those people in the club wouldn't merit her losing her mind. She's killed in the past…what made these people so special that she actually felt remorse for them?"

Tae Hyun took a few seconds to ponder the question. "Would you feel guilty if you killed five ants at once?"

Yoori shook her head.

"How about if you killed two cats at once?"

Yoori slowly understood the point Tae Hyun was making.

He went on, the gentle wind ruffling the short strands of his hair. "In the Underworld, the lives of humans differ in value. Generally, killing other gang members would equate to killing ants. You're taking lives away, but it has no effect on you because you've been trained to kill them. It demands no guilt from you because they are trained to kill you too. So it's kinda like survival of the fittest. On the flip side, killing innocent families or kids hold a higher value in our world. That was why the club massacre incident was so well-known in the Underworld. It's not so much that Soo Jin would dare to kill, but it was more along the lines that she would go so far as killing people who were not a threat to her whatsoever. It's a complicated value in the Underworld that gets mixed up together. Some people, when they've killed enough, feel that they can withstand the weight that comes with killing families and kids."

He gazed at Yoori warily, already knowing the outcome of Soo Jin's fate. "Judging from her desperate need to end her life, it seemed that killing the latter wasn't as easy as she thought it would be."

Yoori nodded understandingly. That made sense. She ventured into her second question. "In my dreams—my memories—I see her kneeling in front of her brother..." She shifted uneasily. "My brother. She was begging him to end her life. This...this is so odd to me. I...I don't understand why she couldn't just kill herself. Why did she give him the needle instead? Why did she need her brother of all people to kill her?"

"She is bound to him by oath."

She was thrown off by his answer. "Bound by oath?"

"This world, as ruthless as it is, still heavily values loyalty and honor. You may not give it to your enemies, but you give it to your family—your Underworld family. When you join crime syndicates in the Underworld, it's like joining a Kingdom of sorts. You not only go through the 'blood in' initiations, but you also take an oath. Your life is sworn to your King, which means that you either die protecting him or die serving him. Committing suicide is considered a betrayal to your gang—to your Underworld King. An Soo Jin was the underboss of the Scorpions gang. If she wanted to die without betraying the oath she took, then she would need his permission...she would need him to kill her."

"This world has a lot of bylaws, doesn't it?" commented Yoori.

"Merely guidelines that people live by," Tae Hyun answered. He regarded her with hesitancy. "You...you're not starting to feel suicidal, are you?"

"What?" she practically shrieked. "No, of course not!"

She didn't like that she was Soo Jin, but there was no way she would kill herself.

"Good." He exhaled in relief. "'Cause I don't care who the hell you were three years ago. I'll kill you if you kill yourself."

She gave him a blank look. "Well, that was a stupid statement."

"Don't be stupid and kill yourself and I won't make a stupid statement like that."

"Okaaaaaay, buddy," Yoori promised, finally letting out a giggle. She took another swig of her alcohol. She gave props to Tae Hyun for saying the most random things to show that he cared.

"I am curious about something that deals with you being Soo Jin," he said quietly, commanding her attention again.

"Go ahead," she prompted, though she was wary of what he may ask.

He drank out of his bottle and began slowly. "It seems that if there's only one person that holds the key to everything…it would be your brother." His eyes locked with her curiously. "Why aren't you more insistent with trying to find him so you can find out more about your past? If it was me, I'd be searching all ends of the world for the one person who could shine some light on my situation and pull me out of the darkness."

"I don't even know where he is…" Her argument was futile and she knew that. It wasn't so much that she didn't want to find him. It was something else she was afraid of.

"Ask me to help you and I'll find him for you." He paused. "Do you even want to find him?"

It was then that she knew Tae Hyun wasn't curious about whether or not she wanted to find her brother. He already knew that she didn't want to find An Young Jae. He was curious as to *why* she didn't want to find him.

Yoori took a long moment to think about her answer before she gave it to Tae Hyun. She gave him the raw, unfiltered answer that she had never voiced out—even to herself.

"Truthfully speaking, I'm not one of those people who *have* to know where they came from. When I woke up in the hospital three years ago and my adoptive family fed me all the lies about me hanging out with a bad crowd, I never once tried to find out who I was. I never once tried to find that bad crowd to find out what I was like in my 'previous' life. I'm not one of those brave people who have to know who they were and where they came from at all costs. I'm really weak and spineless like that. I always run away from my problems and that's the only thing I'm really good at. The only thing I care about is being happy. For as long as I can, I just want to be happy. I don't want to find Young Jae. I don't want to learn more about my past. I don't want to be out of the dark. I like things as they are now—especially right now. I'm really happy right now."

Her gaze went over to Tae Hyun. Though there was a gentle warmness in his gaze, Yoori knew that in many ways, even if he wouldn't admit it to himself, he loved her answer. He loved her answer because what would the world be like if there was no more Tae Hyun and Yoori? As long as Soo Jin was out of the picture, they would always be together.

Yoori laughed. "You knew I was going to say all that, huh?"

"Slightly," he admitted, holding back his smile.

Yoori smiled before venturing into another set of thoughts. "How do you feel about all of this? Me being her? I know you're used to killings and all, but I think killing kids and families is a different level—a level that may be too vicious and barbaric for the Underworld itself. Why aren't you disgusted?"

"She regretted everything enough to want to make things right by killing herself. I don't think anyone can truly be disgusted with that." He tilted his head at Yoori, his eyes holding nothing but an affectionate gaze for her. "Plus, she's you. You may get on my nerves at times, but you could never disgust me."

Yoori frowned at the subtle insult he added in yet chose not to delve deeper into it. She was happy with his answer. This led her to her next random question.

"Would you cry if I died?"

"No," he answered without a moment's hesitation.

What?!

Did the fool drink too much alcohol to speak so irrationally?

He sure knew how to kill a nice moment.

"You're *not* going to cry?" she asked belligerently, nearly having a heart attack from the shock she was experiencing.

"Why would I?" he asked blithely, taking another gulp of his alcohol. His eyes were firmly solidified on her enraged ones as he did this.

"What the hell, jerk-face? Why *wouldn't* you cry if your best friend dies?"

"Best friend?" He nearly choked on his drink. "How the hell did you become my *best friend*?"

"Well, we are, aren't we?"

He made a rude noise. "Shouldn't you get my permission before you label yourself as my best friend? I mean…I didn't even want you to be my friend in the first place. Why the hell would I want you as my *best friend*?"

She was beside herself now. "There you go again, you Snob, always thinking that you're better than me."

"Eh, Choi Yoori," Tae Hyun said sternly, taking offense to her accusation. "Just because I don't want you as a friend doesn't mean I think I'm better than you."

Yoori snorted and looked away. She thought about giving him the "read-between-the-lines" fingers, but decided against it. It was one of those tricks that you could only use on someone once and she now regretted using it on him at the lake house. Surely he deserved the middle finger now more so than before.

"Come on Brat, don't be like this," he urged lightly, trying to get her attention. He sighed when she continued to avoid eye contact. He shook his head at her stubbornness. With a look of exasperation, he said, "Why would I cry if I won't let you die in the first place?"

"You *won't* let me die?" she parroted, turning back to face him with interest. She had expected to see a mocking smile on his face. She was surprised when no mockery marked his countenance. He looked serious.

"I searched an entire city for you when I didn't have to." He shook his head at her like she was out of her mind when she assumed that he wouldn't care. "I'm not going to let you die on me."

Her heart lifted at his answer. She had no doubt she was going to die from a heart attack if he continued to play with her emotions like this.

She was prepared to bury the hatchet until he promptly added, "I mean if you die, who is going to entertain me?"

Yet again, her heart was racing and it was not from being happy.

"Does it look like I have this big red ball on my nose?" she finally snapped, taking another drink out of her nearly empty alcohol bottle.

"What?" he asked incredulously. His eyes noted the nearly empty alcohol bottle in her hand and his eyes twinkled. It seemed he was under the assumption that Yoori was one step closer to getting drunk.

She could feel the effects clouding her vision slightly. She went on, slurring a bit as she spoke. "A cloooooooown! Do I look like a clooooown to you? Here for your own personal amusement? Is that why you're always laughing at me and teasing meeeeee?"

Tae Hyun laughed heartily at her. His eyes spoke of nothing but adoration. He finished his bout of laughter with a sigh. "What am I going to do without you, babe?"

"You'll probably die from boredom," she remarked sarcastically, finishing the last drops of vodka. Once the bottle was empty, she tossed it to the side. The bottle clanked with the other empty alcohol bottles and fell to its place.

Just when Yoori was about to close her eyes and lay her head against the metal chain of the swing, Tae Hyun's next question more than speared the sobriety back into her.

"Would you cry if *I* died?"

She narrowed her eyes onto him. Her gaze blazed with warning. "Kwon Tae Hyun...if you die on me, I'll *kill* you." It was only after Yoori made that statement did she realize, as stupid as it sounded, the statement was more than true.

Logically, it didn't make sense the threats Tae Hyun and Yoori made to each other because how would it be possible that they could kill each other if the other one was already dead? It would probably never make sense to anyone else who heard it, but it made sense to Yoori and she knew that it more than made sense to Tae Hyun. That was the connection they had. It made sense to them – even if they couldn't explain why.

"What a stupid statement," Tae Hyun quipped with a smile.

"Well, don't be stupid and die and I won't make a stupid statement."

"What are you going to do without me, Yoori?" he asked, his riveting brown eyes holding her gaze. "Remember, clowns don't cry..."

Noting that she was no longer drinking, he leaned forward and offered his vodka bottle. It was their last bottle and it seemed that with the contents left within it, it was hers to finish.

"I guess I'm the exception," she stated. She leaned out to grab the alcohol bottle. She sat back in her seat and added, "Plus, you can't die. You haven't found Paris yet."

He regarded her poignantly. "What makes you think I'll find Paris at all?"

"You will," she assured confidently. "I have faith."

"Haven't we established that I don't want to find it?" The content of the question was stern, yet it didn't match his gentle voice.

"That doesn't mean you won't."

He smiled at her insistence. He took a second to wrap his mind around something and then said, "Out of the two of us, who do you think will find it first?"

She deliberated his question. The obvious answer would be her because she was the one seeking Paris. Yet, for whatever reason, Yoori felt it was fair game between them.

"I guess we'll have to live long enough to see."

"Alright," Tae Hyun concluded. "So I guess it's a pact...we won't let each other die..."

"Especially when we haven't found Paris yet," Yoori finished for him, raising her lone vodka bottle as an agreement of their pact.

Guzzling down the liquid contents, Yoori was surprised when she saw Tae Hyun jump off his swing.

"What are you doing?" she asked, pulling the bottle away from her mouth.

Tae Hyun had stopped her swing in place and hunched forward. He was staring down at her and she was staring upward at him.

"It's getting colder," he announced, his cool gaze on her. "We should get going."

The visibility of warm air permeated from her cold lips. "I guess it is time to go home, huh?" she asked sadly, not wanting to leave their little playground.

Despite all the cryptic topics of conversation, this was actually one of the more heartwarming moments she had with Tae Hyun.

She sighed.

Damn the weather...

The weather always had a tendency to ruin things for them.

He smiled, crouching down in front of her. His eyes reflected amusement. "Who says we're going home?"

"But you said it's getting—" She stopped. "Wait, what's going on?"

He tilted his head. "You don't want to see your surprise?"

Her eyes rounded with intrigue. She surveyed the playground. "This wasn't the surprise?"

He laughed. "Not even close." He turned his head and pointed in the direction of the trees that led into the depths of the park.

"Your surprise is in there, I *think*. I'm not too sure. We might have to do some exploring before we find it."

"What's in there?" she asked, looking over in the direction he pointed her in. All she saw were trees.

He shrugged coyly. "You'll have to come with me to see."

"Tae Hyun, it's getting colder," she reminded him, though she didn't see the problem in that.

"Exactly," he said as though that was the reason why they had to leave at that precise moment. He eyed her challengingly. "Are you just going to stay here like a sitting duck or do you want to have your breath taken away?"

Yoori arched an inquiring brow. "A little overconfident with that statement, aren't we?"

"Just confident," Tae Hyun answered smoothly, charm emanating from his smirk. "Come on, if I'm wrong and you don't like it, I'll be your assistant for another week."

He turned around and waited for her. She knew then he was ready to give her a piggyback ride while taking her to the "surprise."

"And if you're right?" she asked, placing her alcohol bottle down and wrapping her arms around his neck with an excited beam.

His smirk grew slowly.

He placed his hands under her legs and made sure she was up and safe around him for the piggyback ride. Rising slowly to his feet, he begun toward the enveloping darkness with the cold wind whipping past them.

"Then it'd be a great night for us, babe."

"You're merely living on borrowed time..."

17: Winter Wonderland

The trip into the inner depths of the park was much longer than Yoori had anticipated. The first time she came to this particular park with Tae Hyun, she had only noticed the playground and the wide-open recreational grass area. She hadn't realized that there was a more extensive part to the park, which led into scenic gardens that were lined with countless trees (green and balding ones alike), bushes, and remnants of rose gardens that had since withered away under the veil of winter.

Apart from the soft radiance of the stone lamps that littered along the pathway, the inner vicinity of the park area they were walking in was secluded with darkness. Normally, such a scene would send chills up Yoori's spine, but the only thing running through her was excitement. It was hard to be afraid of anything when you were with someone like Tae Hyun. The last thing on Yoori's mind was fear. She was too busy thinking about all the possible things Tae Hyun could have planned for her.

Perhaps there was another gazebo in this secluded area?

Or maybe there was a really pretty rose garden he wanted to show her?

The possibilities were endless.

Her sets of possibilities were thrown into a murky swamp when Tae Hyun pulled away from the dirt pathway they were on. Yoori held her breath when she realized he was taking her down a grassy hill. She instinctively tightened her hold around his neck.

Where on earth was he taking her?

"Ah!" she yelped once they reached the flat grassland.

They cut across several bushes, swerved around various trees and stone lamps that stood around the park. They were still in the park vicinity, but she suddenly felt like she was in a forest of sorts. This path was definitely not the regular pathway that other park-goers were accustomed to.

"Tae Hyun, this better be good." She ducked her head when she was near a tree branch. "Where are we going?"

"Choi Yoori, can you exercise a little patience?" Tae Hyun whispered before picking up speed. There was no doubt he was excited. "What fun would it be to tell you now?"

A disturbing paranoia invaded her mind when he jumped over a log. "Oh my God, you're not going to kill me for punishing you this week, are you? Is that what you meant by taking my breath away?"

Tae Hyun snorted at her unreasonable question. "*Yes.* I spent the entire week being obedient, nearly breaking my back to give you your stupid piggyback rides to throw it all away by killing you at the end of the week."

She frowned. "Your sarcasm is not appreciated."

"Nor is your stubborn heart," he whispered, stepping onto broken tree branches.

"And what do you mean nearly breaking your back?" she asked, not hearing what he just whispered. "Are you insinuating that I'm fat?" Before even giving him a chance to answer, Yoori already said, "For your information, I'm *not* fat. I'm deliciously plump."

"I swear, I'm going to spank some sense into that deliciously plump little butt of yours if you don't stop assuming that I think you're fat."

He held on to her more tightly just when he jumped over a pair of twin bushes.

She gaped. "You wouldn't dare spank me!"

"Dare me to do it. I dare you."

"How dare you dare me to dare you? What kinda assistant are you?"

A smug embellished his face. "One who, at the stroke of midnight, will turn back into your boss."

Yoori laughed at his clever response. She played along. "Oooh, you're just a modern day fairytale pumpkin, aren't you?"

"A deliciously plump pumpkin," Tae Hyun corrected lightheartedly. "You got that, my deliciously plump Cinderella?"

"I prefer Princess," Yoori mischievously corrected before casually turning to her side once she spotted a little black blob on her jacket.

"Eek!" Yoori screeched when she saw a big fat spider on the shoulder of her white faux fur jacket. She immediately flicked the spider off and shuddered in disgust. She wanted to be graceful and just smile while waltzing through this maze of plants and trees, but she couldn't help but—

Ah! Another spider!

She whipped it off her hand in disgust and finally let out her frustration. "How much longer is this going to take—"

"We're here," Tae Hyun announced just as they emerged out from the trees.

He slowed his once speed-of-light pace and eventually came to a smooth stop. Very gently and carefully, he set Yoori down onto the ground. While standing with her arms still encircled around Tae Hyun's neck, Yoori found herself completely floored. Her widened eyes took in the scenery before her.

Concealed within the midst of darkness was a secret garden that sparkled like a picturesque painting. The garden had a variety of neatly trimmed bushes, flowers that continued to withstand the test of winter, a modestly huge pond and a white wooden bridge that lingered over it. Encasing this little garden and keeping it hidden from the world were trees—countless trees that surrounded the garden in the shape of a big oval.

Though veiled in darkness, the beautiful features of the garden were more than highlighted with the light from the moon and the various stone lamps that lingered across the region.

Wow, wow, wow, wow, wow.

How was it possible that Tae Hyun seemed to be the only one who knew where all the prettiest places on earth were?

Dazed with wonder, Yoori released her hold from around Tae Hyun's neck. Smiling uncontrollably, she made her way toward the center of the garden where the border between the pond and ground laid. Just as she was a step away from drawing closer to the border, the lights to the stone lamps started to flicker, scaring her out of her wits. The lights died off, leaving only the limited light from the moon to stroke over the darkness.

Albeit she was disappointed with this, Yoori managed to suppress her pout. She turned back to Tae Hyun with the intention of telling him that she really liked his surprise. Though his facial features were slightly covered, she could still see him standing in the darkness.

"It's really pretty here. I really like it," Yoori commented, wondering why Tae Hyun was still standing where he was with his hands buried deep in his pockets.

He looked totally at ease with the fact that they were surrounded by darkness. It was like he expected this to happen.

"Really?" he asked hazily. His silhouette surveyed the garden. "But you can't even see anything. It's so dark."

"I can see enough with the moonlight," she argued, meaning what she said. Lack of light or not, she still thought the garden was gorgeous.

She could feel a smile quirk across his lips. He nodded at her answer. He then sighed dramatically. A bit *too* dramatically.

"I think we need to turn on a couple of lights."

A burst of blue lights illumed from behind her and kissed over his perfect features. Widening her eyes at the sudden presence of light, she whipped her head around. She casted her eyes to the source of light.

In the further outskirts of the trees that encased the garden, there were five trees that twinkled with the embellishment of blue Christmas lights. From the tip of the heads to the roots of the trunks, the dim blue lighting danced across every free space of the trees and even streamed into the bushes and plants that laid below. Right when Yoori was about to turn around to cast her awestruck gaze over to Tae Hyun, another set of lights illuminated over the four sets of trees that stood beside it.

Seconds later, another set of lights appeared...

Then another...

And then another...

Like a domino effect, the world around her ignited with vibrant colors. Yoori's stupefied eyes reflected the blue lights that twirled itself on every tree and marked itself on every plant. To top off the magnificent view, the finale came from the white wooden bridge that hovered over the pond.

Embraced under the veil of the night, blue and white lights emanated from the bridge itself—the final clincher that gave enough light to reveal to Yoori that she was actually standing on an assortment of blue and white rose petals. Nearly keeling over from shock, Yoori was astounded to see that the rose petals not only hid beneath her feet, but they were also present across all the regions of the garden. The petals lay on the plants around her, slept on the soil beneath her, waltzed on the bridge before her and danced on the moonlit pond beside her. The beauty of the rose petals were present everywhere.

And if all of this wasn't enough...

"Oh my God," Yoori whispered, covering her mouth once she felt something white flutter before her mesmerized eyes. Instinctively, she lifted her focus to the dark canvas above. White puff tickled her nose.

It was snowing.

A wide smile appeared on her lips and she sighed in elatedness.

It was official.

She had just stepped out of reality and into a Winter Wonderland.

"Tae Hyun," she called breathlessly, lowering her hands from her lips. She returned her gaze back to him for the first time since the light show took place. Unbeknownst to herself the effect the beautiful scenery took onto her body, she was caught off guard with what occurred next. Her legs, already weakened from the shock of this beautiful surprise, bent like jelly when she turned to him, nearly causing her to fall forward into the inviting pond.

Tae Hyun effortlessly wrapped his arms around her waist and caught her just before she fell into the pond. Helping her to steady herself, he only turned her to face him once the strength returned to her legs. He held her close and gazed down at her with a tender smile. When their eyes met, she could see the satisfaction exude from him. He was unquestionably pleased with her reaction.

"I never told you that finding it would be easy," he whispered, tucking her bangs behind her ears. His eyes lit up, the prelude of his charm already coming underway. "I hope you thought it was worth it though."

"I can't believe you did all this," she managed to utter. Snow cascaded unto them like raindrops. She was so overwhelmed with everything that she couldn't even detect that Tae Hyun had already begun to throw his charms at her again. It may have been cold like the North Pole, but she was suddenly warm like the sun. "Did you seriously do all of this?"

She regretted it as soon as it came out of her mouth. The answer was quite obvious. She wished she didn't just blurt out something so stupid. It wasn't like she was dealing with a considerably nice audience.

Tae Hyun didn't disappoint expectations. He feigned an air of nonchalance. His eyes lazily ran over the beautiful man-made Wonderland before them.

"No, some other Underworld King had a bunch of Serpents climb up on the trees to put up the lights and had Jae Won and Kang Min rip petals from roses and throw it all around this garden. From what my instincts tell me, I think they both tripped over a string of lights and slipped into the pond while dispersing the rose petals…" He shrugged. "But yeah, it wasn't me."

A bout of giggling poured from Yoori's lips. She found entertainment in visualizing the brothers falling into the pond and a bunch of Serpents climbing up on trees and fearing for their lives.

Oh what a sight that would've been…

"Was this why you left so many times during the movie?" She raised a brow at him, knowing now that he was only being problematic in the theater because he wanted to throw her off as to what he was really up to. "And here I thought you were whining about it so much because you hated it."

"I was with you so I suppose the movie wasn't that bad," he admitted with a bemused look. "I was just impatient and wanted to bring you here instead. Why fawn over someone else's story when I can give you your own, right?"

She shook her head at him, not able to think of a proper retort before his smile grew wider.

Releasing his hold from around her waist, he reached out, lifted the hood of her faux fur jacket and placed it just above her head to block it from the downpour of snow, which was now dancing freely around them.

"I hope you like it…Princess," he whispered.

Once he fully lifted the hood over her head, he gave her one of his breathtaking smiles, tucked his hands into his pockets and began to approach the bridge.

The whole time as he did this, Yoori couldn't keep her tipsy eyes off of him.

The scene she found herself in was a dangerous one. She knew, as her heart began to race frantically, that all of this was a dangerous sequel to the last romantic encounter she had with Tae Hyun, which mirrored the magic of this night. She didn't want to think about it, but it was hard not to when she was already weak in the knees.

Was it because she had too much to drink or was it because she was getting drunk on Tae Hyun's charms again?

Probably the first one, she thought hopefully. It was still dangerous though, she reminded herself, especially now since it seemed that Tae Hyun might have unleashed the "charming" side as opposed to the "teasing" side. This was bad news only because Yoori was a weakling when it came to Tae Hyun's charming side.

Taking a second to regain her normal state of breathing and reminding herself that there was nothing going on between her and Tae Hyun, Yoori smiled appreciatively.

"Why on earth did you go all out?" she asked as she followed him. "All of this...this is too amazing..."

Turning slightly, he just shrugged. "We can't take pictures together...so I just wanted to give you memories you'd never forget."

The blue and white rose petals on the foundation of the bridge were now collecting snow as Tae Hyun and Yoori stepped onto the wooden structure. The bridge creaked in response.

"Well...you were right, buddy." She sighed, admiring the beautiful decorations. "You really did steal my breath away."

He smiled slyly, whipping around to face her just after they reached the center of the bridge. Yoori stopped when he did this, nearly bumping into his chest.

"Your breath wasn't what I was trying to steal, you stubborn little minx."

"What'd you just call me?" she shouted, completely disregarding the first part of the statement.

"Nothing, Princess," he voiced almost teasingly. "Now can we sit down? All my sole efforts of walking here took a strain on me. I'd really like to relax now."

Yoori didn't get to register what he said when he took her hand and pulled her down to sit on the bridge with him.

Still dazed and happy with everything, a distracted Yoori was still smiling when they both sat down between a big gap in the railing. Scooting closer to one another, they made sure each fit into that one particular big gap before they hung their legs off the magnificently lit bridge. They rested their chins on the wooden portion of the railing and happily watched the snow cascade around them.

It fell on the petals on land and water alike. It frosted the trees, coated the plants, and sprinkled on to both Yoori and Tae Hyun's hairs as they kept their eyes on the pond that reflected the moon and the Christmas lights above. The entire view was so mesmerizing and relaxing that Yoori couldn't help but breathe in excitement. She kept her happy gaze on the snow falling around them. Everything was delicious candy to her eyes. She was so content that she didn't even feel cold.

"If you keep doing stuff like this," she commented casually, her eyes firmly casted over the pond. "Then my future soul mate will never match up to you."

"Then I guess he wouldn't be your soul mate if he can't match up to me," Tae Hyun said confidently. His eyes proudly scanned the stunning scene around them. He was more than satisfied with the splendor of his creation.

"All of this was a lot of work," Yoori absently observed, not even wanting to surmise how long it took for all his men to set this entire thing up. She faced him. "Why did you do all this?"

"So I can melt your heart," Tae Hyun answered, reclining backward and laying himself across the petal covered bridge. Once the back of his head touched the wooden foundation, he rubbed his temple in a circular motion. It was as if he was now feeling the effects of the alcohol he induced up until that point.

"No, seriously," she insisted, smiling at what she took as a joke.

Always inclined to copy Tae Hyun with whatever he did, she laid herself beside him. Once she was fully situated beside him, she turned her eyes to meet his awaiting ones. She tried not to blush so much when she realized how close they were and how irresistible he looked laying there, his gaze on hers as the snow kissed his skin. It was definitely a sight for the eyes. He looked just like a fallen angel.

There was a haze of emotions in his eyes after hearing her response to his answer. Yoori couldn't decipher what it was he was feeling, but his next actions took her out of that curiosity.

He merely closed his eyes and basked under the cascading snow above them. Heeding his need to enjoy the weather, and excited to close her eyes to do the same, Yoori accepted his silence as a sufficient answer and closed her eyes too.

She wasn't sure how long they laid there, their eyes closed, heads beside one another amongst the myriads of rose petals, Christmas lights, and snow frosting their faces. She wasn't sure how long they laid there as the snow tickled them, as the cold murmured across their skins and as their breathing mingled in relaxation. She wasn't sure how long it was…all that she knew was that she had never felt more at peace. It was like she was living in a frozen dream.

"How is it possible that you've never had a boyfriend as Choi Yoori?" Tae Hyun asked, bringing her out of her reverie. He was careful to distinguish between her and An Soo Jin. Surely they both knew the relationship status of Soo Jin's resumé.

She opened her eyes and met his awaiting ones.

"Why?" she asked jokingly, angling her head to make sure they had direct eye contact with one another. "You think I'm too pretty to be single?"

He laughed at her question, effectively making her blush. "I'm just wondering why that little heart of yours is so stubborn that you've never given any guy a chance to take care of it."

She frowned at the labeling of her heart as "stubborn."

"Because I meet guys like Exhibit A," she replied with teasing judgment in her eyes.

It didn't take long for Tae Hyun to realize that she was referring to him as "Exhibit A."

His eyes widened in shock.

"*Me?*"

The look on his face said it all: he couldn't believe her line of reasoning.

Yoori nodded as if that was the obvious answer.

"What's wrong with me?" he asked defensively, the drunkenness in his eyes somehow escalating with unbridled passion.

It was probably because Yoori was close to being wasted by alcohol because she wasted no time listing her gripes about him.

"You're impatient, insensitive, sarcastic, blunt, argumentative, and more importantly...you're *mean*."

He made a rude noise. Snow fell off his face when he lifted a chin at her. "You just described yourself, Princess."

It was Yoori's turn to be defensive.

"How am I mean?" she asked, snow falling from her face as well.

"You're impatient, insensitive, sarcastic, blunt, and argumentative. As I recall from a reliable source, all those qualities equate to someone being mean." His eyes became more defensive. "And you're drunk, not blind. How can you say all those things about me when you're laying down on rose petals while being surrounded by snow and Christmas lights?"

Yoori grimaced in guilt. He had a good point.

"But you asked what was wrong with you!" she combated weakly.

Tae Hyun regarded her with judgmental eyes. "Now I know why you're single. You don't have a single romantic bone in your body."

Her mouth dropped at his blunt statement. "That's not true!" Even though it was, she wasn't going to give him the satisfaction of being right. Just because he could make her weak in the knees didn't give him the right to diss her nonexistent mating ritual skills.

"Do you even know how to flirt?" It was like he was jabbing her with an eraser. It wasn't enough to harm her, but it was enough to annoy the hell out of her.

"Do *you*?" It was a stupid question because she knew he could. He could do it well in fact.

"Do you really have to ask that?"

She closed her eyes in annoyance, heeding the fact that she shouldn't have asked him such a dumb question. Moving back on to the topic of "abilities to flirt," she said, "Well, of course I know how to flirt!"

"Prove it."

"P—Prove it?"

Tae Hyun nodded with a deviously seductive smile. "Prove it, Princess. Command my unyielding attention. Make me yearn for you. Make me wonder how I ever made it this far without you. Make me think about how miserable I'll be without you. Steal my stubborn heart."

"Wh—Why do you have so many bullet points?"

Tae Hyun closed his eyes in exasperation. "Just prove it," he said impatiently. "I dare you."

"Fine, I will!" Yoori shouted, though she didn't even know where to start. She took a moment to awkwardly stare at his smug face before she gave him a big fake smile, flipped her hair to the side and leaned just a little bit closer to him.

She'd show him...

"Hi, I'm Princess Choi Yoori," she said sneakily, happy that he would have to call her that name if he were to play along with the flirting. Her smile turned into a sexily awkward, but still somewhat sexy smile. "What's your name?"

"Getting attacked by ducks," he replied, holding in a chuckle of laughter.

Her sexy smile faded at the ridiculousness of his pseudonym. "You're 'Getting attacked by ducks'?"

The seriousness on his face remained. "Yeah...do you not like it?"

She spotted the challenging glimmer in his eyes. He was clearly trying to ruin her game.

That experienced bastard.

Well, she'd show him!

"No, no. I like 'Getting attacked by ducks.' I—" She halted and glared when she realized what he tricked her into saying. Not wanting to be made a fool and getting very impatient with him for messing with her, she shouted, "Give me another name!"

"Fine," he complied with a sheepish smile. "Then you can call me 'Sex.'"

Yoori stopped smiling at once.

"Which do you prefer, Princess Choi Yoori?" he prompted with a silky voice. He more than enjoyed the sight of her socially awkward self coming into play.

She gaped at him in bewilderment. "Do I prefer 'Sex' or 'Getting attacked by ducks'?"

She struggled to answer while trying to maintain her "game." There were no fruits of labor for her valiant efforts.

"I—I—I...Hey Kwon Tae Hyun!" she bellowed when she concluded there was no "game" to be saved. "How am I supposed to flirt when you're ruining my game?"

The nerve of this jerk!

"Okay, okay..." he mediated seriously. He rose up slightly, propped his elbow on the wooden foundation and rested his cheek onto one hand. He was gazing down at her directly now.

"Tae Hyun," he replied charmingly, ready to enjoy her efforts. "My name is Kwon Tae Hyun."

Pleased that he was being cooperative, she reorganized her thoughts and sported another sexy smile.

Round two!

She moved closer to where she was laying strictly beneath him. Staring up at him, she made sure the lashes of her big brown eyes would flutter every now and then to further exude the sex appeal she was trying to present. Apparently the effort gained its desired effect when Tae Hyun stiffened up marginally. He clearly realized she was a bit more aggressive than he originally gave her credit for. Though surprised, he seemed impressed with such aggressiveness. If she didn't know better, she would've thought he purposely led her down this topic of conversation with the sole intention of trying to get her to flirt with him...

"So Kwon Tae Hyun," Yoori began, making sure her sultry eyes held his. The snow and petals around her were definitely helping her appear more alluring. "Do you do all this for other girls often?"

"Only you, Princess Choi Yoori," he replied, his voice as alluring as ever. So alluring in fact, Yoori actually felt her heartbeat triple in speed.

Don't get flustered, Yoori, she coached herself. *Show him who he's messing with...*

Keeping composure, she grabbed a blue rose petal and continued with her plan. She was determined to make him flustered.

"Why only me, Kwon Tae Hyun?" she asked again, this time running the rose petal over his chest. Though he was fully covered by the black jacket, she could've sworn she felt his muscles tense up in exhilaration when she did this. His face, however, remained as composed as ever.

"Because you're worth it," he replied, lifting his hand up and allowing it to caress her hair. Then, he allowed his single hand to cup her cheek. His free thumb continuously caressed her cheek as she froze at his actions.

Sweet Jesus, how was she going to survive this?

"Tae Hyun," she began uneasily, her cheeks reddening against his gentle touch.

Damn him for flirting back.

"Yeah?"

"If I didn't know better...I'd think that you're smitten with me already," she bluffed easily, trying so hard to regain her composure. It was working slightly... but only slightly. "Are you sure you want to see me flirt? I might drive you insane."

His eyes sparkled at this proposal. "Do your worst, Princess."

"You're drunk, aren't you?" she accused, catching the sparkle of adoration in his eyes. "That's why you're looking at me like I'm candy."

"So what if I am drunk?"

She knew he had to be. That was the only reason why he would be so flirty and touchy with her. At least that was what she tried to convince herself of.

She didn't answer his question. She was still in competitive mode and her only goal was to win over him.

Her fingers found the zipper to his jacket. Helping herself, she started unzipping it. Very slowly, she allowed the tantalizing sound to ring through his ears before she stopped midway and allowed her hands to stroke the exposed area of his bare chest. He was wearing a white buttoned up shirt underneath and had left a few buttons undone.

"Has anyone told you how good looking you are?" She made sure her nails dug into his shirt when she asked this.

"No one like you," he replied, the composure on his face wavering when she moved her fingers about.

She knew this moment would be the perfect moment to give him a pick up line. "You're so hot, you'll burn me alive."

"We'll burn each other alive," he corrected, his breathing growing heavy.

"How is it possible that you don't have a girlfriend right now?" she asked, very much curious. He could have any girl he wanted. She didn't understand why he was still single.

He smiled, stroking her face. He didn't answer her question. He merely posed questions of his own.

"What would you do right now if I told you that you're the most amazing girl I've ever met?" She froze at his statement as his fingers ran through her snow-frosted hair. "Or if I told you right now that I've been so good all week because I wanted you to get your revenge on me for being your boss. That I wanted you to have your fun so that when this week ends, we can start over on a clean slate." His fingers moved along to her cheek, the flush of it heating up to its core. "Or what if I told you that I can't imagine life without you and that I've fallen for you?"

"I would have to test you to see how genuine you are," she replied, still in her flirting and competitive mode.

She was certain Tae Hyun was also in this competitive mode. She wasn't going to lose to him. She refused to. No matter how weak she felt, she wasn't going to lose to him.

"Test me?"

Yoori nodded, her head moving a couple of rose petals as she did this. "Short set of questions...bullet points..."

He smirked, knowing what she was planning on asking him. "Ask away."

Yoori smiled, allowing the silence to embrace them before beginning...

"Have I commanded your unyielding attention?"

"It's unwaveringly yours."

"...Made you yearn for me?"

"I've never wanted someone more."

"...Wondered how you came this far without me?"

"It was such a long journey without you."

"...Made you think about how miserable you'll be without me?"

"The thought rips me apart."

"...Have I stolen your stubborn heart?"

"Every inch of it, baby."

He answered every question without hesitation. The swiftness left Yoori overwhelmed with awe. He was amazing with his words, she'd give him that much. Even under acting pretenses, he was able to steal her breath away in more ways than one. His voice was also sexy to boot.

Damn him. Damn him for making her lose her senses.

While the silence and the grace of the snow suspended over them, Tae Hyun made sure to keep his enrapturing eyes locked with her for the entirety of the time they laid there. Seconds later, just when more snow began to descend upon them, he lowered himself, stopping only when his lips lingered above her yearning ones.

His warm breath hummed around her lips, leaving her breathless. She fought to keep her mouth from puckering up in anticipation. No matter how hard she tried though, she couldn't control herself. She was losing. She was losing to Tae Hyun's charms.

He dipped lower for her lips. "Have I stolen yours?"

Lost between a world of acting and a world of desire, Yoori's mind was entirely blank. All that she cared about were his lips. His amazingly gorgeous lips that were now descending down to claim hers.

Nothing mattered anymore.

Nothing mattered but him.

She parted her mouth right when their lips were ready to meet. She finally uttered words that would no doubt drive Tae Hyun insane.

"Every inch of—"

She was about to finish her sentence when something startling occurred.

Cracck.

Their eyes enlarged in sober urgency when they heard it.

Cracccck.

The sounds of wood cracking apart...

Craccccccccccccck.

The bridge was breaking apart!

"HAUL ASSSSSSSSSS!" they both shouted, awoken from their little dream world.

Tae Hyun grabbed Yoori's hand and without delay, they scurried off the deteriorating bridge like bats out of Wonderland Hell. Yoori screamed for dear life as they jumped back onto solid ground. Regaining their balance, Yoori and Tae Hyun watched in horror as the deteriorating bridge broke apart. The Christmas lights attached to it blinked in terror while the rose petals on it dove into the awaiting water. Shortly after, the sound of rumbling filtered into the sky and it was followed by a loud splash!

In a matter of seconds, the once solid bridge collapsed into the pond, splattered a billion drops of water into the sky, and submerged into the abyss before Yoori and Tae Hyun could even blink in disbelief.

It was long moments later, as the snow continued to peacefully frost over their heads and the pond remained as calm as ever with rose petals swimming above it, that Yoori parted her shocked lips.

"I think that this is a sign that we shouldn't hang out over a slew of water," Yoori said listlessly, clearly recalling the leaky boat incident at the lake house.

"One of these days," Tae Hyun provided mindlessly, his face pale from what just took place. "The world is going to drown us."

When Yoori gathered her senses and rationale, she turned back to Tae Hyun. He seemed to have also gathered his senses.

"I can't believe you took me out on a faulty bridge," she accused, the drunkenness returning to her eyes.

He gaped at her, the drunkenness also returning to him. "This is *my* fault?" Cursing in disbelief, he turned around and started to venture out of their secret garden. "I can't believe this..." he groaned to himself.

"This is the last time I lay anywhere with you!" she declared, following him as he travelled back out into the trees.

Apparently their little Winter Wonderland was more than over.

"As I seem to recall, the breaking occurred on your side. Why didn't *you* notice?" Tae Hyun accused.

"How could I notice anything when your drunken self was leaning over me? You were my distraction!"

"Distraction?" He nearly tripped over a tree branch when he shouted back at her. "Who the hell was running a freaking rose petal down my chest?"

"You dared me to be flirty!"

"I dared you to flirt. I didn't dare you to tease me!" His pace accelerated.

She jumped over a bush and snorted rudely. "I wasn't the only one teasing, Mr. Touchy Fingers!"

"Oh, here we go again," Tae Hyun stated, already running up a small hill.

Yoori was ready to yell something else at him until she saw that once he reached the top of the hill, he tumbled over slightly.

"Tae Hyun!" Yoori shouted, eyes wide with worry. Running up the small hill, she rushed to Tae Hyun, who was lying on his side on the ground. "Tae Hyun! Tae Hyun! Are you okay?" she cried frantically, turning him on to his back and gently slapping his face awake. "Tae Hyun!" she called, trying to shake him awake. "Are you okay? Wake up, wake up!"

Opening his drowsy eyes, he groaned. "Shit...I think I drank too much."

Her concern for his safety was mixed with lividness.

"You...you idiot!" she screamed, shaking him with worry still pulsing within her. If he couldn't handle the damn alcohol, why the hell did he force himself to drink so much? "Why'd you drink so much to the point where you can't even stand now?"

"I wanted to get you drunk," he slurred, his eyelids seemingly becoming too heavy for him.

"*Why*?"

"'Cause you lie too much when you're sober."

"I lie too much?" Yoori was flabbergasted. "What are you talking about?"

Rather than answering, Tae Hyun merely groaned in weariness. She realized then that he was a lost cause. She wanted to win and get the guy drunk, but she didn't want to take care of him.

Damn it. Damn the shittiness of her luck.

"Let's go home," she whispered, still trying to shake him awake. She made the effort to lift his arm up and wrap it across her shoulder. While holding him close to her, she stood up and allowed him to use her as a crutch to stand up.

"Can I sleep on the warm bed tonight?" he asked meekly, nearly tripping over when they began to walk out onto the pathway.

"Yeah, your punishment ends at midnight," she replied, finding it difficult to hold on to him. It didn't help that she was faintly drunk herself.

"Good," he conceded, his hands digging into his pocket for his car key. "Let's go home."

"You're not driving!" Yoori said at once, grabbing the keys from his grasp.

"I'm fiiine!" he slurred, trying to hold on to the keys but to no avail.

She made sure the keys were out of reach. "No! Friends don't let friends drive drunk!"

"What'd you just call me?" he screamed, his face grimacing when she referred to him as a "friend."

"I'm going to call Kang Min," she declared, ignoring him. Still holding on to him as best as she could, she took out her Blackberry and began to dial.

"Why?" Tae Hyun asked absently.

"So he can come pick us up...duh!" She grimaced at her usage of the word "duh." Apparently she had too much to drink as well. It wasn't enough to get her drunk off her ass, but it was enough to mess with her vocabulary and apparently give her mood swings with Tae Hyun.

"Oh..." Tae Hyun nodded before saying, "Well, call Jae Won too! Someone needs to take the Mercedes back!"

"Oh ho, ho, ho, yeah," she agreed, pressing the Blackberry closer to her ear. "I don't want to leave my poor baby here."

Tae Hyun narrowed his drowsy eyes onto her. "Hey Santa Claus, did you just call my car your baby?"

She paused before nervously laughing. "Err, I meant yours."

No, she loved his car and she definitely meant her baby.

Before Tae Hyun could call her out on her blatant lie, Kang Min had already picked up the phone.

"Hi Kang Min?" Yoori asked excitedly. She flinched at the sound of her own high-pitched, tipsy voice. She had never been drunk, but she could only imagine what an annoying drunk she'd be if she ever became one.

"Hello?" Kang Min's voice was groggy, like he just woke up.

"Honey, who's calling at this hour?" a soft voice asked in the background. It was Hae Jin.

Tae Hyun's brows drew together when he heard that voice.

"Who's that in the background?" Tae Hyun hollered, alarmed that the voice was so familiar to him.

"No one, no one!" Yoori said urgently, not forgetting that Tae Hyun didn't know that Kang Min was seeing (and sleeping) with his baby sister. Struggling to keep him standing, she led him toward the bench that lay on the pathway. "Go sit down, Tae Hyun."

"Yoori?" Kang Min asked, his voice more awake after hearing Tae Hyun in the background. "Are you still at the park with boss?"

After leading Tae Hyun to the bench, Yoori took a couple of steps to the side to speak privately with Kang Min. "Yeah, we're a little bit tipsy. Can you come pick us up?"

She heard him groan over the phone. "Ahhh, but I'm so lazy. Can you just call Jae Won? He's new in the gang. He should get hazed."

Yoori stifled a smile at Kang Min's readiness to throw his older brother under a bus. "Well, he'll actually be coming too because I need him to drive my baby— err—Tae Hyun's Mercedes back."

Kang Min laughed. "You're already staking your claim on his car?"

"It's a fine specimen," she whispered, gazing at Tae Hyun as he rested his entire body on the bench.

"Is that Yoori?" Hae Jin's voice asked, breaking Yoori from her momentary distraction. "Can I talk to her?" Hae Jin's voice was soft and excited.

"Not now, hun," said Kang Min. "I need to go pick her and your brother up."

"Aw, tell her I say hi," Yoori whispered, giggling as she made sure her voice was soft enough so that Tae Hyun couldn't hear while he rested on the bench.

"She says hi," she heard Kang Min relay the message. There was movement on the other line. Kang Min was already getting ready to leave. "Alright Yoori, I'll go pick up my fat ass brother. I'll see you and boss soon."

"Thanks so much!" she shouted, hanging up. She tucked the Blackberry back into her pocket and casted her gaze back to Tae Hyun.

He was sleeping peacefully on the bench. *Damn, he looks so cute sleeping like that*, she thought distractedly when she made her way over to him. She wondered what she would do with a drunk Tae Hyun while they waited to be picked up. She anticipated that she would've just sat there and chilled with him. Yet when she reached him, a wicked thought rippled in her tipsy eyes.

Tae Hyun was drunk and she *wasn't*.

Tae Hyun had lost control and she *hadn't*.

These two thoughts alone were enough to bring a crafty smile upon her face.

Screw watching Tae Hyun sleep! She was going to take advantage of him in his drunken state and she was going to enjoy it.

"You're merely at the end of your rope."

18: Borrowed Time

"Hey, you alright?" Yoori asked Tae Hyun, her voice purposely loud so that she would wake him up. She was so excited to take advantage of him that she didn't even know where to start. Perhaps she'd make him talk about his embarrassing memories? Or maybe she'd have him do something stupid? Oh the possibilities were endless!

Pulling up the hood of her jacket to block off the continuous cascade of snow, she hid a smile when he stirred from hearing her voice. The snow sleeping on him fell when he did this. Not fully asleep yet, Tae Hyun lifted his drowsy lids and stared up at her lethargically. There was anticipation in his riveting brown eyes. It was like he had been waiting for her to come back.

"Are you just going to stare at me all day or are you going to sit down?"

Yoori grimaced in annoyance. It was official. Tae Hyun was still mean as a drunk. No surprise there.

"Well, make room then," she ordered fiercely, waiting for him to lift up his head. "You're hogging the entire bench."

Silently heeding her command, he lifted himself up to give her room to sit. Beckoned by the free space that sprung up, Yoori sat down on the snow-covered bench. She watched as Tae Hyun continued to lift himself up. She thought he was planning to sit up straight beside her or something but instead, before she could even register what occurred, he fell backward. The back of his head gently landed on her lap. His eyes were closed, but there was a coy smile spread across his face.

He wanted this all along...

"Eh! What are you doing?" Yoori asked urgently, shocked by the sudden proximity Tae Hyun had to her thighs.

She felt her skin tingle while the scent of his cologne and heat from his body murmured around her. She swallowed convulsively, suddenly feeling dehydrated. Was it hot out here in Winter Wonderland or was it just her? Her eyes perused the white Winter Wonderland before her. The little balls of white puff were still raining down from the dark sky above. All the stone lamps, plants, trees, and dirt pathway that she had seen moments before they entered the secret garden were now covered with snow. The world around her was still cold and peaceful –

so it was *definitely* just her. She was the only one hot and frantic. All because of Kwon Tae Hyun...

"Tae Hyun, stop playing. Get off," she said sternly, though she made no effort to push him away.

"My head really hurts," he shared. He nuzzled his cheek on her thighs. "I need something to sleep on." He looked completely comfortable and at ease with himself as he laid there with his eyes closed, the snow swaying all around him while he slept on her lap.

"Do I look like your pillow?"

"My deliciously plump pillow," he amended with a smile.

She laughed quietly at his retort. She had forgotten that she was supposed to take advantage of him. It didn't seem like he was the type of drunk who would get easily swayed into talking about embarrassing stuff or doing embarrassing things anyway.

"You're such a bad assistant," she commented, stroking the snow away from his sleeping face.

It disturbed her with how much she enjoyed sitting there with him. She sighed. At least from this angle, she had a good view of his sleeping profile. It was sensual and sinful, just like every other angle on him.

"I always carried you in my arms when you were my assistant," he defended quietly, reminding her of all the times she fell asleep on him. "Just sit still. You're really warm. It's making my headache go away."

There was a subtle slur in his voice that told her he was still drunk. She smiled. It seemed like he was one of those drunks who was able to exercise a bit more control over their drunken state. Any bright ideas of taking advantage of him dissipated from her mind. If anything, it seemed as if he was taking advantage of her right now *because* he was drunk. She could never win with this guy, she thought as his breathing grew soft and the world around them silenced as if endeavoring to not wake him up.

Snow embellished the hood of her jacket while she watched Tae Hyun sleep. Every now and then, her fingers would stroke the layering snow away from his face. The snow was still falling strong, but not strong enough to make Yoori feel that they should take shelter under any roof. The atmosphere around them was nice—her sitting on a snowy bench, him sleeping on her lap and the Winter Wonderland around them covered with snow. She inhaled serenely, lost in her thoughts. She could only imagine what a nice picture this would be if she had a camera.

Everything was peaceful and quiet until a voice permeated the cold air.

"Do you sometimes feel as if you're living on borrowed time?" Tae Hyun suddenly asked, drawing her out of her stupor.

When she lowered her eyes, she was met with his awaiting ones. They were soft, filled with warm curiosity. There was no more drowsiness reveling in them.

"Borrowed time?" she asked, not certain with what he meant.

He nodded with a small smile. He further elaborated. "Like you were never meant to have certain moments in time, but you borrow them anyway, knowing very well that in the end, you'll have to return them to their rightful owner."

Perhaps it was because she knew it had something to do with her, but as she listened to his elaboration, she felt her heart grow heavy with eagerness. "How are you living on borrowed time, Tae Hyun?"

He stole a breath of silence to just gaze up at her, his eyes never appearing more innocent, genuine, and conflicted. Taking another minute as if to gather the strength his alcohol-induced body could give him, he explained to her what was on his mind.

"When I stole you from your world, I was never supposed to keep you for this long. You were never supposed to come this far. It was only supposed to be a temporary thing."

Her ears perked up in attentiveness. "What do you mean?"

"I only needed your assistance for a brief time," he slurred again, his eyes never leaving hers. "Just for a couple of things because I was really busy. It was never supposed to be for this long."

She swallowed tightly. She never knew she had such a short timeline when it came to working for him. "When were you supposed to let me go?"

"Do you remember the night when we went shopping and we both slipped in the grocery store? The night where I spoke to you about the two things that I wanted and I chose choice number one?"

Yoori nodded, clearly recalling the events of that night.

"I was supposed to let you go after my meeting with Shin Dong Min. I was supposed to return you to your world when I came back home that night – the night right before your initiation."

Okay, so he was supposed to fire her...

She was all ears. "What happened?"

It wasn't like Tae Hyun ever truly shared much about his thoughts to her. Even though he was all over the place with the things he shared, she didn't mind. She didn't mind in the least bit. She sighed. Thank God he was drunk on alcohol. He would never in his sober mind tell her all of this if he wasn't swayed by alcohol. And she was thankful. She was thankful that she had a chance to listen to all this.

She waited as he casted his gaze over to an undetectable part of the scenery. He contemplated her question. His eyes were dim when they recalled what took place.

"I came in and I saw you standing in front of the elevator, and I couldn't even fathom the thought of letting you go...at least not at that moment. It was funny because when I was on my motorcycle, I was so prepared to lay you off as my assistant and send you on your way back to the real world...but when I saw you, I figured we could just hang out for a bit before I let you go." He exhaled, a smile gracing his lips. "I continued to debate on this issue when we drove here for the first time that night. I was still thinking about it when I was holding you in my arms."

His smile grew slightly wider after he recalled something random. "Do you realize that you fit perfectly in my arms? Even though I'm the one holding you, I don't know why I feel safe and warm as well."

Yoori stroked the snow away from his profile as he continued.

"I decided that it couldn't hurt to keep you with me for a bit longer just because you have that presence about you that always leaves me yearning for more. There's something about you that just calms me and makes me happy. There's just something about you that makes me feel normal..."

His smile faded when an unpleasant memory materialized.

"But when I received that call from Ju Won, I knew I should've let you go that night. I should've *never* allowed you to meet them." He shook his head, silently scolding himself. "Yet when you threatened to run away again, I *still* wanted you. So, being as stupid as I was, I let you come with me...knowing the dangers involved with being around the Advisors."

"I insisted on going. It wasn't your fault," she provided once she heard the guilt in his voice.

She hated that he placed so much of the weight on his shoulders. She was an adult. It was her choice to go and it was no one else's fault.

"You didn't know what you were getting yourself into," he countered at once, his face plagued with remorse.

Another bout of silence overcame them. Tae Hyun stared at the falling snow. Yoori watched patiently. Tae Hyun didn't say anything, yet she could almost feel the overwhelming sounds of his thoughts. He was so tense as he slept on her lap, so troubled as he tried to organize his thoughts.

And then, as Yoori stroked more snow away from his profile, he spoke again, his soft and troubled voice stroking a nerve she never knew existed.

"When they trained us...they told us we'd become better than human—that we'd become Gods. They said that dependency on anything other than your family – your gang – would mark you as human...as weak." He swallowed roughly. "So I grew up having control over what I did. I never drank too much, never smoked, never did drugs, never gambled because I was too good for all of that. I was too good to be addicted to weakness. I was too good to be human." He smirked to himself, a self-mocking laughter following suit. "They never told us about that agonizing moment though...when your human self returns to you. People have a tendency to leave that part out when they are training kids to kill. They leave that part out as they watch you snap necks apart and shoot people without batting an eyelash."

He reverted his gaze back up at her. Yoori couldn't explain what was going on in her mind. She was so overwhelmed with emotions that she couldn't comprehend. It was like for the first time, as strange as it was, she felt like someone understood her. For the first time, she felt like she truly understood Tae Hyun.

He favored her with a smile, his eyes growing warmer with her holding his gaze. "I hate that I like being around you—that I'm addicted to you. I hate that even though I choose to accept this as my weakness, I continue to keep you around so I can continue to become *more* attached to you." His voice lowered with guilt. "I remember when I came home that night after your initiation. I remember walking into our room and seeing you on the bed. The bedroom was dark, but I could still see the light of your tears as you slept. I remember walking to your side of the bed and suddenly kneeling beside it. Something went off inside me when I realized that you had been crying."

He averted his gaze from hers, finding it difficult to keep eye contact as another current of thoughts coursed through him.

"Ever since I took over the Serpents' throne, I rarely show emotions for things, especially ones that involve feeling guilty and despondent – the weakest of all the emotions. I rarely show it because I don't get affected anymore. My soul has deteriorated from all the years of being in the Underworld that I thought I was past being affected by all those weaknesses...especially for someone who wasn't even my family member or a part of my gang."

His sad eyes met hers and at that moment, Yoori felt her heart grow heavier. She struggled to keep the tears from forming in her eyes. She could feel the pain that he felt and she couldn't help but be affected by it. How could she not be affected when it was Tae Hyun who was suffering so much by himself?

He continued to speak, the snow around them falling more fiercely.

"When I kneeled beside you that night, I didn't know what came over me. I didn't know why it pained me so much to know that you had been crying. I didn't know why it felt like someone had just ripped something out of me as I kneeled there beside you, wiping the tears away. I didn't even know how long I was beside you that night. All that I knew was that I was contemplating it again...letting you go before you got pulled any deeper into the Underworld...." He bit his lips. "But then, when I started thinking about that...the pain became more substantial. I still wanted you with me. I still wanted to be with you..."

A hint of warmness reveled in his voice. "That was why I took you to the lake house. I knew it'd help make you feel better if I took you away for a while—even if it was only for a short time."

A gust of wind whirled pass them and he snuggled closer to her. He held a bittersweet gaze, one torn between being thankful and being remorseful.

"From the moment you fell asleep on the dock, a big part of me knew I shouldn't have brought you—*us*—to the lake house. I knew it was a mistake when

I started opening up on the boat. I knew it was a mistake when we played the drinking game. I knew it was a mistake when we danced under that gazebo and I knew it was a big mistake when we—" He stopped, clearly recalling the most fundamental memory of the trip. "When we kissed."

Yoori's lips quivered at the mention of the epic portion of the trip. This was the first time either of them had brought it up since it occurred.

"After you ran off…I sat there on the railing for God knows how long. There was so much running through my mind, but the only thing…the only thing I knew was that I made the biggest mistake of my life."

When he caught the despondence in her eyes, he went on quickly, dead set on sharing everything with her.

"Yoori…" he began, his eyes never wavering from hers. "When I kissed you, I realized that I had never been as happy as I was at that moment. In all my years as a God…in all my twenty-three years of existence, I had never been happier than the moment I held you in my arms and kissed you. When I kissed you…I wasn't a God…I wasn't the King of Serpents…and I wasn't a crime lord…I was just Kwon Tae Hyun. There was no complexity to it. I was just Tae Hyun kissing Yoori. I was just a guy kissing a girl who drove him crazy. I was just a guy…who realized he has never known true happiness until that moment."

His gaze grew more poignant on her. Yoori struggled to steady her breathing as she listened to words that would forever engrain themselves into her mind.

"Do you realize how damning that is for an Underworld King? To realize that even as a God…he has never truly known heaven? To realize that the one moment he chooses to give into temptation…the one moment he chooses to be human…he found heaven? I couldn't speak to you afterward because I was still trying to wrap my head around everything that happened. I was still trying to figure out how I lost all the control I once had." He smirked at himself. "I figured I was just drugged emotionally…that all I needed was time and it would all fade away. I figured I'd find faults in you and you'd fade away and I wouldn't be weak anymore."

Another self-mocking laugh came before his next statement. "The world was cruel when it sent you out to the balcony to find me. It was so cruel when it sat you there next to me. I hate that no matter how hard I try to avoid you, all you had to do was blink and I'd give you all the attention in the world. I hated it even more when you told me you were An Soo Jin, when you told me that you were starting to remember everything again. I should've been happy then. I should've been happy when the world gave me the fault I wanted from you. You being An Soo Jin should've been the clincher for me. It really should've been. But…I never could've imagined the pain to follow when I wasn't disgusted, but worried that I would have to let you go now. It was then that I realized it was finally time to let you go. I have been living on borrowed time with you for too long and it was time to return you to the world I stole you from."

He took in a sharp, painful breath. "I never could've imagined how hard it would be to just walk away from you. How hard it was to see you in so much pain...how hard it was to ignore you as you followed me, trying to talk to me with your voice softer and more broken than I've ever heard it. I could've never imagined how heart wrenching it would be to open that door and have you tell me that you needed me and beg me not to leave. Those seconds I stood there with my back turned to you were the most miserable seconds of my life. The hardest part was just walking away, knowing that I couldn't take care of you when I should've—when I wanted to."

Yoori took in a sharp, agonizing breath and continued to listen.

"You would think after all that, it would've been easy for me to leave, but I just stood there. I just stood there thinking about nothing but you." He briefly closed his eyes. "I knew as I stood there that I was screwed. I knew then that I had fallen and was no longer a God. I knew as I fell beside that wall, the pain ripping me apart like none I had ever known, that I was finally human again. Against all odds, I fell for the biggest weakness—the biggest temptation—of all and became human again."

He opened his eyes and called for her.

"Yoori..."

"Hmm?" she asked, still dazed with everything she had just heard.

Tae Hyun wasn't the only one who was drunk on that bench. Yoori was drunk too. Drunk on alcohol and apparently on Tae Hyun. Her mind was everywhere yet nowhere.

"You're one of my best friends...you know that, right?" he slurred, a smile taking over his now carefree face. "I care about you...*a lot*...so don't you ever forget it."

She nodded dubiously, thankful that they had returned to the carefree portion of the conversation. God knows she needed to absorb everything when she was sober, not when there were endless amounts of alcohol swimming inside her.

"And you're one of mine," she said genuinely. "You know that too, right?"

"How much do you care for me?" he asked, gazing up at her with anticipation.

"More than I should," she said honestly, stroking the piling snow away from his profile.

He nodded, more than satisfied with her answer. He closed his eyes and began to nuzzle closer to her.

"Do you see what I mean now when I say that I've been living on borrowed time?" Though his eyes were closed, he was still speaking directly to her. "This is your chance now, Yoori...your choice. If you want to go back to your world, I'll take you back now. I'll send you to another country and I'll make sure no one in the Underworld is able to find you. I'll make sure you're safe...even if I'm not there to watch over you. You just have to let me know though...do you want to go back to your world?"

"You're so drunk right now, Tae Hyun," she commented delicately, not wanting to answer his question.

"I'm not," he insisted, his eyes still closed while he laid one side of his cheek on her lap. "You didn't answer the question..."

She sighed, stroking his defined jawline. "We're both living in the same world, Tae Hyun. If you return me...you still have to come with me. Do you know why?"

"Why?"

She smiled sadly. "Because you're not the only one living on borrowed time...I am too. Why do you put so much pressure on yourself to be the one to let go when you have none of those powers in the first place?"

He was quiet, listening intently as she went on.

"You don't get to decide whether or not you can keep having me around. *I* decide if I want to stay or not and if *I* want to leave so badly, then I'll run away again...it's not that hard."

"You'll always come back to me," he warned with a charming smirk on his sleeping countenance. "You know why, right?"

"'Cause I'm your boomerang?"

He shook his head. "'Cause you fell for me...just like I did for you."

Panic blared inside her at his blunt answer. The walls around her began to form when she realized how true that statement might've been.

No.

She couldn't do this. She couldn't fall for Tae Hyun. No. They would never work out...no.

Trying so hard to maintain her composure, she stiffened up, swallowed tightly and said, "Well, that was an arrogant statement on your part."

"It's alright, assistant," he easily appeased in his drunken state. "It's okay that you fell for me. You're actually pretty amazing to have held out for so long."

Her heart raced some more.

She couldn't have this.

Enough was enough!

"Get off, get off, get off," Yoori demanded, attempting to push Tae Hyun's head off her lap. "I refuse to listen to all of this. You weren't even drunk when you said all of that, were you?" she accused mindlessly. Her main intention now was to get away from this topic. "Which parts were lies and which were truths?"

"No, I was just kiiiiidding!" Tae Hyun slurred, referencing to him saying that they fell for each other. He was not even listening to Yoori's accusatory questions. She kept trying to push him off. He pouted and fought to sleep on her lap. He nearly fell off before a panicked Yoori caught him in time. She wanted him off, but she didn't want him to get hurt.

"Damn it! Why did you drink so much?" she shouted, knowing now that everything he said was a mixture of truth and over-exaggerated drunkenness. He was messing with her. Even when he was drunk, he was messing with her.

"I can't believe you're so drunk that all you want to do is sleep on my lap and joke about us falling for each other. Don't you know that's a no-no in BFF land?"

"Are you cussing at me?" he suddenly accused, his eyes widening in outrage.

"Am I—wh—*what*?"

"What the hell is 'BFF'?"

"Oh! 'Best Friends Forever,'" she explained. If this were any other situation, she would've laughed at him for his cuteness in not knowing the acronym. However, this was definitely not the time considering she had other worries coursing through her already heavy mind.

"What the fuck..." he remarked bewilderingly. "Why would I want to be your best friend *forever*? I thought it was just a stage."

"A—A stage?" she stuttered dubiously. "Like there's another level that comes after that title? What the hell did you think comes after being my best friend?"

"You're so confusing," he replied, already closing his eyes and falling back asleep.

"Hey Kwon Tae Hyun! You know that you're talking to Choi Yoori, right?" she shouted, so confused as to what was going on. Did he know he was speaking to her and not someone else? "You're not harboring some pent up feelings for some other mystery girl in your past and telling me all this stuff because you're confused, right?"

Silence met her.

He had already fallen asleep.

Now it was Yoori who was left downright unsatisfied.

Bitterness gushed through her and her heart raced in confusion. Her eyes held his sleeping countenance in its gaze, never faltering its attention to anything else. Yoori concluded that it was probably better that he had fallen asleep. She would be able to have some peace to herself and her own thoughts.

She thought back to his words.

Everything that he said...were they really true or were they just exaggerated lies?

The silence mocked her as she waited for an epiphany.

Nothing came.

The only one who could really answer her question was asleep and who knew if his drunken self would even remember saying all that stuff to her?

She sighed, stroking the snow away from his sleeping face and from his jacket. She casted her attentive gaze over to him again. She gradually found herself lost in just staring.

The snow was still falling gracefully around them. The soft glow of the moonlight speared dimly through the white tipped trees, its affectionate rays kissing over Tae Hyun's perfectly crafted features.

One would think Yoori would use the peaceful time wisely and use it to recollect her thoughts. Yet, all she could think about was him, the handsome devil sleeping like an angel on her lap.

Kwon Tae Hyun, Kwon Tae Hyun, Kwon Tae Hyun....

She was lost, so lost in an enrapturing daze...

Before she could catch herself, her fingers had already ventured on to the contour of his jaw. Ever so slowly, she slid her finger down the defined line and rested it on the skin of his smooth cheek.

Yoori couldn't decide why, despite all her gripes about him, she was so fascinated with Kwon Tae Hyun. *Do I like him because he's handsome or do I like him because he's Kwon Tae Hyun?* The question may appear redundant, but it posed as a significant query for Yoori. She had always thrown her attraction for Tae Hyun as nothing but a crush because he was more than easy on the eyes. She accepted the fact that she may be a bit superficial, but if that were the case, then wouldn't she have the toughest time choosing between him and Ji Hoon? Her attachment, loyalty, and feelings were all given to Tae Hyun and to this day, she didn't know why he commanded such an unyielding attachment from her.

There was an off-handed charm that Tae Hyun possessed, which made him more alluring and addicting for Yoori. She thought about all the qualities he possessed—good and bad. Tae Hyun could be sweet when he wanted to be, but he could also be a jackass if he wanted to be. It was funny because she actually felt that she could handle the asshole side better than the sweet side of Tae Hyun. At least with the asshole side, she could have enough sense to argue back. But on reserved occasions where Tae Hyun threw his charms at her, there was never a moment where Yoori didn't feel weak in the knees and completely lose all her senses.

She exhaled, her eyes straying on to the contents of his sexy lips.

What an enticing moment.

My, my...how inviting they look under the glow of the soft moon...

A naughty thought occurred to her. She knew she shouldn't do it because it was like playing with fire, but yet...she had the biggest yearning to do it. Why not, right? He was asleep. It wouldn't count as anything.

Yeah, her confused and tipsy self urged. Her eyes were still marked on those enticing lips of his. Maybe it wouldn't hurt if she did it fast. It wouldn't hurt if she just—

Without a second's hesitation, Yoori, with all her inhibition thrown into an abyss, leaned forward and pecked his tempting lips with hers.

It was quick with intention, but powerful enough by nature to send a fire to sprout on her lips.

She gasped quietly and straightened herself up. Her eyes still locked on him, she gulped in disbelief at what she had done. Her lips burned, begging for more of his lips as her heart pounded fiercely against her chest.

She just took advantage of Tae Hyun and kissed him!

She tried.

She tried so hard to bite her lips to prevent a smile from overtaking it, but her nerves were too overwhelmed. It was nice. The stolen kiss was so nice. It was so nice that she wanted another one, but with whatever strength she had left, she somehow managed to anchor herself from giving into another round of temptation. She had already taken advantage of Tae Hyun's drunken state…surely she couldn't do it again.

The implications of her actions only rained down on her when she caressed the short strands of his hair, her eyes feasting on the features of Tae Hyun's countenance.

Her thoughts ran amuck while she admired him.

He looked just like a fallen angel while he slept. Even the moon favored him as it kissed his smooth skin. It all felt like a dream, like a complete dream until—

"Can I have another?"

Shit! Yoori cursed in her head, panicking when she realized that he was awake. He wasn't actually asleep?

"Huh?" she managed to squeak out, her eyes enlarged in urgency. She gaped at his still sleeping countenance, unsure if she just heard right.

"No, no, no, don't stop…another," he murmured again, his eyes still closed.

Her heart breathed in relief when she realized that he was only dreaming. "*Thank you*," she mouthed while gazing toward the sky. "Thank you so much."

"BOSSES!" Yoori heard two voices call out from the side.

At the sound of the voices, a once dreaming Tae Hyun woke up to see Yoori staring down at him. She tried her best to stay relaxed when she observed that, through the drowsiness in his eyes, he was actually staring at her strangely.

He looked unsure as he continued to stare. And then, just as more snow graced his face, he parted his lips and said, "Did…did you do something to me while I was sleeping?"

"Excuse me?" she spluttered out, snorting as if she couldn't believe how ridiculous he was being—even though she was worried shitless. "What would *I* do to *you*?"

She bit her lips, but immediately stopped when she saw that Tae Hyun was biting his lips too.

He was still staring at her suspiciously.

Was it just her or was he eyeing her guilty lips?

Great.

This was her karma for taking advantage of her BFF.

No more drinking for her!

"They…they're here!" she announced, desperately trying to change the subject.

She was saved when the brothers, both dressed in jeans, black puffy jackets, and beanies, finally reached them. The brothers looked sleepy and a little bit bitter to be in the park. No doubt they were reminded of the pond they fell into.

"Hey Boss Kwon, you alright?" Jae Won asked warily when he saw that Tae Hyun was still laying his head on Yoori's lap.

"Did we interrupt something?" Kang Min asked, heeding his brother's apprehension when he concluded that the scene before them looked suspiciously provocative.

"Tae Hyun's drunk and I'm a bit tipsy," Yoori explained, wanting to telepathically hug them for coming just in the nick of time. Heroes. That was what these two were. They were her heroes.

"I'm not drunk," Tae Hyun stated defensively. He lifted his head from her lap and sat upright on the bench. "I'm just tipsy too."

Kang Min smiled and then looked at Yoori. "Yeah Yoori, boss *rarely* gets drunk. He can handle his liquor."

Yoori let out a round of laughter when she thought about how ridiculous Tae Hyun had been acting throughout the night. "Oh you didn't see how drunk he was when he was speaking to me earlier—"

Yoori only quietly stopped laughing when she realized a dawning of realization had illuminated in the brothers' eyes when they heard what she said.

The brothers quietly averted their gazes over to Tae Hyun, who was sitting pretty on the bench. His lethargic eyes met their questioning ones.

It was an odd scene for Yoori because she didn't quite understand what was happening. It was like the brothers and Tae Hyun were having a telepathic conversation while they stared at one another in silence. Was it one of those guy things where they didn't have to say anything yet they completely understood each other? It seemed that way when the brothers finally blinked in comprehension.

Then, as if nothing occurred, they turned back to Yoori with a hidden smile on their faces and merely said, "You ready to go?"

Still flustered as to what had just taken place, she turned to Tae Hyun. He was staring at her with innocence in his eyes.

"You ready?" he also asked.

She nodded apprehensively. She was ready to go, but she was not ready for whatever it was that Tae Hyun had planned for her.

As innocent as his eyes appeared, there was still a sultry light within them that left her on the edge of her seat. If her womanly intuition concerning the matter was any indication, then the interesting night she was having was far from over. If anything, the *epic* portion of their already eventful night was ready to take place.

"Rest assured..."

19: Confessions of a King

The ride back home was an uneventful one. Afraid that they'd throw up in Tae Hyun's Mercedes, both Yoori and Tae Hyun insisted that they ride in the backseat of Kang Min's blue BMW instead. That suggestion was much to the delight of Jae Won, who was psyched that he got to drive the Mercedes and was able to get out of riding with the drunk people. It was a suggestion that was much to the bitter dismay of Kang Min, whose eyes nearly watered when he heard the news that the drunk people were riding in his precious car.

Kang Min, clearly afraid that driving too fast (and using his brakes too much) would trigger the barf-mode in his passengers, made sure the ride was safe and smooth. After a couple of friendly green lights and several stoplights, they reached Tae Hyun's apartment just as the snow stopped falling. Jae Won, who had gotten to the apartment before them, ran out of the car to help carry Tae Hyun out after they parked.

The journey back up to the apartment was smooth too.

As soon as they helped Yoori and Tae Hyun into the elevator, Yoori informed the brothers that she could take care of Tae Hyun and thanked them for all their help.

Casting an unreadable gaze over to Tae Hyun, who was listlessly leaning against the elevator wall, the brothers gave another hidden smile and waved goodbye to Yoori, who was too sleepy to notice that any strange interaction had occurred. Once they reached the apartment, Yoori directed Tae Hyun, who still seemed like he was having trouble walking on his own, to the shower so that he could wash up and perhaps clear his drunken mind.

Yoori changed into her black tank top and her drawstring pink and white plaid pants while Tae Hyun showered in the bathroom. While brushing her teeth over the kitchen sink, Yoori cast her thoughts back to the naughty kiss she stole from Tae Hyun. She bit her lips, feeling the remnants of the heavenly fire she felt when she gave him a quick peck. She was so drunk and she couldn't even deny it anymore. Why the heck would she steal a kiss from Tae Hyun if she weren't drunk?

She frowned and scolded herself. She was such a bad girl. She was thankful that the night was ending. They could just sleep and have everything return to normal in the morning. Who knew what a sexually deprived Yoori would do to a fox like Tae Hyun if the night continued on? She would probably continue to take advantage of him...that much was for sure.

"Hey!" Yoori shouted, knocking on the bathroom door when she felt that Tae Hyun was in there for far too long. "Are you okay in there?"

"Yeah," he answered through the door. He switched off the shower.

Relieved that he was okay, Yoori walked back into the kitchen and opened the fridge. She reached in to grab a water bottle for the night. Just as she drank from the water bottle, she heard the bathroom door open. Tae Hyun walked out with a white towel wrapped around his waist.

Yoori felt the perversion in her eyes grow at the fleeting sight of this. Shaking her head like she was shaking the sinful bug off of her, Yoori turned back to the fridge, closed it, and sat on the sofa. She drank from the water bottle and waited to make sure she gave Tae Hyun enough time to change into his pajamas before she walked into the bedroom and prepared for bed.

"Hey!" she hollered, tossing the water bottle back into the fridge. She took a couple of strides forward and waited in the hall for his answer. "Are you done changing?"

"Come in," he answered through the closed door.

"Okay." She turned the doorknob and walked in.

Boy oh boy was she ready for bed—*OH MY GAWD!*

Yoori nearly had a heart attack when she walked into the bedroom and saw that Tae Hyun was still dressed (or underdressed) in his white towel. He was standing beside the window, his arm lifted up as he dried the short strands of his hair with another white towel.

Yoori's eyes instinctively ran over his deliciously sculpted arms, his marvelously chiseled chest and rock hard abdomen. He stood before her in obliviousness of the perversion enrapturing her mind. It didn't help that his entire body was still misty from the shower he just took.

She was still so drunk, she was sure of it. She was sure of it because she couldn't even be subtle and take her eyes off of him.

*My goodness...*Yoori fought for breath, her eyes feasting on the sight before her.

Sex.

Kwon Tae Hyun was made for sex.

She swallowed convulsively at the living aphrodisiac that was now staring at her with curiosity. He no longer appeared drunk, merely amused with her unabashed gaping.

Good lord, she thought desperately.

How would she survive this?

"Err, are—are you feeling better?" she stammered clumsily, trying so hard to act normal.

Why? Why didn't he change? Why must he torture her like this? Didn't he know that she wasn't a good girl? There was no innocence in her eyes whenever she gaped at him!

"A lot better," he answered easily. He tossed the towel he was using to dry his hair aside. The muscles on his body rippled teasingly when he did this. It nearly drove Yoori insane.

Making his way toward her, there was a look of concern, coupled with amusement, on his face.

"Yoori, are you okay?" he asked delicately, clearly noticing how odd she was behaving.

He reached her before she was able to back away. She could've sworn his eyes were sultry, teasing even. She thought about it again and quickly vetoed the idea that he was giving her the "sexy bedroom eyes." She was just going crazy because he was half naked and she was still drunk with perversion.

"I—I'm okay," she stuttered, nearly keeling over when she felt the warm heat from his body whisper around her.

He was too close. Too close and it was too damn uncomfortable for Yoori.

Not believing her, he placed a warm hand over her forehead. She went still. Goodness, if she wasn't exercising so much control, she would've ran her hands down his amazing body already. If only he was drunk too…then she probably would've taken advantage of him at this moment. But it seemed like he was no longer drunk. It seemed as if—

"Is it just me, or are you hot right now?" he asked.

Mystification besieged her.

The tone of his voice, coupled with the gaze in his eyes, gave it away.

Yoori gasped mentally when she realized that the sultry gleam in his eyes wasn't her imagination. He was actually looking at her like that!

"I – I don't know," Yoori replied, moving away from the touch of his hand. She retreated and stopped only when she backed into a wall, not realizing that it may have been a bad idea to trap herself between a wall and Tae Hyun.

"Yoori…you're acting really strange," he commented, tilting his head at her. His voice was supple, sensual even.

"I—I think I'm really drunk," she confessed, trembling in her stance.

Holy crap. What the hell was going on with her?

"Are you really?" He casually drew closer to her. There was much interest when he asked this.

She nodded, hiding her hands behind her back to keep from reaching out and molesting Tae Hyun.

"How do you know you're drunk?" he inquired.

"Be—Because..." she answered, her eyes strategically placed on the tiles so she wouldn't have to look at him. "You look really different to me right now."

He smiled uncertainly. "I—I look different?"

She nodded again, contemplating running into the bathroom so she could take a cold shower. She wanted to, but she didn't want to make a scene. She laughed fretfully, desperately wanting to appease the sudden burst of desire that was scorching through her.

"Okay, you're going to laugh when you hear this. Hahaha um...um...right now...I think it's seriously the alcohol in me...but I don't know...it feels like you're hitting on me right now. Which I know is *not* happening. So I'm just a bit freaked out with myself right now. That's all...heh, heh, heh—"

"I *am* hitting on you," Tae Hyun remarked without any hesitation.

WHAT?

Her eyes nearly fell out of her sockets.

She did her best to ignore the thumping of her eager heart. "You...you're joking, right?"

He shook his head, his body already drawing closer to her. When there was a considerable space between them, he placed a hand on her hip and pulled her just a bit closer to him.

"I have a confession to make."

"Wh—What is it?"

"I've been holding back on you," he whispered, his free hand running up her bare shoulder. He ran his fingers down from her shoulder, to her arms and all the way to the palm of her hands. He continued this hypnotizing motion as they spoke.

"Hold—Holding back on what?" she stuttered.

She was downright stupefied with all that was happening to her. She was going crazy with the enrapturing touch his dancing fingers were performing for her arms. His riveting brown eyes stared deep into hers, the adulation within them making it appear as if his eyes were only made for her. It was then that she knew what it was he had been holding back on. He confirmed her speculations by verbally answering her.

"All these months...I've held back from you. I've wanted you for God knows how long, but I've held back because I thought it was merely infatuation." He smiled, stroking her hair before lifting her chin up with his fingers. "I'm seeing things clearly now and I've decided that I'm not going to hold back on you anymore."

216

He sighed and rested his hand back on her hips.

Yoori tried not to whimper in pleasure from his casual touch. With her confused eyes on him, she did her best to maintain the control that she was slowly losing.

"I've decided that I want you, Choi Yoori," he continued, his expression desirous and serious. "I want your warmth, your body, your essence, your heart – all of you. There will be no more beating around the bushes, no more subtleties. I want you and there's no more doubt in my mind about that."

"This…this is so wrong," Yoori spluttered out, the socially awkward side of her coming out.

He smiled seductively, anticipating her being uncomfortable with his forward nature. He lightly grabbed her shaking hand and laid it above his bare chest, over his heart.

Yoori fought for air when he did this.

Air!

Where the hell did all the air go?

If Yoori thought Tae Hyun was good at seduction before, she was in for a hell of a show now…

"Was it wrong when we kissed at the lake house?" he asked delicately, dipping down and nipping his nose with hers, never kissing her yet attracting her lips like magnets. His warm breath lingered around her, enticing her further.

Yoori restrained herself when she saw that her lips were following his as his nose nipped hers upward. She could feel her lips yearning for his. No. It was *burning* for him.

Damn her weak lips, she cursed in her head. Damn her weak body!

He continued, his voice smooth and sexy, stroking over her senses. It was like his voice was just made for her and her alone.

"Was it wrong when we were about to kiss on the bridge?" He nuzzled his chin against her neck, leaving her with the strongest desire to bring her hands up and just hold him there. He moved his lips against her ears. "The only thing that's been wrong," he began, his warm breath caressing her skin, "is us denying each other all these months."

"This…this is only infatuation," Yoori struggled to answer. She combated the urge to wrap her arms around him and kiss him until the fire burned her alive. "Your words right now are just infatuation."

"It's not."

"Yes, yes it is!" she yelled, wondering why she had no strength to just push him away. "This…this isn't right, Tae Hyun. We're not meant for each other."

If her words spiked any pain within him, he surely didn't show it. In lieu of saying anything, he merely held the wrist of her hand, which was still pressed firmly above his chest—above his heart.

"This…" he began, never flickering his gaze from her, "is all yours."

She could feel the heat from his skin and the beating of his heart, and she wondered if it was true.

As if anticipating her doubt, he moved her hand downward, slowly—*very slowly*—past the muscles of his chest, past his breathing abdomen and stopping only when her hand reached the hem of the towel that wrapped around his waist.

"All of this...is *entirely* yours."

With her hand still hanging over his towel, he released his hold on her and allowed her to make her own decision on what she wanted to do next.

"Make the first move, Yoori," said Tae Hyun, his voice fine and smooth like seductive chocolate. His voice, however seductive it was, was also veiled with a light of apprehension. He wasn't going to force her to do anything she didn't want to do. It was her choice. All her choice...

"Just let me know," he stated gently, his desire for her driving her crazy as well. "Let me know that you want me just as much as I want you and I'll take care of the rest."

He smiled warmly at her, taking her breath away with the mere handsomeness of his stare.

It was working, he was breaking through the barriers of her senses and he was commanding the attention and desire of every fiber on her body. All she wanted to do now was rip off his towel.

Damn him, she thought. Damn him for making her lose control. Damn him for making her do what she was about to do. Damn this hot bastard for making her give into her temptations, especially with the last of his words that drove her over the edge.

"I promise it'll all be worth it. Every splendid, euphoric and magical moment of it will be worth it. You'll have me, baby...all of me."

Dazed with disjointed thoughts, Yoori found herself mindlessly touching his abdomen, her shaky fingers floating around the towel for God knows how long. The silky heat of his skin embraced her touch and warmed her senses. Her fingers murmured over the tight packs of his stomach, moving up and down between each packs. Breathing was definitely becoming an issue for her. Trying to breathe regularly while also trying to stay alive from the hormones raging through her was suffocating her. Then, as the fire seared within her, she traced her fingers over his torso, the journey of which led her eyes back to the hem of his towel and the little knot that held it up.

She could only imagine what lied beneath all that cloth.

All the while she did this, Tae Hyun stood still, his body breathing quietly, encouraging a still dazed Yoori to continue. His voice was barely audible, yet she could hear him say, *Touch all you want...*

How much longer could a girl resist the temptations of a guy who had driven her crazy since she first met him? Yoori wanted to think that she could hold out longer because she didn't want to be that weak girl who gave in so easily, especially to guys like Tae Hyun who had more than his share of beautiful girls. She wanted to be guarded, but her mind's desires and her body's desires were two separate things that were at war at the moment.

"This...this is all a dream, isn't it?" Yoori asked, her heart growing heavy. There was a tremendous surge of hope soaring through her, telling her it was actually happening. Nevertheless, with a heavy heart, Yoori pushed those thoughts aside. There was just no way this could be real. No possible way.

How was it possible that Kwon Tae Hyun was throwing himself at her and how was it possible that she was ready to accept this offer?

"It's a dream, Yoori," he confirmed, his head nodding steadily.

Her heart dropped to her stomach at the news. It *was* a dream after all.

He reached out to her and began to run his fingers through her hair, his expression adorned with longing.

Yoori bit her lips in agony. Even if he only was a figment of her perverted imagination, he definitely knew how to make a girl go crazy just by staring at her.

Yet...something was unsettling for her as she felt him stroke her hair.

"Really?" she asked again, her voice soft with remnants of melancholy.

But something was odd. His touch felt so real.

He nodded again, causing all the hope to deteriorate from her confused body. "This is all a dream, Yoori. None of this is really happening."

Her breath lodged in her throat after hearing his reply. She knew it. It was because she was too drunk.

"So what's the harm in us doing what comes naturally if this is all a dream, right?" he suggested seductively.

Yoori was ready to nod in agreement when she detected a certain mischief in Tae Hyun's voice. *What the?* Without another thought, she abruptly lifted her groping hand off the silk of his abs and grabbed a handful of his right bicep. Granted there was no fat for her to pinch, there was enough muscle for her to at least squeeze as hard as she could. And that was what Yoori did, she pinched Tae Hyun like he was a cute fat kid.

"Ow!" he roared, pulling his tensed bicep away from her pinch. "What are you doing?"

"I was making sure if this was a dream or not!"

He gaped at her incredulously. "What the hell? Why didn't you pinch *yourself?*"

"'Cause I didn't want to hurt myself!" she shouted back, realizing now that everything was truly happening and that Tae Hyun was lying to her. She gaped at him with a mixture of horror, disbelief and drunkenness. "You...you..." She pointed accusingly. "You were trying to trick me!"

A smile graced the sexy curves of his lips. He tilted his head at her with guiltless charm. "You think, babe?"

Yoori's heart fluttered at the smile he presented her. Why did he have to appear so dashing whenever he called her "babe"?

"Why'd you try to trick me?" she asked, trying to sound infuriated when she was only confused.

He shrugged carelessly. Sighing with boredom, he reached a hand out and started playing with the pink strings that held her pajama pants up. She froze instantly, afraid that the slightest movement would have her pajama pants falling faster than the speed-of-light.

"Wouldn't you be more inclined to follow your inner desires if this was a dream?" he asked ingeniously, slowly undoing one string. One string was left to work alone as the puny knot helplessly held up her pants.

"So you were telling me it was a dream so I'd ripped your towel off?" she asked, pushing herself against the wall like he was holding a gun to her stomach. Of course, she wouldn't dare say that a gun would turn her on as much as Tae Hyun.

"No," he replied, tugging at the final string that held the knot for her pants. "I was telling you it was a dream so I could rip *your* clothes off."

Oh no! Yoori gasped inwardly, feeling the tingle stream through her quivering body. That really turned her on!

And then, much to her horror, he did it. He pulled the other string, his eyes glittering as if he was expecting his birthday present to appear before him.

Yoori held her breath, expecting a whiff of cool air to touch her skin. Surprisingly, all she felt was the same reserved warmth. Confused, she stared down. She saw that the elastic band was still sturdy enough to hold her pants up.

"What the fuck, Yoori," Tae Hyun complained, clearly pissed that the pants didn't fall according to plan. "You should cut those strings if they don't even help hold your pants up. It's misleading..."

"It's for stylistic purposes," a drunken Yoori explained before it occurred to her that Tae Hyun was actually trying to strip her naked!

Though it was impossible for her to go anywhere, Yoori pushed herself harder against the wall as her defense mechanism. Acting just like a scared child, she brought her hands up and covered her face, only unveiling the brown orbs in her eyes through the spaces between each fingers.

"Tae Hyun! You're so drunk!" she cried desperately. "You have to stop playing! I'm *really* drunk and I'll rip off your towel if you don't stop this soon!"

"You think I'm drunk right now?" Tae Hyun began, gently grabbing her wrists and pulling her hands down from her face. "I've never been more sober in my life."

"But at the park—you—you were slurring—and you couldn't even stand by yourself—"

He sighed at the confusion in her voice. "If you knew that I was sober the entire time, would you have listened to all my confessions?"

The murky confusion streaming in her mind cleared at his simple question. His confessions…his confessions at the park. The confessions she played off as insincere because he was drunk and the ones she was afraid to take seriously because it meant that she would have to confront certain things that she didn't want to confront.

"Would you have listened to everything I had to say, without running away or trying to change the subject?" he asked, his eyes noting that there was fear in her tentative eyes.

No, Yoori answered in her mind. She scratched her head briefly, trying so hard to reorganize her drunken thoughts away from her sober thoughts.

Shit.

It wasn't working. Everything was mixed together. Damn. How she wished she didn't drink so much. She apprehensively played with her nails and avoided eye contact with Tae Hyun. He was still standing in front of her, looking as tempting as ever. Just then, another important tidbit filtered into her already stupefied mind. She gasped. The park bench!

She gazed up at him worriedly. "Were…were you actually asleep while we were sitting on the bench?"

A coy smile spread across his face. "I was falling asleep," he drawled out before adding, "But then something woke me up."

Heat reddened her already blushing cheeks. "Something…something woke you? So – So you were pretending to dream?"

She cursed in her mind, somehow already knowing the answer just by analyzing Tae Hyun's sneaky face. Why did it suddenly feel like someone had just stripped her naked and threw her out into a stadium filled with millions of Tae Hyuns? How mortifying!

Rather than answering, Tae Hyun simply released his hold on her wrists and laid both of his hands flat against the wall behind her. With his strong arms to either side of her, he leaned in, his enrapturing cologne filling bliss in her nostrils. Temptingly, he maneuvered himself so that his lips were hovering above hers.

Yoori bit her lips to keep from instinctively puckering them up for him.

"You stole something from me, Princess," he stated simply. The scorch of desire enhanced his voice, mesmerizing her. "Give it back."

"Give…give it back?" she stuttered, blushing even more.

She shook her head at the command. How the hell did this tease expect her to kiss him again? She was only brave enough to do it when he was asleep. Now that he was wide-awake, gazing at her with those sex eyes of his, Yoori knew she couldn't do it. She could already hear his critique in her head: *"Your kiss was salty, just like last time."* Yoori shuddered at the thought. Damn it. The first time she did something naughty and stole a kiss from a guy, she got punished. The world sucks.

"You...you take it back," she countered. There was no way she could kiss him again—even though she really wanted to. She didn't have the nerve to do it again. Yoori, as blunt as she may be at times, was very socially awkward when it came to romantic things pertaining to the good-looking opposite sex.

Amusement enveloped his eyes. He raised a curious brow. He had no problem teasing her further. "You were the one who stole it, Princess. It should be you who returns it."

Yoori stubbornly shook her head. The fiery blush on her cheeks resembled that of a red rose. "Take it yourself or leave me alone and go tease someone else."

He frowned. "You still think I'm playing around?"

She nodded, though she knew better. It didn't help that she was not only afraid of him now, but it also didn't help that she was becoming awkward and was yearning for him.

"You really believe that, Yoori?" he asked, his cunning voice now a soothing whisper. He leaned in and nipped his nose with hers, causing her to hold her breath as she bit her lips harder to keep from being magnetized to his lips.

"I...I...I..."

It was official.

She was now a babbling buffoon.

Even in her wildest fantasies, Tae Hyun didn't get *this* sexy and irresistible. Was it because he was actually this sexy or was it because she was drunk? She wanted to think the latter, but deep in her desirous heart, she knew better. Tae Hyun always had the charms. Apparently the tease never showed up until this fateful night.

"You really can't see how much I want you right now?" he continued. "How much I want to rip those clothes off of you? How much I want to throw you on that bed? I want you so badly, I swear I'll die from the need unless I can have you."

"Oh Jesus Christ, Tae Hyun please stop this," Yoori cried, nearly falling to her knees when the implication of his words seared through her. "I'm so socially awkward right now it's not even funny!"

It was getting harder; it was getting so much harder to resist Tae Hyun. God help her, she was so caught off guard with everything that she felt like wax. She was melting under the fire that exuded out of him and she resented that she *liked* the feeling. It was at times like this that she hated her own body for reacting the way a woman should when an attractive guy hits on them.

With her back still pressed against the wall, she unknowingly wrapped each of her hands around his arms, her nails digging into his biceps. The purpose was to hold on to him to keep her from crashing to the ground. Surely it would be a horrible idea to fall to her knees while Tae Hyun was only wearing a diminutive towel over that sinfully enticing body of his. But good heavens, the feel of his warm muscles under her hold was only doing worse things to her body.

"Please stop," she breathed out weakly. The air around her was not sufficient enough to keep her sane. "This is crazy, Tae Hyun! We...we can't do this."

"You're not curious, Yoori?" he crooned, nipping his nose with hers and pretending that he didn't hear her plea.

Yoori felt her lips part in eagerness when his nose tempted hers. Who knew nose nipping could be so tantalizing?

Tae Hyun went on, further driving her crazy. "I just told you that my entire body is yours and you're not curious?"

He pulled away from her, allowing air to fill the space between them. He lifted his hands off the wall and grabbed hold of both her hands. He pulled them off his biceps and instead brought them to his stomach. Laying her hands flat on the hard plane of his abdomen, he moved her hands downward, slowly allowing her to revel in the feel of the muscles beneath her hand. His stomach muscles contorted and rippled under her touch. It seemed to Yoori that Tae Hyun knew well that her weakness was his abs and he was damn well ready to use it against her. Being the perfect tease that he was, Tae Hyun stopped the trail once her hands touched the small knot that held his towel up.

"You're not curious about what else belongs to you?"

By now, Yoori didn't even know how it was possible that she was still breathing. She was losing her breath and was very close to losing her mind.

"Sweet merciful Lord, why are you so hot?" The words came out before she had any chance to filter it. It came out and it couldn't have been more loyal to how she truly felt.

Pleased with what he heard, Tae Hyun grinned bashfully. This acknowledgement was all that he needed to know that she was melting in the palm of his hands. He persisted with his teasing prompts, evoking more whispers of possibilities to swim through her foggy mind.

"Can you imagine it, baby?" he asked, pulling her to the side so they could have the perfect view of their beckoning bed.

Baby. She never thought she'd be one of those girls who appreciated it when their lovers called them by that name so affectionately.

"Can you imagine me and you on that bed?" Before giving her even a semblance of a chance to try and regain her sanity, his lips found her ear. He nibbled on it with care and continued to speak, his hot breath intoxicating her senses. "My lips on your naked body...your hands running over mine...our inhibitions shot to hell while I worship every inch of that beautiful body of yours? Can you see your nails clawing at my skin? That pretty little voice of yours screaming out my name as you beg for more? It'll be amazing. It'll be magic, baby. Timeless magic."

"Just—Just—*Just do it then,*" Yoori voiced breathlessly.

And clearly, that was when she lost it.

It was hopeless to deny it anymore and she knew it.

How could she not want him? How could she not want any of the things he was offering? She was after all merely a mortal girl. How could she deny someone like Tae Hyun, who seemed to have the persuasion and charisma of an epically amazing sex demon?

"Why are you torturing me?" she begrudgingly whispered when she felt him draw his hovering lips away from her.

His poignant gaze returned to her unhappy ones. He took stock of the desperation in her eyes. "I have to know if you want it as much as I do," Tae Hyun said instantly, his eyes swirling with need. He cupped her flushed face, his thumbs moving over her lips. "I want you. I want you so badly that I'm burning right now. But I won't force anything on you. I won't do anything to you unless you're ready—unless you want it as much as I do."

If she had energy, she would've snorted in his face. "My body is on fire right now and you don't know if I want you too?"

He grinned at the frustration in her question. "You're hot. I know that already."

She wanted to roll her eyes at the suggestiveness in his double meaning statement. She resisted the temptation. She instead rested her hands flat against his chest, causing him to catch his breath in surprise.

What a horrible addiction he had become to her.

Screw having control over her feelings.

Tae Hyun wasn't the only one who could tease and she'd be damned if she allowed him to be the one who dictated how this night would proceed.

"What do you want me to do, baby?" she asked, leaning closer to him.

Before she could comprehend what she was doing, Yoori had already circled around him, her body more alive than she had ever known it to be. Alive with needs, wants, and desires of its own. How easily was it for her to just go from a babbling buffoon to a woman tempting the one who was trying to seduce her?

She rested her flushed cheek against his back, embracing him from behind. She ran her hands up from his abs and stopped only when she reached his chest. His heart thumped wildly against the skin of her hand, telling her that her touch was driving him insane.

"Do you want me to tell you that you drive me crazy too?" she asked. "That I've never in my life felt more like a woman as I'm standing here right now, stroking your body like you actually belong to me?"

It was the first time where she felt her heart ache when the words finally came out of her mouth. It felt like a ton of brick had just fallen on her. She remembered now why she was so hesitant with going on this road with him. How foolish it was for her to drown in her desires and completely forget the reality of the situation. How foolish it was for her to follow the commands of her body—*and quite possibly her heart*—instead of the rationale in her mind. Tae Hyun and her...they would *never* work. Everything was against them ever working out.

"I do," he breathed out roughly. His eyes fluttered shut. It was as though he was using all the control within him to restrain himself from whipping around and just wrapping her into his arms. "All yours...only yours."

There was such genuine conviction in his voice that she wondered if he knew what he was saying.

She shook her head.

"You're so drunk right now. Just like me, you're so drunk..." she went on swiftly before Tae Hyun could get a word in. "Not drunk on alcohol, but drunk on the belief that we would actually work."

She closed her eyes, burying her cheek closer to his skin. God, she loved the feel of him; she loved his warmth. It was like fire tasting rain. She was dying under his touch, but it couldn't be more euphoric for her.

"Why do you torture me like this," she murmured, repositioning herself so that her forehead was now resting on his back.

She endeavored to diffuse the aching in her heart. Her efforts failed as his skin further tempted and tormented her. This man would be her downfall. He would be her epic downfall.

"Don't you know what a mistake all of this is?"

Despite the pain in her words, the desire on her lips overshadowed the urge to just pull herself away from him. Instead, she raised herself on her tiptoes and kissed his shoulder blade, no longer able to resist at least feeling his skin against her lips. And God, she loved it. She loved it so much that she continued to place kisses all along his spine, stopping only as she slowly returned her heels back to earth.

"*You* torture me," Tae Hyun whispered back, his voice hoarse. He breathed in roughly.

Now it was finally a courtship between a man and a woman.

"Everyday since we've met, you torture me. I've never in my life held this much control and I've never in my life wanted someone more than I've wanted you. Now I'm bearing my soul to you and you tell me this is all a mistake?"

He whipped around, facing her agonized eyes.

"What do you want to happen, baby?" he asked delicately, his hands finding the hem of her tank top. Slowly, he began to lift it up, the palm of his hands whispering up her bare hips along the way.

Her breath lodged itself in her lungs. Her body heated up in anticipation. If this continued on, she would die from lack of air before the night was over.

While he lifted her tank top like he was lifting up curtains, Tae Hyun lowered himself to his knees. His eyes reveled in the temptation of her soft skin as it became revealed. He didn't allow the fabric of her top to ride higher than he needed it to rise though, despite the fact that Yoori knew, from the shaking of his fingers, that it was only because he was restraining himself from completely ripping the shirt off of her. He stopped, only allowing the fabric to raise and stay just above her navel.

"Do you want all of this to merely be a dream?" His poignant eyes stared up at her as his hands caressed the flat plane of her stomach. "Do you want me to just get dressed?" He lowered his eyes from hers and leaned in. He kissed the area around her navel. "Do you want to just ignore what's happening right now?" His hands explored the exposed area of her stomach and settled onto the small of her back. "Should we just get into bed, sleep on our separate sides, and act like nothing happened?"

"Yes," Yoori answered without delay. The answer speared itself like knives into her soul. She was stuck. Stuck between heaven and hell. She wanted him, yet she didn't want to want him.

Though lost in limbo, Yoori allowed her mind to override her body's needs. Using all that she had, she pushed herself away from Tae Hyun's hold. It was instant. The coldness of winter instantly enveloped her once she left his warmth.

"Let's forget any of this happened," she said sternly, pulling the hem of her top back down. While doing so, she wondered to herself how she managed to garner such a harsh tone when all she wanted was to throw herself at him.

All of this temptation would've been easier if he took the decision away from her—if he just grabbed her and pressed his lips against her mouth. It would be easier to melt that way. She would never be able to blame herself for anything and she would get to have him.

Tae Hyun rose to his full height. Although there was need in his gaze, there was also annoyance. He didn't like that she drew away from him.

Despite the difficulty of everything, she continued on like she was angry and annoyed. "If you won't take me yourself, then you can just go to sleep dreaming about it. I won't be the one to start this mistake. *I won't*." Even though she really wanted to. She desperately wanted to pull the towel off and worship his body like it was meant to be worshipped.

"You're being a fucking brat-ass prude right now," Tae Hyun bit out, showing very openly how unhappy he was that she had the nerve to pull away from him.

A forest fire lit inside her.

Even under the veil of thick sexual tension, Yoori and Tae Hyun still managed to argue about the most ridiculous of things.

"And you're being a disillusioned, horny snob," Yoori retorted, her argumentative side surging out of her. It was mixing with the desire she had for Tae Hyun. Fire mixing with fire. It was something that would be her undoing. "Did you really think it was going to work? Seducing me while you're only in your towel?"

"Seduce?" He shook his head in hilarity. His laughter stroked over the coldness of the room. "No baby, the towel was to tease you. The merchandise beneath it was the good that would've 'seduced' the living hell out of you."

"You're such a slut," Yoori insulted, growing hotter for him.

Clearly offended, Tae Hyun gaped disbelievingly at Yoori's labeling of him. He scoffed, muttering a curse to the ceiling.

"Yes," he agreed with scorn. "I'm a slut. I'm a slut for not sleeping with other women since I've met you. I'm a slut for being solely devoted to you and I'm a slut for trying to squash the unbearable sexual tension that has been floating around us since we've met." He cursed to himself again at the ridiculousness of her definition of "slut." "I can't believe the state that I'm finding myself in right now."

Resentment adorning his visage, he narrowed his furious eyes onto her. "You know what? I'm going to un-slut myself." He motioned his hands up and down his body. "I take it back. *None* of this is yours," he declared angrily. "There. I'm a prude just like you now."

Yoori's mouth hung open. Possessiveness overpowered her, acting like gasoline to the fire already scorching within her. She pointed at him in outrage. "Y—You can't take it back. You gave me that—*all of that*. It's mine."

He was no longer listening to her. He simply drew past her and headed straight for the drawer that held his pajamas. "It's cold. I'm getting dressed."

Her angry eyes followed him like a hawk. "Kwon Tae Hyun! Don't you dare put on your clothes while you're talking to me!"

"Try and stop me, *Princess*," he dared with male arrogance. He pulled the top drawer open and reached in for his clothes.

"KWON TAE HYUN!" Yoori shouted with rage.

Any sense of her control obliterated at Tae Hyun's dare. Whipping around with wrath, the next thing that happened occurred so fast that Yoori didn't even realize it happened. Before she could stop herself, she had already sprinted toward Tae Hyun, lifted herself in the air and then jumped on him.

As if expecting her to do this, he easily caught her as she wrapped her legs around his hips.

This was the part where Yoori knew that she had lost her mind. Encircling her arms around his neck, she dove her lips for his and instantly felt a tsunami of pleasure overtake her. A flash of white-hot sensation cascaded over her as she kissed Tae Hyun like there was absolutely no tomorrow.

A victorious grin waltzed across Tae Hyun's face. He held her against him with eagerness.

"You know I was kidding right, babe?" he asked in between their ardor kisses, subtly revealing that he had purposely planned this argument with her to get her fired up. "Everything's still yours."

"Mine," she stated territorially, not even listening to him. Her fingers combed through the short strands of his hair in fervor. "All mine," she continued, apparently not only getting drunk off the bottles of alcohol she drank earlier, but more so off Tae Hyun's addicting kisses.

"All yours," he vehemently agreed, their kiss becoming more intense. He held her tighter against him. "Only yours."

It was only minutes later, when she felt her lips grow numb, did she pull out of the kiss. Revelation dawned on her.

"You planned this all along, didn't you?" she accused, gaping at him with the fires of desire still dancing in her eyes. Her chest was heaving up and down, synchronizing greatly with Tae Hyun's chest.

The sexy curves of those lips formed into a devilish smirk. The sight made her grow hotter with yearning. "You think after months of being with you...teasing you....I won't know what to do to get you to pounce on me?"

"You tricked me," she said in abhorrence.

He chuckled darkly. "No, my sexy little kitten, that was called foreplay." A wicked glint sparkled in his eyes. "*Now* it's time to play."

Next thing Yoori knew, she was bouncing on their bed. Tae Hyun laid above her, showering her with kisses around her neck while moaning into her skin.

Months. After months of ignoring the ticking time bomb of the sexual tension that surrounded them, Yoori and Tae Hyun were now feeling the effects of the bomb as it detonated all around them.

The world was a kaleidoscope for Yoori—a kaleidoscope of heat, desire, passion and most importantly, pleasure. Squirming and whimpering in Tae Hyun's hold, all she knew was pleasure. Pleasure and magic. Blurred with nothing but need, Yoori wrapped her arms firmly around his neck, pulled herself up, and then violently pushed his back against the headboard of their bed. A loud thud sounded when the back of Tae Hyun's head collided with their bedframe. Instead of screaming out in pain, Tae Hyun's countenance merely contorted in approval.

With her bent thighs on either side of his legs, she rose up an inch higher and continued to kiss him like she was a super vixen.

Clearly turned on with the aggressiveness that Yoori displayed, Tae Hyun smiled in childish excitement. He continued to kiss her with zeal, his hands holding on to her hips with the utmost care.

Lost, so lost in everything, Yoori was only able to regain some fragments of sanity when she bit his lower lip in need. She needed...she needed something to help with all of this...

"Cuffs," she commanded, her lips eagerly finding his earlobe. She nibbled on it like she was a hungry little kitten. "The handcuffs. Take them out."

"The...the handcuffs?" he asked breathlessly, his chest heaving up and down with exhilaration. Tae Hyun, being as shocked as he was, gawked at Yoori in astonishment. It was clear by the gaze in his eyes: he didn't realize that she was *this* kinky.

"Holy fucking shit!" he cried once she found the sensitive area of his earlobe and began to nibble more roughly. "God, you're going to kill me," he whispered, lost in his own ocean of pleasure.

"The cuffs…" she whispered into his ear. Her lips lowered from his sensitized earlobe, to his perfectly structured jawline, then to his neck, and finally resting on his shoulder.

She needed those cuffs…

Before Yoori could even endeavor to stop it, she had already bared her teeth and bit into the skin of his shoulder. God help her, she wanted him so badly that she could eat him alive. If it was anyone else, then Yoori was certain that biting into skin would cause a guy to scream out in pain. But Tae Hyun was different. He didn't scream out in pain. He merely moaned in approval.

"*Now*," she demanded for the handcuffs, going crazy with just being in his arms.

Heeding her command, but not wanting to release her body from his hold, he struggled to embrace her with one hand while mindlessly reaching his hand out to the counter beside the bed. Pulling the top drawer out, he blindly reached in to retrieve the handcuffs. While doing so, his face was contorting in pleasure from the bliss Yoori was bestowing him.

She had just relieved his shoulder of her kisses and was now venturing lower, kissing the warm skin on his chest, traveling her kisses down to the muscled packs that lined his abs. One hand caressed his torso while the other stroked his biceps with love. If the look on his face was any indication, then it was clear that Yoori was driving him over the edge.

"Tae Hyun," she cried, kissing the last line of packs before the muscles traveled under the veil of his teasing towel. "I can't take it anymore." She pulled herself back up and found his lips again. "I need those cuffs *now*."

Encouraged by the plea in her voice, Tae Hyun, being as disoriented as he was, was still trying to kiss her and blindly find the cuffs at the same time. A groan of relief tore from his chest when he finally ripped the silver cuffs from the confines of the top drawer. It had been a while since the cuffs made an appearance in their bed and it seemed that he was more than excited about the prospect of using it. He handed the cuffs to Yoori and pulled her closer to him. He dove for her neck, showering her with adoring kisses that merited whimpers from her lips.

Disoriented with everything, Yoori struggled to pull his exploring hand toward her. After long seconds of trying to retrieve it, and while trying to keep herself from fainting at the love bites Tae Hyun was giving her, Yoori was finally able to cuff his left wrist.

"Oh God, Tae Hyun!" Yoori cried once Tae Hyun started to nibble on her earlobe, nearly causing her to faint from all the pleasure. Damn, why did he have to know where all her weaknesses were?

Breathing sharply, she finally raised his hand up with the cuff and was finally able to cuff the other brace to the bedpost. Relieved that she was finally able to cuff him, Yoori gave into her inhibitions and found herself lost in nirvana. Their lips found each other's again, her hands and Tae Hyun's one free hand traveling all throughout the bare corners of their bodies with passion and care.

Just a bit more, she told herself. *Just a bit more and then I'll—*

And then, before a moan could escape her lips, Yoori abruptly pulled herself out from the kiss, fell backward on the bed, bounced off, and fell to the floor where she was hyperventilating like she had just ran twenty miles. She kneeled there, her hands lying in front of her like she was worshipping a God.

She gazed up at Tae Hyun. He was gaping at her in dismay.

"Oh shit," Tae Hyun cursed once he focused his eyes onto the cuffs imprisoning him to the bed. He just realized that Yoori might not have been as kinky as he led himself to believe.

"Yoori," he prompted in alarm. "Please don't tell me you're doing what I think you're doing…"

Pulling her jelly-like legs up, as they were still succumbing to the aftermath of the pleasure Tae Hyun had placed them through, Yoori stood up regrettably.

"I'm so drunk right now, Tae Hyun," she whispered, her eyes narrowing onto his naked upper body with lust. "I've never lost control like this. You have no idea how much I want you right now. I think I would've raped you if I didn't manage to hold on to some control and cuff you to that bedpost."

"Yes!" he shouted, agreeing with her. "Yes!"

She gawked at him strangely, the desire having yet to leave her body. "I don't need you to agree with me that I was about to rape you."

"No, I'm saying 'Yes,'" he clarified in aggravation. He rose to his knees and tried to pull against the cuff on the bedpost. His efforts were fruitless as he was still stuck there. "It's not rape if I say yes and I'm saying YES."

"I—I'm sorry," she replied, still determined to keep him cuffed so he wouldn't be able to touch her or tempt her further. As long as she was away from those seductive lips of his, she would be able to retain some control.

"Yoori, please don't do this," Tae Hyun pleaded, desperation rippling in his voice. "Don't tempt me like this and then just leave me cuffed to our bed…"

Yoori's heart broke at the plea in his voice.

Her eyes traveled from his pleading face to the scrumptious body that called out for her touch. Tae Hyun being cuffed to that bed, more than ready to bring her all the pleasures in the world, looked just like a delicious aphrodisiac that was being presented as a sensual offering to her. He was like chocolate and she was like a cute fat kid on a diet. Oh how she was dying to just jump on that bed, pounce on him again and devour every inch of that amazing physique of his.

But she couldn't.

This is my karma for kicking a fucking duck, she declared remorsefully, thinking back to what occurred earlier in the day. She had lost control and kicked an innocent duck in front of a cute fat kid. Now it seemed that karma had just returned and it was biting her in the ass. Yoori was ready to cry as she backed away from him. She got ready to excuse herself out of their bedroom so she didn't actually rape him while he was cuffed to the bed.

"Tae Hyun," she began while he fought the grip the cuffs had on him. He was going crazy with trying to free himself. "For what it's worth, you didn't have to seduce me. I would've ripped off your towel as soon as you turned away from me."

"Oh fuck, don't say that," Tae Hyun groaned, clearly regretting wasting so much time with the teasing and the seduction when he could've just turned around and permitted her the opportunity to rip off his towel.

No doubt, if it was any other time, then he would've had the energy to break the bedpost, run to her, grab her, and throw her onto the bed. But Yoori knew despite his strength, Tae Hyun was too frazzled with everything to successfully direct his energy into breaking anything.

"We can discuss this further in the morning...when we're both sober," she continued, her hand finding the doorknob. She was still drunk and she was sure the pleasure from Tae Hyun's kisses had completely overshadowed the alcohol that previously inundated her body.

"Yoori, don't do this," he gritted through his teeth as he watched her pull the door open. Her remorseful eyes were still on him. "Come back here and be with me," he coaxed, his chest rising up and down with frustration. "You don't belong anywhere else but in this bed, *completely naked*, with me."

Her heart stopped beating at the sexiness in Tae Hyun's distressed voice. Maybe it wouldn't hurt if she just...

"I hate you! I hate you! Why are you so fucking hot, you sexy bastard?" Running like a little cheetah, she jumped back onto the bed and fell into his embrace again. She attacked his lips with hers. His free arm hooked around her, holding on to her as they grew lost in the desperate kiss.

"Un-cuff me...un-cuff me now, Yoori," he urged, slanting his head to deepen his kiss with her. "Un-cuff me now. You know you want to be in this bed with me."

"I—I—Oh God, Tae Hyun," she struggled to voice between their kiss. "Tomorrow...I'll un-cuff...you...tomorrow."

Right before Tae Hyun could protest her decree, Yoori pulled herself away from his tightening embrace, fell backward and effectively screeched in pain when her butt collided with the cold tiles.

"Ow! Ow!" Yoori cried, rubbing her butt after she rose to her feet.

"Holy fucking shit," he moaned in self-pity. He closed his eyes in exhaustion. "I can't believe this is happening to me."

Yoori wanted to cry. She missed being with him already. She was drunk in the worst way possible. The large consumption of alcohol was more than clouding her judgment and the charm Tae Hyun was throwing at her was turning her on in ways she didn't know was possible. She had to leave and she had to leave *now*. Otherwise, she'd really end up spending the night screaming his name.

"Choi Yoori!" Tae Hyun growled, nearly going crazy as he watched her retreat like a scared little kitten toward the door. "Don't you dare walk out that door! I swear to God if you walk out, I'm going to spank that pretty little ass of yours so hard you won't be able to walk for a week!"

Oh goodness gracious, that should *not* have sounded so hot.

"Stop turning me on!" Yoori shouted desperately, her hands finding the lock on the doorknob. If she didn't lock this door, then it was almost guaranteed that she would run back inside later and just fall right back into his seducing arms.

"Yoori! What are you doing? Why the hell are you locking the door?"

"So I won't be tempted to come in and rape you later on tonight!"

"*What?*"

She didn't give Tae Hyun a chance to change her mind.

Yoori quickly slid behind the door and pulled the door close. She soon realized, just when the door clicked close and the last of Tae Hyun's words filtered into the hall, that it might have been a *very* bad idea to lock the door.

"HOW THE HELL ARE YOU GOING TO COME BACK INSIDE AND UN-CUFF ME IN THE MORNING?"

Uh oh.

Squeezing the knob with her hands, she struggled to open the now locked door. Oh man, oh man. How was she supposed to go back in? She kept trying to open it but it was useless. There was no getting inside unless she figured something out. Morning. *I'll do it in the morning*, she appeased herself, already feeling tired from everything that took place. She would do it in the morning when she wasn't so drunk.

"Tae Hyun!" She stood closer to the door. "Just go to sleep. I'll figure out a way to get to you in the morning!"

She pressed her ear against the door and heard nothing but his angry grunts. She knew then that he was pass talking to her. His only concern was trying to un-cuff himself from the bedpost. She shook her head at his resilience. Quite tired as the alcohol from her body had fully immersed her senses, Yoori quietly backed away from the door.

Yoori was beside her drunken self. She couldn't believe she just gave up on having amazing sex with Tae Hyun. She couldn't believe she just gave up on something that thousands of other girls would die for. Yoori was sure of it, she was going to regret this in the morning and this knowledge in it of itself would be the worst hangover of her life.

Retreating into the cold living room, she pitifully grabbed the purple blanket that Tae Hyun bought for her and curled up on the lonely couch. She rested her eyes and dreamed about embracing Tae Hyun. She wasn't sure who she tortured more tonight. Despite appearances, she was positive she tortured herself more than she ever tortured Tae Hyun. At least the hot one got the warm bed as opposed to getting the lonely, cold and uncomfortable couch.

Yoori groaned in misery. With the bitterness set in her, Yoori forced herself to fall asleep before she found herself succumbing to the urge to grab an ax and break through the door so she could actually bring her desires to fruition and make love to Tae Hyun like they were energizer bunnies in heat.

What a hell of a night that would've been, she thought bitterly before another worried thought streamed through her mind.

She had a bad feeling already.

She should definitely get some sleep because it was going to be a hell of an experience when morning arrived. Because heavens help her, who knows what Tae Hyun would do to her once she un-cuffs him in the morning.

"You will not always be this powerful."

20: Morning Seduction

Yoori dreamt that she was in bed with Tae Hyun, sleeping as he held her close to his chest, embracing her with his warmth. She could feel his beating heart as her rosy cheek laid upon him, her mouth so close to his skin that she couldn't help but press her lips into the pectoral muscle beneath her face.

A quirk of a satisfied smile appeared upon her sleeping face. She could've sworn she felt "dream Tae Hyun" exhale in bliss when she did this.

Wanting to further molest "dream Tae Hyun," Yoori permitted her hand to roam up his body, causing satisfied murmuring to escape from the deep recesses of his chest. She moved her slender fingers up to his neck, moved along to his shoulder, and murmured down to his biceps. Yoori felt the butterflies quake in her tummy when she felt his muscles tighten at her every touch.

Inspired by the pleasurable effects all this molestation was having on her "dream Tae Hyun" and herself, Yoori gradually moved her fingers over to his abs—the tight abs that she loved so much. Flattening her hand on to the hard planes, she gradually moved up from the lower packs to the upper packs, reveling in the feel of him breathing in pleasure. Once her hand reached the upper packs, Yoori allowed her hand to venture lower again. Lower and lower and low—

It wasn't until she felt a hand grab her wrist, and stop her fingers just beneath the skin at his lower abs, did she realize that this dream may be a *bit* too realistic for her...

"Stop you little tease. You drive me crazy enough."

This was all that Yoori needed to hear to realize that none of this was a dream.

Snapping her eyes opened, her frenetic heart skipping more than a couple of beats, she was horrified to find that she was actually sleeping with Tae Hyun and that she was truly harassing him in reality.

"Oh shit," Yoori cried out. She was set to propel out of bed like a rocket—that was until Tae Hyun held on to her wrist, grabbed her by the waist and pinned her to the bed.

He rose above her. His gorgeous face peered down on her while the sun hovered into their bedroom, kissing the exposed area of Tae Hyun's shoulder. He propped himself above her, his elbows on either side of her. Amused with her behavior, he grinned lazily at her.

"How...how did I get in this bed?" she asked earnestly. Her heart was thumping so hysterically that she was sure it would pop right out if she didn't get answers soon.

She paused.

She didn't break in to rape him, did she?

Yoori moved her hands underneath the little purple blanket that was still covering her. She touched her stomach and legs. She still had her clothes so raping him wasn't a possibility. Whew!

"I carried you in," he replied easily, virtue radiating in his voice. Even when his eyes were teasing, he could still exhibit such innocence with his answer. He made it sound like he rescued her from an orphanage somewhere in the storm.

Still flustered, she asked the obvious question. "How...how did you get out of the cuffs?"

"Magic," he answered simply, his eyes rising up to stare up at the cuffs in question.

Yoori wanted to yell at him for his stupidity in always giving her that answer, but she made the executive decision to refrain from yelling at him or bringing up the cuffs. It was more than likely that she would end up staring at the cuffs too. And someone help her, she didn't need to be subjected to that temptation. She could already feel her body warm up at the mere thought of seeing it. She couldn't believe she actually used a pair of cuffs to restrain this sex demon in bed.

Dazed with lethargy and confusion, her gaze involuntarily shifted onto the small office desk in the further corner of their bedroom. Her eyes rounded when she saw that Tae Hyun's teasing white towel was hanging off the chair. She then noted that she could feel his body heat. Because the purple blanket was still covering her, she couldn't feel much of him on her. All that she knew was that he was shirtless and the big comforter veiling over him hid any further knowledge to whether or not he was fully naked.

A gush of panic heaved through her all the same, acting as a catalyst for the stilling of her already frantic heart. Her eyes returned to Tae Hyun. His enrapturing brown eyes stared coolly down at her. He knew that she noted he was no longer wearing that sinful towel.

"Please tell me you're not naked under the comforter right now."

There was hope in her voice. She was worried that if he were really naked, then it would just lead her down another path of sexual temptation. Truthfully, she didn't want to deal with it in the early morning. It didn't help that she didn't have the excuse of "being drunk" to use as her crutch. She could kill herself. Would a drunk recall everything that occurred the night before? Apparently she wasn't a piss drunk. She was still a rational drunk. This realization scared the hell out of her because she realized that she jumped on Tae Hyun because of her desires, not because the alcohol clouded her better judgment. What a damning thing to realize in the early morning when the sex God himself was teasing her again.

"What if I am?" he drawled lazily.

Yoori gasped. "Are you?"

He shrugged idly. "I just showered. That towel was irritating me. This little minx that I was trying to seduce last night was supposed to rip it off so I could play with her. The girl instead tricked me, chained me to a bed, and left me to die here as she went to sleep on a couch."

He shook his head. His eyes turned bitter at the reminder. No longer keen on beating around the bushes, Tae Hyun carried on with the confrontation Yoori was sure he had been dying to have with her.

"I can't believe you did that," he confronted heatedly. "I mean…I *seduced* you last night. I've never had to seduce any girl in my entire life and I actually seduced you. I even called you 'baby' countless times." He cringed at the word. "Do you know how much that word makes me feel nauseous? I never call anyone 'baby.' I feel like I'm whipped every time I say it, but I say it because I know that you get turned on by it. And what do you do? You made me think you were going to have sex with me, you cuffed me to a bed, you ran out on me begging you not to go, you locked the door, and you slept on a couch instead."

He frowned, his eyes becoming more offended than bitter now.

"You slept on a *couch* instead of sleeping in the same bed with *me*," he reiterated to Yoori as though she had committed some sort of blasphemy and missed Sunday church. "It's official, *Choi*. You really suck at life."

"Don't call me *Choi* like that, *Kwon*," Yoori retaliated by shoving his shoulder. The aftermath of a crazy night aside, Yoori wasn't about to just lie down like a weakling and have him pick on her. "If you don't like calling me 'baby', then you shouldn't have started it last night. I can't help that I react to it because I know that your sorry ass hardly say anything sweet to me unless you're trying to bed me. *And…*" she added, bitterly raising an index finger. "*And* you got me calling you 'baby' last night too. Ugh, I can't believe you, you perv! How could you do this to an innocent, susceptible drunk girl?"

Granted she wasn't really drunk, she wasn't about to let Tae Hyun in on that secret.

"Oh give me a break, you weren't drunk," he called out like he had just read her mind. "Your sentences and thoughts were coherent. You only felt drunk because your control was wavering. I can't seduce someone who doesn't want to be seduced—drunk or not. You enjoyed every bit of it. Even when I offered you the opportunity to make the first move, I knew you were going to take it. So stop denying that."

Heat jumped onto her cheeks. "Well, of course I wanted to be seduced," she defended meekly. "What girl wouldn't want to be seduced like that?" She remembered his earlier insult and felt the extreme need to add, "Oh and for your information, I wasn't the one who got tricked and was cuffed to the bed all night. I may suck at life…but you *fail* at life."

Tae Hyun's jaw clenched. Though he seemed extremely angry, it was apparent he was more upset with himself than with her.

"You're right. That was an epic failure on my part last night. I should've known you weren't that kinky. I was too wasted on being hopeful than being realistic. I won't make the same mistake again though."

His voice was marked with male arrogance. It was a tone that scared her because it only meant that Tae Hyun would more than prevail over her now that he knew how cunning she could be.

"Yes, of course you wouldn't make the same mistake again," she retorted with the hopes of moving the battle to her favor. "You almost ruined our friendship. Luckily we didn't do anything. Things can still be saved, Tae Hyun. We can still keep things as they were. We can still keep our friendship safe and healthy."

He laughed incredulously. "Are you kidding? You chained me to a bed in fear of 'raping me.' In the shorter scheme of things, we didn't do the deed, but at least I know now where your head is at. And to be perfectly honest, I don't give a damn about keeping our 'friendship' safe and healthy. Our friendship can burn in friendship hell for all I care."

Yoori wanted to gasp at Tae Hyun's display of hatred for the term she used to describe them. She resisted the urge. She was too angry to even want to loiter on the topic for any significant amount of time.

"You're such a delusional fool." A small part of her wondered if she meant that insult to be directed at both him *and* her. "Anyway, answer my question now. Are you actually naked under the comforter?"

"Of course I am," he answered after studying her for a bit.

She gasped.

Not giving her a chance to delve in the glory of his naked body hovering over her, he continued on, his eyes filled with resolution and determination. "Anyway, we should talk about what happened last night."

"Aren't we talking about it right now?" she asked, still not over the fact that her "friend" was naked above her.

"We're talking about the seduction part—not about the part that really matters."

Yoori stiffened. She'd rather talk about the seduction part than venture into the part where Tae Hyun told her that he wanted more with her (and where she confessed that she wanted more with him as well). The part that "mattered" was harder for her to have a discussion about.

Tae Hyun persevered, ignoring her reticence with this topic. "I told you that I'm done beating around the bush and I'm not joking about that. I meant everything I said last night. I want you and I want something more with you."

"I don't want to talk about this," Yoori muttered stubbornly. She knew how immature she sounded, but it couldn't be helped. She really didn't want to talk about it.

Amusement gleamed in his determined eyes. "Should I bring out the charms again to seduce you into having this conversation?"

"Oh, please don't," she pleaded a bit too urgently. She knew that she sucked at life when it came to trying to resist his charms. She was only able to skirt away from him last night because she chained him to the bed. She doubted Tae Hyun would allot her the same opportunity this time around.

"Why are you so afraid of all this?" Though his voice was soft, it was powerful enough to lift the walls she had begun to place up.

"Because we're friends," Yoori combated feebly. It was such a stupid statement because after what occurred last night, how could she even label them as friends? But she had to try. God help her if she didn't fight this. She was already melting under him and that was a stupid move for her. It was one thing to lust after him; it was another to even dare to consider having something more with him.

Yoori may be stubborn, but she knew Tae Hyun was just as stubborn as her.

A charismatic grin waltzed across his sexy lips. He caressed her hair and bestowed her with a kiss on the forehead. Yoori held in the need to whimper when he did this.

Oh crap, he was starting.

Seduction, Round two: *On.*

"You cuff your 'friends' to the bedpost in fear of losing control and sleeping with them?" he crooned temptingly.

Yoori braced herself.

"I was drunk last night," she defended, her cheeks flushing more fiercely.

"I don't want to be your friend," he replied with a sigh.

His gaze ran over the glow of her skin in the early morning. With the boredom of not being able to touch her sparked within him, Tae Hyun brought up a hand, rested his fingers on her cheek and begun to trace it slowly. He was aware that even mere touches from him drove Yoori insane.

Yoori resisted the urge to blink and breathe in pleasure. Though his eyes were still dazed with interest, Yoori knew better. Tae Hyun made it appear as if he didn't know that his casual touch was driving her insane, but Yoori knew that Tae Hyun, being the talented tease that he was, knew exactly what he had to do to get her to give into temptation. It appeared that his tactic was working. She was already beginning to melt under his teasing caress.

Garnering all the control she had, she went on to say, "But you'll be my *best* friend. Remember? BFF? That's more special."

"Chae Young has that title. I don't like to share," he dismissed, distractedly tracing his fingers down to the collar of her bone. Yoori felt her stomach perform cartwheels. She eyed his striking face and then ran her gaze over the teeth mark that was left on his shoulder, left by her the night before.

"But you'll be the boy best friend," she went on desperately, knowing fairly well that her "control" was being pushed over the edge again. "That's special too."

"Hmmm…" he hummed pleasingly, suddenly extracting his fingers away from her skin.

Yoori's body was ready to weep at the absence of his touch until she realized that Tae Hyun's only intention was to give up on the foreplay of merely teasing her skin with his fingers. Slowly, he dipped down, his warm lips finding the side of her chin. Feathering delicate kisses on her, his lips trailed up her jaw and then found the delicateness of her right ear.

Parting his lips over the earlobe, he began to nibble on it before whispering, "That's tempting, but I'll pass…"

"Tae Hyun!" Yoori whimpered once his tongue teased her sensitive earlobe.

Her breathing was now utterly shallow. Yoori knew that the best thing to do was to push him off for putting her through this sinful enticement once more. She should push him off. It was *that* easy. It was that easy yet she didn't have the strength to do it. She didn't have the desire to push him away. It couldn't hurt if she just allowed that amazing mouth of his to nibble on her ears a bit more…it wasn't like he hadn't done it before…

"Can't I just be your boyfriend?" he negotiated with an innocent murmur. He nibbled again, making Yoori squirm from the pleasure. He hastened to add, "I promise I'll be the best boyfriend."

Bastard. Bastard. Bastard.

He was trying to seduce her into being his girlfriend and it was working! Bastard! Why did he have to be so skillful? Yoori squirmed uncontrollably, finally letting out a little whimper.

Maybe it couldn't hurt to just ask, right? She already knew he was talented in the seductive and physical stuff…

"Will I like being your girlfriend?" Yoori asked stupidly and mindlessly. Her defenses were completely obliterated as she felt his hot breath grin in victory at her question. She was screwed and she knew it.

He gave her a kiss on her cheek and then rose back up on his elbows. He shook his head at her question and then readjusted his naked body under the comforter. He gazed down at her sensually, his cologne filling her nostrils more so than it did before.

"No, you'll hate it," he said, the smile having yet to leave his countenance.

A storm of perplexity came into her lustful eyes.

Noting the bewilderment in her gaze, his smile widened. He dipped down again, his lips finding her bare shoulder. "You'll hate it because I'll spoil you rotten." His warm breath and tongue teased the burning skin on her shoulder.

Yoori held back the urge to blink in delight. Surely she must exhibit *some* control, right?

He went on, his voice shrouded with unbridled sensuality. "You'll hate it because I'll always be on your mind – even more so than now." His lips moved toward her neck. Yoori instinctively arched herself to give Tae Hyun better access to her neck. "You'll hate it because you'll get used to my warmth, my embrace, my kisses..."

Yoori gasped for breath once she felt him suckling and giving love bites on the sensitive skin of her neck. He knew after last night that it was her weakness. It should be a cardinal sin that this guy was so damn sexy and so damn good at making her burn with desire.

After spending a couple of seconds on the spot during which Yoori was breathing in approval, Tae Hyun showered her with kisses all around her neck, her collarbones and then moved up to her chin and finally rested his lips just above hers. His lips weren't touching hers, but his hot breath continued to act as a sexual stimulant that made her want to pounce on him.

"You'll love my presence and loathe my absence," he went on mercilessly, his captivating eyes clearly seeing the control dissipate out of Yoori. "It'll get so bad that you'll wonder how you ever came this far without me..."

Needless to say, Yoori was more than losing her senses. It wasn't until Tae Hyun broke eye contact to stare up at something did Yoori fall out of her staring state. Overcome with the spell he placed her in, she involuntarily followed his gaze.

"I'll be your drug, your addictive drug," he continued alluringly when she caught sight of the handcuff dangling off the bed post, a souvenir of what took place on their bed the night before. Her body grew warm at the remembrance. His lips were still hovering over her lips, teasing her and seducing her further.

And then it happened.

Snaking his powerful arms behind her back, he smiled when he raised her up to face him. There was a wicked gleam in his eyes that mirrored the look of last night. He was ready again—ready to strip her of her final control. "You'll be at my mercy, baby...just like I'm at yours."

That was it for Yoori.

Her arms instinctively encircled around his neck and all was lost when his teasing lips finally claimed her yearning ones.

"Tae Hyun..." Yoori whispered breathlessly.

Their lips parted and his kiss consumed her. She was completely and utterly lost in a world of ecstasy.

"I'm all yours," he reminded her, pulling her closer to his chest. Their lips crushed upon one another with more passion and care. Yoori was going crazy. She was absolutely going crazy with the longing blazing inside her.

"Are you all mine?" he prompted in breathless anticipation.

Panting with fervor, her lips continued to seek out Tae Hyun's. As the passion swallowed her whole, Yoori finally gave Tae Hyun her unbridled answer.

"I—I'm really afraid, Tae Hyun," she whispered in between their kiss, meaning it with all her heart. Her fear wrapped over her, pulling her out of the blissful trance Tae Hyun worked so hard to place her in. She hated herself. She hated the unknown fears that just pushed her away from Tae Hyun. "I'm so afraid..."

He stilled at the trepidation emanating from her trembling body.

"Why are you so afraid?" he asked, pulling out of the kiss. His right hand caressed and held her cheek. His eyes swirled with questions. He was trying to understand why she was afraid and Yoori felt horrible because she didn't know the reason herself.

With her arms still wrapped securely around his neck, Yoori just impulsively lied and said, "Because I like being friends with you."

It was a horrible lie because that wasn't the reason. If she knew, she would tell him. But that was the thing, she didn't know what the answer was. She just knew it existed and it was coiling in the pit of her stomach.

Annoyance dimmed his gaze. He knew that wasn't the reason why she was so afraid. However, he didn't push her on it.

"No offense, but I've never considered you as a friend," he instead bit out.

"But I considered you a friend," she retorted before quietly muttering, "My BFF."

"What do you want me to do about that, Yoori?" he asked impatiently. She could tell he was annoyed with her using the same old excuse. She didn't blame him. She was annoying herself too. "Any chance of us going back to the way things were was pretty much shot to hell when you jumped on me last night."

Yoori blushed. How was a girl supposed to respond to that?

His face softened at the sight of her blush. "You really know how to ruin the mood, don't you?" He eased himself away from her slightly. "You're killing me, Brat," he persisted wearily. "I've never had to seduce a girl like this and I've never been this sappy with any girl. So just put me out of my misery and awkwardness. Just tell me what I need to do to convince you that it'll all be worth it."

Yoori admired his persistence. She wished she had his confidence and bravery. She had always been spineless. If things got too hard, she would run from them. It was a habit of hers and it was one that was still alive and well in her.

"Are you saying it'll be easy?" If it was, then she would've agreed to it last night, but it wasn't. She may have been drunk, but she knew she was on to something. No matter how much they both may want it, they didn't belong together. They wouldn't have a happy ending together.

"I only said it would be worth it," he replied, disappointed with her penchant for the easier choice in life. "Nothing worth fighting for will ever be easy in this world."

Yoori wallowed in the same disappointment. How would she even begin to explain to him that there was something that she was so afraid of? There was something scaring her, but she didn't know what it was. What kind of crazy explanation could she give him? It was hopeless.

Heeding the uncertainty in her eyes, Tae Hyun stroked her cheek again and slowly lowered her back to the bed. Yoori sadly uncurled her arms from around his neck. He rested her head back on the pillow and laid on his elbow again. He framed her cheek with one hand, his thumb kissing over her sensitized lips.

"I wish you would tell me why you're so afraid," he murmured. "Why you're always running away from this."

His eyes held hers. Silent promises swam in those enchanting brown eyes. It was a gift, Yoori concluded as she stared up at him, her heart breathing faintly against her chest. A dangerous gift for a man to possess over her and Tae Hyun had that gift. He had that gift in his eyes that made her want to drown in his silent promises—promises that if she gave herself to him, then he would give her the world. And she wanted to give herself to him. She wanted to eradicate that gnawing feeling of fear in her stomach. She wanted to simply place her fears aside and drown in him. But wishful thinking wasn't an option for her—not if she wanted to protect herself and protect the relationship they had. If they moved to a different level, then they could never go back to the way they were. Things would get harder and Yoori wasn't ready for that. She wasn't strong enough for that.

Desperate to change the tone of the conversation, Yoori did what she did best: she changed the topic.

"I think your disillusionments about wanting to be with me has softened you," Yoori noted with joking humor. "So does this mean you're not going to pick on me anymore?"

Maybe there was a silver lining to this whole thing after all. Maybe Tae Hyun would only see her as a woman now and perhaps he would realize it was inappropriate to pick on a woman so much.

His next words crushed her surging hope. "Did you kick another duck today or something? Are you crazy? My joy in life is torturing you. Whether it be teasing you or charming the social awkwardness out of you."

Her jaw dropped.

"I knew you weren't the seductive prince charming you were trying to be!" she snapped, unknowing to herself how her plan of lightening the mood actually worked. Funny what short attention spans they both had.

"No," he agreed. "But I'll be your boyfriend before the week is over, you stubborn little Brat."

She gave him an unladylike snort. "Don't hold your breath, you overconfident Snob."

"I'll hold yours instead," he whispered, dipping in and nipping his tempting nose with hers.

Danger!

Yoori instinctively closed her eyes when he did this, holding her breath in anticipation. She could've sworn she felt his lips brush against hers as well, but she wasn't too sure. She was probably too desperate to kiss him and was imagining a meeting of their lips.

"Honestly speaking," he said, easing upward from her and allotting her the chance to open her eyes again. "Do you really think you'll be able to survive my charms if I don't offset it with playful teasing?"

"Words spoken by a true bully," she retorted, unimpressed.

Tae Hyun opened his mouth, ready to impart words of witty retort until something crossed his mind. "Actually before I forget…just a reminder…I hope you haven't forgotten, we have a busy night the day after tomorrow."

"What are you talking about?"

He eyed her skeptically. "I didn't tell you last night?"

She blinked at him blankly. "Um no. You were a bit too busy with walking around in a towel and seducing the hell out of me."

"You recall a lot for someone who was too drunk to remember anything, huh my little prude?" he quipped with amusement.

Yoori moved uncomfortably at the remark.

"Okay, so what's going on Friday?" she asked, bringing him back on topic.

"Apparently Hae Jin and Chae Young invited themselves, along with Kang Min and Jae Won, over for dinner." An iota of annoyance bore into his eyes. "We're providing the food."

"Hae Jin and Chae Young?" Her interest perked up. "Wait, you've been talking to Chae Young? Since when?"

"Since you ran off last week and slept at her place. Remember? I told you I went to see Chae Young at the diner to try and find you. You weren't at her place and then I went and found you at Vertical VII." He smiled. "You really have bad memory, don't you?"

Yeah, I have amnesia, buddy, she wanted to reply to him, but held in the inclination. "Things got overshadowed when a certain someone decided to fall off the building of a luxury hotel," she replied vacantly. "Okay, okay go on," she prompted, interested in knowing how it came to be that she and Tae Hyun were hosting a dinner.

"Well, I went to visit Hae Jin a couple of days ago, when my 'boss' had the cravings for ice cream in the middle of winter." Yoori smiled innocently as he narrowed his eyes on her before finishing. "Chae Young, Kang Min and Jae Won were there too. I was talking to them for a little bit and next thing I knew, those two short girls were standing in front of me and thanking me for dinner invitations that I never gave."

Yoori laughed at the imagery of Tae Hyun, the feared King of Serpents, getting coerced into planning a dinner party by his baby sister and her best friend.

He smirked. "I thought I told you, but I guess I was too exhausted with how much my 'boss' from last week overworked me." He sighed, weariness inhabiting his eyes. "Now close your eyes."

"Why?"

"I'm naked. And now I'm getting out of bed. Surely you don't want to catch a glimpse of anything when I get up, right?" There was a gleam of wickedness in his sultry eyes. It was like he was daring her to keep her eyes opened.

Of course I do.

"Of course not," Yoori replied, lowering her eyelids. She squirmed suddenly, tightening her eyes even more when she felt Tae Hyun pinch her nose.

"Don't pinch me when my eyes are closed!" she chastised, moving her nose away from his line of fire.

She heard him chuckle over her.

"Just making sure you're closing them as tightly as possible," Tae Hyun stated. She could hear the smile in his crafty voice. The guy could care less if her eyes were closed tightly. He just wanted an excuse to pinch her nose.

"What are you waiting for? *Tomorrow*? Hurry and get off," she shouted impatiently.

Tae Hyun chuckled at her impatience. Yoori instantly felt the weight of the comforter fall onto her once Tae Hyun lifted himself up and crawled out of bed. As the darkness surrounded her, her eyes twitched in interest. *Hmm...* She knew it would be a horrible thing to sneak a peak, but she was so curious. She was so curious to how amazing *it* would look. Maybe it wouldn't hurt if she just—

She lifted one eyelid.

Shock overcame her when instead of seeing his naked defined ass, she saw his cute butt veiled with blue and white plaid pajama pants.

"I thought you said you were naked under the comforter—"

As soon as the words came out, Yoori covered her mouth with her hands. Fuck.

This was the part where she wanted to find a hole to crawl into so she could die in it. Damn her and her unfiltered mouth.

"Really Choi Yoori, it had only been ten seconds since I got out of bed." He gave her a teasing wink before grabbing the towel off the chair. He threw it over his neck and allowed each side to hang off his shoulders. "I thought you would've restrained yourself from peeking for a little bit longer..."

He tugged on either ends of the towel and sauntered over to her with a devilish grin tugging his lips. Once he reached the bed, he crouched down on the floor and stared up at Yoori in hilarity.

"You asked me if I was naked under the comforter," he explained coyly. "The brand of this pajama pant is '*Comforter*.'" He carefully pulled her hands away from her mouth. "Were you disappointed?"

"I—I was just curious about the male anatomy," she whispered, the fires of hell warming her needy body. When she knew she was caught, she involuntarily added, "Oh I hate you. I really hate you. I can't believe you lied to me. You know what I meant when I asked if you were naked. You're such a…"

Tae Hyun cocked his brow in interest. "What?"

"Tease."

He grinned. He peered up at the handcuffs on the bedpost with a mixture of boredom and disapproval. "As far as I'm concerned, you're still the champion tease in this bedroom."

She smirked bitterly. "I'm excited for the next couple of days since we'll be apart. I get to hang out with other people and get away from all the hormones raging out of you, *Kwon*."

"Say that again the next time your hormones rage out of control and you bite my shoulder while screaming out my name, *Choi*," he replied slyly.

Before a caught-off-guard Yoori was able to give her own witty reply, Tae Hyun's Blackberry sounded off from the bed counter beside them. The melodic ring tone blared through the bedroom, shaking both Yoori and Tae Hyun out of their blissful bubble.

Something in Yoori's gut pulsed in worry as the music thundered through her senses. *Don't pick it up!* she wanted to scream out to Tae Hyun once she felt a wave of chills pierce through her skin. She was too late. Tae Hyun picked up his Blackberry from the counter, looked at the unknown number on the screen, sat down on the side of the bed and answered.

"Hello?"

"Tae Hyun, my boy," the familiar, senile voice swam through the receiver and into the room. It was clear to Tae Hyun and clearer to Yoori who it was: Ju Won.

The pit of fear increased in her stomach. She hated the sound of Ju Won's voice and she hated it more that he called. Ju Won was her reminder of the Underworld. He was her reminder of why she was so hesitant with moving forward with Tae Hyun. The reasons for her were blurry earlier, but it was all crystal clear now.

They didn't belong together.

They couldn't be together…especially when people like Ju Won were in their lives.

"What do you want?" Tae Hyun's rough tone left nothing to the imagination. He was annoyed that Ju Won called and wasted no time sugar coating this feeling. The last time Tae Hyun saw Ju Won was after her five-minute initiation. Yoori had the feeling Tae Hyun gave Ju Won the same piece of mind he was giving him over the phone.

Yoori moved closer to Tae Hyun to listen. She ignored the look of warning he gave her to not eavesdrop. He made a move to walk away, but Yoori's nails dug into his shoulder, her silent promise that she would give him a world of hell if he dared to move away from her. He glared at Yoori for a brief second and settled back on the bed, permitting her full disclosure to the conversation at hand.

"We haven't spoken since the night after Choi Yoori's initiation," Ju Won replied calmly, unaffected by the angry tone Tae Hyun directed at him. His voice was more amused than angry. "I heard about your altercation with Ji Hoon at Vertical VII. I wanted to see how you were. You've disappeared from the Underworld for quite some time now. People are starting to wonder about what had happened to their beloved King of Serpents." A purposeful silence filled the other line. "We should meet today, Tae Hyun."

"I'm busy," Tae Hyun answered at once.

"Tae Hyun," came another voice on the line. It was Dong Min's voice. His tone matched none of the amusement Ju Won displayed. It thundered with gravity and concern. "There are many whispers rippling around our world right now. People are saying that you may not have what it takes to lead our world."

Tae Hyun stiffened at the concern in his Advisor's voice. He had little to no respect for Ju Won, but Yoori could see it in Tae Hyun's demeanor that although he wasn't afraid of Dong Min, he still respected him immensely.

"You've been distracted for too long and people are noticing—even your supporters. The Royals in the 1st layer are starting to ask questions. This is serious. Ju Won and I wouldn't be calling if we didn't think your standing has been compromised. Come meet with us so we can fix this before it gets any worse."

Akin to Dong Min's words being a splash of cold water for him, unease washed over Tae Hyun.

"When and where?" he asked. His voice, however controlled it was, was throbbing with strain. Tae Hyun, like Yoori, could tell that there was more to what Dong Min was letting on—more serious matters at hand.

Even though she saw it coming, Yoori couldn't control the unscrupulous dread that formed in her heart after she heard Tae Hyun give into the demands of the Advisors as soon as he heard that his candidacy to be the Lord of the Underworld was in jeopardy.

She had always known that this candidacy was more important to Tae Hyun than anything else. She had always known this. It was just that, in the course of the recent weeks and all that had happened between them, she thought his priorities *might* have changed. It was a silly hope on a silly girl's part, but as she watched him harden at the knowledge that his position was challenged in the Underworld, she knew that Tae Hyun was still eager for power in this world. It didn't matter what occurred in this bedroom or the night before, power continued to prevail over Tae Hyun's needs and this fact alone was enough for her to justify her actions in not giving into him.

They didn't belong together. This very moment proved it.

"In an hour. The Stadium," Dong Min stated before adding, "And Tae Hyun?"

"Yes?"

"Stop distracting yourself. It'll do no good for you in the end."

The line went dead.

Dong Min's words were simple, but it felt like scalding knives.

Yoori stared at Tae Hyun in worry when he hung up.

"What?" He feigned obliviousness, but she knew in his eyes that he knew why she was so concerned. Even then, she knew that Tae Hyun was just trying to ease the stress away from her. He never enjoyed it whenever she had fear spread on her face.

"They know that you've been too distracted with me?"

"They know that I haven't been as active in the Underworld," he corrected, still subtly attempting to ease the worry away from her.

"And they know it's because of me," she persisted, worry spreading through her like cancer.

She knew that the Advisors didn't approve of her being with him. She doubted the entire Underworld would've approved of her being with him if and when everyone else found out. She knew all of this, but she hadn't realized what a big deal all of it was until now. Despite Tae Hyun's nonchalance, Yoori knew the situation was graver than he was letting on.

"Don't worry about it."

"But—"

"It'll be okay, Yoori," he insisted. "I can deal with them. I was born into this world. I know how to play the politics. Plus, everyone in this world knows that Ji Hoon will never do a better job than me. I'm the only one who could lead this world in the way that it needs to be led."

"What if they find someone else for the position and pit them against you?" The question came out before she could stop it. It wasn't the right time to ask, but it was undeniably appropriate.

"Who?" he inquired, his question coming out faster than he could catch it as well. "Who in this world has the power to challenge me? Who in this world has the power to bring me down?"

Yoori didn't give Tae Hyun a name. She just stared at him, her eyes dark with storms of worry. While there were no words exchanged, Yoori knew that Tae Hyun could tell who she was thinking about. They were the only two who knew about her existence and knew *who* she was in a past life. Judging by her notoriety in this world, Yoori knew her past self was more than capable of being considered a candidate, especially with a fickle old man like Ju Won who seemed to constantly change his mind about who his favorite potential heir was.

Yoori had always assumed that despite the fact that he was angry that Soo Jin had yet to complete a deed he wanted her to perform before she died, he still favored her most. Yoori believed that until she thought about it further. At this very moment, there was no doubt that it was Tae Hyun that Ju Won favored. Not Soo Jin, or Ji Hoon or anyone else. It was just Tae Hyun. Of course, with an untrustworthy man like Ju Won, he could very well be leading all the heirs to believe that he was favoring all of them. This also seemed like a likely scenario. Anything was possible with the cunning old Advisor.

"I—I'm just really worried," she answered truthfully, unable to ignore the sinking feeling in her stomach.

A tinge of remorse sparked in Tae Hyun's eyes. Yoori knew it only sparked because he hated seeing her worry. She wished she had better control of her emotions. She was still troubled. Her fears were well-founded fears and that was enough to keep the sting of terror going within her. It wasn't so much the fact that the Advisors were unhappy with him, but it was more due to the fact that the Advisors were powerful enough to sway opinions. If they wanted the Underworld to turn on Tae Hyun, then it would be a simple task, especially considering that there were already whispers about him being too "distracted" with her.

"Come on, Brat," he whispered. Desperation was present in his voice. "I hate it when you get like this. Stop worrying. It'll be fine—" He stopped talking when his eyes enlarged in alarm. He pointed his index finger out dramatically. "YOORI, SPIDER!"

"Eeep!" Yoori shrieked like a little mouse.

She hopped over to Tae Hyun's side of the bed and shook nonstop at the fear that a big spider had crawled onto her. Her eyes scanned the bed for the spider in question. It was only until she felt Tae Hyun grab her wrist and swiftly entangle something cold around it did she realize he had tricked her.

Yoori narrowed her eyes onto the bedpost.

Fear embalmed her eyes.

She had just been handcuffed to the bed!

"Uh oh..."

Standing smugly to the side with his hands tugging on each end of the towel, Tae Hyun smirked at the pathetic state Yoori found herself in.

"You still worried?" he asked warmly, playfully nipping her nose with his thumb. "Please stop worrying. I can't stand it when you worry like that."

Yoori crinkled her nose. Only Tae Hyun would attempt to make her feel better by distracting her and scaring her about something else entirely. Her worry about the Advisors and the Underworld dispelled as she glared at Tae Hyun. Who the hell would try to make someone feel better by cuffing them to a bed?

"Very funny, *Kwon*. Yeah, okay I'm not worried anymore. I'm pissed at you. Now grow up and let me go."

She tugged against the cuffs. It was as strong as she remembered it. It was impenetrable without a key.

"Why should I let you go?" He folded his arms across his chest. "You tortured me like this last night, remember?"

Yoori smiled uneasily. "We shouldn't live in a world filled with the vicious cycles of revenge."

Tae Hyun shook his head at her attempt to assuage his needs. "I can't. No matter how much I like you," Tae Hyun replied almost apologetically. His tone was still lighthearted. "I'm a very vengeful person. I won't be able to go on with my day unless I get you back for what you did to me last night."

Butterflies played in her tummy. "Heh, so what are you going to do? Just leave me chained here all day while you tease me by taking your clothes off?" She didn't know why she said that, but she did and she was slightly hopeful that he would consider her question. They didn't belong together, but she could still lust after him and joke with him, right?

He raised a curious brow. "Are you suggesting something, *Choi*?"

"It was merely a question," she replied before some sensibility rained over her. "Anyway, stop playing. Don't you have evil, five-minute beating Advisors to meet? Let me go."

"I don't have to meet them for another hour," he drawled. "Until then, you can hang out there while I make you suffer."

"You're such a jerk-face. You just got done trying to seduce me, trying to ease me of worry, and now you're punishing me?"

Tae Hyun laughed affectionately. Instead of answering her, he merely sat himself back down on the edge of the bed beside her. He framed his hands over her cheeks and pulled her back to him. His lips brushed over hers. The kiss that came unto her lips was slow and deliberate, one that she didn't protest as she closed her eyes and puckered her lips for him. She was a loser and she acknowledged it. Even when she was frustrated and determined not to have a relationship with the guy, she still gave into the temptation he threw out because she desired him so. She had to be honest. She was chained to a bed with a guy who was strutting his stuff without his shirt on...what girl wouldn't close her eyes to enjoy a simple kiss? And Yoori did just that. She enjoyed the kiss and allowed it to detonate her senses. The stolen kiss was fast, memorable, and over too quickly when Tae Hyun pulled away from the kiss, leaving her to yearn for more.

"So...you're going to kiss me to death?" she finally spoke out, her eyes glazed from the aftermath of the quick and addicting kiss.

"No," he replied. "That was my apology to you."

It should have sounded scary, but it didn't. Yoori wasn't afraid of Tae Hyun. She was just apprehensive about some of the punishments he might come up with. She didn't want to have to deal with it. They knew each other too well and unfortunately for Yoori, weaknesses were more than included in this tree of knowledge.

"Tae Hyun…don't be mean." Her voice was soft, but it wasn't a plea. It was a subtle command—one that Tae Hyun didn't miss.

"See, if you were my girlfriend, I'd actually listen to you," he cleverly emphasized, reminding her that he wasn't over the fact that he still wanted her as his girlfriend. "But you're not so…"

"What…what are you going to do to your BFF?"

Tae Hyun sighed airily and leaned forward, strategically placing his lips right beside her ear.

"How do you feel about me making us the most decadent of breakfasts?" he whispered sultrily, just as he did the night prior while trying to seduce her. Yoori whimpered at the thought and he went on, encouraged by her weak reaction. "Can you imagine it, *baby*?" His hot breath painted a clear and juicy picture for her. "The works: pancakes, sausages, scrambled eggs, syrup, orange juice, rice, bacon, fresh fruits and your favorite…tater tots."

She wanted to ask him if he would ever consider switching occupations and becoming a commercial actor instead. He could probably do a commercial ad for TV. She was sure whatever the hell he advertised with that sexy voice of his would sell out in a matter of seconds. He was *that* convincing. He would make one lucky company a lot of money if they ever signed him. Regrettably for Yoori, Tae Hyun was content with using his skills on her and her alone.

"Can you imagine me and you on this bed," he continued relentlessly, "eating all that food as the syrup and the taste of heaven roll around in our mouths? Can you already taste those deliciously plump tater tots as you roll it around in ketchup? The ecstasies in your mouth as you close your eyes and cry out in the biggest of bliss?"

Yoori nodded sadly, hating Tae Hyun for making her so hungry. "You're going to go make it, aren't you? And then…you're going to torture me by eating all of it in front of me."

The crafty smile that quirked on to Tae Hyun's face was confirmation to Yoori that this was his exact plan. "Unless you convince me otherwise."

"How?" Yoori breathed out in agony. She was so hungry now.

"A kiss."

"A kiss?" She gaped at him confusingly. "But you just kissed me."

"A kiss *from* you," he reiterated. His eyes rested on the poutiness of her lips. "Just a kiss. I'll be putty in your hands and I'll un-cuff you."

"I won't be blackmailed into giving you a kiss, Tae Hyun," she said sternly, wondering how the hell she managed to speak so severely when all she wanted to do was give in to him. It was times such as these, even when she was in handcuffs, that Yoori was amazed the lengths her mind went in terms of veiling control over her.

"Damn," he replied exhaustively. "You're always so stubborn." He stood up and reached for the cuffs above her. Taking out a key from his pocket, he surprised her by un-cuffing her from the bedpost.

Yoori gawked at him. "What happened to being a vengeful person?"

"I can forgive you." His voice was concise, but very much genuine.

"Have you forgiven in the past?" Her question was swift, just like many she voiced to him earlier in the day.

"No," he answered quickly, and she knew it was the truth. "But there's a first time for everything, right?"

His words ignited something inside her. Yoori didn't know what came over her, but when she watched him retreat to the closet to get dressed, she reached up, grabbed each ends of his towel and brought him back down.

Wrapping her arms around his neck, she pulled him toward her and pressed her lips over his upper lip, teasing him with the half-kiss until he wrapped his arms around her waist and pulled her up, slanting his face so that his lips would get the full treatment from her. It was a quick, passionate, and a hell of a kiss. One that ended too soon when Yoori used all her bearings and pulled herself away from him. It could never extend longer than a quick kiss. Both herself and Tae Hyun weren't strong enough in the morning for a long and passionate kiss. They would never leave the bed if that occurred.

"What was that for?" he asked, his eyes gleaming with content.

"That wasn't a kiss," Yoori elaborated, releasing her grip on either side of his towel, allowing him to stand back up. "I'm just returning what I stole last night."

"I was under the impression that you weren't giving it back."

"There's a first time for everything."

He smiled, almost ready to get up again when Yoori held on to his arm.

"Tae Hyun," she voiced worriedly. "I can hear it in their voices. They're angry with you." No matter how distracted she was, she couldn't shake the fear off of her, especially when she knew he was getting ready to meet them.

"I know they are." His gaze on her was confident, unafraid. Rising up, he drew across the room and approached the closet where he pulled out a gray, long sleeved dress shirt and black pants. "But at the end the day, their power is to merely advise. They have no direct power over me." Running his hand through a sleeve of his shirt, Tae Hyun also said, "Now close your eyes."

Seeing that he was in the process of changing his pants, she did as she was told.

"Just…just don't underestimate them," she warned with her eyes shut, listening as his pajama pants fell to the floor.

"I never do." She heard him murmur before long seconds later, a warm palm touched her face.

Yoori opened her eyes and saw that Tae Hyun was staring down at her with a smile that nearly had her keeling over for air. He was fully dressed and he looked as mouthwatering as ever.

"Thanks for the concern though, Brat." Natural charm radiated from him even when he wasn't trying to exude it. He extracted his hand from her cheek and reached for his Blackberry. "It's nice to know that you're attached to me enough."

Spurred with the walls of her defense, she said, "If you get hurt, then I'll have to take care of you. I'm too lazy for that." She didn't mean any of it and she knew he didn't believe any of it. She just had to get it out there for the record.

She jumped off the bed and followed a laughing Tae Hyun as he ventured out of the room and into the living room. Their living room illumed with natural sunlight. It invigorated Yoori to see such a sight.

"Call Jae Won or Kang Min if you want to go anywhere," he instructed, already grabbing his keys from the coffee table. He headed straight for the door. "And if you see them, ask them what they want for dinner."

In light of all the new developments that had occurred, Yoori had momentarily forgotten about the dinner party they were having. A small tread of hope kindled within her. At least there were still good things happening, she thought distractedly before chasing after him.

"Wait!" she cried, running barefoot behind him as he wore his black leather shoes. "Hey, I have last words for you."

"What is it?" he asked tiredly. His hand was already pulling the door open.

In lieu of saying anything, Yoori simply stomped up to him with the intention of yelling at him one last time for seducing her the night prior and warning him to be careful with the Advisors. She had intended to merely voice all of that, but instead, she did the unthinkable.

She *shoved* him.

"Have you *lost* your mind?" Tae Hyun asked bewilderingly, flabbergasted by the unexpected show of violence on Yoori's part.

"That was for trying to seduce me last night. You perv, I can't believe you actually grabbed my hands and ran them down your chest and stomach. You know I have a thing for your abs." She shoved him again. "And you better be careful with them or I'll kill you. I don't want to host that stupid dinner all by myself." She finished that warning with a final shove that left him to stare at her in annoyance. "And that's for just being you. I hate you."

"You know what, Choi Yoori?" Tae Hyun asked through gritted teeth. His patience was visibly pushed over the edge.

"What?"

And then he did the unthinkable: he *shoved* her as well.

Nearly causing her to collide with the wall behind her, he caught her just in time before any damage was done to her body. After that, he picked her up and pressed her against the wall, causing her to instinctively wrap her legs around his hips. Yoori's first inclination was to fight to get out of his hold, but her body's first reaction was to wrap her arms around his neck. And that was what she did. She wrapped her arms around his neck like she was his beloved girlfriend rather than an uninterested personal assistant.

Tae Hyun's lips swept over hers, his kiss filled with hunger and need. Fire spread through Yoori's lips, spikes of warmth and bliss surged from the crown of her head to the tip of her toes. It was a kiss they had been dying to have since morning resumed. Reveling in the feel of his lips whispering on hers, Yoori was almost lost in it when he abruptly pulled away, panting fiercely.

He brought a palm up and framed her cheek with it. "*That* was for cuffing me to the bed last night." His lips met hers again. It was short, but still filled with immeasurable fire. "*That* was for rejecting me when I asked to be your boyfriend." He nipped her lips again. "*That's* so you don't forget how much you want me."

While pulling away, he allowed Yoori to fall back against the wall, holding on to her to keep her from crashing to the ground. He then cupped her face and kissed her again, *one last time*. This one was longer, wilder and more passionate— all of which left Yoori stunned with so much ecstasy that she was certain she would pass out if Tae Hyun hadn't pulled away from her in time.

"What…what was that last one for?" she asked, panting for air with Tae Hyun.

"I'm not giving it back to you," he simply stated. He closed his eyes and briefly pressed his forehead against hers. Their yearning breaths mingled in excitement as they both fought for air.

Still flustered, she said, "Give what back?"

He didn't answer her. Bestowing her with one last kiss on the forehead, he finally pulled himself away. He approached the opened door like he never got into a "I-have-to-have-you-now-kiss" with Yoori, who still looked mesmerized. Her eyes were still dreary from the kiss.

"Don't miss me too much," he imparted with a sultry grin.

The door clicked shut behind him, leaving Yoori lost in wonderment. Her back was still pressed against the wall, her body still adjusting to the kiss that just took place.

"I'm not giving it back to you," she repeated in her fragmented mind. Was he talking about the "stolen" kiss or something else? What the hell did he mean by that? She was lost in a series of unanswerable questions until the sound of soft knocking left her staring at the door.

Under the impression that it was Tae Hyun, Yoori, who quickly fixed her hair to look presentable and composed, meandered over to the door and opened it without looking through the peephole.

"Did you want another dramatic goodbye—?"

Yoori's heart stalled when it was clear that the person she was talking to wasn't Tae Hyun. It was someone else. Someone else she didn't want to see and someone she was deathly afraid of seeing.

Shin Jung Min.

"Yoori," Jung Min greeted.

His lips quirked into a smile that didn't reach his cold eyes. He looked just as intimidating as when she last saw him at Ju Won's mansion, if not more intimidating. He was an old man, yet he still towered over her, reminding her of how powerful he was when he beat her through her five-minute initiation.

"Tae…Tae Hyun isn't here," was all Yoori could muster out. Her nails dug into the knob of the door. She was tempted to slam the door in his face, but she resisted. She didn't know Jung Min that well, but she knew the old man was strong. He wasn't someone to piss off.

His face displayed no emotion to the news.

"I know," he stated simply. "I came here to see you."

"Me?"

He nodded, still stoic and dangerous.

"Can I have a few moments with you?" His tone was a warning one. It was one that hinted that he wouldn't take no for an answer and that he would use other forces to convince her if necessary. He didn't raise his voice, nor did he glare at her, nor did he make threats, but his calm demeanor sent chills up her spine all the same.

Yoori wanted to refuse him. She was getting ready to find an excuse when the words of protest lodged itself against her throat after Jung Min gravely added, "It'll only be a few moments."

His eyes dimmed in forewarning.

"Tae Hyun is being given a few moments to decide how he wants to get rid of you. You should have a few moments to decide the same."

"The time will come..."

21: Lord of the Underworld

CenYen Mist.

That was where Shin Jung Min brought her. He brought her to a contemporary teahouse that has been a luxury staple in Seoul for years now. Surrounded by indoor waterfalls as walls in every corner, the teahouse oozed of wealth and power. The atmosphere was serene. There were only a couple of guests in the big central room that stretched over the entire vicinity. It gave a "homey" feeling of sorts.

From what Yoori heard, CenYen Mist had an exclusive clientele. If you weren't a prominent figure in Seoul's society, you wouldn't be able to book a reservation for months. And apparently, Shin Jung Min was one of those prominent figures in society as he commanded one of the bigger tables that sat in a secluded area of the teahouse.

Dressed in a light brown sweater and brown pants, Jung Min looked like he would be a regular uncle that you would have tea with—that was if your uncle was one of the top Advisors in the Underworld.

The serenity of the teahouse should have relaxed Yoori, who was sitting in a wooden chair across from Jung Min.

A waitress placed their expensive tea in front of them.

"How were you after your initiation?" Jung Min asked casually, sipping from his tea.

The waitress gave them a polite bow, loosened the green chiffon drape to give them privacy and left.

Yoori swallowed her green tea and fidgeted in her seat. Caught off guard that Jung Min of all people was at her doorstep, Yoori only cared enough to grab Tae Hyun's black hoodie as her source of warmth. It was ironic, she thought, to be talking about the initiation when she was wearing the exact same hoodie that she was beaten in.

"I was fine," she answered meekly, careful to not divulge into so much information.

She wondered why Jung Min was wasting so much time with small talk. After that cryptic message at her doorstep, Yoori hoped he would give her some respect and just stop beating around the bushes. She was still feeling uneasy.

"Tae Hyun must've taken good care of you afterward," said Jung Min, his eyes cold as ever.

"He did." Never being one for patience, small talk evaded Yoori. She felt compelled to address the pink elephant in the room. "I just wanted you to know that I'm not who you think I am."

"Don't patronize me," Jung Min said severely. Evidently, he was not a fan of useless small talk either.

Yoori had to use all her strength to not flinch from the fear that raced through her. Although he didn't raise his voice, there was something about Jung Min that just terrified her.

Now they were getting right down to business.

"You may be able to fool Ji Hoon, you may be able to fool Kang Min and Jae Won, and you may be able to fool Tae Hyun...but you can't fool me." His gaze on her grew stronger. "I was there in the hospital with your mother and father when you were born. I was there for each and every one of your birthdays. I was the one who trained you for ten years, so don't you dare patronize me and say that you're not the person I *know* you are. The three of us know who you are, Soo Jin. We're just respecting your wishes and the new life you've created for yourself."

"What new life have I created for myself?" Yoori asked, maintaining her composure and continuing to play dumb. She hadn't anticipated Jung Min to go into details about being there for her in the past. It caught her by surprise. She was certain it wouldn't be the last thing he says that would catch her by surprise today.

"Right now, you're either lying to me or you did something to yourself and now you've completely lost your memory." He sighed knowingly and almost mockingly. "And with what happened the other night...the way you 'allowed' us to beat you down like you were a dog, I'm betting on the latter. You used one of the test drugs we concocted, didn't you? You faked your death, injected yourself with the shot that brought forth your blissful amnesia and now here you are, a completely new person who is more than free from the guilt of what she did to that poor family in the club."

Yoori visibly stilled at the mention of the club incident. She wondered how much Jung Min knew about that incident. She debated asking him about it. The longer she pondered the decision, the more afraid she became. There was a cruel smile on his face, one that hid the knowledge of the things that would literally rip her soul apart if she asked for more details. Still hell-bent on playing dumb, she chose not to address that. She simply stared at him. She had hoped her nonchalance would make him believe that she wasn't Soo Jin. She heavily doubted her efforts were working with how he was looking at her.

He smirked reprovingly. His fingers wrapped around his teacup so roughly that she had no doubt it would crack to pieces if he didn't let go of it soon. "You may have left this world a legend, but you died a disappointment in everything that we've taught you."

There was so much venom in his voice that Yoori wondered if she should be drinking anything around him. He despised her and was immensely disappointed in her. She couldn't imagine what Soo Jin did that would piss Jung Min off so much.

"You chose to 'kill' yourself. You chose the easy way out and that's something that will come back to haunt you. It's something you'll have to pay for when everything comes full circle again."

"Why am I here, sir?" Yoori asked impatiently, not even validating his guess with a proper reply. All she wanted to do was humor him by coming here so he didn't get aggressive with her. Now that she was here, all that she wanted to do was leave. She didn't want to listen to the old man complain to her about the disappointment that was Soo Jin. Hell, she hated Soo Jin too. She didn't need to listen to anything more that dealt with her.

"Stay away from Tae Hyun," Jung Min warned, getting right to the point of why he came. "He didn't get to the level of where he's at for no reason. Tae Hyun is very well-known to be ruthless in our world. His soul deteriorated long after he killed his own brother for the Serpents' throne. Right now, any charm that he's showing you is inauthentic, well rehearsed to make it appear as if he has human emotions left. Don't be fooled by it. He's a bastard and he'll be more than willing to sacrifice you to get what he wants in the end."

"Why should I listen to anything you have to say about Tae Hyun?" Yoori asked, only developing a backbone when it came to having to defend Tae Hyun. She would be damned if she just sat there and allowed Jung Min to talk about someone she cared about like that. "I saw how you interacted with him, *Jung Min*. You despise him. I don't think you're someone I would go to for advice about what type of person he is."

Yoori could've sworn she saw steam coming out of his ears after hearing her blunt statement. If it was even possible, his eyes grew more deadly.

"The next time you use that patronizing tone with me as you say my name, I'll cut your tongue out to remind you never to speak to me that way again."

"Is that why you came, *sir*?" Yoori asked sweetly, purposely pushing him to see how much further she could go. Jung Min was intimidating, but as Yoori was quickly starting to learn, he also seemed very hesitant on hurting her. "You wanted to pick on Tae Hyun's girlfriend?"

She wondered if he was afraid of hurting her because she was "Tae Hyun's girlfriend" or if it was because she was "An Soo Jin." Yoori had a feeling it dealt with both factors.

"I'm here to help you. I'm not here to threaten you," Jung Min said sternly, his voice strained with impatience. Veins started to appear on his neck, outlining the angry crow lines that were adjacent to his dark eyes. "Stay away from him. Right now, all that you are to him is his shiny new toy—his little trophy that he shows off to the world. But it won't be long when he sees that you're not the trophy he wants."

He smirked at her once he caught the concern that betrayed her eyes.

"You're a fool, *Choi Yoori*. What kind of world do you think you're in right now? Do you think Kwon Tae Hyun is just another gang leader off the streets? Do you think he's a gang leader who would hold your hand and run around in alleys with you all day? This world isn't the street gang that you're used to seeing in the fucking media. Our world is bigger than that—better than anything the outside world could dream us to be. We have infiltrated every facet of this country and countries all over the world. The street gangs are merely on the streets to perform our biddings as we see fit, but this world is ran by the most educated and the most cunning people there are. And right now, Tae Hyun is at the apex of all of that. He is being considered as the King who will take over all facets of this organized Underworld and become one of the most powerful men the world will ever know."

His eyes scrutinized her.

"Do you envision all of that when he whispers sweet nothings in your ear? When he promises you the world? Do you even know who he is, *Yoori*? You only know that he is powerful. You don't know just how powerful he is and how much power is at stake for him. What do you think Ju Won and Dong Min are talking to him about right now?"

Yoori's heart stilled at the question.

"They're telling him to get rid of you, to cut you loose. They're telling him to kill you if he has to." He uncrossed his leg and leaned in closer to her. "You see Yoori, three years ago, Soo Jin was the beloved protégé. The one the three Advisors loved like a daughter and the one the Underworld revered as a beloved Queen. But things have changed since then. An Soo Jin is still revered as a beloved young Queen in death, but right now there are two young Kings who are more than overshadowing anything she ever did. In the course of the last three years, Lee Ji Hoon and Kwon Tae Hyun have brought this world to heights it has never seen. In the course of the last three years, this world has never been more ready to revere one of them as the official Lord of the Underworld. *That's* how far they've come. *That's* what is at stake here."

"What does this have to do with me?"

"At one point in time, Soo Jin was Ju Won's favorite. But she's not anymore. She never succeeded in what he needed her to do and even in death, he has not forgiven her. He's been deciding between Tae Hyun and Ji Hoon. The sole fact that Ji Hoon reminds Ju Won of the embarrassment that Soo Jin was to him is the reason why Ji Hoon isn't reigning as the prime candidate for the position. Right now, the one closest to the throne is Tae Hyun."

Jung Min's jaw clenched in distaste.

"Though it sickens me that this little punk, who was never trained to fill the role of a King for our society, is gaining such power, I do have to give him credit for one thing: he's proven time and time again that he's a force to be reckoned with. He may be young and inexperienced, but no other King in history has ever had such a strong following. The fact that he has the 1st layer in the palm of his hands is the reason why he offers so much appeal to Ju Won. No King in history has ever had the appeal to command such respect from the 1st layer. It has *only* been Tae Hyun."

"Why are you telling me all of this?"

"*That's* what you're standing in the way of, Yoori. His greatness. This is what Dong Min is reminding Tae Hyun of right now. My brother is angry...very angry that his protégé is being so irresponsible that he's allowing a girl to ruin everything that he's been working toward. He's angry...just like I am with Ji Hoon for allowing you to cloud his judgment. I heard about what happened at Vertical VII and I couldn't be more disgusted at the behavior both exhibited. It is one thing to fight, but it is another to fight over a girl."

He swallowed roughly, his face softening when reminded of Ji Hoon.

"I understand what Ji Hoon is going through after seeing you with Tae Hyun, and I can empathize with his pain. Dong Min, however, isn't as understanding with Tae Hyun. Right now, he's reminding Tae Hyun of all the power he has and all the power he will lose if he continues to allow you to distract him. And because it seems that Tae Hyun is Ju Won's favorite for the time being, Ju Won is right there as well, convincing Tae Hyun to get rid of you before you ruin everything."

As if sensing how uncomfortable Yoori had gotten, Jung Min showed an uncharacteristic trait. He became more understanding.

"He may love you now, but he won't love you for long. Tae Hyun is just like any other man who has ever walked the earth. He only seeks things that are untainted. He only seeks things that aren't damaged. He would never love you. He would *never* love Soo Jin. Because if there was only one thing Soo Jin was remembered for, it was her hatred for the Serpents family. She had always been very loyal like that. Above all else, her loyalty had always been with her father and her brother. Kwon Ho Young killed her father and nearly killed her older brother in the process. Soo Jin made the promise over her father's grave that she'll exterminate the entire Serpents existence if it was the last thing she did."

He chuckled cruelly. "It is ironic, isn't it? You pretend to die, you somehow give yourself amnesia, you start a new life and now you find yourself in bed with the same person who represents the one gang that you despise most in this world."

"I'm not her." Yoori's voice was strained as she fought to keep her cool.

Something Jung Min said struck her. It speared a stake through her heart.

He was right.

Tae Hyun could never love Soo Jin—just like Soo Jin could never love Tae Hyun.

"But you are and trust me, Dong Min is telling him all of that this very second," Jung Min persisted, feeding on the depression consuming her eyes. "Ju Won is right there with him as Dong Min tells him how much you despise him and his family. He's telling him if he isn't careful, you'll be the first to kill him once he lets his guard down."

"Tae Hyun won't hurt me," Yoori said inflexibly, the fire searing through her as she tried to make sense of the emotions that Jung Min evoked from her. She sharpened her eyes onto him and she saw Jung Min stiffen. Even if it was brief, she could see that her anger scared him.

He sighed, seemingly used to her hardheadedness. He gazed at her, like a father would at a daughter who was about to make the biggest mistake of her life.

"You were the daughter I never had. I'm here right now, not because I want to hurt you, but because I want what's best for you." The intimidation dissipated from his eyes. There was nothing left there but concern. "I favor Ji Hoon, not only because I know he'll lead our world well, but because he loved you and sacrificed everything for you. The reason why everyone in this world favors Tae Hyun is because he would *never* do the same for you. I can't stress this enough. If forced to choose between you or the throne, he'll choose his throne. And right now, that's what he's doing as he's sitting there, listening to Dong Min and Ju Won."

With pity, he dutifully poured more tea into her empty teacup.

Yoori, who was so frazzled with emotions, couldn't even keep her eyes set on him. All she could think about was...everything.

"You're living on the brink with him right now, Yoori." His voice swam over her and continued to drown her. "It's not too late, but it will be if you don't wrap your mind around the severity of this situation. Get yourself out of this before Tae Hyun shows his true colors and gets rid of you himself."

"You don't know him like I do," Yoori replied, recalling his personality when he was around her. Always caring, always loving. "You don't see how he is around me. He cares about me...a lot. He'll never hurt me."

"He'll hurt you if he's provoked. And you *will* provoke him." Heeding the questionable gaze in her eyes, he went on. "You're merely living on borrowed time. You can't escape from your past, no matter how desperate you are. One day, you'll remember everything. You'll remember that you're a trained killer, you'll remember that you need to kill to survive, and you'll remember who you despise with all your soul. Soo Jin will overpower you and Tae Hyun won't see you as his beloved girlfriend anymore. He'll just see you as he sees Ji Hoon. He'll see you as his rival, his enemy, and the one he needs to kill to get to the top. Get out of this now. I don't want to be there when he puts a bullet through your heart."

If it was anyone else, then Yoori was sure that the girl would be fretting in her pants. But Yoori wasn't anyone else and she knew that. Despite her hatred for Soo Jin, the one thing she would thank Soo Jin for was the ability to read someone that she had grown up with all her life. Yoori didn't have any memories of Jung

Min. However, she did possess the residual power to read him just as Soo Jin was able to read him. After sitting with him for quite some time now, observing his every move and analyzing the fluctuations in his voice, a once dazed Yoori knew better now. She could tell that Jung Min was being genuine with his concern – just as he was being inauthentic.

"Why did you really come to see me, Jung Min?" she asked stoically, her eyes unyielding as she stood up from her seat, ready to leave and get away from this man.

He was up to something and she knew it. And judging by the smirk that appeared on his once "concerned" face, Yoori knew she was right in thinking that she wasn't dealing with a caring man who was once a father figure to Soo Jin. She was dealing with an experienced Advisor who was an expert with manipulation.

"Second chances for people like us are rare, my child," he began, sitting peacefully in his seat. Too peacefully. "It's been three years since you've left our world and this world still reveres you like you're its Queen. Regardless of the fact that you were never an official gang leader, your reverence has only grown stronger throughout your absence. Now you're back and you have two Kings in the palm of your hands. Ji Hoon would give you this world; Tae Hyun would fight you for it."

He narrowed his fierce eyes onto her. "We gave you back your gun. This is your second chance from all of us, Soo Jin – from all three Advisors. We can forgive you for everything, as long as you finish the deed we assigned you that fateful night. Get rid of Tae Hyun and finish what you started that night in the club."

"Wh—What do I have to finish?" Yoori asked, now more curious than ever about what the fuck Soo Jin was doing in that nightclub. She sat back down, her eyes dimmed with anticipation.

Jung Min stood up. He threw a stash of cash on the table and gazed ominously at Yoori. "You wasted three whole years. All you have to know is that you were a disappointment three years ago and if you don't finish what you have agreed to finish, then the next time you die, it will be a sure thing."

"Wait," she spoke before he walked away. Desperation teemed in her voice. "Don't go yet."

Jung Min sighed and sat back down. When he was settled in his seat, Yoori continued tentatively. "Can...can you tell me more about Soo Jin?"

Despite knowing that it was a bad idea to go down this route, Yoori still wanted to learn more about Soo Jin.

The corner of his lips lifted. "You haven't been enlightened by your boyfriends?"

"Tae Hyun did not know her, he has only heard rumors about her. Ji Hoon was her boyfriend, his view on her is tinted." She regarded him intently. "I want to hear it from you…the one who was there when she was born—the one who trained her all her life."

Jung Min pondered her words for a few moments before saying, "Do you know why she was Ju Won's favorite?"

She shook her head.

"Because out of all the Underworld Royals, she lost her soul the quickest."

When Yoori remained quiet, he went on. "She was a natural born killer. Even with no training, she knew what she had to do to survive." His eyes grew brighter. It was as though he was reminiscing a warm memory of his own child. "During the eighth month of her training, Ju Won decided to pit her against three well-known assassins in the Underworld. She was only ten and she had yet to be fully trained. There was absolutely no chance she'd come out victorious in that battle. Yet the night before the match, Soo Jin did something that surprised all of us. Whereas other young Royals took their chances to be beaten by these three killers, Soo Jin decided that she wanted to win. She did not want to lose to them; she wanted to conquer them."

Yoori swallowed tightly. "What did she do?"

"She put rat poison in their food and poisoned them before the match."

Yoori pushed her teacup away, suddenly losing her appetite.

Jung Min did not share the same distaste. If anything, he seemed to grow fonder of the story he was sharing. "When I asked her why she cheated, she said it was because she was their Queen. 'The Queen always wins.'"

He looked at Yoori. "*That* is the type of person Soo Jin was. Even at a young age, she was merciless. She does not play by the rules. Her only goal is to conquer and win. If she cannot beat someone the conventional way, then she will find other ways to be victorious." He smiled, his eyes becoming mocking. "How do you think she will play if she was to fight your beloved Tae Hyun for the Underworld throne? Do you think she will play fairly…or will she revert back to her old ways?"

When Yoori exhaled painfully, Jung Min shook his head. "You will never get to keep him. If and when your memories ever return, Soo Jin will never let you keep him. You said that Tae Hyun will never hurt you, but Soo Jin does not have the same qualms. She will hurt him and in turn, he will forget about you and wage a war against her as well. "

He leaned in, his eyes never straying from hers.

"Your love will never conquer what this society raised them to be. There is no happy ending for you…but there is still your second chance. Like I said, get rid of Tae Hyun and finish everything you started."

"I do not know what was started that night," she voiced with anguish. Pain ripped through her. All of his words were echoes of the thoughts already percolating in her mind. He didn't have to tell her that it was inevitable Soo Jin and Tae Hyun would wage a war against one another if they "met" —she already knew that. She took in a weary breath. "How can I finish it when I do not even know where to begin?"

He looked at her with pity. "The answer lies in your memories. The concoction given to you is strong, but no doubt it has weakened with time. All you have to do is let go of the walls you're holding up and let Soo Jin out. You do not need to know how it started, you just need to let her finish it."

Realization dawned over Yoori. She examined him with clarity in her eyes. "This is the true reason for your visit, isn't it? To resurrect Soo Jin?"

Jung Min smirked before making his true exit this time.

"You may not realize it now, but a war is coming. The stadium for this war has been set. Soon, Tae Hyun will appear in that stadium and you will join him. You will not fight beside him; you will be his adversary. There will be a war of the Gods and when it ends, one of you will become the Lord of the Underworld and one of you will die. Which would you prefer, Yoori? Would you rather become an eternal God in this society, or finally know true death?"

"When you will have to step down from being a God..."

22: Dinner Party

Yoori couldn't stop thinking about her unexpected meeting with Jung Min when the following night came around. Tae Hyun hadn't come home after he left that day. This fact did little to calm her nerves about what type of things Ju Won and Dong Min may have told him when he met with them.

She was disjointed with concerns that were founded and unfounded. If Jung Min's primary goal was to make her paranoid, then he succeeded because Yoori was more worried than ever. She sat around in the apartment, mulling over everything he said. She was worried about all of this and she was concerned about Tae Hyun's safety.

Yoori was only reassured that things were possibly still fine when Jae Won and Kang Min stopped by to check up on her. They informed her that Tae Hyun was busy catching up with Serpents business. They told her he wouldn't make an appearance at home until the night of the dinner gathering. Yoori had hoped that she would at least be able to converse with Kang Min and Jae Won about what happened. The need escaped her when she saw how tired they were and how quickly they had to leave to deal with Serpents business. She made the executive decision to not tell them. She was afraid they'd share that she met with Jung Min with Tae Hyun. She didn't want him to worry.

Everything else aside, Yoori still had to vent this entire thing out to someone and she knew she couldn't vent out to anyone else but her best friend. Chae Young and Yoori had been constantly on the phone since their meeting at the grocery store. As such, it wasn't atypical when Yoori invited Chae Young over the next night to catch up. She caught Chae Young up on everything that happened: the movie date, the park date, the seduction, the morning after and the meeting with Jung Min.

Of course, she conveniently left out incriminating information about anything pertaining to her being An Soo Jin. She just vaguely told Chae Young that Jung Min told Yoori to stay away from Tae Hyun because she was a distraction and that if she didn't, Tae Hyun would eventually get rid of her himself. It wasn't that she didn't trust Chae Young. Yoori would trust Chae Young with her life. However, there were just some things that Chae Young, for her own safety, didn't need to be privy to. Yoori being Soo Jin was one of those things.

"What a paranoid old man. Tae Hyun would never hurt you!" Chae Young cried after hearing Yoori's story.

She was lying across the sofa in the living room, covering herself with Yoori's purple blanket. All that was visible was the faux lined hood of her white jacket and her black pajama pants.

"You should've seen that boy when he came into the diner and asked me where you were. He was chalk white. You couldn't tell he was a crime lord until he started glaring at me after I yelled at him for making you cry."

Dressed in a white sweater and black silk lounge pants, Yoori frowned protectively on the nearby couch. "What an ass. He gave you 'the glare'?" she asked angrily, pissed that Tae Hyun would dare disrespect her friend like that. She shook her head. "I'm sorry for that. He's someone who is used to getting his way. Just continue to speak to him as you would to anyone else. He needs to be grounded. In the meantime, I'll yell at him for you."

"No, no, he was nice," Chae Young mediated with a wave of dismissal. "I think he was just shocked when I told him you were crying. But you should've seen how antsy he was when I wrote my address on a napkin for him and offered him the spare key. He just grabbed the napkin, said he didn't need the key, and sprinted out." Chae Young shrugged. "What I'm saying is that it's obvious the guy is in love with you. When I'm with Jae Won, Kang Min, and Hae Jin, all they would talk about is how obvious it is that he's fallen for you. I mean, it would be stupid of him to take what those old men tell him to heart. Just because you resemble this An Soo Jin, it doesn't mean anything. I mean, you had a life. You're from Taecin for heaven's sake!"

Yoori smiled meekly at the lie that Chae Young still believed to be the truth. "Well, I haven't seen him since he left to meet them. Jae Won, Kang Min, and Hae Jin have been busy with the Underworld stuff too. He had Kang Min and Jae Won come check up on me briefly, but that was it…" It was silly, but Yoori couldn't help but venture on to the darker trails of possibilities. "What if…what if he actually takes them seriously and—"

"You enslaved the guy for a week, Yoori," Chae Young assured, catching on to where Yoori was heading with her question. "He's a 'King' in this society. He has a lot of stuff to catch up on. Don't be stupid and think anything else of it. Right now, you're just walking into a trap. These Advisors sound like they're instigators. You can't allow them to affect you. You're the only one who has been with Tae Hyun. You're the only one who knows who he truly is. You can't allow someone else to mess with that knowledge because once you do, everything will just fall to shit."

Yoori nodded vehemently at Chae Young's advice. This was why Yoori loved speaking to Chae Young. Yoori always had the voice of reason reveling in her mind, but Chae Young was always the ultimate voice of reason. Though she was a year younger than Yoori, Yoori was almost sure that Chae Young was older and wiser than her. She truly believed Chae Young was a ninety-year-old woman who was stuck in a beautiful twenty-two-year-old's body.

"You're right," Yoori conceded thankfully. "It's always so easy to get off track in this world. I'm glad I have you to keep me in line. I would be going crazy right now if I didn't have someone to talk to about this."

Chae Young smiled, giving Yoori an air-pat on the shoulder. "Now let's move the topic along to something more fun. I'm really excited for dinner tomorrow!"

Yoori shared in this genuine excitement. It was the only thing she had been looking forward to…spending time with her good friends and seeing Tae Hyun again.

"I am too. I've never had a dinner gathering with friends before."

It was a true story. Yoori didn't have any friends in Taecin and only had Chae Young as a good friend before she met Tae Hyun. Now her group of good friends had expanded and Yoori was immensely grateful.

"Speaking of which, I have something for you," Chae Young announced in a sing-songy voice. She reached behind her for one of the shopping bags she brought in when she came to visit Yoori. She pulled out a sparkly red gift bag.

"From Hae Jin and I," she said happily, reaching across to hand the bag over to Yoori.

Yoori was floored by the gesture. "But I didn't get anything for you," she said faintly, grabbing the bag with hesitation.

Chae Young waved her hand as if she was warding off a fly. "Don't worry about it. It was just something that we saw while shopping. We just wanted to get it for you. Wear it for the dinner tomorrow, okay?"

"What the hell, this is so nice!" Yoori shouted, her eyes blossoming at the sight of a pair of diamond earrings and a diamond bracelet. The gorgeous jewelry layered over a silk, chiffon white dress that sat humbly beneath it. "The two of you just decided to buy me a beautiful dress and diamonds?"

Chae Young shrugged languidly. "Well, Jae Won and Kang Min picked out the diamond set. We all chipped in." She laughed, jumping over to hug Yoori, who was gazing at the items with disbelief. "No tag-backs, okay?" Chae Young exclaimed. "You have to keep all of it and you have to wear it tomorrow!"

"But—"

"Uh!" Chae Young raised a silencing finger to Yoori, who was trying to pack everything up and give it back to her. "Don't bother because I'm not taking it back. We shredded the receipt already. Now you better wear it tomorrow and be the pretty hostess that you are."

Despite the beauty of the diamonds sparkling before her, she was more entranced with the short dress that sat below it. Yoori rasped her fingers over the dress in awe. "Do you think—?"

"Tae Hyun will like it?" Chae Young finished for Yoori, her smile conveying that this was the plan. "He'll fall to his knees once he sees you in this."

■ ■ ■

Yoori's hair was swept up the next night. Diamond pins held her hair up like clouds, leaving only a few loose strands to swim close to her ears. She glided across the living room, placing the fine China on the enormous dinner table that Tae Hyun had shipped in specifically for this little dinner party.

Yoori had never styled her hair in this manner. It had always been too stylish for her. Yet, as soon as the white sleeveless dress came over her chest and fell to her thighs, Yoori knew she couldn't do justice to the beauty of this dress, or the diamond earrings and diamond bracelet that her friends bought for her, if she had allowed her long black hair to stay down as she usually allowed it to. So she placed her hair up and magic happened.

Even as she stood in front of the full-length mirror, she could see how the light adored her and the outfit she wore. Her bare shoulders glowed in the light, giving off a purity shine of sorts. She even wore diamond-encrusted heels to match. It was silly to say, but she felt like a princess. It was irony to the situation she found herself in. She was in anything but a fairytale story. Regardless, she smiled gently and twirled around, lost in a world where she felt like she was dancing on clouds.

No matter how blissful this moment was, it couldn't have matched the feeling she felt when Tae Hyun, after about two days of not seeing him, walked into the apartment just as she was lining the champagne glasses.

His expression was weary when he walked in. However, as soon as he laid eyes on her, Yoori could see the light shine through his eyes. He stopped in his tracks and gazed at her like she was the most beautiful thing he had ever seen.

Feeling her breath lodge itself in her chest, Yoori discounted the assumption that he was actually looking at her like he had never seen such beauty. Needless to say, it was a bit conceited of her to acknowledge that, but it was honest to how she really thought he felt. Or was it what she *hoped* he felt? Yoori wasn't sure. The only thing she was certain of was that she had never felt more beautiful until Tae Hyun walked in and stared at her like she was a dream.

"Thanks for leaving me with all the work, jerk-face," Yoori casually greeted, breaking the unearthly silence that suspended over them. She hoped there wouldn't be any tension from his meeting with the Advisors that would transpire here. "This was your dinner party to set up and now, I'm stuck doing all the work."

"Isn't that the duty of an assistant?" he asked with warm amusement.

Yoori felt her heart lift. At least he was still in a good mood when he was talking to her. His expression still had remnants of awe sprinkled over them. His lingering gaze fell on her. Shortly after, he broke his attention away. He placed the boxes of dessert on the kitchen counter.

"Speaking of which, I think we have to talk about your job," he announced, nearly causing Yoori to knock over a champagne glass because she was so thrown with his words.

"As fun as this has been, I think it's time for us to end this 'working relationship.' I've already decided that your last day would be tomorrow."

Despite the casualness of his voice, trepidation still swung inside her. The meeting with Jung Min flashed through her mind, along with the concern about things changing between them because of all these external factors.

Yoori attempted to hide the disappointment in her voice. She doubted she was too successful. "You decided all of that after you met with Ju Won and Dong Min?"

Tae Hyun tensed at the soft accusation in her question. He shook his head. His gaze never left her as he continued to speak. "I've been thinking about it for a while now." His steady voice made her believe that this statement was true. "I've stolen you from your world for long enough, and you've already helped me with more than I could ever imagine. In saying that, I think it's time for you to go on to bigger and better things." He smiled reassuringly at her. "I'm doing that thing where I push the bird away from the nest, I guess. Plus, I've already spoken to Hyun Woo and Daniel."

"Your best friends in the 1st layer," Yoori provided when it seemed like Tae Hyun was about to remind her who they were.

He nodded. "Hyun Woo and Daniel are pretty much the Princes in the 1st layer. Their empires extend everywhere. I spoke to them and I told them about you. I told them how you were interested in the business field and told them how great you are. Whatever field you want to work in, wherever you want to get started in, they can make it happen. And if you're worried about being further associated with the Underworld, you don't have to worry. The Underworld association for the 1st layer only pertains to the executives at the top. They never seep down to the employees. Their empires are still legit. It's just that some of the executives have ties and investments to the 2nd and 3rd layer too."

"That sounds like such a great opportunity," Yoori commented with a forced smile.

However lucky she felt to have such great connections through Tae Hyun, she couldn't shake the sad feeling spreading through her like a forest fire. It wasn't that she didn't have higher aspirations of becoming a more successful person in life. It was just sad that this was Tae Hyun's subtle way of kicking her to the curb.

He had finally chosen to get rid of her as his distraction.

She thought she at least deserved better than this. She paused after a moment's thought. She couldn't complain too much. At least she would have a job waiting for her after this ordeal was over. It just sucked that they had to go out like this. Then again, she couldn't blame Tae Hyun. He worked tirelessly to get into his position of power in the Underworld. She could understand why he would get rid of anything that stood in the way of his greatness over this world.

"So I'll start packing up then," she said weakly, fidgeting nervously with her nails. She no longer felt like a Princess...just frumpy old Cinderella.

Tae Hyun looked at her like she had just gone crazy and kicked another duck. "*Why?*"

Yoori returned the "what-the-hell-have-you-been-smoking" stare. "Well, I won't be your assistant after tomorrow night. You don't need me around here anymore."

"What the fuck, Yoori? Who says you're moving out? I said you're done being my assistant; I didn't say anything about you moving out. Are you kidding me?" He fastened his eyes on the bedroom and pointed at it. "Do you know how time consuming it was to move all my clothes from the closet to the drawers so I can make room for your clothes? I didn't do all that work for nothing. You're not moving out."

"You said you're kicking the bird out of the nest, you confusing butthole!"

"I meant the 'work' nest so you can be on the road to ruling over the corporate world, you inattentive loser."

Although she was relieved with his answer, it was clear to her that she was too paranoid about the Advisors and their "advices" having an adverse effect on their relationship. She couldn't pretend to talk about other stuff until they addressed it.

"Tae Hyun, let's stop beating around the bush. We have to talk about what happened a couple of days ago. What did Ju Won and Dong Min say to you when you met with them?"

Tae Hyun's eyes dimmed at the reminder.

He took a moment to close his eyes. He squeezed the bridge of his nose with his thumb and forefinger and said, "Do we really have to talk about this now?"

Yoori could see that whatever the hell they said to him had been swimming around in his mind too—just like Jung Min's words were swimming around in hers.

Yoori assertively placed her hands on her silk, chiffon covered hips. "Yes. Now."

"They told me to stay away from you," he shared, extracting his fingers from his face. He shrugged and was quiet for a moment before he asked, "What did Jung Min say to you?"

"To stay away from you," Yoori replied, surprised that Tae Hyun knew about Jung Min. "You knew?"

He blinked his eyes in confirmation. "I told you at the lake house that the Advisors, as mentoring as they can be at times, have the biggest inclination to pit people against each other. Dong Min has invested a lot into me, he's concerned about the toll it's taking on my reputation—my status as the potential first Lord of this world."

"What else did they say?" Yoori asked, certain that Dong Min and Ju Won made it their mission to insert more poisonous things into Tae Hyun's mind. Did they tell him what type of person Soo Jin was? That she was a vengeful person? That she hated the Serpents with all that she was?

"It's not important, Yoori," Tae Hyun assured. He approached the table with an opened bottle of Cristal. "I didn't listen to them; I won't ever listen to them. I know you...I care about you a lot and I'm not letting you go. It doesn't matter what their advisements are."

Yoori smiled a little at his assurance. She still felt the need to resolve everything.

"We still need to talk about what they said to us," she persisted, despite her own aversion to it. "Their questionable intentions aside, I still think what they said was valid. We...we should address it."

"And we will...on another night," he agreed unenthusiastically. "But for now, let's enjoy this night. It's our night."

Yoori nodded slowly. She wasn't excited either, but it was one of those things that they couldn't avoid talking about. Normally, Yoori would be all about avoiding complicating issues. However, she knew she couldn't run away from this one, especially when it dealt so heavily with Tae Hyun and his safety in this world.

"Tae Hyun," she whispered, placing a bowl of salad on the table.

"Hmm?"

"I trust you," she emphasized to him. "I really do."

And she meant it. Every bit of it.

"I trust you too," he replied and she knew he meant every word. "I always have."

Relieved that they could place all of that in the backburner for the night, Yoori went back to the lighter issues at hand. "So no more boss and assistant, huh?"

Tae Hyun grinned, pouring Cristal into the champagne glass. "No more."

"I'm not going to miss it," she stated with relief. "Being your personal assistant sucks."

"You were the worst assistant a boss could ask for," Tae Hyun retaliated with the same tone of relief. "You suck at everything, especially at washing the dishes. Whenever you're in the shower, I always run my ass over to the sink to rewash the dishes because you failed so miserably at it."

Yoori's mouth hung open at this new revelation. "You seriously did that?"

His careless shrug was his answer. Yoori entertained throwing another insult his way, but she was too distracted with the yummy dishes. What was the point of bickering when there was such beautiful cuisine in front of her?

"By the way, these look delicious." She placed a big plate of Korean barbeque pork beside the gargantuan plate of sushi and enormous plate of chow mein. In addition to the three biggest dinner plates on the table, there were also plates of white rice, fried rice, lasagna, turkey, chicken, and an impressive selection of overpriced drinks that Yoori couldn't believe Tae Hyun bought. It was definitely a feast fit for a gala as opposed to some small dinner. Yoori wasn't complaining. Her mouth was already watering for the barbeque pork, beef and the kimchi.

Lifting up her gaze, she saw that Tae Hyun had since stopped pouring Cristal into the champagne glass. He was merely holding the bottle in his hand. His eyes were gentle, filled with a different poignancy that Yoori hadn't seen before. It was enough to cause something in her heart to warm; it was enough to beckon the butterflies in her stomach to come out. She wanted to ask him what he was thinking. She found the words frozen at her lips.

He spoke in her place.

"You're breathtaking." His voice was simple, but its content rippled with verity.

He made her breathless.

There was a lingering tone in his voice, like he wanted to use another adjective to describe how beautiful he thought she looked. But instead of using that lingering adjective, Tae Hyun merely said, "I've been trying to think up the right word to say once I saw you in that dress, but the best I've come up with is that I'm speechless. 'Breathtaking' is the only mortal vocabulary that would do justice to anything I'm feeling right now."

Yoori smiled bashfully. Her cheeks were as rosy as ever. "You know how to annoy and charm me at the same time, don't you?"

Tae Hyun shrugged lazily, flashing her a smile that would be the downfall of women all over the world. "It's a gift."

"Well, you look good too," she replied, feigning casualness.

He was wearing a black dress shirt and casual gray pants. He would've looked like the boy next door if he weren't sporting a big fat Rolex that was blinging off his right wrist. The sleeves of his shirt were rolled up to his forearms to permit easier access to handling drinks and food. It failed to hide the wealth he possessed on his wrist.

She wanted to say to him, "You're breathtaking too," but restrained the temptation to save face and to not sound too much like a fan girl.

Before allowing one of those awkward "lovers'" silences to befall them, Yoori broke the silence by casually stating, "I didn't realize dinner parties were your thing."

"They're not. I could care less," he answered truthfully, pouring Cristal into the final champagne glass. "I do it to humor my baby sister and Chae Young, both of whom say that I don't share you with them enough and that I owe them a good dinner party to make up for all my 'selfishness.' Plus, I know how close you are to those four. This is more to entertain you than them."

Yoori laughed, purposely ignoring the last bit for it caused her rosy cheeks to turn scarlet. He definitely had a way with words.

She placed her hands on her hips and surveyed the big feast surrounding them. It was odd how normal it felt to be standing with Tae Hyun like this – like they were just a normal couple celebrating dinner with friends. It couldn't have been more heartwarming for Yoori. She had never done something like this before.

"Do you think we could finish all of this?"

"Are you kidding?" he asked incredulously. "We're *under*-serving with the pigs coming to town." He paused. "Well, not Hae Jin or Chae Young, but the other two."

"Don't say that," Yoori warned, even though she secretly laughed at his comment.

"But have you seen Jae Won?" he persisted with a playful chuckle. "He's gained a bit of weight since joining the gang. I actually joked about it offhandedly when I was talking to both of them and the whole 'your ass is fat' caught on from then."

Yoori's eyes bloomed like a rose. "*You* were the one who started the insult?"

This came out of nowhere. She thought it was Kang Min who came up with the insult this entire time!

Tae Hyun nodded, his face showing a hint of guilt. "I said it to shut him up about something and it worked. Some of the guys have been saying it, but it just happened to be me who vocalized it first. The bad thing for him was that Kang Min was there so the insult within the gang pretty much spread like fire. I actually feel a bit bad, but his reactions are just so entertaining."

"So you're really close to them, aren't you?" It was a question Yoori never really thought to ask. She had always just assumed that Kang Min was deathly afraid of Tae Hyun and that Jae Won, after the whole "I just kicked your ass so your gang has to merge with my gang" fiasco, hated Tae Hyun like no other.

It just proved how self-involved Yoori had been. She hadn't taken notice at the park where the brothers were both so comfortable around Tae Hyun – even Jae Won, who she still hadn't forgotten had told her he didn't know if Tae Hyun could be trusted. Though Kang Min rescinded his statement, Jae Won had yet to rescind his and that bothered her. She trusted Jae Won like he was her younger brother and it perturbed her that he didn't trust Tae Hyun fully.

"I've always been close to Kang Min," he shared distractedly, fixing some of the dinner plates around to make it look more presentable. "Jae Won was annoying to deal with in the beginning but we've seen eye-to-eye on a couple of things and I think he's getting more comfortable now." He smiled to himself. "Possibly a bit too comfortable, but all in all, we're close enough."

The doorbell rang when Tae Hyun finished speaking. The melody was soon followed by two hard knocks that had Tae Hyun approaching the door and Yoori standing beside the dinner table, inwardly clapping at the prospect of her friends finally arriving.

"Oppa!" Hae Jin's excited voice sang through the apartment once the door flew open.

Like a child, she threw herself into her older brother's arms. She hung from his neck as he picked her up with care. Laughing, Tae Hyun effortlessly lifted her up and embraced her as well. Hae Jin was wearing a black trench coat over her black halter dress and she couldn't have looked cuter.

"What the hell, lil sis?" he asked playfully, shaking her around like she was a rag doll. From the looks of it, it seemed that Tae Hyun gave this greeting to Hae Jin often. "Why are you still so skinny?"

"I gained weight!" Hae Jin retorted when he placed her down.

"She's lying! This punk hardly eats!" Kang Min stated heartily, smiling after he walked in and gave a quick bow to Tae Hyun.

Kang Min was sporting a black leather jacket over his black slacks. Tae Hyun nodded as his means of greeting Kang Min and returned his attention to his sister.

"Traitor!" Hae Jin berated at a laughing Kang Min. She playfully shoved Kang Min before turning to her brother. "I do eat, oppa."

"Apparently not enough," Tae Hyun observed. He gently pushed her to the dinner table. "Hurry and eat before you get blown away when the wind comes."

Kang Min laughed as Tae Hyun gave him a quick pat on the shoulder. "Should we test that theory?"

"Bah!" Hae Jin bitterly replied before she spotted Yoori. "Yoori!" she squealed happily, her arms already stretched out as she ran to her.

"Hae Jin!" Yoori squealed back. Under normal circumstances, Yoori wouldn't be the type of girl who would squeal. Yet, it was hard not to be affected when someone as bubbly as Hae Jin runs to you like you're the most amazing thing on earth.

Damn Kwon siblings, Yoori thought. *They have so much charm.*

She watched Tae Hyun greet Jae Won and Chae Young.

"Tae Hyun, everything looks so yummy! Good job!" Chae Young exclaimed with approval. She gave him a hug. She was also dressed in a black dress. The only difference was that she wore a black cardigan over it to make it look a bit more preppy. "And you ordered the dishes we requested too!"

"Yes, I appreciated the long list you guys gave me," he replied with warm sarcasm. "We could've gone to a buffet and it would've cost me less money."

"But what fun is that, Boss Kwon?" Jae Won greeted with a quick bow. He wore a maroon dress shirt and black slacks too. He and Chae Young looked like the perfect preppy couple. "Happy girlfriends, happy lives, right?" he said as Chae Young stood to the side and started gaping at the feast before her.

Tae Hyun nodded before they moved to the dining table. "True saying."

"Oh man, you got the barbeque beef I requested too!" Jae Won shouted like he just won the lottery.

"You're not eating that," Tae Hyun stated inflexibly, snapping Jae Won out of his euphoria.

"Wait, what?" Jae Won asked with confusion. His face was covered with disappointment.

"Yoori's been eyeing that," Tae Hyun explained, already pushing Jae Won away from the food he was saving for her. "You can eat something else."

"But—"

"Happy girlfriends, happy lives, right?"

That statement was the last thing Yoori heard Tae Hyun say before she got distracted.

"Yoori, are you done staring at your lover or can we meet again?" Kang Min joked, appearing beside Hae Jin, who was smiling nonstop at the fact that Yoori was gaping at her older brother instead of paying attention to the people around her.

"For your information, I was staring at the food," Yoori tried to contend. She swiftly pulled her eyes away from Tae Hyun. She hoped her acting worked. Judging by the expressions on her audience members' faces, she doubted it.

Kang Min pursed his lips in confusion. "I didn't realize that the food on the table was that tall. Did you know that, Hae Jin?"

Hae Jin pursed her lips in bafflement too. She shook her head, her curly black hair swishing about. "I don't know…the table looks pretty short to me. Unless 'food' equals my brother."

Yoori crinkled her nose. "You two haven't seen me for a while and instead of being super nice to me for neglecting me because of your 'Underworld stuff,' you decide to gang up on me?"

"We're just kidding, Yoori," said Hae Jin, grabbing Yoori's hand and swaying it about to show her playfulness.

Yoori gave them both a big smile. "So is everything good between you guys?" She made sure her voice was barely above a whisper so that only they could hear her. She hadn't forgotten that Tae Hyun wasn't privy to their relationship.

Hae Jin and Kang Min gazed at one another and nodded. Big, bright smiles lit up their faces. The sight of such happiness caused Yoori's heart to warm.

"Yooooooooooooriiiiiiiiiii!"

"Bosssssss Choiiiiiiii!"

Chae Young and Jae Won shouted in unison. They came running toward her. Yoori had an inkling that Jae Won was just passively mimicking his girlfriend, which was why she couldn't stop laughing when they reached her.

"Boss, you look like a Christmas ornament!"

The laughing ended after she hugged them. Yoori scowled at the comment.

Your ass is fat! Your ass is fat! Your ass is fat! Yoori felt like screaming out. She refrained from doing so just because she looked so cute in the dress. She didn't want to ruin her demure image.

"Christmas ornament?" Kang Min scoffed from the corner when Yoori pulled out of the embrace. Jae Won was standing to one side with Chae Young beside him, Hae Jin beside her, and Kang Min beside Hae Jin. "Why would you say that to a girl?"

"It was a compliment," Jae Won defended, his eyes distraught that anyone could consider his compliment to be an insult.

"What girl in her right mind would be flattered if she was compared to a short, fat and bald ball?"

"You fuc—!" Jae Won curbed the inclination to curse when he noted there were a good amount of females around him. Merely biting his tongue, he said, "I wouldn't mind jabbing you with a broken ornament right now."

"Just compliment me," Kang Min huffed back. "I'm sure it'll hurt more."

"Why you little—!"

"Are we at a family reunion or something?" Tae Hyun's voice thundered over the brothers, causing them to shut up immediately.

He was standing beside the dinner table, his face shrouded with impatience. It appeared that he had been ready to eat for quite some time now and was only waiting for everyone to finish their greetings.

"You two." He pointed at the brothers. "You were the ones who requested the most food. Now it's all here for you. Get your asses over here and start eating before I toss both of you out the window."

That was how dinner got started, with Tae Hyun berating Kang Min and Jae Won like they were his younger brothers and everyone happily taking a seat at the dinner table. The girls sat on one side and the boys sat on the other. They were all excited for the great company and the amazing feast before them.

As dinner progressed, there were a couple of interesting things that Yoori learned. In the amount of time that she had spent separately from Tae Hyun and the brothers, she never once thought they would be as close as they were. When Tae Hyun told her they were "close enough," she couldn't have imagined the scene before her. They didn't look like close friends – they looked like brothers.

With Tae Hyun sitting in the middle, he looked just like an older brother as he laughed, joked, and picked on Kang Min and Jae Won. It was actually entertaining for her. She was silently praising the Lord for a break from all of Tae Hyun's teasing.

Yay for Kang Min and Jae Won getting the sharp end of Tae Hyun's mean wit instead of her!

The relationship was the same way with Hae Jin, Chae Young and herself. Like long lost sisters, Yoori and the girls would whisper things amongst themselves. Such an act would have the boys leaning in to eavesdrop. Yoori was elated with how good dinner was. In her three years worth of memories, she had never experienced a dinner like this. With all the bickering and laughter included, Yoori only realized now how blissful she felt. She actually had friends now. Good friends.

"We were sitting on it, amongst all the rose petals that Kang Min and Jae Won happily spread around, and then the bridge started falling apart!" Tae Hyun shared in disbelief, reliving the events of the night at the park. Of course Tae Hyun, being the gentleman that he was, edited out all the flirting, making out, and questionable use of handcuffs—basically anything incriminating from that very eventful night.

The brothers laughed boisterously.

"I prayed for that to happen!" Jae Won shouted proudly.

"Me too!" Kang Min shouted, high-fiving Jae Won.

"We didn't fall in the water though," Tae Hyun said mockingly. "Unlike these two idiots I know."

Jae Won and Kang Min reddened and shut up immediately.

"So did anything productive happen after we dropped you guys off?" Kang Min asked subtly, drinking from his champagne glass.

Everyone grew quiet to listen to the answer.

Damn him! Yoori knew someone was going to be nosy and start snooping around for more naughty answers. Who knew the first nosy kid was going to be Kang Min?

"We slept," Yoori assured them as Tae Hyun bit into his sushi, his bored face somehow not corroborating her lie. He seemed bitter at the reminder that nothing happened for him that night.

Jae Won furrowed his brows while he bit into his lasagna. "A whole gang of Serpents were climbing on trees and drowning in water and you guys just slept?"

"I…I…" Yoori assumed that Tae Hyun would jump in to save her. To her indignation, he merely took another careless bite out of his sushi. His eyes were glued on her. He, too, was awaiting her answer.

"I—I—Don't talk with your mouth full, you rude person!" Yoori spluttered out at Jae Won.

Jae Won sulked at her command. He looked away, stuffed another sushi into his mouth and went silent.

"Oppa, you should host more dinners like this. It's so fun!" Hae Jin exclaimed from the side, smiling at her brother from across the table.

"Yeah, you throw one hell of a feast, Tae Hyun," Chae Young agreed, stuffing herself with lasagna.

Tae Hyun smiled at the girls. "Yes, I do enjoy throwing dinner parties the two of you invite yourselves to before I even knew I was throwing it."

"You don't share Yoori enough," Chae Young explained. There was no guilt in her smile as she patted Yoori's shoulder with adoration.

"Which reminds me...excuse us," Hae Jin announced suddenly, standing up and grabbing Yoori's hand.

A look of knowledge spread across her face and Chae Young stood up too.

"Wait, where are you three going?" asked Kang Min. His mouth was still stuffed with chow mein.

"The bathroom," Chae Young stated simply.

"There's only one toilet in the bathroom," Jae Won ingeniously proclaimed.

"So?" Hae Jin replied blankly. Her hand was still on a confused Yoori, who didn't know why the hell she was being led to the bathroom. "We're going to have girl talk."

"Since when is it appropriate to discriminate against genders?" Kang Min stated. His face was cloaked with worry as to why the girls were sequestering themselves.

"What are you, a baby?" Chae Young asked jokingly, clearly unhappy that he was bringing gender discrimination into their "girl talk." "Are you going to cry now?"

Kang Min grimaced. "No, that was just a question. Damn, Chae *No-Fun*, that was mean."

Chae Young smiled apologetically. "You know I was just kidding."

"Uh huh," Jae Won voiced with approval, smiling uncontrollably at the sight of his girlfriend picking on his younger brother.

"Just let them go," Tae Hyun said in a brisk tone. "They'll be much nicer to us if they can complain about us in the bathroom."

"But that's why we shouldn't let them go in there!" Jae Won protested.

Kang Min was about to agree with Jae Won when their Blackberries sounded off, interrupting any intentions of keeping the girls from the bathroom.

It happened instantly—just as it did when Tae Hyun's phone rang in their bedroom the other day. A cold chill ran over Yoori's skin as she watched their faces read the text on the screen. They looked troubled.

"We'll be out on the balcony," Tae Hyun announced, already rising to his feet and approaching the balcony. He slid the door open and the brothers followed. They instantly dialed a number and got on to the phone.

"What's going on?" Yoori asked, watching worriedly as the boys stood outside.

"It's nothing," Hae Jin said with a reassuring smile, though even her smile wasn't too certain. "Tonight is the five-minute initiation for the new recruits that are joining the Serpents. The only ones not there right now are my brother, Kang Min, and Jae Won. It's a big event. There are about one hundred and thirty being initiated tonight alone. Everyone is at the Serpents estate right now, setting up. We're all just here for dinner before we go back and get things rolling."

"Serpents estate?" Yoori asked, never hearing Tae Hyun speak of any Serpents estate before. She was never even introduced to it...

"It's where we have our meetings. It's one of the biggest estates in the country, very secluded. It's a secretive place. You'll only know where it is and be able to go inside if you were an actual Serpent," Hae Jin explained, noting the curiosity in Yoori's eyes. "Oppa has never introduced that place to you because he didn't want to directly initiate you into the gang. He wanted to keep you away from all of that."

Yoori nodded absentmindedly before asking, "So what do you guys do for the five-minute initiation?"

One hundred and thirty people in one night? Yoori was certain something more drastic took place for anyone who wanted to join Tae Hyun's gang. As Yoori recalled, the Advisors said that her chances of survival were higher if *they* initiated her. She couldn't imagine how much more violent things could get if any other gang initiated her.

Hae Jin bit her lips. "Sorry Yoori, I would tell you, but we're all put under oath."

Yoori nodded, realizing that although she had known Tae Hyun for quite some time, she really only knew him as Tae Hyun—not the Underworld King, who was so connected that he was deemed as one of the most powerful men in the country. This realization hit her like a splash of artic water. She had always known this, but to realize it to this degree was staggering. Tae Hyun, with all intents and purposes, was going to become a God in this world. If forced to make a decision, why in the world would he choose her over being a revered Lord in the Underworld? This knowledge stung her. It stung her badly.

"Yoori, did you hear what I just said?" Hae Jin's voice came rippling into her ears seconds later.

Yoori snapped out of her stupor and gazed at Hae Jin questionably. "Wh – What did you say?"

"It's something Tae Hyun doesn't want you to know," Chae Young said with a smile. The content of the statement should've sounded cryptic, but there was eagerness in Chae Young's voice. It made Yoori curious.

"What is it?"

"It's his birthday tomorrow."

"*What?*" Yoori wanted to screech out, only to have Chae Young and Hae Jin cover her mouth.

"Shhhhh!" they whispered together, nearly causing her to fall backward.

She pulled their hands off her mouth and then craned her neck in Tae Hyun's direction. He was still on the balcony, leaning against the wall and speaking to the brothers. As though sensing her eyes on him, he met her gaze briefly. Yoori panicked and turned back around to face Chae Young and Hae Jin.

"Why am I just finding out about this now? Why didn't he tell me?"

"Oppa hates celebrating his birthday," Hae Jin explained after a sigh. "Every time we try to do something for him, he either kicks us out or doesn't go out to dinner with us."

Chae Young nudged Yoori suggestively. "But I'm sure if it's just the two of you, you can make something special out of it..."

Chae Young was right. Yoori had to do something special for it. There were no ifs, ands, or buts. Bad things happening aside, Tae Hyun's birthday was still important.

"But what am I going to do for him?" Yoori thought in horror. She felt like she was under pressure to throw the biggest party of all time. She focused her eyes on Chae Young. "Cake! I wanna bake him a cake. Will you help me bake him a cake?"

"I've never heard 'cake' and 'bake' so much in a request, but yeah! I'll help you."

"Great, thank you," Yoori said efficiently before whipping her attention back to Hae Jin. "What's his favorite cake?"

"Red Velvet," Hae Jin answered at once.

Yoori looked at Hae Jin blankly. "What the eff is a 'Red Velvet'?"

"It's a red cake," Hae Jin explained. "Oppa loves them. If you give it to him, he'll be putty in your hands." Hae Jin paused. "Well, more so than usual."

"Will you help me bake it too?" Yoori asked, her eyes blossoming so wide that she felt like Bambi.

"Aww, I would, but I'm hanging out with him during the day. I'll have Kang Min come help. He knows how to do all that baking stuff better than me anyway."

"He won't be busy?"

"I can talk Jae Won into taking over some of his duties," Chae Young assured. "Don't worry, Yoori! Just tell Tae Hyun you want to hang out with me all day. You can shop for him with Kang Min and just come into the diner to bake the cake. Afterward, you can surprise him when you go home."

"Ooooh, that sounds good," Yoori voiced gratefully. An uneasy inkling settled within her. "But will your dad not kill me, since you know...I quit without giving a valid notice?"

Not that it was her fault, of course. It was Tae Hyun's fault. And now she was going to bake him a birthday cake...in the very same diner he stole her from. *Go figure.*

Chae Young waved her hand dismissively. "Don't worry, my dad's mean to you, but he still loves you. I told him that you just had emergency stuff to take care of and he understood. Plus, he's out of town so it won't be an issue."

Woot, woot! Yoori cheered in her head. "Okay, that sounds good. We'll reconvene tomorrow."

"Aye aye, Captain," Hae Jin and Chae Young joked with a salute before the sound of the door opening caught all their attention.

The boys were back.

"Is everything okay?" Yoori asked, seeing the boys pile back in.

Kang Min and Jae Won were shaking from the cold while Tae Hyun was as composed as ever. Yoori wondered if the guy ever got cold. It didn't seem like it.

"We're leaving a bit earlier than expected," Tae Hyun shared, stuffing his Blackberry into his pocket.

"Aw, so dinner's over?" Chae Young complained sadly.

"We'll do it another time," Tae Hyun assured her. Walking into the dining area with Jae Won and Kang Min, he stopped the brothers as each of them grabbed an empty plate to place in the sink.

"I was kidding," he told them amiably. "I'll clean up myself. Just take the girls home and do what you need to do. I'll see you guys there soon."

The brothers smiled appreciatively at Tae Hyun and set the plates down.

"Thanks for dinner, boss," the brothers chimed at the same time.

"Thanks for letting me know and thanks in advance for your help," he responded to them just as Hae Jin walked over to give her brother a hug. Yoori wondered what it was they informed him of and what they were helping him with.

"Aww, thanks for dinner, oppa."

"I'm still seeing you tomorrow, right?" Tae Hyun asked while pulling his sister into an embrace.

Hae Jin laughed merrily and faked a careless shrug,

Tae Hyun pointed at Kang Min when she did this. "You're her best friend. Remind her to hang out with me tomorrow."

"I will," Kang Min confirmed with an amused nod. It was evident that he was always the one Tae Hyun counted on to remind Hae Jin to keep her appointments.

"It's going to be a long night, isn't it?" Jae Won asked wearily, already looking tired. He rubbed his temples in woe.

As Kang Min nodded, Hae Jin said, "After tonight, oppa will lead the single largest gang our society has ever known. So yes, it would be a busy night. We have our work cut out for us."

Perching herself against a nearby wall, Yoori watched quietly while the four official Serpents members grew lost in their conversation about how long the night ahead would be. Yoori watched in utter stillness, her attention focused exclusively on Tae Hyun. He was standing at the other side of the room, laughing while he perched himself against the wall. He was speaking and nodding intently with his sister, Kang Min, and Jae Won. It was a simple sight that was the catalyst for a landslide of emotions that inundated Yoori.

"He may love you now, but he won't love you for long. Tae Hyun is just like any other man who has ever walked the earth. He only seeks things that are untainted. He only seeks things that aren't damaged. He would never love you. He would never love Soo Jin…"

It was funny how life worked. For months now, she threw her attraction for Tae Hyun as mere lust—physical attraction if anything. She knew that she liked him, but she was sure the attraction didn't go past anything physical. Yet as she watched Tae Hyun, realizing how easily he could be taken away from her due to circumstances she couldn't control, she realized something she couldn't deny to herself anymore.

She had fallen for him…*hard*.

Yoori swallowed tightly and fought against the impending sobs that threatened to escape from her dry throat. Realizing that you've fallen for someone shouldn't have this effect on a girl. Yoori was aware of this. Still, she found it difficult to ignore the pain that ripped through her when it was clear that, despite all that was against her, she still cared about him with all her heart.

The air stilled inside her and she acknowledged her stupidity. Out of everyone to fall for, out of all the times to fall out of denial, she chose *this* time to admit that she had fallen for Tae Hyun. Of all people, she had to fall for Tae Hyun…the one who was about to lead the Underworld and the one she was standing in the way of.

"Yoori, are you okay?" Chae Young's voice came over her delicately.

Chae Young stood in front of her and rested a worried hand on Yoori's shoulder. From the angle the other group was in, if they had turned in their direction, it would seem like she was having an intimate conversation with Chae Young. It was a vantage point that she took advantage of. She was so consumed with emotions that she didn't even answer Chae Young. She just continued to peek over in Tae Hyun's direction.

Her eyes ran over his striking features. Her ears bathed in the sound of his laughter vibrating across the walls. He laughed a lot with her and she liked that. Whenever he laughed, he'd make her laugh too. Even when he was teasing her, deep down, she didn't mind it at all if it made him happy. He had the most amazing laughter that would make anything in her world appear brighter.

"I think…I've fallen for him."

Yoori didn't say anymore while she stood there with Chae Young. She didn't delve deeper because she knew Chae Young could read what was going on in her eyes.

There were no more ifs, ands, or buts. After denying it for so long, the truth was finally there for her. There were no fireworks, trumpets, or stopping of worlds. It was just the simple realization that she had fallen for Kwon Tae Hyun.

That simple realization was also the most complex thing she'd ever felt in her life. It was overwhelming and exhilarating for Yoori, who had never felt this way about any other man in her life. How ironic that it was only when she feared that he would be taken away from her did she realize how much she had fallen for him?

Life was cruel.

Her heart clenched.

She realized now what he meant when he said, "I'm not giving *it* back to you."

It was her heart.

He wasn't giving her back her heart.

Her breathing grew shallow.

There was so much working through her body…so much she wanted to cry about. The emotions were overpowering. She was standing in a dining room with her best friends in the world, never feeling happier and now, she felt the need to cry. All of this happiness, all of this love only existed for Tae Hyun's Yoori. It didn't exist for An Soo Jin. No matter how hard she tried to separate herself from Soo Jin, Yoori knew in the end, it was an impossible separation. Soo Jin would always haunt her. If not through memories of her past, then she would haunt her with the prospect of ruining her future. Tae Hyun loved Yoori, *not* Soo Jin. And when the time comes, he'll leave Yoori *because* she's An Soo Jin.

And as Chae Young held her hands, her knowing eyes staring into Yoori's tentative ones, it was then that Yoori knew that Chae Young saw what it was she was feeling. It was a girl thing so to speak, a non-biological sisterhood bond that they shared. She doubted that Chae Young knew exactly what was happening in her mind, but she knew that Chae Young knew enough. She knew that Yoori had just realized how important Tae Hyun was to her—how much she wanted to be with him.

"We'll make sure you bake the best cake for him," Chae Young whispered, her voice dimmed so that only Yoori heard what she said.

There were countless fears running through Yoori as she nodded, countless fears running through her as her guests left, countless fears streaming through her as she helped Tae Hyun clean up, and countless fears tearing through her as Tae Hyun continued to sweep her off her feet while they spent an hour together before he left for the initiation. Despite the fears, she still wanted to give him a great birthday. She still had a few more moments of borrowed time with him and it would be silly to let the moment pass her by without making more good memories.

"What are you thinking about, Brat?" he asked, pressing his forehead against hers.

He stood in the doorway, preparing to leave for the initiation that would change the course of his life forever.

After this, he'd be one step closer to becoming the revered Lord of the Underworld. He would also be a step further from being with her. This was how "love" and "power" worked in the Underworld. It worked inversely...never moving in the same direction.

"How much you fail at life," Yoori joked, smiling innocently at Tae Hyun.

He scoffed in disbelief at her unwarranted insult. She hoped that her stupid little insult would mask the pain that inhabited every nerve in her body. She had never felt so naked and so vulnerable in her life.

"You know how to kill the mood, don't you?" he asked playfully. Walking past her, he proceeded to the door. He gave her a smile before walking out. "Remember, I'm still firing you tomorrow. Better get the tissues out and ready."

"Yes and I'm excited to kill the mood even more when I quit before you fire me tomorrow!" Yoori replied coyly, already excited about surprising him with the birthday cake.

All pain coursing through her aside, Yoori knew his birthday would be a great night for them. She was determined for that. The world owed them that much. They deserved at least one more great night before the world stepped in and pulled them apart. Yoori was bound and determined to make the most out of all the borrowed time she had left with Tae Hyun because in her heart of hearts, she knew it would all be over soon.

It would all be over and everything occurring now would merely be a distant memory in the future.

"And become human again."

23: Birthday Cake

"Do you think Tae Hyun would like this?" Yoori asked the following evening.

She settled herself over the counter in the kitchen diner and cast her gaze down to the circular red cake before her. Having informed Tae Hyun the night before that she was planning on hanging out with Chae Young for the majority of the late afternoon, it was a pretty easy task for Yoori to escape from the apartment, especially because Tae Hyun had gotten in really late and was still sleeping in. It was luck that the birthday boy couldn't find time to snoop around and find out what she was up to. Yoori was grateful for this. She was never too good with holding in secrets and she doubted she could hold many secrets from Tae Hyun if he really wanted to know something from her.

"He'll love it!" Chae Young exclaimed, pushing the black birthday gift bag to the side so she could get a better view of the cake. It was sitting between Yoori and Kang Min.

The birthday present was one of the hardest gifts that Yoori had to purchase to date. She was extremely thankful that Kang Min was there to help her buy it. She was also thankful for him as he ran around the grocery store with her, making sure they found all the ingredients for the cake before they went to the diner where Chae Young awaited them.

"Are you kidding?" Kang Min answered, helping Yoori as they frosted the red cake together. "He'll love anything you make him."

"You make it sound like Tae Hyun's freaking hypnotized by me. Do you not know how blunt he is?" She distractedly spread frosting over the cake. "Homeboy would be more likely to criticize me to death and make me eat it before he'll ever put it in his precious mouth."

It was a true story. Everyone kept telling her how much Tae Hyun would like anything she gave him. Although Yoori knew this too, she also knew that Tae Hyun wouldn't let any opportunity to make fun of her pass him by—even if that meant teasing her about a possibly poisonous birthday cake.

"Well, we tasted the sample we made!" said Chae Young. "It tasted good!"

Yoori was still skeptical. "Yeah, but what if only that sample was good and the rest is just shitty?"

"Then I guess you offer him your body instead," Kang Min suggested jokingly. "Should we pack a cup of frosting in your bag in case you need to resort to Plan XXX?"

He quit laughing when he received a scolding smack from Yoori, who nearly fell off the counter when she put all her force into that hit.

He was wearing a navy blue hoodie with blue jeans. Yoori was sure she left a flour handprint on his hoodie when she smacked him. Because he made her bitter, she made the executive decision to not tell him she vandalized his clothes.

"You dare speak to me like that?"

Kang Min made a bitter face at Yoori. He ceased with the frosting and shook off the pain of her smack. "It's not perverted because you're like my big sister."

"Just disturbed," Chae Young pointed out, sticking her hands in her apron. She was wearing black jeans and a red turtleneck top underneath the white apron. On typical occasions, it would be unusual for Chae Young to hang out in the kitchen, but since there were no customers and the kitchen staff had left early, Chae Young was able to help out more so than Yoori could imagine.

To a degree, it made Yoori feel bad because Chae Young shared with them that the diner hadn't been doing so well in terms of business. There were always just a couple of nights where the diner didn't have any customers. Yoori recalled this trend when she worked here. Due to this fact, the diner closed early on certain days. Tonight was one of those nights where it worked in Yoori's favor.

"Ew, that's true," Kang Min conceded after hearing Chae Young's thought-provoking argument. He shook his head and returned his attention to frosting the remainder of the cake. They were almost done. "I gotta tell you, I feel a bit girly right now. How was it that I got stuck with the shopping and cake duty?"

"Jae Won hates shopping and he would've taste-tested the whole cake if he was here," Chae Young replied with a big smile when reminded of her boyfriend. "Plus, he's busy helping Tae Hyun with some Underworld stuff from what I heard."

"Okay, done!" Yoori announced when the cake was completely snowed in by the frosting. She motioned at Chae Young to approach the counter with the red icing. There was no way she was writing the message herself when she could get a talented person to do it. "Chae Young, go!"

"Okay, what do you want it to say?" Chae Young asked, standing in front of the chubby frosted cake. "Happy Birthday, Tae Hyunnie? Happy Birthday, Sweetie? Happy Birthday, Hun?"

"Happy Birthday, *Snob*," Yoori said proudly.

Well, she was proud until a boisterous round of laughter emitted from Kang Min and Chae Young.

"Good one!" Kang Min and Chae Young laughed at Yoori's joke, or what they thought to be a joke until they realized she was serious.

"What?" Yoori asked, her expression utterly offended. She thought it was cute.

"Yoori, you're such a loser-face," Chae Young criticized bluntly. "Do you not have a single romantic bone in your body?"

Yoori wanted to huff and puff at her friend's critical words. She controlled herself. She was still grateful that Chae Young was kind enough to help her with Tae Hyun's birthday surprise.

"Um, did you not see me bake this cake," Yoori began defensively before muttering under her breath, "*under your supervision*, and buy him the birthday gift, *under Kang Min's supervision?*"

When the unimpressed gazes remained on their faces, Yoori silently added, "It's...it's our thing."

"And sometimes I get annoyed when Hae Jin calls me 'Suga Bear,'" Kang Min voiced, shaking his head at how unromantic Yoori was.

Yoori's mouth twitched. Suga Bear? There was definitely not enough time to make fun of that.

"Oh, just do it!" Yoori instructed to Chae Young, who began to carefully place the icing on the white frosted cake. "Hurry! I need to go before the storm comes and it snows!"

"Okay! Okay!" said Chae Young, steadying herself. She quickly wrote the message. "Here! I did all the hard work." She handed Yoori the icing. "Just write 'Snob.'"

Yoori eyed the icing apprehensively. She didn't want to mess up the cake. "Why?"

"It'll be like your signature on the cake," Chae Young explained, stuffing it in Yoori's hand.

"Oh...okay, good idea!" Yoori acknowledged, trembling as she wrote "Snob" on the cake.

Kang Min nodded in amazement. "Damn Chae Young, you're like an expert on everything, aren't you?"

"You better recognize, *Suga Bear*," Chae Young mocked in a falsetto voice. She laughed while Kang Min gave her the death glare. Apparently no one but Hae Jin was allowed to call him "Suga Bear."

"Okay, done!" Yoori declared, breaking up an argument that would've commenced between Chae Young and Kang Min. "How does it look?"

"Oooh, looks delicious," they approved.

"Okay, hurry before the storm comes," Chae Young urged, grabbing a white to-go cake box from underneath one of the shelves. She placed it on the counter as Kang Min helped Yoori pick up the red plate beneath the cake. She carefully deposited it into the to-go box. Once the cake was safely inside, Yoori shut the box and tucked it into an awaiting shopping bag that Chae Young had held out for her. As she did this, Kang Min ran to the side to grab his keys.

"Thank you!" Yoori cooed, jumping excitedly to hug Chae Young. "Thank you so much for helping! I lub you!"

"You're welcome." She pushed Kang Min and Yoori out of the diner. "Now go! Seduce the hell out of birthday boy!"

Yoori heard that snow was falling tonight and she was determined to see Tae Hyun before it fell. Maybe if it worked out well, she could have him blowing out the cake just as the first snowflake fell. That would definitely be romantic.

"Oh crap, it's cold!" Yoori cried once a puff of cold air slammed against her, causing her long black hair to fly all the way to one side. She wore a black zip up hoodie and baby blue lounge pants and now, she was paying the price as the cold seeped through her clothing and molested her skin.

After hearing Kang Min unlock his BMW, which was parallel parked right beside the diner, she instantly pulled the passenger door open and threw herself in.

"Yoori seduce someone?" She heard Kang Min joke after he ran into the car. "I'd pay to see that."

"Hey, I flirted on the bridge," Yoori argued.

The car started and she waved appreciatively at Chae Young, who ran back into the diner to get ready to close up.

Darkness had crept over the city since she was last outside and Yoori was more excited than ever to see Tae Hyun. She felt silly admitting it, but she missed him.

"Didn't the bridge fall apart afterwards?" Kang Min asked with humor.

"I *hate* you," was all that Yoori could muster out when Kang Min placed his BMW into gear and sped through the streets, swerving left and right, cutting through thickening and then thinning traffic that led back to the apartment.

All the while, as the nightlife of the city passed her by, Yoori's full attention was placed on the cake box that was sitting quietly on her lap. Her heart was beating loudly against her chest as she sat patiently in the car. It continued to pound as she ran out of Kang Min's car and sped into the apartment complex. It was hyperventilating against her chest as she stood in the elevator with Kang Min, waiting to be whisked up to the apartment. Smiling proudly, she pressed the cake box closer against her thumping chest.

You better appreciate it or I'll cake you, she threatened telepathically when Tae Hyun's face came into her mind. She was so excited. She couldn't wait to give it to him.

"I can't believe you tripped," a soft voice meandered through the hall when the elevator doors slid open. "You're such a loser."

Stepping out of the elevator with Kang Min, Yoori curiously craned her neck to see who was in the hall with them. In the further end of the bright hall, she found Hae Jin walking out of the apartment with Jae Won, who was limping beside her. He was hissing in annoyance.

"You think your 'Suga Bear' would've done better if he was walking around in the dark?" Jae Won grunted in pain.

"What's going on?" Yoori asked, approaching them in curiosity.

Like drapes in the wind, Jae Won and Hae Jin turned at the sound of Yoori's voice. Hae Jin was wearing a long maxi pink dress and Jae Won was in a blue jacket and dark jeans. A big smile spread across Hae Jin's face while a smile of agonized pain took over Jae Won's.

"Yoori!" Hae Jin greeted happily, rushing over to Yoori.

Jae Won limped pathetically behind her.

"Boss," he grunted, struggling to stand up straight once they reached the still curious Yoori and Kang Min.

"What's wrong?" She was unable to take her eyes off Jae Won and his overly tormented (and dramatic) face. "What happened?"

Hae Jin groaned like she thought Jae Won was being such a drama queen. "The electricity in the apartment somehow went off when I was having dinner with my brother. Oppa called Jae Won here to go and buy candles and help brighten the place up." She sharpened her eyes on Jae Won. "Genius here, while helping set up the candles, couldn't handle the darkness, tripped and knocked over a candle, nearly setting the apartment on fire. Oppa got pissed, thanked us for our help, and kicked us out."

"Way to go, smart one," Kang Min voiced to his brother. He reached out for Hae Jin's hand and pulled her to him. "It would make sense that *you* would be the one to ruin boss's birthday with his girlfriend."

"Nothing caught on fire," Jae Won defended sullenly. "Plus, he'll be fine." His eyes caught sight of the cake box in Yoori's hands. "Especially when little boss here walks in with that little present."

Little boss? If she had the energy, she would've smack his head for calling her "*little boss*" like she was a neighborhood elf. Instead of voicing her anger, she moved on to more important matters at hand.

"So he's not in a good mood?" Yoori asked tentatively, a bit pissed off that Jae Won may have ruined Tae Hyun's mood on his own birthday.

"He'll be fine once he sees you," Hae Jin answered. She glanced at the cake box. Her smile grew wider in approval. It was a smile that Yoori realized mirrored that of Kang Min and Jae Won's.

Yoori eyed them oddly, suddenly feeling the suspicious nerve on her skin spark up.

"Why are you guys smiling and *smiling* so much?"

Kang Min became suspiciously panicky at her observation. "Alright, stop wasting time. Go in, Yoori," he ushered, pushing her toward the door.

"Wait, what's going on?" Yoori's eyes were wide as she stared up at the three musketeers, who were now gawking at her as if they were watching their kid go off to prom.

"TaeRi Fighting!" Hae Jin encouraged with a raised fist.

Yoori blinked at Hae Jin.

"What the eff is a TaeRi?" Yoori asked with confusion.

No one answered her. Instead, Jae Won merely gave a stiff nod to Kang Min and Hae Jin to move ahead.

"Actually, before you go in, can I talk to you for a minute, boss?" Jae Won requested, already pulling Yoori to the side.

Kang Min and Hae Jin had already walked into the elevator. They stood inside it, their hands stretched out to keep the elevator door from closing. They waited for Jae Won.

"What is it?" Yoori prompted. Tae Hyun's cake box was still pressed with care against her chest.

Jae Won glanced his eyes over to Kang Min, who was still waiting patiently inside the elevator. His silence was a hint that he was listening to everything with approval. Yoori involuntarily followed his gaze before refocusing her attention to Jae Won.

"Jae Won?"

He looked at her, his eyes veiled with something that was along the lines of a brother's approval of something.

"I just wanted you to know...for what it's worth...I trust Tae Hyun too."

"Come again?"

She heard what he said, but she couldn't *believe* what she just heard.

"That night, when we were in the limo, Kang Min and I told you that we weren't sure if Tae Hyun could be trusted," he reminded quietly, his voice purposely soft so Hae Jin wouldn't overhear them. A gleam of approval continued to touch his eyes. "I just wanted you to know that for what it's worth, I trust him too. I trust that he truly cares for you and that he'll do anything to protect you. And that's enough for me and Kang Min."

"What brought on this change?" Yoori asked, already feeling a rock lift off her chest.

Out of the two brothers, it had always been Jae Won who was the most cautious when it came to Tae Hyun. Yoori had always presumed that this "distrust" for Tae Hyun would always continue because Jae Won was forced to merge gangs under coercion as opposed to voluntary choice. Yoori knew that Jae Won, despite his carefreeness at times, took his job seriously when it came to watching over her. Kang Min grew up working for Tae Hyun, so she could understand how he was the first one to rescind his statement that Tae Hyun couldn't be trusted. But when it came to Jae Won, she couldn't help but wonder what exactly made him change his mind.

"I think you should go inside now, boss," he instead urged, merely glancing at the door with a small smile. "Boss Kwon isn't the most patient guy in the world and he's dying to see you. I think he misses you."

Jae Won bestowed Yoori with a small bow and then descended to the elevator where his younger brother and his younger brother's girlfriend awaited him.

"Have fun!" the three shouted, waving ecstatically at Yoori.

With the weight of the cake growing heavy in her grasp, she smiled and waved back. Seconds later, the elevator doors slid close, leaving her alone in the decadent hall.

She took a preparatory breath and faced the door. A million things ran through her mind as she eyed the doorknob. Her meeting with Jung Min, Tae Hyun's meeting with Ju Won and Dong Min, Ji Hoon, An Soo Jin, Kang Min and Jae Won, Hae Jin and Chae Young…everything flashed through her mind. Then, it all stopped when she lowered her eyes to the cake box she held – the cake she made for the one person who mattered the most: the jerk who stole her heart.

The weight of the world lifted from her shoulders and all that consumed her was excitement. *Finally*. It should be a sin that any one man could possess such talent, a talent that could have her feeling safe and content even when the world was against her. It was a sin, but Tae Hyun possessed that talent, that power over her. Nothing else mattered. She was too excited to see him.

Shaking with exhilaration, Yoori slid the card key. The door buzzed open for her entrance. It was only after she walked in did she realize that Tae Hyun might have been planning a surprise for her today as well.

"And when that time comes..."

24: Paris Is Worth It

Throngs of cold air greeted Yoori when she stepped into the dark apartment. The cold startled her, nearly causing her to drop the cake box. Muttering a muted curse, she was ready to switch on the lights when it occurred to her that the electricity had been turned off. Or that was what she continued to believe until she saw that the dark apartment was filled with a myriad of candles that illuminated almost every corner of the room.

A gasp escaped from her when the door closed shut behind her.

Her stunned eyes roamed the room. Its gaze reflected the candles that laid on nearly every available surface of the apartment. The notion of the electricity dying out in the apartment was shot to hell when she saw white icicle lights dangle extravagantly from the ceiling, giving the room a more Parisian feel. A big smile kissed her lips. She suspected that Tae Hyun may have planned a nice little dinner tonight to celebrate Yoori being "fired" as his assistant, but she couldn't have anticipated the guy to go all out for it.

Freaking Tae Hyun, she thought, holding the cake box against her chest with a mixture of bitterness and appreciation. He was always outdoing her surprises. How was she supposed to compete with breathtaking decorations? He knew she had a thing for lights and now, he was spoiling her with it. Determined to yell at him for stealing her "I-want-to-surprise-you" thunder, she continued through the apartment.

"Tae Hyun?"

She expected him to appear out from the hall, but there was no response.

As she steadily walked in, her black boots sounding off on the squeaky clean tiles, Yoori's eyes moved to the torrent of wind that was flowing into the apartment. The sliding door to the balcony was left open, allowing the fresh cool air to filter through. The fireplace in the living room was left on—a first since Yoori moved into the apartment.

She looked at the sliding door. She didn't need to think twice about where he was. She knew for sure that he was hanging outside the balcony. She shook her head. He was definitely not a mere mortal. How he was able to withstand the cold and hang out like it was a cool summer's night was beyond Yoori. She just thanked the fates that her body was becoming more tolerant in regards to handling the cold.

Prepping her lungs for the attack of frostiness to come, Yoori sped toward the sliding door. Her breath stilled in her chest at the sight of everything outside. If she thought the décor of the living room was a beauty, then Yoori could only describe the decorated balcony outside as breathtaking.

Her heart raced, basking in the scene before her.

Every inch of the balcony was adorned with icicle lights that twinkled like stars in the calm night. White and blue rose petals covered the deck while various candles embellished the floor. Her surroundings were extraordinary, unreal. It was like she was floating in her own little heaven above the city sky, and she loved every bit of it.

If the secluded garden at the park was like a Winter Wonderland, then this…this was something else altogether. There was a different aura to the balcony than at the park. As much as she loved the park, it could never compare to the sense of security that always washed over her whenever she entered Tae Hyun's apartment. She didn't know how to fully explain it. She just loved how the apartment reminded her of Tae Hyun and how safe it made her feel.

"Took you long enough to come home," Tae Hyun's warm voice cascaded over her, pulling her out of her thoughts.

She cast her gaze over to him. Her heart skipped a couple of beats. It had been a while since she had seen him and she had missed him.

He was sitting on a table. He had a black hoodie and his blue and black striped lounge pants on. His eyes were focused on the blinking city when he spoke to her. To her, he looked just like a fallen angel who was ready for bed.

"Should've used your spidey senses to find me," Yoori retorted jokingly, already drawing over to Tae Hyun.

He turned his gaze over to her, the impetuous smile on his face clearly displaying his delight in finally seeing her.

Yoori placed the cake box on top of the table and pushed it forward. With Tae Hyun helping to pull her up, Yoori was soon sitting beside him. They smiled when they moved closer together, drowning in each other's heat while the cold rippled around them. The wind was constant, but not overbearing. It brought forth air that was fresh and warned of descending snow. Yoori hoped it would snow soon. It would be a pretty sight to sit out on the balcony and enjoy the feel of snowflakes on her skin with Tae Hyun beside her.

"So I heard that the electricity went out," she drawled, her eyes noting the icicle lights that reflected on the glass structure on the balcony.

Her eyes focused onto the string of icicle lights beside her boots and the icicle lights that were hanging over all four sides of the table like a bed cloth. She was unable to contain her knowing smile when she raised her eyes up to meet Tae Hyun's.

He was smiling expectantly at her.

"How is it possible that you have such a lightshow going on when the electricity is down?"

"Magic," Tae Hyun answered easily, playful humor in his brown eyes.

She laughed. "That's your answer for everything, isn't it?"

"It's a good generic answer for the things I could pull off." His eyes wandered over the scenery. "The lamp lights were insufficient for what I needed so I opted for candles, icicle lights, and city lights instead." He elicited a careless shrug, trying to make it seem like this set up was more of a whim than an actual plan. "I figured I could kill two birds with one stone and give you the 'romantic dinner' I promised you while celebrating your last day as my assistant. Pretty smart, huh?"

"So there's no other occasion you decorated today for?" Yoori asked, bringing her knee to her chest to block off the wave of chills that was pooling around her.

She counted on him saying that it was his birthday since it was obvious with the cake box that she knew. However, she doubted Tae Hyun would easily admit the existence to such a day—even when the proof of his cake was sitting right beside him.

He shook his head, his eyes clearly eyeing the cake box before they returned their gaze to her. Though he knew what was in it, Tae Hyun continued to purposely dance around the topic with the minutia of small talk.

"You haven't seen me all day, Choi Yoori. Missed me?"

"Didn't even know you were gone," Yoori lied, smiling nonstop.

Tae Hyun laughed. He easily pulled her closer to him once he noticed that she was shaking from the cold. "Oh yeah, that pretty little smile of yours is a good telltale sign that you're not happy to see me."

No longer keen on keeping her exhilaration in, Yoori gave up on beating around the bushes. She wanted to show off her surprise for him.

"That's because I have something for you, *birthday boy*," she exclaimed. She pulled the cake box up. She placed it between her chest and her bent knees. She proceeded to place her hands over the cover.

"Oh God," Tae Hyun moaned, bashfully running his fingers through his hair. "I was really praying that you just decided to buy a cake for the sake of getting a cake."

Yoori's eyes transformed into evil slits. "Oh and I appreciate you letting me know that you're firing me on your birthday." Her sour voice was killed off by her uncontrollable smile.

"I didn't realize it was the same day until *after* I told you I was firing you yesterday," he explained, tilting his head to get a better view of the cake. The cover skewed his vision. It was only Yoori who saw what was inside the box.

"You have to promise to eat it and finish it no matter what," she pre-negotiated. She kept the cover slightly opened with her fingers. She refused to show him the cake unless he agreed to her terms.

Worry pooled in his eyes like thunderstorms. "What kind of stipulation is that?"

"Just hurry and promise me. After that, you can look at it and eat it."

"Is this your get-out-of-jail-free-card? Make me agree to eat it regardless of what it does to me?"

"Yes," she confirmed instantly. "*And* you have to smile when you eat it too."

"You know…for most girls…when they give their boyfriends something to eat, they're a bit more modest about it. They usually say, 'I don't know if it's good or not so you don't have to eat it.' Then, I'll feel guilty and eat it regardless of how it tastes."

"What are you, my relationship coach?" Yoori asked impatiently. "I think it's pretty clear that I'm not like most girls, so don't compare me to the rest. Oh and you're not my boyfriend, so don't get confused on that either. BFF, remember?"

Despite her newly acknowledged feelings for Tae Hyun, Yoori was still uneasy about admitting it to him. She felt safer just being his BFF, no matter how ridiculous and annoying it sounded to her now. She was mature enough to get out of denial with herself. However, she wasn't mature enough to let him know that.

Tae Hyun frowned at the term. She could tell that she was getting on his nerves with the BFF thing. She didn't blame him for being annoyed; she was annoyed with it herself.

"I know that BFF isn't exactly a curse word, but why does it feel like you're cussing at me every time you shove that term in my face?"

Mindlessly, he grabbed a handful of rose petals from the table and threw it into the air. The petals danced for a moment and flew away with the wind.

"BFF you, Tae Hyun," Yoori instigated, knowing that it would piss him off. It was terrible of her, but she loved pushing his buttons.

The glare on his face told her it worked. "You know what, Choi Yoori?" he prompted gravely. His eyes were firm.

"What Kwon Tae Hyun?"

He held up three consecutive fingers and then said, "BFF you, Choi Yoori."

"You're supposed to say, 'read between the lines,'" she said cleverly, thinking she outsmarted him.

"I'm sure you did already, Princess."

"I…I…I…"

Damn it! She did! She *did* read between the lines herself! Damn!

She couldn't even maintain any further energy to bug him to love her cake. She was too pissed off about allowing him to outplay her in her own "read between the lines" game.

"Here!" She shoved the box into his hands. She needed something to cheer her up before she spent the entire night being bitter. "Open your gift!"

Though he spoke of apprehensiveness against her gift, Tae Hyun's eyes were only filled with excitement when he finally lifted the cake box up. Sitting modestly in the to-go box, the white frosted cake stared up shyly at Tae Hyun, who was staring at it quietly, his eyes running over the calligraphy-like writing that said "*Happy Birthday*," and the messy red writing that said "Snob."

"I don't know if it's good or not," Yoori provided tentatively, not even caring to play around anymore. She made sure to use Tae Hyun's coaching advice, not because he told her to, but because she actually meant it. "This is my first time baking and Chae Young and Kang Min were helping me. Hae Jin said that you really liked Red Velvet cake so Chae Young and I went online and got the recipe from some forum. The recipe got good reviews from that site, so I tried my best to follow the directions."

She gazed at him gently. "If it doesn't taste good, don't force yourself to eat it. I won't be mad." She didn't want Tae Hyun to think that he would have to guiltily digest the cake just because he didn't want to hurt her feelings. "Does it at least look presentable?"

"You baked it?" he asked, not even calling her out on using his "coaching" advice. He took more interest in the fact that this was something she actually made herself.

Yoori beamed proudly. "This is a once-in-a-lifetime event so you better treasure it." She smiled timidly, her expression not matching the severity in her words. She shrugged, pretending to be nonchalant. "It's not much. I was actually thinking about buying a cake, but I figured it'd mean more if I baked it. You know the whole 'it's the thought that counts' thing. But like I said, you don't have to—"

"It looks perfect," he spoke up, gazing at her like she had just brought him a cake from heaven. "Thank you." His voice was so genuine that Yoori knew he was more grateful than he led on. This made her crazy happy. He went on, unaware that she was inwardly doing cartwheels. "I've been craving for Red Velvet cake for some time. I'm honored to be the guinea pig for Choi Yoori's first baked good."

Although there was teasing humor in his voice, he looked really excited. He couldn't even take his focus off the cake. His eyes journeyed over the inscription on the cake again. His lips quirked in amusement. She knew he was focusing on "Snob."

"And thank you for the harmonically beautiful pet name, Brat. I'm sure all the romantics out there are envying me right now."

"Wouldn't you be freaked out if I called you 'Suga Bear' instead?"

Tae Hyun shuddered. She didn't know if it was from the cold or if it was because Tae Hyun was disgusted with that name. She had a hunch that he most definitely preferred "Snob."

"I wish you would've told me that you wanted this place to be decorated for your birthday," she commented while he admired his cake. She glanced around the balcony and craned her neck to look inside the decorated apartment. "I would've helped."

"This isn't for my birthday," he said offhandedly.

"So this is just for the 'romantic dinner' and the 'I'm so happy to be firing Choi Yoori' day?"

He chuckled. "This is actually all for you."

His answer didn't make sense to her.

He didn't give her a chance to ask a follow up question when he abruptly jumped off the table. His bare feet slammed against the foundation with a thud. He bent down and picked up something.

Air left Yoori's lungs. Her eyes blossomed as she watched Tae Hyun place a white, transparent covered cake box on the table. He lifted the lid and Yoori saw it: Oreo Cookies and Cream ice cream cake. Her absolute favorite cake.

A torrent of emotions flooded through her. She fought back the tears that were ready to glaze over her eyes.

How did he...how did he know?

She didn't even remember.

How did Tae Hyun know?

Presenting her with a smile that would melt hearts, Yoori was left breathless when Tae Hyun finally uttered words she never had the opportunity to cherish.

"Happy birthday, Yoori."

There was not much that Yoori could tell you about her past. If you asked Yoori how she was raised to become the person she had become, she wouldn't be able to give you a straight answer. If you asked her about the lessons she learned as a child, then she wouldn't be able to tell you either.

This was one of the precise reasons why she never cared to remember when her actual birthday was. To date, Yoori only had three birthdays. She spent the first one with her adoptive parents. The only thing she remembered from that night was them fighting about spending too much money on a cake that they couldn't finish. It wasn't a happy day for her because she was traumatized over not remembering anything about her life. The second birthday occurred shortly after her home in Taecin caught on fire. Needless to say, Yoori wasn't in the mood to celebrate anything. She was alone in a new city and she was staying at a shady motel while trying to make ends meet with the little money she had. She also hadn't found a job yet, adding to the stress and depression. The third birthday was spent with Chae Young who, despite Yoori's protests, insisted on taking her out for sushi before they called it a night from work. They were close then, but not close enough where Yoori was able to feel at ease with herself. Overall, her birthdays never carried too much weight for Yoori.

To a degree, she made the subconscious decision to forget about it. It didn't matter so much to her because she didn't feel that she had someone who cared about it enough to make a big deal out of it anyway.

It didn't matter.

It didn't matter until Tae Hyun came along.

"Happy birthday, Yoori."

His words echoed in her mind like the softest melody, causing a tidal wave of euphoria to submerge her. The simple words lifted sadness off her and replaced it with bliss that she didn't even realize she yearned for until this very moment.

"How…how did you know?" She was barely able to form a discernible sound from her dumbfounded mouth. She was still astounded with everything.

"When we had our dinner, the guys and I went outside to deal with some trouble that was brewing with the initiation for our new recruits. After we settled that problem, Kang Min and Jae Won used the opportunity to tell me that there was something about you that I needed to know. They told me that Chae Young informed them that your birthday had passed recently. She was going to set up a belated party for you, but then she thought that *I* might want to do something special for it. So she had the guys tell me instead."

Yoori recalled the dinner where Hae Jin and Chae Young pulled her aside and told her about Tae Hyun's birthday.

Those four…they planned everything…

Tae Hyun went on. "I asked them for the date that passed and I realized that it was the same weekend that we left for the lake house. That whole day, when we were sitting on the dock till a little after midnight, when we were on the boat, when we played the drinking game and when we danced in the gazebo…that was your birthday." His eyes flashed at the remembrance of their first weekend away. "Why didn't you tell me?"

"I…I didn't remember," she replied honestly. Then, something clicked in her mind that made her smile. "So the dress and jewelry they got me – "

"Your birthday gift from them."

"And dinner yesterday?"

"Our birthday dinner with them."

"So they all knew?"

Tae Hyun nodded. "Hae Jin and Jae Won were here helping me set up for your gift. And I guess Chae Young and Kang Min were helping you with mine."

And just like that, Yoori found the air lodged in her chest. She recalled all the other birthdays that never resulted into much of anything. Her birthday had long came and went (and God knows if it was even the right "birthday"), but she couldn't help but smile as her eyes gleamed with gratitude.

"But today is *your* day," she breathed out, feeling incredibly emotional. Her friends and Tae Hyun were taking her breath away. It was something so simple. A birthday. Something so simple and it was making her emotional.

"You think I would make a big deal out of this day if I wasn't celebrating your birthday too?" He laughed. "To be honest, I've never been a big fan of my own birthday. It'll be nice to take the spotlight off me and give it to my girlfriend instead."

"BFF," Yoori corrected out of habit. She wanted to smack herself thereafter. It was extremely annoying. Yet, it was the only thing she could use to protect herself from her feelings.

"Maybe it's time you read between the lines when you use those words with me," Tae Hyun said sternly, stroking the bangs away from her eyes just after a puff of wind darted through them. He smiled, gazing back at the two cakes staring at them. "Should we put candles on the cakes?"

Yoori bobbed her head, still feeling dazed. She reached into the pocket of her pants and took out a package of multicolored candles and a lighter. When she pulled it out, she saw that Tae Hyun had the same package of candles. He also had the same red colored lighter.

"It's too windy," he complained, having trouble getting the candles to stay lit. The harsh wind continued to ripple around them.

"Yeah," Yoori agreed, flinching when the fire from her candles burned her slightly before flickering into oblivion.

"You know what this means, right?" Tae Hyun asked coyly, staring at her and then at the table. He was still standing beside it and by the show of things, he wasn't planning on jumping back on.

Yoori grinned knowingly. She blew out the rest of the flickering candles.

Delicately placing his hands on her hips, he helped her jump down. After Yoori landed on her feet, both reached out with their lighters in hand and picked up their respective cakes.

"Duck kickers first," Tae Hyun offered, motioning to the area underneath the table.

"Duck lovers first," Yoori counter offered.

"Did you get attacked by another duck today? You know I'm not going in until you go in first. So hurry up. My ass is freezing right now."

"You sure know how to do bed talk, don't you?"

"You know it, baby. Now get your pretty little butt in there."

"Don't stare at anything," Yoori warned, bending her knees and pushing the cake in before she crawled in under the table too.

"I wouldn't dream of it," he replied, tilting his head and shamelessly staring at her butt. If the look on his face was any indication, he loved what he saw.

Fully situating herself underneath the table, Yoori waited eagerly as Tae Hyun lowered himself, pushed his cake in, and slid underneath the table. He started lighting the candles to the cakes.

As she sat with the icicle lights hanging off the table and hovering all around them, Yoori didn't feel the cold. The candles from the cake warmed her under the secluded shelter. It was a beautiful feeling. She felt like she was in another world.

"Okay, you ready?" Yoori asked after she was done helping light the candles. Twenty-four candles for Tae Hyun and twenty-four candles for her.

"I was just waiting for you, slowpoke."

"Should we sing?"

"Please don't make me," Tae Hyun begged, his voice mirroring that of a little kid's.

Yoori laughed at the child-like innocence exuding out of him when he said that. How adorable!

"Okay, fine." She raised his cake up instead. "Should we just blow the candles at the same time then?"

He nodded, relieved that they didn't have to sing.

"What's your one wish tonight, Yoori?" Tae Hyun asked when he held her cake higher.

"What's your one wish tonight, Tae Hyun?" she replied, holding his cake higher. "Wait, wait," she cried. "We can't tell each other or else it won't come true."

"Fine," Tae Hyun said with amusement. "At the count of three then…" he instructed, watching as Yoori nodded in agreement.

"One…"

"Two…"

"Three…"

Forty-eight strings of smoke sashayed and dissolved under the weight of the wind as Yoori and Tae Hyun settled their cakes before them. Streams of smoke waltzed around the icicle lights and filtered into the air. Then, it was unexpectedly ripped apart by white particles that had begun to descend from the dark winter sky above.

Snow.

Finally snow.

Extending her right palm into the outer vicinity that surrounded the rectangular table, Yoori collected pieces of snowflakes that started melting over the heat of her skin. Compelled to do something her drunken self wasn't sober enough to do the other night, Yoori took off her black boots and then unzipped her black hoodie.

"Choi Yoori!" Tae Hyun shouted after Yoori tossed her boots and jacket in one corner. "What the hell are you doing?"

Only dressed in her black camisole tank top and her lounge pants, Yoori smiled wickedly at Tae Hyun. She slid herself out from the table. She threw herself under the grandeur of the icy night.

For as long as she could remember, she had always loved snow. It was a strange habit of hers to run outside and just prance in the wintriness of the night, basking under the touch of the snow as it kissed her bare shoulders and danced underneath her bare feet. Yoori didn't get to enforce this habit the other night, when the first snow of winter fell while she was with Tae Hyun at the park. She was drunk and occupied, but she promised herself she wouldn't let this moment pass again.

She stood in the center of the balcony and inclined her head. Yoori closed her eyes and felt her body relax as the snow touched every uncovered area of her skin, leaving her to feel not only the chills, but also a sense of renewal. The ice melted on her, fulfilling her need to be cleansed under the care of nature.

"Did you drink tonight without telling me?" Tae Hyun's voice swam over her like a tidal wave, drawing her out of her serene state.

She lowered her head and opened her eyes. She smiled at Tae Hyun, who had his arms folded before his chest. He was staring oddly at her.

"Take off your hoodie," Yoori commanded, wanting Tae Hyun to enjoy the same serene splendor she felt.

"What am I, your personal stripper?"

"Just do it. You were willing the other night," Yoori reminded, though she wanted to say, *"Yes, yes! Be my personal stripper!"*

"Can I hold you if I take it off?" he negotiated with charm. He drew toward her, his eyes speaking of nothing but desire for her. "I haven't seen you all day and I've missed you. I've been good and held off my charms until now. It also doesn't help that you're not wearing a jacket and it's cold out. My first instinct is to hold you and keep you warm."

"And here I thought your seductive charms were over for the time being."

"It *was* over," he said slickly. "But now it's alive and well again."

If only it was as simple for her to give in. If it were that easy, she would've already jumped into his arms. Yoori resisted the impulse to do so when the fog of recent events milled around the fortress of her heart. She would like nothing more than to forget everything. Despite this desire, she couldn't ignore all the fears that continued to tread through her. No matter how wonderful this night had been, she couldn't allow herself to get lost in it completely.

"You can take it off or you don't have to," Yoori said impatiently, though she secretly hoped that he would just take the hoodie off. She wanted him to enjoy this with her. "I don't care."

"Prude," he complained under his breath. He was already ripping the hoodie off his shoulders and tossing it onto the table. He drew closer to Yoori, stood beside her, closed his eyes and awkwardly lifted his head up to meet the skies.

Yoori realized what a mistake it was to offer him the opportunity to enjoy this with her. If she were smart, then she wouldn't have offered him this moment, only because seeing him in the black muscled shirt, the fabric of which wrapped snugly around his upper body, more than enticed her eyes. The sight of him standing there while the snow caressed his skin tempted her. It made her want to do the same. It was evident that he found no enjoyment (or peacefulness) in standing barefooted with no jacket, freezing his ass off. He only did it for her and by God, he couldn't have looked more adorable doing it.

"Close your eyes," Tae Hyun said suddenly, turning around to face her.

Using all her strength to not flinch at the fact he caught her staring at him, she said, "Why should I do what you tell me?"

"Because I'm still your boss and I want to take advantage of you."

Yoori wanted to snort at his incriminating reply. "You know this can be considered sexual harassment, right?"

"I didn't hear you say 'no' to the sexual advances the other night."

Under any other circumstances, Yoori would've put up a fight and objected just because she was used to objecting to Tae Hyun. But because he got her with his statement, she merely blushed and closed her eyes. She was too bashful to look at him after the reminder of the "sexual advances" the other night.

"You're not going to strip down to only your towel again, are you?" Yoori asked with humor and a hint of hope. She was such a pervert for him, but she accepted this long ago. She concluded that she wouldn't be too healthy if she weren't like this for him. No woman would be able to resist him.

"Me? Strip for you in the snow?" There was interest in his voice. "Is that one of your fantasies, Yoori?"

"You're so hot, I bet you'd melt all this snow into rain as soon as you take off your clothes." The words came out of her laughing mouth too quickly, but it made her giggle like no other. The same effect wasn't lost on the one she addressed it to.

"You're lucky you're a cute one." Tae Hyun laughed. "Because you would not get any action with those sucky pick up lines of yours." He sighed and then moved forward with his intentions. She could feel the anticipation in his voice. "This will only take a couple of seconds…"

"Oka—"

His warm lips pressed against hers, holding prisoner a snowflake that fell between their lips. Yoori stilled at the unexpected kiss.

"*Just enjoy this with me.*" She heard him whisper before he pulled her closer to him.

The snow melted onto her lips and caressed over her as Tae Hyun pressed deeper, his hands framing her warm cheeks and trapping more snow between the heat of their yearning bodies. Yoori was ready to wrap her arms around him when Tae Hyun abruptly pulled away from the kiss.

He pressed his forehead against hers. His eyes mirrored hers. It teemed with suppressed longing and need.

"Dance with me?" he asked, his hands already finding a comfortable hold on her hips.

"There's no music though," she noted quietly. Despite this observation, she wrapped her arms around his neck anyway.

"It doesn't matter," Tae Hyun assured. "I don't need music. I don't need anything to dance with you. I just need you."

Warmth rolled over her. How could she say no to that?

"Okay," she uttered. She followed Tae Hyun's lead and began to move with the rhythm of the falling snow.

Silence surrounded them and they moved like petals to the wind. There was no music. There was just the whispers of the wind, the company of the cold, and the innocence of the snow dancing all around them.

"I've missed you," he whispered simply. He kissed the top of her head, holding on to her tightly. Snow continued to frost over them. She knew he was talking about not seeing her today and not seeing her for all those days where he was too preoccupied with Serpents business.

"I've missed you too," Yoori replied, unable to hide her feelings with a witty comeback. All she had as they danced under the cloak of the night's snow was honesty. "I've missed you a lot."

The snow spilled over them, caressing their skins, melting on them and sheltering them from the wind that lingered in the night. It should've been cold, but Yoori felt none of it. She was numb. All she felt was Tae Hyun. She was lost, lost in the spell of Wonderland.

Framing his cold hand over her cheek, Tae Hyun made sure their eyes met before he said, "I don't want to go through another day wondering where we're at in our relationship. I want to settle this and I want to settle this tonight."

There was so much determination in his voice, so much determination and hope that it tortured Yoori. His words were like knives that cut her out of her bliss.

Fear returned to her with full force.

"I'm not ready to settle it tonight—if ever," she admitted, hating that she was so afraid of what was coming. There were so many reasons why she was afraid, so many reasons why they would never work out together.

"Why are you so afraid?" he asked, stroking her cheek with his fingers. His eyes pleaded for her answer.

"Because I am," she whispered, feeling so numb that she didn't even feel the sting of cold beneath her heels.

"Why?" he persisted, standing in his place.

It took her a while to realize that they had stopped dancing. She was now avoiding his gaze. "There are so many reasons."

"Tell me."

She shook her head while backing away from him. She was still determined not to answer.

"Yoori," he said sternly, stepping forward to reach out to her.

Unable to hold back any longer, she said, "I'm afraid of you."

Tae Hyun stopped inches away from her. His eyes flashed with confusion. "*Me*?" He was stunned with her answer. "Out of all the answers you could've given me, you say that you're afraid of *me* of all things? Do you really think I would hurt you?"

Yoori shook her head. Her heart was clenching like fists at the pain in his voice. "It's not a question of whether or not you would hurt me. The only thing that matters is that you have the power to."

The liveliness of the wintery night had since dimmed as they finally journeyed on to a topic that agonized Yoori to talk about. The candles had burned out from the wind, the icicle lights had dimmed under the cloak of snow and the city lights had flickered away in the distance. It was a silly thought, but Yoori could've also sworn she saw the stars above diffuse in its vibrancy. It was as though they were watching her and Tae Hyun with pity in their eyes. It felt like the whole world was watching them with nothing but sympathy in its silence.

"I forgave you for leaving me that night," she began faintly, using all her efforts to keep her voice steady. She couldn't allow her voice to break. "I forgave you, but I'll never forget what happened. I know that you never actually left me that night...but when I thought that you did, I waited for you. I counted down the minutes and I waited for you. I waited until the tears started to soak my eyes. I waited until my heart began to rip itself apart. I waited until I became one of those girls...one of those girls who was sitting beside a wall...crying over a guy."

She went on as the sting of fear circled around her. Her chest had tightened in such agony that she wondered how she could stand for so long without keeling over.

Throughout her ordeal, Tae Hyun remained silent, attentive. Although he said nothing, she could sense his anguish all the same.

"I've always been spineless; I always run away from things. I may be a coward, but I never cry. I never cry...yet that was all I did that night. You broke me. You mean so much more to me than I'll ever want to admit. You left me then...but you came back. But what about next time? What about next time when you leave...and you don't come back?"

Her body shook from her own words. She hoped she was shaking because of the cold, but Yoori knew better. At this point, the cold weather couldn't match up to the inner storm raging inside her body.

Tae Hyun attempted to say something. "Yoori. I won't—"

"You keep secrets from me," Yoori interrupted, backing further away from him once she saw that he was trying to reach out to her. She would only torture herself more if she allowed him to hold her. She couldn't allow herself to get lost in his arms. She wanted to stay strong for the things to come...for the things she would probably have to do once their night ended. She knew she was such a fool to think that she could stay here with him like this—*especially* when a myriad of obstacles threatened their future. But she could make things right. She could make it right by confronting Tae Hyun with one of the things she knew would be her way out.

Based on the shock in his eyes, Yoori knew she was on the right track.

The air escaped her when she verbalized thoughts she always feared voicing out loud. "I've told you in the past, Tae Hyun. I've always trusted you…but when we were on the balcony that night and you ran out on me, you told me you ran out because you needed time to process that I'm An Soo Jin and I understand that."

She gazed intently into his eyes.

"But I know that wasn't the *entire* reason why you left. For months now, I've allowed myself to be oblivious to whatever secrets you've kept from me. I don't snoop around and try to find out what you're keeping from me because, deep down, I know that I'm afraid to find out. But how could you stand here and ask for something more with me when you don't even trust me enough to share all that you've kept from me? Do you think I deserve someone like that? Someone who keeps things from me? I mean…do I even know who you really are?"

Tae Hyun froze at her question.

She hated that her voice broke. Her heart ripped itself apart as it yearned for her to stop pushing herself away from him. The truth was…she would've accepted anything about him because if there was one thing she knew, it was that she knew the real Tae Hyun. Not the Underworld King, not the Serpents leader, but Kwon Tae Hyun himself. Nonetheless, her hopes continued to drop all the same. Perhaps Tae Hyun would make this separation easier for her. She had hoped that she sounded pushy enough to turn him off. But as he nodded, his eyes glazed with so much pain that it ached her to just see it, Yoori knew she was far from pushing Tae Hyun away. She was actually opening him up.

A million different emotions filtered in and out of his poignant eyes. Yet, when he finally parted his lips and spoke, all Yoori heard was truth and desperation. There were no more reservations with Tae Hyun.

"I'm not the type of gang leader that you're used to hearing about," he began. The wind spun around them, twirling mixes of rose petals and snow in the air. The icicle lights clinked above when the harsh wind billowed about.

"I'm not the type who has never killed anyone. I've killed countless people. I've grown so used to it that it doesn't even faze me whether I kill one person or ten people at once. I don't have much of a soul…the majority of it died with the people I've killed over the years."

Even then, Tae Hyun was still good at keeping the even composure in his voice. It didn't matter how much his eyes betrayed him.

"I'm not the good guy in this story. I'm greedy and selfish—in every way possible. Just like the rest who has walked this life, I'm just another villain with a corrupted soul. I live to collect power and I live to pursue endless power." He smirked dryly. "I wish I could tell you differently. I wish I could tell you that I've changed completely from all of that. I haven't. I can still kill without a care in the world. I still seek power because I love it. I love it when people fear me and I love it even more when they kneel before me."

"If you love it so much, then why do you insist on being with me?" Her chin wobbled uncontrollably. "Don't you realize that I'm standing in the way of all of that? Didn't Ju Won and Dong Min reiterate that to you when they told you to get rid of me?"

"Do you think I want this right now?" he asked swiftly, breathing in painfully once he saw the hurt breed like cancer in her eyes. "Do you think it's easy for me to stand here like this? To yearn for you so much that I begin to forget why I'm here in the first place?"

He smiled dryly to himself, taking a moment to stare off into the snow-drizzling horizon. "I wish that none of this is happening right now. I wish I could've met you later...when I had no more soul. Maybe then, I wouldn't be here right now...like this. I wouldn't be torn between wanting something I've wanted my entire life and something that has just occurred to me that I may want for the rest of my life." He exhaled sharply while Yoori tried to coordinate her breathing. "I still want power, but I want you more. And this factor alone has been killing me. If I had the choice, I would give everything up just so I could be with you. Haven't you realized how much you mean to me by now?"

His eyes showed no tears, but his voice spoke of every pain that she felt.

Yoori felt hopeless. She felt like she was barely hanging on in a world that just wanted to drown her.

She did.

She did realize how much she meant to him and how much he meant to her.

"Can't you just run away with me?"

The words slipped past her lips as easily as the air she exhaled. Her lips trembled when she asked this, immeasurable anguish seeping into her eyes. There were no thoughts attached to that question, just hope. Just the faintest hope in her desperate heart that she could just run away with him and go somewhere where they could start over. Where they could just be safe and normal.

She noted his reluctance and she continued. It was pathetic. She was pleading for him to give her the easy way out because she wanted to be with him so much.

"It's so hard to be with you in this world," she breathed out, her lungs fighting for air. "Can't you just run away with me so we can start over somewhere else? Somewhere where I know you'll be safe if you were with me? Somewhere I won't be reminded of Soo Jin? Somewhere where we can just live a normal life?"

Tae Hyun took in a sharp breath. It pained him to see her like this and it pained him to not be able to give her what she pleaded him for.

"I can't run away with you, Yoori," he whispered, the finality in his voice causing Yoori's heart to drop. "If you had asked me for anything else, then I would give it to you without batting an eyelash. But this…I can't give you this. I can't disappear. I can't disappear like Young Jae because he was never a candidate to become the Lord of the Underworld. He never reached the level that I have reached."

He swallowed tightly. "Right now, I'm vying for the most powerful position this world has ever known. My position in this world has been marked. I either die trying to be the Lord of the Underworld or I die as the Lord of the Underworld. There's no in-between in this world. I have too many enemies and they are waiting to see me fall. I can't run. This society would hunt me and it would hunt you down too. If I stay as I am, then I have my gang and the 1st layer to watch over me—*us*. If I run with you, I'll lose both. I'll lose the ability protect you and then I'll lose you."

Yoori bit her quivering lips, fighting back sobs that threatened to flood out of her chest. So that was it. There was absolutely no option for them. She was ready to give up and walk away when she was suddenly pulled against him. His warmth enraptured her. Raking his fingers through her snow-covered hair, Tae Hyun bit his own lips as he stared into her agonized eyes. His eyes were deep, poignant, and mirrored the pain in hers.

"I know the right thing to do would be to let you go right now because there's no future for us. I wish I could be less selfish and just let you go because you deserve better than me. You deserve better than this life. I wish the little soul I have within me would stop yearning for you so I could just let you walk out of my life…so I could just go back to being happy with the life I led. That way, things would be easier and I wouldn't have to stand here…never in my life feeling weaker or feeling guiltier for all the things that I've done…"

He continued to caress her hair, his eyes holding hers with nothing but desperation.

"I've made mistakes in the past, Yoori," he shared, going back to the first concern she brought up. It seemed that this issue had been plaguing him for quite some time. "Mistakes that I was raised to believe were necessary to get me the ultimate power and keep me alive in this world. Mistakes that are irreparable…mistakes that will probably disgust you to a degree where you won't be able to look at me again…"

"Tae Hyun," Yoori started, her voice trembling. She struggled to understand why he was so worried. "What have you done?"

"I would understand if you couldn't look at me afterwards…if you hated me after you found out everything."

Yoori had never seen such fear embalm his eyes. It was like he was afraid of losing her.

"Just tell me," Yoori whispered, wanting to cry for him more than for herself.

"But please know that I've fallen for you," he pleaded, still so apprehensive with telling her everything. It broke Yoori's heart to see him so afraid. "I wish I didn't care for you this much…that I need you this much, but you have everything of mine. My heart and what's left of my soul. Everything is yours, all yours and only yours. And come tomorrow, I'll tell you everything—everything that I've kept from you. But for now, can you trust that I'll take care of you? That ultimately, your well-being and your safety will always be what comes first?"

"Tomorrow?" Yoori asked, pressing her forehead against his. She was shaking with emotions.

He was borrowing more time and she allowed him, not because it pained her to see how hurt he was, *even though it pained her greatly*, but mainly because she was afraid of what she would learn. What had Tae Hyun done that was so horrible that she wouldn't be able to look at him afterward? Yoori knew that if she thought about it long and hard, she would know the answer. But that was the thing…she didn't want to know the answer. Deep down, she wanted to prolong anything that may cause her to push herself away from him. She was so afraid; she wanted borrowed time as well.

"Tomorrow," he confirmed, his fingers gliding over her cheek.

Even though one thing was settled, Yoori still saw one more obstacle in their way. They dealt with Tae Hyun's past mistakes…now they had to deal with Yoori's past self.

She asked the dreaded question. "What if…what if I remember everything and An Soo Jin takes over? I'm pretty sure the drug is wearing off because I feel myself changing everyday…I feel her taking over more and more everyday. She hates you, Tae Hyun. I can feel it in my gut whenever I contemplate wanting something more with you. I can feel her disgust and her hatred for you."

Yoori swallowed past the tears threatening to rise up in her throat.

"What if I wake up one day and I'm no longer me? What if I wake up one day and I'm *her* again? When I remember everything…we're not going to be the same. I won't be here with you anymore. I'll be trapped within Soo Jin. All I'll be able to do is watch as she hurts you. All I'll be able to do is watch, completely powerless, as we become enemies. Don't you realize that, Tae Hyun? Don't you realize that's our future if we keep going down this road?"

"You think none of this crossed my mind?" he asked, framing his hand over her tear stained cheek, wiping the fresh tears that were streaming out.

She was crying again. She didn't even realize she was crying.

"You think the fact that you're Soo Jin hasn't been on my mind? The fact that at any point in time, something could trigger inside you and you'll remember everything? That you'll remember it was Ji Hoon you loved and it was me you hated? That you'll remember it was my brother who killed your father? That *I* represent everything you despise? That it's very likely I'll find you pointing a gun at me, shooting at me like you've never spilled coffee on me, like you've never bickered with me, like you've never been handcuffed with me, like you've never kissed me…like you've never spoken about Paris to me?"

He laughed to himself. "I thought about that…I've thought about it long before the Advisors ever met with me, long before they ever told me I should kill you. I've considered letting you go, but time and time again, I just can't. No matter how selfless I try to be, I just can't let you go. I could deal with anything and everything that may come my way. I could deal with all the obstacles and I could deal with dying if I have to…but please don't leave me because of all this. Don't leave me because of things we can't control. I can't be without you, Yoori."

Snow continued to drizzle over them as they stood like statues on the balcony.

"It's so hard to love you in this world, Tae Hyun," Yoori replied, her voice shaking relentlessly as she tried to stay strong for him. "I don't know if I'm ready for it…even though I care about you so much. I don't know if I'll be able to withstand it. I'm not a strong person. I'll fall apart if anything happens." She reached up and caressed her fingers over his cheek, reveling in the feel of his smooth skin against hers. "What if I allow myself to completely fall for you and *you* get taken away from me? What if I allow myself to completely fall for you and *I* get taken away from you?"

She bit her lips, trying to smother the sobs that would've escaped from her if she hadn't bit her lips till it bled. It was her worst fear…to fall completely in love with Tae Hyun and have her soul ripped to shreds when the world tears them apart.

It wasn't until Tae Hyun touched her biting lips did Yoori stop biting the blood out of them. It wasn't until he pulled her into a deep embrace did Yoori still in his hold. Burying his chin into the side of her neck, he gave her a kiss that calmed her nerves and soothed her soul.

It was a kiss that she needed.

"As of late," he whispered, his warm breath calming her, "I've come to realize that life is not always about a past filled with mysteries or a future filled with endless dark possibilities…it is also about a present filled with timeless distractions."

He wiped the tears that froze on her cheeks and kissed away the tears that threatened to slip from her eyes.

"Do you remember your definition of Paris on the dock that night at the lake house?"

The reminder of Paris evoked a stroke of inner strength she didn't know existed. It had been so long since that night…

Tae Hyun smiled at her attentive silence. "You said that Paris is the city of love. You can't go to Paris unless you're madly in love with the person who is taking you. And not just the type of 'love' where you tell one another that you can't live without each other. No…not *that* type of 'love'. But the type of love that is unconditional—the type that is *undying*. You know…the type that can withstand anything…one of those…."

"Once-in-a-lifetime love," Yoori finished for him.

He framed his hand against her cheek, caressing her skin. "No one said finding Paris would be easy…"

"They only said it would be worth it," she mindlessly provided, never feeling so much bravery and fear in her life.

"You're worth it for me, Yoori," he told her with confidence. "All the obstacles, all the hardships, all the heartaches, all the pain, all the hell to come… you're worth *all* of it to me."

Yoori's hyperventilating heart lifted at his words. It lifted even more when he asked, "Do you not want to find Paris with me, Yoori?"

"I do," Yoori replied quickly, never meaning something more in her life. There was strength that she didn't even know existed. "You know I do. I want to find it with you, *only you*."

He nodded, his eyes smiling at her ardent answer.

"Are you all mine?" he asked finally, nipping his nose with hers. His warm breath lingered over her, tempting her and thawing the cold from her skin.

There was no hesitancy this time, no more denial. "Yours. All yours," she conceded. She buried her face into his chest and allowed the wintriness silence to fill them. The snow continued to dance all around them, surrounding them with its innocence.

"You'll be the death of me," Yoori finally whispered long seconds later, gazing up at Tae Hyun.

He was staring down at her with so much love in his eyes that she wondered how it was possible she was able to resist the one who had stolen her heart for so long.

"And you'll be mine," Tae Hyun whispered back. Taking a moment to stroke her face with adoration, Tae Hyun, no longer able to control his needs, leaned down and pressed his lips against hers, stealing her breath as he bestowed bliss unto the kiss.

A world of timeless magic.

That was where Tae Hyun took her as she, for the first time in her life, kissed without reservations. For the first time in her life, she allowed herself to get lost as she fell in Tae Hyun's embrace. Tears of worry stained her lips, yet Tae Hyun swept it all away with his lips. Fear drowned her, but Tae Hyun pulled her back up with his embrace. Hell called out to her, but Tae Hyun held her in a world amongst the heavens, never letting her go. Despite knowing everything that could go wrong, she continued to kiss him because it was the only thing that felt right.

When she pulled away from the kiss, Yoori just stared at Tae Hyun, her eyes glazing over with fresh tears when she realized that after so long, they were finally at this point.

"I bet you didn't know you were going to be outside in the cold, freezing your ass off and kissing me like this when you came into the diner that day."

Yoori laughed as the final tears slipped from the side of her eyes.

Tae Hyun joined in her laughter, shaking from the cold. He wiped away her final tears of the night. "Definitely not. My defined ass would've ran away from your deliciously plump ass if I knew you were going to put me through such hell."

"Which reminds me, I quit as your assistant," Yoori announced smugly.

Oh how she wanted to quit for so long.

"You can't quit. I fire you," Tae Hyun countered, getting back into the normalcy of their bickering. Even after a heartfelt conversation, they were still the same couple.

"You can't fire me. I do not deserve to be fired. I've made your life easier. Who dealt with all the miscellaneous stuff?"

His expression mocked her. "What do you actually do?"

"I wash the dishes."

"And I told you the other night that I rewash them because you suck at scrubbing."

"I do laundry."

"No, *I* do laundry. You just close the lid and take credit for it."

She started to get flustered. "I...I help with administrative gang stuff."

"Your handwriting is like chicken shit. I have to secretly take my own notes to know what's going on. As far as I'm concerned, it was like I was your assistant."

Oh wow. She *did* suck as an assistant.

"Sucker," she drawled, pinching his nose. "That's what you get for falling for your employee."

She laughed when he shook his head at her, turning away from her and blushing like a tomato.

"Anyway, can we go inside now?" Yoori asked when the wind picked up.

"Why? I thought you liked the snow?"

"Um, because I'm not wearing a jacket or shoes and my deliciously plump ass is freezing right now."

Tae Hyun gave her a blank, unimpressed stare. "You're really good at bed talk, aren't you?"

Yoori snorted at his passive insult. "Hurry up and take me back inside before I break up with you."

Tae Hyun raised his brow. "What the hell? Why are you abusing the privileges already? I can't believe you just used that as a threat. It took me forever to convince you to be my girlfriend and now you're threatening to break up with me?"

"That's right, baby," Yoori cooed jokingly, laughing as she leaned in and kissed his jawline.

"I probably should've thought things out better before I made that big speech about finding Paris with you," Tae Hyun voiced bitterly, already melting under her kiss. He picked her up and carried her bridal style into the living room. "Now I'm stuck with you through thick and thin."

"Loser-face," Yoori giggled, falling onto the couch.

Tae Hyun settled beside her. He covered the purple throw blanket over their bodies. He wrapped himself over her and laid his chin above her head. Both shook from the remnants of snow on their skins. They were soon warmed from the fireplace and the comfort of being indoors.

"You're not going to strip down to your towel?" Yoori asked suggestively, tracing her finger down his chest. She moved closer to him. "I promise I'll rip it off this time."

"You little perv. Was that why you agreed to be my girlfriend? So you can reap the benefits?"

Although Yoori smiled, there was no veiling of her fear. They haven't changed as a couple, but their future was still uncertain.

"I'm still afraid," she admitted meekly. It was the honest truth. No matter how excited she was that they were finally together, she was still afraid.

His eyes professed the same concern. "I am too."

"But you're worth it," Yoori assured, tightening her embrace around Tae Hyun. "You're the only one I would do this for."

"You're the only one I would do this for," Tae Hyun agreed. He kissed her again and ran his fingers through her hair. The kiss was shrouded with fire and passion. It brought the most blissful of pleasures to her lips. He wasn't kissing her as Tae Hyun, he was kissing her as her boyfriend.

Finally her boyfriend.

"No one said finding Paris would be easy; they only said it would be worth it."

These words echoed in Yoori's mind as she rested her head on Tae Hyun's chest, never in her life feeling like she belonged with someone more. She knew as she laid with Tae Hyun that there were going to be countless obstacles in their way. The world they were in was just waiting to rip them apart. She had no idea how they were going to get through this—if they truly had the strength as a couple to get through this *together*. It was going to be hard. It was going to be so hard that Yoori wondered if she truly had the power to go through all the hardships to come. It wouldn't be easy and that knowledge in it of itself continued to frighten Yoori. She was almost lost in another world of uncertainty when she felt Tae Hyun caress the bare skin on her shoulder. He touched her and all her fears vacated.

Staring into the rich tone of his brilliant brown eyes, Yoori smiled at the fact that she was still in Tae Hyun's arms. She was still in the arms of the one who stole her stubborn heart.

"You're worth all of it," he reminded her delicately.

Yoori smiled and leaned forward. She gave him three quick pecks on his lips.

"This isn't a dream, right?" she asked, casually grabbing a handful of his bicep.

"No. We're finally together." He narrowed his eyes onto the big chunk of bicep she was pinching when she asked her question. "And I appreciate the fact that you're always pinching me instead of yourself whenever you ask that question."

She laughed guiltily. She released her grip and grinned sheepishly at Tae Hyun. Her eyes had become drowsy.

"Are you ready for what's to come?" she asked, listening closely to the beating of his heart.

"I think so," Tae Hyun replied, closing his eyes before he placed a tender kiss above her head. "Are you?"

"I hope I am..."

Putting her worried thoughts aside for that night, Yoori allowed the joy of being with Tae Hyun to overtake her. She ignored the sinking feeling in her gut as his breath warmed her skin. She ignored the trepidation in her nerves as Tae Hyun's enrapturing cologne soothed and embraced her. Sleep soon beckoned them and Yoori wished that they could freeze time and remain in this blissful moment forever.

The storms were coming and she knew that. She knew that she was in for a world of pain, tears, agony, heartaches, and anything else that would arise from trying to find Paris with Tae Hyun in a world where blood streamed through snow like water. She knew that they were living on borrowed time…but she had no idea how quickly they were going to have to pay for all the time they borrowed.

She had no idea how quickly things would change once she woke up the next morning.

Finding Paris would definitely be worth it, but the unforgiving storms to come would make it damn near impossible for them to find.

"You won't only have to face your demons…"

25: Killing Demons

Huff…
Huff…
Huff…
Claps of thunder boomed over the dark horizon as she plunged the sole of her boots into the muddy grass. Her legs trembled beneath her, begging her to stop.

Treacherous rain clouded her vision, drenched her hair, devoured her clothes, and inundated the entire world beneath her yet she continued on, blood that didn't belong to her seeping from her clenched fists.

Her lungs were struggling for air, yet she paid no attention to it.

She had to hurry.

She kicked down a door and burst into the dark room. Her heart hammered brutally against her chest. She looked from left to right. Only shadows surrounded her. Her frantic eyes focused on the room at the further end of the abandoned hall.

While fiercely holding on to the item in her bloodstained palm, she kicked another door down. The door nearly flew off its hinges. Jumping and passing over several steps, she landed on the seventh step and continued to run.

Huff…
Huff…
Huff…
Darkness…darkness everywhere.

The storm continued to echo in the far distance as she lunged onto the ground. She fought through spider webs and dust before reaching a brick in the wall. Her heart throbbed in her ears. She kneeled on the ground. She pulled out the brick, revealing a hollow space within the yellow stained wall.

Panting quietly, she held out her trembling hand. It was too dark to see it, but she knew exactly what she was holding. She could still feel the strings of blood adorning it.

57…

Red-hot tears threatened to mist her eyes while she took a moment to ponder its value. Anger. Scorn. Hatred. Disgust. All these emotions ripped through her, drowning her. No longer able to stand it, she threw it into the hollow space. She

---

313

filled the brick in that space, blocking off any knowledge that the wall was disturbed.

No one else could know...

Just as the distant thunder roared outside, she rose to her feet, sprinted out of the room, sprung out into the hall, and flew into the awaiting storm. As if anticipating her return, the dark sky illumed with lightning, revealing the spacious lawn she was running on and the splatters of blood staining her dark clothes.

No one could know where she hid it. It would be her secret; one that she would take to her grave if she had to.

Huffing and puffing, she continued to run despite the violence of the weather. She continued to run despite the pain and desperation tearing through her.

I'm doing the right thing, she told herself. *I'm doing the right thing. There's no other choice...*

Yoori woke up with a quiet gasp after she felt a chill slither up her spine. Her heart drummed against her chest. Her dreary eyes surveyed her surroundings in momentary confusion. What the hell did she just dream about? Yoori couldn't remember much...just that in the dream, it was really dark, rainy, cold, and there was a lot of running. Too much running and too much anxiety.

Yoori sighed to herself. She hated her dreams.

She nuzzled into her pillow. It took her a while to realize that she wasn't sleeping on her bed and that she wasn't nuzzling into a pillow. She was sleeping on a couch and nuzzling into Tae Hyun's chest...her boyfriend's chest.

Her mood lifted instantaneously. The stress and fear that once coursed through her vacated when Yoori noted that she was safe in Tae Hyun's arms. They were still sleeping underneath their purple blanket and the waves of icicle lights that glimmered above their ceiling.

What a breathtaking sight.

Butterflies quaked in her stomach at the reminder of what took place the night before. It wasn't a dream. All of this was still real. She smiled blissfully at Tae Hyun, who was still sleeping soundly. He looked so handsome and he was all hers now.

Unable to help herself, she allowed her fingers to stroke over his smooth face. She was so tempted to just kiss him. As her fingers moved from his cheek, to his jaw and then whispered down to his neck, Yoori's eyes blossomed when she remembered that she hadn't given Tae Hyun the birthday gift she bought him.

The diner.

She had forgotten his birthday gift at the diner!

Yoori wanted to smack herself. In the process of rushing out of the diner, she had completely forgotten Tae Hyun's gift bag on the kitchen counter. She was so angry. How could she forget something as important as Tae Hyun's birthday gift?

Something clicked in Yoori's mind. The diner was closed, but she still had the keys. Wouldn't it be nicer if she went to the diner, got the birthday gift, came back and cuddled with him as she presents the gift when he wakes up? Yoori glanced at a sleeping Tae Hyun.

She smiled at the thought.

It would be quick. She would just drive his Mercedes, fetch the gift and come back before he even knew she was gone. She doubted she would run into any gang members because she only planned on running into the diner for two seconds to get her gift. Worst comes to worst, she would just drive back home if she sensed suspicious people near the diner. What were the odds that she would run into any danger if she was away from Tae Hyun for a couple of minutes? She couldn't stay under his protective wings forever. She had to do things for herself.

Decision set, she quietly untangled herself from Tae Hyun's embrace. She lifted herself off the couch and lowered her bare feet onto the cold tiles. She watched cautiously as Tae Hyun moaned a soft protest and shifted on the couch, moving around like a little puppy. It was as though he was searching for her in his sleep.

Relieved that she hadn't woken him up, Yoori descended into the bedroom where she grabbed Tae Hyun's white hoodie, put it on and grabbed his keys from the counter. She wore her black boots over her pajama pants and sped out of their apartment.

Yoori noted that it was 4:17 in the morning as she drove Tae Hyun's Mercedes.

She looked around.

The world was unusually quiet.

Though night had long past, the sun continued to hide behind the dark clouds that floated above the city. Snow had risen to a couple of inches and there were barely any people out on the streets. Yoori shivered despite the strength of the heat eliciting from the car. Something was making her...uneasy. She had long gotten out of the cold so she didn't understand why she was receiving chills. Yoori sighed, stepping on the gas in an attempt to get to the diner faster.

It's because you're up at an ungodly hour and outside in ungodly weather, Yoori sullenly told herself.

Though she was bitter, Yoori was more than encouraged by the fact that she was doing all of this for Tae Hyun. She wanted her first day as an official girlfriend to be a good one, hence the unusual behavior of waking up at an ungodly hour and doing something sweet for him. She smiled to herself again. She was too excited about giving him the gift when he woke up. She was also too excited about jumping into his arms again.

She was so lost in a daydreaming bliss that Yoori hadn't realized she reached the diner until she nearly drove past it. She hastily stepped on the brakes, placed the car in reverse and carefully backed into the parallel parking space a couple of feet away from the diner. Just as she switched off the headlights and killed the engine, an onslaught of panic came over her.

Like a hawk, her eyes zeroed in onto the diner door.

The door had the "Closed" sign on it.

Uneasiness clawed at her.

Something felt...*off* to her.

She examined the dark streets. Everything appeared normal. It was quieter than usual, but Yoori attributed this to the cold weather. Everything appeared in order, but the simple fact that her stomach was coiling itself in dread was enough to make her wary.

Yoori depressed the auto-lock for the car doors as a safety precaution. She sat in the dark with her Blackberry in hand. She was tempted to run into the diner to just grab the gift, but the better part of her instincts was screaming at her to leave. She could feel it in her tense hands, her shivering skin, the tightness in her chest, and the uneasiness in her gut. Something was wrong here. Knowing very well that her gut instinct had done nothing but serve her well in the past, Yoori was ready to leave when she suddenly heard voices.

On instinct, she threw her back against the leather seat and slid down in an attempt to hide from detectable view. Her heart slowed when she registered that the voices were coming out of the diner. It was only when Yoori craned her neck out did her heart completely stop at the sight of bodies materializing after the voices.

Chae Young.

Chae Young was the first thought that came to Yoori's frantic mind. Her eyes locked on the men piling out of the diner.

She counted.

One...two....five...eight...eleven...

Eleven...

Eleven men and...and...and...Chae Young?

As if injected with adrenaline, her heart rate raced from zero to one-hundred. Nausea overcame her while her stomach twisted into unbearable knots. Holding in her gasp with her shaking hand, Yoori instantly speed-dialed Tae Hyun's number. She kept her eyes solely focused on the men who were disappearing into the dark distance.

She shook uncontrollably in her seat.

It took three rings before Tae Hyun's voice came over the other line.

"Yoori, where are you?" he prompted frantically. From the sounds of disarray in the background, Yoori could discern that he was already getting dressed once he realized she wasn't in the apartment.

"Tae Hyun!" Yoori gasped desperately. She spoke to him, her mind running in circles. "Tae Hyun! I—I came to—to get your present f—from the diner—" She could hear him running out the door. "And I saw *eleven* men walk out from the diner."

She inhaled sharply.

Her eyes continued to stay on the group of men who were disappearing into the shadows. They were all dressed in dark colored puffer jackets, jeans, and dark colored beanies.

Her horrified eyes swiveled back to the diner. "Oh my God, I—I think Chae Young is in there and they did something to her! Oh God, Tae Hyun! She's in there! She's in there! What do I do?"

She was losing it. The only image in her mind was of her best friend: smiling and helping her bake a cake before hugging her goodbye.

"Yoori!" Tae Hyun shouted, clearly sensing that she was in a state of disarray. "Do *not* get out of the car! Do you hear me?"

It was clear to her he was running like a maniac down the apartment stairs. He was coming.

"What if she's hurt?" Yoori trembled like a leaf as she thought about all the possible things they could've done to her.

Eleven men and Chae Young...

There was only one possibility that Yoori could surmise and she prayed it didn't happen to Chae Young.

"I—I have to go in," Yoori stuttered, already unlocking the door. The men were out of sight and she couldn't stomach hiding out in the car anymore. Not if her friend needed her. "I have to make sure she's okay."

"Yoori, don't! I'll be there soon!" Tae Hyun shouted, the heavy wind taking form on his line, making her believe that he was probably running to his motorcycle. "You don't know if there are still people in there. You don't even know if Chae Young is in there."

"I—I have to go make sure she's okay." With no more reservations, Yoori hurled herself out of the car, ran into the billowing wind and sprinted toward the diner.

"Yoori! Don—"

"Please hurry," was the last thing Yoori said to Tae Hyun before she hung up. It was foolish of her to go in by herself, especially if there were still people in there. But she didn't care. She didn't give a fuck about anything but her best friend.

She could feel the tears coat her eyes. She could feel her heart wrench in agony and she could feel the anxiety puncture itself through every nerve in her body. Yoori veered through the opened door. The darkness in the diner threw her off, rendering her blind for a split second. The distraction was enough for her to slip on a piece of fabric. She fell forward. Her chest slammed onto the hard tiles before her Blackberry slipped free from her grasp.

Spikes of pain attacked her chest, causing Yoori to gasp painfully for air. Groaning, Yoori reached for her Blackberry. Her vision had gradually acclimated to the darkness. Once she saw something twinkle in the shadows, she reached out for it and found her phone. Her eyes widened when she observed that the fabric she slipped on was a turtleneck. Chae Young's red turtleneck. The fine hairs on the back of her neck stood, not because she realized she slipped on Chae Young's top, but because she realized that the screen of the phone was wet...wet with blood.

"Chae Young!" Yoori sprang to her feet.

Her eyes roamed the room in horror. It was Chae Young's blood. She had no doubt about it. Yoori's surveying eyes caught sight of something in the corner. Chae Young's white apron hung on one of the booths. Her eyes continued to roam the room and there on the floor, she saw something that drained the color from her face.

Chae Young was sprawled on the floor, naked and unmoving.

She was covered in blood.

The world stood still as Yoori froze there, the seconds distending to eternities. Other than the screams of anguish bellowing within her, nothing was discernible to her ears. Her eyes ran over the blood, the torn clothes, and Chae Young's lifeless body.

Yoori was ready to keel over when she heard soft moaning. The dark spiral she felt herself being dragged into was lifted when light held on to her.

Chae Young was still alive.

"CHAE YOUNG!" Yoori shouted. She ran over to Chae Young so fast that she almost slipped on the trail of blood that led up to her body. "Oh God, oh God. Thank God!"

Yoori fell to the ground, picked Chae Young's head up, and carefully placed her knee underneath Chae Young's neck.

"Chae Young, please open your eyes," Yoori pleaded, her chest tightening in agony. Tears threatened to rise up through her. She gently slapped Chae Young's cheek so that she would lift her lids. Chae Young was ice cold and it was killing Yoori, ripping her apart to see her friend like this. "Please...Please look at me."

"*Yoori?*" Chae Young finally whispered, opening her bruised and swollen eyes slightly. Her eyes were merely slits, its full bloom prevented by the huge swelling surrounding her eyes.

"I'm here, I'm here," Yoori assured, warming her cold cheeks with her hands.

Tears welled up in Chae Young's eyes. She gazed up at Yoori with such horror that it tugged at Yoori's heartstrings. Sobs began to filter from her lips.

"Y—Yoo—Yoori," she cried, shaking with tears. Her bloody fingers gripped on to Yoori like she couldn't believe she was still alive to see her.

"I'm here. You're going to be okay, sweetie," Yoori whispered. She lifted her arms up and took off her hoodie. She placed it over Chae Young's upper body as a means to keep her warm. "Can you keep your eyes open for me?" Yoori struggled to dial for help. "I'm calling for help now."

Her fingers were shaking as she held back her own tears. She was trying to stay strong for Chae Young, but she was losing it, especially when she realized that she couldn't make the phone call. The battery to her phone was missing. It must've broken off when she tripped earlier.

"Fuck! The battery!" Yoori hissed, whipping around as Chae Young continued to shake with sobs in the background.

Carefully placing Chae Young's head back on the tiles, Yoori crawled on her hands and knees. She tried to find the battery for her phone. She was going crazy. She was hurting from hearing Chae Young cry in the background and she was losing it herself. Where was it? Where the *fuck* was the battery?

"You better be ready to jog when I come pick you up in a bit..."

Yoori's gaze snapped toward the door once she heard the male voice stream from outside. As if hearing her savior, Yoori staggered to her feet and barreled out of the diner, catching a jogger on the phone just before he swept past the diner.

"Please help me!" she cried, opening the door and catching the teenage boy in time. He wore a black workout jacket and windbreakers. He nearly jumped off the sidewalk when she came out.

She went on, barely able to keep her own sanity intact. "M—My friend was attacked! I—I need a phone!"

"Oh God!" Instantly heeding Yoori's plea, the boy immediately hung up on his friend. He ran back into the diner with Yoori and dialed for help.

"Hurry! She was attacked. She's lost a lot of blood!" The boy shouted into the phone. Blood drained from his face once he saw the condition Chae Young was in. He didn't look a day over fifteen and he looked petrified.

"Hey hun, you're going to be okay," Yoori whispered, her voice shaking once she got back onto the ground and stroked Chae Young's forehead. Sobs choked her chest yet she held it in.

As though it was hurting for her to breathe, Chae Young inhaled sharply, held back her sobs, and said something that chilled Yoori's blood.

"Y—Yoori—you shouldn't be here," she cried desperately.

All of a sudden, she tried to push Yoori away from her. She was too weak. Yoori didn't even budge. She didn't budge physically, but mentally, Yoori was being pushed over the brink of insanity.

"Wh—What?" Yoori whispered as she heard the boy tell the operator on the other line the condition Chae Young was in.

Chae Young's eyes were coated with fear as she spoke. "They—They..." She gasped for air. She seemed delirious. "Y—You can't be here—they're coming back—they're coming back—and they'll do this to you too!"

"They won't, they won't. They're gone," Yoori assured Chae Young, biting her lips to keep from screaming in frustration. It pained Yoori to see Chae Young so afraid.

More sobs elicited from her lips. Chae Young shook her head. "Th—They said they'd come back for me." Violence overtook her shaking body. She chaotically recalled what they did to her. "Th—They said they'll keep me alive because they w—wanted to come back for me." Tears slid down her bloodstained face. "They—They took *turns*. They used knives and—they—they took their clothes off and—th—they took *turns* with me..."

Unable to finish, Chae Young just shook and shook, her tears mixing with her blood.

The entire time, as Yoori absorbed Chae Young's words, she felt her heart grow heavy with anger. Every word Chae Young spoke, it felt like nails were being drilled into her. Yoori knew that Chae Young had been raped...*mercilessly and heinously*. But to hear her best friend, the one she loved so much, voice it out loud and to see the fear in her eyes....

Yoori's eyes narrowed onto the cuts on Chae Young. She took stock of the bruises, the blood covering her and her naked body. She ran the scenario in her furious mind, the control she held already withering under the fire of rage burning within her.

Those bastards raped Chae Young. They slit her skin, beat her and tortured her...and they told Chae Young they would come back for her.

Yoori's blood boiled.

No, she wouldn't let them come back for Chae Young.

She wouldn't.

She wouldn't let those fuckers come back.

Those fuckers...

Those fuckers were *never* coming back!

"Where are you going?" the boy shouted when Yoori pushed past him and ran out of the diner.

She didn't answer him.

Everything had faded in her world, but Chae Young's pain, the eleven bastards and the knowledge of what they did to Chae Young.

The fires of hell singed in her eyes.

At that moment, all excess emotions were stripped out of her soul.

All that was left within her was wrath.

Pure, unadulterated wrath.

Blood...

It was all that she sought as she ran like a predatory wolf.

Their agonized screams...

It was all that she wanted to hear as she barreled through a group of joggers, causing them to fall every which way. She jumped over their bodies and continued down the snow-strewn sidewalk.

The feel of her hands ripping their skins apart...

That was all that mattered to her as she bent down, never slowing down her pace to grab an empty beer bottle near the curb.

The feel of their blood squirting on to her skin...

That was what she wanted to feel as she smashed the bottle on to the side of a building. Trinkets of broken glass flew into the sky like crystals and then fell back down, snipping her skin as she continued to run, her eyes unblinking with rage. Jagged edges ornamented the broken bottle.

Holding on to it with the strongest of grips, Yoori swung it up and down, her nostrils flaring.

Yoori cared about nothing.

Nothing but making them suffer.

Those fuckers would pay...

They would pay for everything they did.

They would pay for everything they did to Chae Young.

26: Wrath of the Queen

Yoori swung past a row of dilapidated buildings that were well-known for harboring street gangs. It was a neighborhood that cops purposely deviated from and it was a block that Yoori purposely threw herself into because she knew the people she was looking for were there.

"That was the best fuck I've had," said a laughing voice. "I'm tempted to go back."

"Bitch put up a hell of a fight. I had to knife her a couple of times to get her to stay still."

"We should do it again."

"You know where she works and where she lives. If the bitch isn't dead, I'm sure you can pay her another visit."

Yoori stopped running once she saw them. She could feel the hatred flow like acid in her veins as she listened to them gloat about what they did to Chae Young.

Fucking bastards.

"Look boys, we have a lost kitten," one of the fatter, bald men in his early thirties spoke. Standing at about 6'1", he was one of the biggest in the group. The other men were almost as big and just as intimidating, but this one just radiated arrogance that told Yoori he was the leader.

He was the one who probably raped Chae Young first...

He was the one who should die first.

She tightened her grasp on the bottle, revolted that this pig was breathing in the same air that she was. Yoori didn't say anything when she walked in, her boots stepping on the snow that lined the alleyway. The alley was big. Big enough for her to do what she needed to do and narrow enough for her to take them all on at once. It was the perfect killing field.

"Now will you look at that little weapon she's holding." The leader's eyes glittered. He rubbed his chin in glee. It was clear to him where Yoori came from and what she found in the diner.

"Did you like the present we left you at that diner, baby? Was she your friend?" His voice pulsed with guiltless mockery. He didn't wait for her answer. He already knew by the anger emanating from her stance. "That whore friend of yours has a hell of a pussy..."

His eyes glistened as more of his gang members piled out of a nearby building and walked into the alley.

Eleven. There were eleven of them now. Some were sitting on the steps, some were leaning against the walls and some were standing in the center of the alley. They were all staring at her, their perverted gazes already undressing her and fantasizing about all the things they would do to her in this secluded place.

"But I'm sure your pussy is a hell of a lot better than hers, isn't it?" he continued to croon, laughing. He pulled a pocketknife from his back pocket. He lifted the blade. The sharpness of the tip winked in her direction. Snow had just descended, layering the once quiet alley with white fluff. He carefully pointed it in her direction. The rest watched in the background, amusement covering their faces.

"Don't hurt her too badly, Spi," one reminded the leader.

"She'll be alive," Spi sneered. "She'll be more than damaged and she'll be begging for death, but she'll be alive." He sharpened his eyes on her, smiling as though he expected her to be kneeling in the seconds to come. "Who do you think you are walking into this alley like you own it, you stupid little bitch?"

Yoori's face was still stoic, deadly.

"Show me what you got and I'll show you who the little bitch is," Yoori stated gravely. There was a different tone to her voice. It was one that was unfamiliar to her and one that didn't belong to her.

Mocking laughter saturated the alleyway.

Spi's eyes became vicious. He was ready to make her pay for her insulting words. "I'm going to make you scream, my little bitch."

And then, with his knife faced out, he charged at her with glee on his face.

She watched him accelerate, his boots digging into the snow beneath them. She waited for him to draw closer. When he was an inch away from her, he snarled, lowering his knife with the intent of stabbing her in the hip.

She couldn't have that.

Finally picking her legs off the ground, Yoori sped to him and swerved to the side. He swished the knife toward her hip and missed her by an inch. As his eyes enlarged at her evasion, he was thrown into an even bigger shock when Yoori doubled back for him, extended her glass weapon and pierced it through his left cheek, causing a hole to form as the jagged edge buried into the flesh of his face. His head bashed against the wall at the force of her attack. He screamed in agony. He shook at the feel of his skin hanging off his cheek by mere strips.

Yoori was far from done.

With the bottle still pierced in his cheek, Yoori, who had nothing but hatred in her eyes, twisted the bottle like clockwork. The meat of his skin began to rip. He tried to wiggle out of her hold. Her strength proved to be unyielding. He cried against her grasp, begging her to let him go.

He wasn't so pompous anymore.

Yoori smiled when the blood from his cheeks doused the snow beneath them. She leaned in close to his shaking ear.

"Did she tremble like this when you raped her? Did you show her any mercy when she begged you to let her go?"

Yoori knew he didn't and she wouldn't give him any mercy either.

She twisted the bottle again, tearing into the finalities of the meat on his cheek. It tore like fabric…slowly, easily, and painfully.

"Go to hell, motherfucker," she spat out before pulling the bottle out of his cheek. She proceeded to stab it into his right temple, causing another scream to emit while she grabbed the pocketknife from his trembling hand and stabbed him below, right through the jeans of his pants and cutting off his penis in the process.

His eyes dilated in the purest of agony. He opened his mouth to scream. Nothing came out. He had no power to scream when Yoori finished the attack by stabbing into his neck and hitting a jugular vein. Nothing but blood sprayed on to her once she pulled the knife out of his neck.

She stared into his eyes, watching him take his final breath.

No guilt overcame her. Just satisfaction.

She let go and allowed his heavy figure to fall lifelessly to the ground with a big thud. It was easy. It was *that* easy to kill a piece of shit. She turned her blood-splattered face over to the ten remaining men. They were gaping at the scene before them in horror.

The curve of a small smile appeared on her lips. It was like a part of her had just been woken up; it was like a part of her just surged with life.

One down.

Ten more to go.

"Let's play."

Snapped out of his trance before the others, one pulled a knife from behind his back.

"You bitch!" he screamed, determined to slit her throat. He made the same mistake as his leader, thinking he could take her down by fighting her with a measly knife. He was no match for her.

Running as well, Yoori easily jumped off a step for a boost. She flew in the snow filled air, kicked the side of the alley wall and spun toward him. She extended her leg out and kicked him down just before he reached her. His skull collided with the ground after he fell backward. When Yoori landed back down, she made sure the heels of her boots slammed down onto his fingers. Sounds of bones cracking spilled into the air with his screams.

"You…" she said gravely, staring down at his petrified face. "*All* of you will pay for everything that you did."

She reached down and stabbed the side of his face, cutting through the skin and effectively cutting off an ear. She recalled he was one of the ones who wanted to go back to see Chae Young. For good measure, she pulled the knife out, grabbed the back of his head, and pounded his face into the alley wall. She bashed his head three times—once to break his nose, twice to break his forehead and the third to turn his face into mush. His blood sprayed on to her and she smiled. His blood wasn't enough. She wanted more.

When Yoori was satisfied, she threw his screaming body to the floor. She stood to her feet and anxiously watched as the rest charged for her.

"You fucking bitch! I'm going to shoot your brains out!"

The two ahead of the pack were smarter than the previous two. Instead of deeming her to be someone they could easily overpower with the force of a knife, they pulled out their black guns to shoot her down instead. The rest were running behind them, seemingly afraid to use their guns as they might fire on their own.

Idiots, she thought with a smile.

Reacting quickly while dodging the bullets, Yoori grabbed two knives from the ground. She strategically raised her arms, recoiled them backward, and threw the knives straight toward each of the men. The sharpness of the tip pierced into the bull's eye of their foreheads, sending them to brutally snap their necks backward before their lifeless bodies fell to the ground.

Seven more remained.

More shots came in her direction.

"Augh!" The bullets ricocheted off the walls of the alley, slicing through Yoori's arm and slicing off her skin. The heat of the pain ripped through her, but she couldn't waste time tending to her wounds. She still had bastards to kill.

She retreated back to grab the guns from the fallen men behind her. Yoori wiped away the splatters of blood that were streaming down her face and grabbed the guns. She wasted no time in raising her guns. There was nothing to grow accustomed to. To Yoori, holding the guns and knives just felt right.

Like the focus lens on a sniper gun, she narrowed her eyes onto them and began to shoot. The bullets flew out chaotically, yet it met her targets with precision. The bullets went into kneecaps, buried into arms, punctured into chests, shot off pieces of ears and shot off fingers that held guns.

Pain.

She was determined to give them pain and torture before they died.

One by one, they fell, their blood and the flesh from their bodies garnishing the snow. They groaned in agony.

It was funny how, even then, Yoori felt like she was showing them mercy. They would never know that she could do worse than all of this.

"You will *never* touch her again." That was the last thing Yoori said before she relished in their screams and began to fire at their heads. The gunshots sounded off, causing sprays of blood and particles of brain tissue to fly into the snow drenched sky. The rage pumped in her veins and she glorified in the scene in front of her. Death surrounded her and for the first time this morning, Yoori felt...satisfaction.

The time to revel in this feeling ended when a loud sound elicited in the alley, leaving Yoori distracted with new company.

Clearly having heard all the commotion from outside, the door to one of the buildings burst open. Three more gang members came out with AK-47's in their hands. Their eyes grew wide at the carnage before them and with no hesitation, they began to shoot at Yoori.

She instinctively fell to the floor. She picked up two of the fallen men and shielded their bodies over her. The bullets slammed into their bodies and she tried to think of what to do next. It was like the strength had left her after killing those eleven men.

Now, she was just Yoori again.

Now, she was defenseless again.

The continuous firing of the three guns penetrated the silence around them.

These two bodies could only hold off the bullets for so long. She could hear their descending footsteps as they came closer to her. Just another foot closer and they'd have a good aim at her and her brains would be blown out.

When all was lost and it seemed that it was due time for Yoori to meet the bullets, three gunshots roared into the alleyway.

The three men died instantly. Their faces buried head first in the snow when they fell to the ground.

She was saved.

Yoori turned. Her eyes widened when she saw Tae Hyun walking into the alleyway like a dark knight.

He was wearing black from head to toe. A black zip up jacket, black pants and black leather shoes. The snow danced around him. Yoori gazed at the two silver guns in his hands. It was clear he was the one who shot those men.

"Yoori." He was beside her at once. He placed his guns on the snow. He framed a hand over her cheek. The softness returned to his once hard features. His gentle eyes skimmed over her in worry. "Are you okay?"

Yoori shook under his touch, still reeling from everything that happened to her. Before answering him, Yoori's ears perked up when she heard sounds of shuffling. More gang members were coming and they were getting closer.

"Tae Hyun, there's more—!"

"Keep them covering you," he ordered, already knowing that there were more on their way. His enhanced hearing was as good as hers.

He picked up his guns from the snow and sprinted toward the door where more gang members were piling out with knives and guns in their possessions.

Yoori's heart dropped when she saw that there were also snipers on the roof. They were lying across the foundation, getting into position to shoot Tae Hyun just as he was fighting the dozens of men whom were barreling into the alley like a hound of dogs. Yoori was ready to run out and help him until she saw that he was more than capable of taking care of himself.

326

Jumping in the air while kicking down three men with a powerful spin kick, Tae Hyun raised his guns in the air and began shooting at the snipers who loitered on each side of the buildings.

The impressive part?

He didn't need to focus his eyes on them when he shot them. He was too busy sweeping his leg on the ground, creating a tornado of snow in the air and throwing several gang members off their feet. He didn't focus his eyes on the snipers, yet one by one, in sequential order, six of the snipers fell like deadweights to the ground.

"You shouldn't have messed with my girlfriend," Tae Hyun growled just as he punched several eyeballs out. He was clearly pissed that she had to resort to hiding behind dead carcasses as her shield from their bullets. "You just made the biggest mistake of your lives."

While shooting upward, Tae Hyun was also kicking and elbowing each of the gang members charging at him, skillfully maneuvering around their swiping knives. There were a couple of gunshots that sprang into the alley but, each time, Yoori only heard sounds of other men groaning. Tae Hyun had allotted opportunities for himself to use others around him as shields. Seizing their arms and throwing others in front of him, they all began to stab, slit throats, and buried bullets into one another while Tae Hyun acted as their puppet master.

He shot upward again, this time shooting the last remaining snipers who had just taken a swipe at him, slicing off skin from his shoulder and piercing the heart of a gang member beside him.

"Who the fuck are you?" one shouted just before Tae Hyun bashed his head against the wall. Bones cracked and his face turned to mush at the powerful impact.

"Your fucking King," Tae Hyun answered regally, performing a roundhouse kick to three gang members while aiming his guns upward. Another sniper bullet had just missed him. He threw his guns high into the air after he shot them. While doing this, Tae Hyun grabbed the heads of the gang members surrounding him with his unoccupied hands and began to snap their necks like twigs.

One...two...five...eight...

He successfully snapped eight necks apart before his guns fell back into the safety of his awaiting hands.

Once the last remaining snipers tumbled from the sky and fell onto several gang members on the ground, Tae Hyun averted his full attention to the dozens still standing before him. With no more evasions or distractions, Tae Hyun began to shoot at them, alternating each time by jumping onto alley walls and firing bullets from the air. The bullets plunged into the top of their heads. Once his heels fell back onto the foundations of earth, he began delivering bone-crushing blows with his elbows and the backend of his silver guns.

Yoori was in awe as she analyzed all his moves. His reflexes and agility were to be envied...even by Yoori, who realized what a challenging opponent he would be if she were to wage a battle with him.

In the alley with Jae Won's gang, when Yoori was first given a taste of Tae Hyun in action, she realized now that Tae Hyun was showing mercy when he fought with the Dragons gang. Considering what she was seeing now, she knew he could've easily overpowered Jae Won's gang. He could've easily been more vicious...

The last sound of gunshots, breaking of bones, and snapping of necks swam into the once hectic alley, stealing Yoori out of her trance. The world around them was quiet again as dozens upon dozens of bodies laid in the alley like a river of death.

Tae Hyun was done.

Averting his attention back to her, Tae Hyun stuffed his guns into the holsters behind his back and ran back to Yoori. There were splatters of blood on his face and body. She wasn't even fazed by the fact that he just murdered countless people in front of her.

That should've been Yoori's first clue that something was changing within her because all she felt was relief that he was okay. When he came closer, she noticed that he had some bruises on his face. She examined him. There were knife wounds on his upper body and his legs as well. He may have come out of the battle victorious, but he definitely hadn't come out unscathed.

"Yoori."

As Tae Hyun stood above her, his face gentle with her as ever, Yoori suddenly realized something...

She lowered her eyes onto the snow when she finally felt the blood drip off her face. The blood didn't belong to her. It was only after she surveyed the scene before her did it all come together for her...

It was like an out of body experience.

Akin to waking up from a stupor, Yoori's eyes expanded when she stared at the bodies she was using to cover her. She peered at the dead men behind her and gazed at the blood covering her hands. She touched the splatters of blood on her face. A gasp ran through her soul. She just killed...She just killed all eleven of them.

A scream emitted from her lips and she started to gasp for air. "I just – I just killed—!"

"Shh, it's okay, Yoori. It's okay." She felt Tae Hyun crouch beside her. He whispered calming words to soothe her, yet she heard none of it. She closed her eyes and covered her muffled screams. What did she just do?

"I just killed them, Tae Hyun! With my bare hands!" The thought inundated her mind. It drowned her.

"They all deserved to die," he appeased, though she could hear in his voice that he was worried for her too.

It was no secret that An Soo Jin was trained to be a ruthless killer. The simple fact that Yoori was able to tap into those killer instincts only meant one thing: she was not only changing everyday, but it also meant that An Soo Jin, even in a fleeting moment, had woken up and made her brief appearance in the Underworld.

For a horrified Yoori, she feared it wouldn't be the last time Soo Jin made an appearance.

"Chae Young needs you, Yoori," Tae Hyun whispered, changing the subject. He knew Yoori would wallow in misery if he didn't pull her out in time. He cupped his hands over her cheeks and brought up the one thing he knew would pull her back to earth. He stared down at her, his eyes noting the distraught in her eyes. Yoori knew that he could read what she was feeling.

At the reminder of Chae Young, Yoori felt her heart wrench again. She also felt some sanity return to her.

He went on, noting the calmness in her eyes. "I know that you're hurting right now...that you're overwhelmed with everything going on right now. But you have to stay strong for her. We have to go see her now."

"Where is she—?"

"She's at the hospital." He began to wipe away the splatters of blood on her face. "Jae Won is rushing over there to see her."

"But someone needs to be with Jae—"

"Kang Min and Hae Jin are there with him."

"Her dad—"

"He's already been contacted," he interrupted understandably, still wiping the blood off with his thumbs. "He's coming."

She was still perplexed. Her mind was still all over the place. "But is she going to be ok—"

"She'll be fine. I've already called the hospital and requested one of the best doctors to oversee her. She'll get the best treatment and she'll be fine. But she won't want to see you like this. She's been through a lot. You're going to have to stay strong for her. Can you do that, Yoori?"

At his soothing words, Yoori nodded slowly. Tae Hyun was right. She couldn't go to the hospital and attempt to be by Chae Young's side if she wasn't stronger.

Tae Hyun smiled when she nodded. "Good." He pulled his hands away and tore off the black jacket he was wearing. He wrapped it around her and kissed her forehead.

"I'm taking you home first. You need to wash away all this blood before you walk into that hospital." He carefully pulled her up, wrapped her in his arms, and allowed her to lean against his body as they walked back to his awaiting motorcycle.

Snow continued to encircle them and, for the first time, Yoori felt the coldness.

"You did nothing wrong," Tae Hyun assured her, knowing fairly well that she would be consumed with remorse if he didn't mend the guilt for her now. "Death for them was too kind."

Those words were the last thing a dazed Yoori remembered before she got onto the motorcycle, wrapped her arms around Tae Hyun's back, and fell into a trance as they drove back to the apartment before they went to see Chae Young.

She was still so out of it.

She never turned back to look at the carnage she created. She knew she didn't have to look back. She knew that this very moment would catch up with her regardless. She just viciously murdered eleven gang members. There was no way to forget that or sweep it under the rug.

It was like opening Pandora's Box. Even subconsciously, Yoori knew it was only a matter of time before all other aspects of Soo Jin's "being" came out of her as well.

This fact scared her.

It scared the living hell out of her.

"Your time has come."

27: Revenge

When they arrived at the hospital, Yoori and Tae Hyun waited in the corridor beside the emergency room with Hae Jin, Kang Min, and Jae Won. No one spoke as they waited. Hae Jin and Kang Min were sitting on the tiles against the wall, each on either side of Jae Won. He was pale as a ghost while he sat there, his eyes lost in a distraught trance. Yoori was no better. She sat on a small bench with Tae Hyun, her eyes lost in a similar daze.

Tae Hyun held her in his arms, whispering soothing words every now and then to make sure she was okay. Everyone was depressed. It was a complete 180 from their boisterous dinner two nights ago.

"She's going to be okay," Tae Hyun whispered into her ear, holding her hand.

Yoori didn't say anything, but she bathed in his reassuring words. His voice, his warmth, his presence…it was the only thing keeping her sane and it was the only thing that comforted her.

In the course of this waiting period, Yoori also had to speak to two cops. They asked her the usual questions about how she found Chae Young and whatnot. Her fragmented mind proved to be beneficial to her as the cops were very sympathetic to her pain and didn't purge for more information that dealt with her running out on the scene. They just accepted her answer that she was distraught (which was true) and just couldn't handle seeing her best friend in such a condition.

In this timeframe, Chae Young's father, Mr. Lee arrived. Mr. Lee had always been a tough boss to Yoori, but she loved him all the same because behind the tough exterior, she knew he was a sweet man. It broke her heart that she had to reunite with him in the worst of situations. Mr. Lee, although frantic and panic-stricken, was incredibly appreciative of Yoori for being the one to find Chae Young. He couldn't stop thanking her and hugging her. He was crying too, which broke her heart even more.

Soon after, Chae Young was finally out of the emergency room and was moved to a private room that Tae Hyun arranged for. If there was one thing that continued to surprise Yoori, it was Tae Hyun's stature in this city. All he had to do was make a call, say that it was Kwon Tae Hyun calling and doors would open at the sound of his name. For Chae Young, that was what Tae Hyun did in terms of getting her one of the best doctors and getting her a private room for recovery (all at his own expense).

When she was moved to her room, the cops went in to speak to Chae Young. After they left, Chae Young's father went in to see her. He came out crying twenty minutes later. He motioned for Yoori to come in.

"She only wants to see you," he whispered in between sobs. "She's not ready to see anyone else."

Everything still felt surreal to Yoori. Turning around, she gazed at Jae Won wearily. "Do you want to go in with me?"

"Go in first," he replied, his gaze following Mr. Lee, who was sitting on a bench, crying to himself. "She wants to see you first."

She knew Jae Won was dying to see Chae Young though. He had been worried sick for his girlfriend. If Yoori weren't lost in such a stupor, then she would've put more effort into bringing him in with her. But she had no energy either. She just wanted to see her friend.

"I'm going to go make sure he's alright."

That was the last thing Yoori heard before Jae Won walked over to Mr. Lee to no doubt comfort his girlfriend's father. It was the last thing she heard before she left Tae Hyun's side and stepped into Chae Young's room alone.

Chae Young had fallen asleep in the short amount of time that her father left her. Her face was free from blood now. There were stitches on her forehead, cheeks, and stitches that could be seen on her bare arms. Physically, she looked better than this morning, but psychologically, Yoori knew Chae Young was no better.

"Chae Young?" Yoori asked, reticent with disturbing her sleep.

Yoori nearly jumped out of her skin when Chae Young started screaming in her sleep.

"Yoori, Yoori!" Her eyes snapped open and she surveyed the room in panic.

Yoori ran to her. She leaned over and framed her hands over her cheeks. "I'm here, I'm here. I'm here, hun."

"Yoori!" Chae Young shouted at once. Terror consumed her teary eyes. "Yoori, you have to be careful!"

Yoori swallowed painfully. She nodded at Chae Yong, understanding how traumatic this had been for her. "Chae Young, it's okay. Tae Hyun took care of those guys," she lied. "They won't ever come back to bother you."

Chae Young shook her head, fresh tears forming in her red-shot eyes. She grabbed onto Yoori's hand. Worry pulsed in her voice as she coherently said, "No, no, no! You have to listen to me, Yoori! Th—They came for *you*!"

Yoori's heart stopped. "What?"

The distress escalated in Chae Young's voice. "Th—They wanted me to call you...to lure you out alone. But I wouldn't do it." Her chest started to rise and fall, sobs threatening to tear out of her. She struggled to tell Yoori everything. It was as

332

if she was afraid Yoori would be attacked right then and there. "And – And then they took out their knives and the girl..." Horror embalmed her eyes at the reminder of the girl. "Th—The girl told them to do this to me. She told them to do whatever they needed to do to—"

"A girl?" Yoori asked vigilantly. Fire seared through her soul again. "What girl?"

"Something Jin..." Chae Young breathed out. She was having trouble breathing normally. "J—Jin..."

"Ae," Yoori completed for Chae Young.

It was Jin Ae. It was Ju Won's niece.

The residual anger pumping through her blood was ignited at this knowledge. It was the same girl who instructed her men to rape Yoori.

It was Jin Ae.

Rage imploded inside her.

It was fucking Jin Ae all along!

"IT WAS JIN AE! IT WAS THAT *FUCKING BITCH* ALL ALONG!" Yoori screamed, running out of the hospital room.

She crashed into Tae Hyun. He was speaking softly to Mr. Lee and Jae Won. He caught her midway. He pulled her to the side, shushed her and brought her to the corner where people were craning over to see what the commotion was all about.

"Calm down, Yoori. Calm down," he hushed her gently. "You're scaring Mr. Lee."

Seeing that the elevator doors were wide open with no occupants, Tae Hyun pulled Yoori into it. Just as the doors slid close behind them, he pressed on the emergency button to stall the elevator and said, "What did you just say?"

"Jin Ae!" Yoori cried. "Chae Young said that Jin Ae was there and she was trying to force Chae Young to call me so that I would come meet her alone!"

Anger rose through her as Tae Hyun's eyes widened in fury.

Jin Ae was taking her revenge.

She was taking her revenge on Yoori for having to kneel before her that night.

"I'm going to kill her," Yoori declared ruthlessly. The image of Chae Young crying at the diner and crying on her hospital bed was like fuel to the fire. Wrath poisoned her rationale. "I don't care if she's Ju Won's niece. I'm going to kill that bitch!"

"Yoori, stop!" Tae Hyun shouted, though his eyes were also severe with anger. "If you want someone dead then *I'll* take care of it! Ju Won won't be able to touch me if I kill her, but he'll be able to send people after you if you hurt her. I won't risk that."

"I don't give a fuck about Ju Won!" Yoori shouted hysterically. For her, it was just black and white. There was no gray area in wanting to kill Jin Ae for what she put Chae Young through.

"I don't give a fuck about him either!" Tae Hyun bellowed out. "I give a fuck about you!"

Yoori wasn't able to see reason in his argument. She was too blinded with her emotions.

"She did this to Chae Young! You weren't there to see how Chae Young was! You weren't there to see the fear in her eyes! You weren't there to see how amazed she was that she was still alive and how much she *hated* that she was still alive! All of this happened to her because Jin Ae wanted me! She had *eleven* men rape Chae Young because she knew that it would kill *me*! All of this happened to Chae Young because…because…of *me*."

Yoori's own words hit her like a ton of bricks, finally pushing her over the edge she had been trying so hard to hang on to. She covered her mouth and started to hyperventilate. Tears bubbled in her eyes.

"All of this happened because *I* brought her into this world. It happened because *I* was her friend. It happened because she was there to help me bake a cake. She was raped because of me. Me. It's all my fault."

"Yoori, stop. Stop saying that," Tae Hyun voiced when he saw the state of misery she was falling into. "She wouldn't have made it if you hadn't gone back."

Yoori wasn't listening. "She was late…she stayed late at the diner because she was helping me bake your cake." Her heart twisted in knots. "And Kang Min and I left her…all alone while we laughed in the car and drove away."

Yoori could see it all so clearly. She could see herself laughing and smiling with Tae Hyun on the balcony while on the other end of the city, Chae Young was begging and crying as those fuckers raped her.

The air escaped her.

"It's all my fault…this is all my fault."

That was the last thing Yoori said to herself before her body finally gave up on her. It was the last thing Yoori said before darkness consumed her and before she fell unconscious into Tae Hyun's arms.

"You can't keep me in the dark anymore."

28: Betrayal of Gods

"You have to eat," Tae Hyun whispered, gathering her long hair away from her face and letting it drift to the other side.

Crouched on the floor beside her, he gazed at her with gentle puppy dog eyes that she knew he was purposely giving her. He had just brought soup to her for the fifth time today. "Please?"

It had been about a day since Yoori passed out in the elevator. She had been dazed out of her mind and hadn't had much of an appetite to eat. She hadn't even been able to visit Chae Young because she was afraid of breaking out in another hysterical fit that would merit her passing out again. The last thing any of them needed was for her to be stuck in a hospital bed.

The afternoon snow glowed elegantly outside their bedroom window, yet it failed to harmonize with the disarray Yoori was feeling.

"I'm not hungry," she mumbled, lying on her stomach with the pillow underneath her. Her eyes were still on the white bedspread. She hadn't been as hysterical as the day before, but the guilt was still there with her—along with other thoughts that continued to drown her.

The fact that Chae Young was tortured because of her, the fact that she went crazy and killed a bunch of gang members, the fact that she couldn't get rid of this queasy feeling, the fact that she was still so angry that she could rip off Jin Ae's head if she ever saw her again, the fact that she was still worried about her relationship with Tae Hyun, the fact that she felt An Soo Jin was slowly but surely devouring her, and the fact that she was still in the Underworld...everything in her life was simply *drowning* her.

The only one who wasn't drowning her was Tae Hyun.

Throughout this whole ordeal, he had been by her side. He had sat in bed with her as she spoke about her guilt, as she slept away her sorrow, and as she wallowed in her own misery. Yoori had always prayed that she would be one of those people who could stand strong and continue on with their lives when tribulations came their way. But as she slept in bed with her comforter covering her, she couldn't deny that she was only strong enough to wallow.

Everything was too much for her.

She needed time to be in her own state of misery.

It hadn't occurred to Yoori that Tae Hyun had been indirectly wallowing along with her until she returned her gaze to him.

"Have you eaten yet?" she asked.

It wasn't possible that he did. She had been in his arms all day. If she didn't eat, she doubted he had a chance to eat.

She reached out and ran her fingers down his cheek. He was dressed in his pajamas, just as she was. The heater was on full blast in their apartment so he was only wearing a white shirt and his black lounge pants. He looked pale. There were dark circles under his eyes and he looked extremely exhausted. If there was a mirror, Yoori was sure she looked exactly like him.

"No," he answered, confirming her assumption. He smiled lightly at her. Even under the veil of lethargy, he still looked like her personal fallen angel. It was weird for Yoori. Even after having the official "boyfriend and girlfriend" label, they were still the same two people. Nothing changed with the exception that they could touch and kiss each other without having to have a conversation about "sexual harassment".

Yoori sighed. She unthinkingly poked at the lips she loved so much. "Why haven't you eaten?"

She pulled her poking finger away just as those enticing lips parted.

"I don't have much of an appetite when my girlfriend is in bed, wallowing in her own misery and starving herself," he answered gently, laying his chin on the bed. He continued to stare up at her with his puppy dog eyes.

Yoori frowned at his bluntness and the cuteness exuding out of him. She still felt fragmented with confusion, but it was easily melting away. Being around Tae Hyun always had that effect on her. He always had that innate ability to make her feel better.

"I'm allowed days like this where I can just be miserable in bed," she shared weakly, still intent on not eating.

"Then I'm allowed to be miserable with you," he swiftly retorted, though she could see in his expression that it was hard for him to see her like this.

Yoori smiled tightly at his comment. "You dummy. Why are you punishing yourself?"

"You're the dumb one who's punishing yourself first," he argued, tracing his fingers over her pale face. He sighed. "You can't change what happened and blaming yourself isn't going to help. *None* of this was your fault. You couldn't have known what was going to happen. If you knew even the slightest bit, do you think you would have allowed it to happen?"

Yoori knew what he said was true, yet she couldn't deny that the entire situation continued to weigh her down.

"I just have so much on my mind," she said honestly, the guilt having yet to leave her.

"I know you do."

336

"And I'm already so *fed up* with all of it. I'm not punishing myself. I'm just…not hungry."

"Fine, you little *Brat*." Tae Hyun sighed, officially giving up. Weary from another one of his failed attempts to get her to eat, Tae Hyun lifted himself onto the bed, draped one arm over her comforter-covered tummy and wrapped one leg over her legs.

"I guess I'm not hungry either then," he told her after he brushed his lips against the side of her neck. Yoori restrained the satisfied whimper that fought to emit from her lips. Was he trying to seduce her into eating?

Yoori only sprung out of her daze when she heard his stomach growl. She frowned again. She could feel him smile guiltily when the growl burst into the room. She guessed that he got close to her so that she would hear it. Tae Hyun always had his creative quirks when it came to trying to make her feel better. Apparently, convincing her to eat by starving himself was also a tactic of his.

Fortunately for him, it worked.

She turned her body around to meet his face. "If I eat, you eat?"

She wasn't hungry, but she would eat for him.

He nodded. The breathtaking smile illuminated on to his lips, causing her to smile too. The guy was too charming for his own good.

"Okay," she conceded. "I'll eat now then."

She sat upright and reached for the soup on the counter. It escaped her grasp when Tae Hyun was right beside it, holding the white bowl in his hands.

"It's gotten cold," he told her. "I'll warm it up for you first. Just drink the tea I made you."

He picked up the teapot from a red tray and poured tea for her.

Yoori grinned at the strings of aroma wiggling out of the red teacup. It was the tea she loved.

He handed Yoori the teacup and rushed out to warm up her soup. "I'll be right back."

She pulled off the comforter and hung her legs over the edge of the bed. She drank the tea. Though it had only been a day since she became a zombie, she could've sworn it felt like it had been decades since she rested on that bed in misery. She pushed away all the horrible thoughts that were beginning to plague her and just thought about the one good thing in her life.

Tae Hyun.

Tae Hyun was the only thing that pushed all the nightmares aside. He was the only thing in her life that made her smile. Yoori grinned gratefully, feeling fortunate to have him by her side. Just then, her hold on the teacup loosened and before she could catch it, the teacup fell to the floor.

Sounds of broken glass spilled into the room as the content of the warm tea and remnants of the teacup polluted the tiles.

Yoori groaned to herself and gazed up at the half opened doorway. The sound was loud, but if the microwave was on, she doubted Tae Hyun heard it. She jumped off the bed, leaned down and carefully reached under the mattress to retrieve the big cracked piece. It had rolled underneath the bed. While under there, she touched something else and pulled it out.

Yoori laughed to herself when the mystery object came into view.

It was Tae Hyun's red hat, the one he wore when they first met. It felt like it had been ages since that fateful moment. Her face lit up as she ran her finger over the curves of the brand new hat. Then, like a light bulb going off, a sudden thought dawned over Yoori...

"Well, you should've worn a hat or something!" she remembered yelling at him after their movie date.

"Well then maybe we shouldn't watch a movie like that next time because I hate wearing hats."

If Tae Hyun hated wearing hats so much, why did he wear a brand new hat when he first met her? Her thoughts went into overdrive and her memory of when she first saw Chae Young again at the grocery store came into view.

"...All we had was the surveillance tape of you talking to some guy in a red cap and you following him after he left seconds later," Chae Young had said to her.

Surveillance camera...

The Underworld was all about confidentiality. Tae Hyun would only wear a baseball hat if he knew beforehand that the diner had a security camera. He would only know if he had planned to come into the diner all along...

Then, Yoori remembered that he ordered coffee. Yet, for as long as she had been with him, he never once drank coffee. The memory of when she spilled coffee on him was her next recollection.

"What the hell is wrong with you?" he shouted, rubbing his hands together in agony.

"I'm—I'm so sorry!" she cried, genuinely apologetic. She grabbed a handful of napkins from the dispenser and started drying his red-hot hands with them. It was true that Yoori didn't like the guy, but she never wished to harm him like this! This was what she got for talking shit about someone in her head. Her vision became blurred with confusion as she tried to make sense of what happened. "Th—th—the handle just suddenly broke—I...oh God...are you okay?"*

She looked at his hands. They were blazing red.

She only left the coffee pot alone with him for a few seconds. Was it possible that he did something to it in such a short time span? Like a sequential effect, the rest came to her as easily as one domino falling on the other. The night when he broke into her apartment and cuffed her for the first time came into her mind.

"Look," he started, staring into her eyes while he slid a bit closer to make peace. "I'm ready to get past this. Can you come back to work?"*

Yoori gawked at him. After all that happened, he still wanted her back? Mystification assailed her. Did this guy need an assistant that badly?

He stared at her expectantly, those enticing brown eyes holding her gaze. "Please?"

Out of everyone, he just wanted her so badly. And he would need her because...

The moment she first met Jae Won entered her mind.

Tae Hyun spared a glance at Yoori.

She was still staring uncomfortably at Jae Won.

"This is just the tip of the iceberg. Take a long and hard look at everything. Realize who is on our side and why we are the best."

And just as the door swung open, Yoori's world tilted on its axis. Her stomach twisted in agonizing knots.

No...

It couldn't be possible...it couldn't be possible...

"Hey, just sit down. I'll take care of it."

In an instant, Tae Hyun was by her side, pushing her away from the broken glasses while dousing the tiles with paper towels.

Yoori sat on the bed and watched Tae Hyun carefully. Her lips had grown numb from shock. Her eyes lingered upon him, the only one who had been there for her since she was first introduced to this world. The one she shared so many laughs, so many secrets, and so much trust with.

Now, for the first time, she felt that she didn't know him anymore. For the first time, she felt like she was staring at a stranger instead of her Tae Hyun.

She thought back to the secret Tae Hyun promised he'd share with her, the secret he feared would be so horrible that she wouldn't be able to look at him afterward. After everything that happened to her, Yoori couldn't help but feel her heart clench itself in fear. It was as if it was begging her to not dig any deeper into all this. It was as if it was begging her not to say anything because it needed Tae Hyun so much.

"Tae Hyun," she prompted tentatively. The next words boiled in her throat, begging to be set free. She couldn't be in the dark anymore.

"Hmm?" he responded distractedly. He had just picked up the broken glass and was placing it on the damp paper towel.

"If you could explain to me how you were raised to be the person you are...to justify the things that you have done...what would you say to me?"

She wanted to understand everything. She wanted to understand why he did the things that he did.

A piece of glass pricked his finger just when she asked this.

Paying no mind to the cut, Tae Hyun gazed up, his eyes cloaked with turbulence when he finally noticed the red hat she was holding in her hands.

It was clear that he wasn't mentally prepared for this.

"Yoori—"

"It's an experiment," Yoori assured, feigning a light smile when she sensed his need to stall the conversation. "To see how well I know you since we've met."

She noted the stress exuding out of his once carefree stature. Tae Hyun rarely got nervous and he seldom showed it. This moment was a rarity.

"I don't—"

"Just humor me. Please?" Yoori insisted with another one of her bright smiles. "What is the typical thing you say to someone you've just recruited?" Once she saw the obvious uncertainty in his eyes, she smiled wider. "*Please?*"

She needed this moment to prepare for what was to come. She needed this moment to just be with him for a little while longer before the downpour of emotions rippled around her and drowned her.

"There's a list of rules...that has been passed down from Underworld Kings to Underworld Kings," he began apprehensively. So many emotions twisted in his eyes, yet she couldn't read any of them. "I was taught to memorize it when I started my training at ten-years-old. It's a series of statements that I, as well as other Royals, repeat to ourselves every morning."

"Can you share it with me?"

Tae Hyun was unreceptive to the request.

"I think you should eat first and rest. We can talk about this another day...when you're feeling better," he amended delicately.

He picked up the broken glasses with the damp paper towel, walked out, and tossed it into the trash outside before he returned to the room.

He was picking up the bowl of soup for her when Yoori said, "How about I eat while you tell me?"

She wouldn't let him push it to another day. Their agreement was that he would tell her the day after she agreed to be his girlfriend. He was supposed to tell her the day she found Chae Young in the diner.

That day had long passed.

The nerves in his jaw clenched. When it was clear that he was backed into a corner, Tae Hyun nodded stiffly, picked up the bowl and walked over to her. He sat on the side of the bed with her, picked up the silver spoon, dug into the soup, and fed Yoori her first spoonful. The heat of the soup warmed her tongue when he spoke.

"Our world is different from the rest," he said just as she chewed some meat and vegetable from the soup.

It took all of her control not to free the sob from her chest once she heard the strain in his voice—the guilt echoing from him. The strain confirmed that all of her speculations were accurate. He really *had* been using her since the beginning. How ironic was it that she knew him well enough to detect guilt in his voice, yet she hadn't known he was using her all along?

340

"Some people find themselves stumbling into it whether willing or unwillingly..."

"How did you fall into it?" Yoori asked when she sensed his hesitation to continue. She parted her lips for the soup, her additional silent encouragement for him to go on.

"I was born into it," he answered wearily, feeding her another spoonful of soup. His face was paler now, completely drained of color. "That's why I'm here right now. That's why I have this much power. That's why I can do whatever I want."

Yoori nodded while she swallowed her soup, understanding that indeed he did have so much power in this world.

"To be the leading hand in this world, you have to be flexible with your morals. You can't allow yourself to be weak. You have to be able to punish people without fear."

She also understood the lengths he was willing to go to further extend his power. Kwon Tae Hyun would sacrifice anything for power and using Yoori like she was an object was no exception to his determination.

"Wrong or right, you have to stick by your decisions. Because if you don't...you'd end up destroying yourself. You can never forgive the ones who betrayed you. You have to make an example of them by reminding them what you're capable of."

He betrayed her. From the beginning, he betrayed her and this comprehension tortured Yoori. She swallowed past the tears rising through her as she thought about the feelings she had for him.

Tae Hyun would never know the things he did to her, how much power he had over her. And now, to realize how that power was contrived, how it was purposeful instead of natural, Yoori couldn't have felt more betrayed. She not only felt stupidity, but she also felt immeasurable pain for this duplicity. Before she could help it, tears had already bubbled in her eyes as Tae Hyun fed her another spoonful of soup.

The truth hurts...

"Notoriety is everything. Make sure that they will never betray you again...finish them off. Remember this step...it's the most important one."

He swallowed miserably when he saw the tears bubble in her eyes. It looked like someone had just stabbed him in the chest. Yoori wondered what he felt terrible about. Was he miserable because she was crying or because he was caught?

He stopped talking and was silent with guilt until Yoori parted her mouth and waited patiently for another spoonful of soup. It was her quiet and *painful* way of telling him to go on—to finish telling her the list of Underworld guidelines as she gathered her final strength for the turbulent conversation to come.

Tae Hyun went on with difficulty. "Kindness...is overrated. You have to be able to kill people like they are worth nothing. Even when you know for a fact, that's not true. You have to...show no remorse. If you show just an ounce of weakness...just one ounce...then you're done in this world."

He showed her kindness. That was why she fell for him. She thought he was different. She thought *she* was different. She thought she had changed him and that she had touched a part of his soul. It was a silly wish on a hopeful girl's part and now, she was paying for her naivety.

He used her.

He was able to use her because she was worth nothing to him.

She wasn't different.

She was just worthless.

"That's why I am one of the best..." He exhaled in pain when he saw the first teardrop fall from her eye.

Tae Hyun's betrayal...it was more painful than anything a knife or a bullet could ever hope to inflict on her. Hurt, humiliation and anger...was it possible for a single teardrop to contain all those emotions?

"It's truly a terrible thing," he added, his voice breaking faintly when he watched tears ease out of her eyes. "Terrible how unjust this world can be."

No longer able to hold back, Tae Hyun reached out with the sole intent of wiping her tears away...*to hold her in his arms perhaps...*

Yoori wouldn't have any of it. She backed away from a worried Tae Hyun and crashed hard onto the headboard behind her. She refused to allow him to touch her. The strings of her heart twisted in agonizing knots. God help her if he touched her. If he showed her more thoughtfulness, then she would never be able to do what she had to do.

"It is only unjust for the people who kneel before you," Yoori finally breathed out with difficulty. "But just like all things in life, you should know that what goes around comes around."

Her gaze became colder.

"No world can be unjust for so long. For every lie...there is a truth. For every injustice...there is revenge. For every empire...there is a downfall. For every temptation...there is a God who falls." She smirked. "Just because you're more powerful than human, just because the world kneels before you...does not mean you're exempt from the cruelties of life."

Her eyes ran over his taut face. "You're merely living on borrowed time. You're merely at the end of your rope. Rest assured...you will not always be this powerful. The time will come when you will have to step down from being a God and become human again. And when that time comes, you won't only have to face your demons...but you'll also have to answer to the people you've hurt."

She leveled her eyes with his.

"Your time has come," Yoori prompted decisively, swallowing past the lump of tears and fury rising through her.

Her once weakened eyes became cold, *unforgiving*.

Their borrowed time was up.

"You can't keep me in the dark anymore. It's time you told your side of the story."

"It's time you told your side of the story."

29: The Separation of Gods

"Was it your plan all along?" Yoori incited without delay. She had no more inclination to beat around the bushes. "To steal Ji Hoon's girl? To use An Soo Jin's lookalike to help you get to the top? To secure your position as the next Lord of the Underworld?"

She watched him rise quietly to his feet. Walking over to the shelf, he placed the soup bowl above it. His back was turned to her as if to gather his nerves for everything to come. It was like he was preparing himself for an impending storm.

He turned around, his countenance paled with nothing but desolation. His enrapturing brown eyes held hers. There was nothing but unease in his gaze. Though all of this was seemingly difficult for him, he looked more than ready to tell her the truth.

"The plan was never to steal you from Ji Hoon. That thought didn't cross my mind when I first saw you."

Yoori ignored the whip of pain that slapped her face once she *finally* heard his words of confirmation—once he finally confirmed that everything was planned from the beginning.

It was like she was living in a nightmare she couldn't wake up from.

"When did you first see me?" Yoori asked swiftly, moving the conversation along before her emotions got the best of her.

"I saw you two weeks before I met you at the diner," Tae Hyun admitted, standing across from her.

He never appeared more human to her than at that moment. With all the power he had in this world, he didn't have enough power to change the past. He didn't have enough power to change the mistakes that would scar them forever. It was ironic. Their entire relationship was ironic.

"You were sitting on a bench in the business district, reading a book when you caught my eye. I didn't know who you were, but I couldn't take my eyes off of you. It wasn't until the Serpents beside me caught sight of you, did they tell me that you were An Soo Jin."

Yoori smirked to herself. So there was actually a moment in time where he knew of her existence long before she ever knew of his…

"And even then, I didn't believe it. I had never met Soo Jin, so I wouldn't know right from left when it came to her, but I knew the things an Underworld Royal would do. I asked them, 'Why the hell would An Soo Jin hang out in the busy business district when she was supposed to be dead?' I really believed that you were just someone who resembled Soo Jin. It was too ironic that you were out there in the open for everyone to see and you were so aloof about it. So I dismissed it as nothing. I dismissed it as nothing, but I had a couple of my Serpents keep an eye on you." He shamefully looked away when he said the next part. "I stumbled upon an An Soo Jin lookalike. I made sure to keep a close leash on you just in case I ever needed you in the future."

Her chest tightened, the air around her becoming insufficient.

"...just in case I ever needed you in the future..."

His words taunted her.

How was it possible that this was the same person who stole her heart? The very same person who made her feel so much love? The emotions bearing down on her were overwhelming, but she endured it. She had to listen to everything before she allowed her emotions to drown her.

He went on with difficulty, like he could sense the toll it was taking on her. Even then, she could see the concern for her bubble in his eyes.

"Then two weeks after, I saw on the news that the Skulls had left a carnage of dead gang members in a building in Echo District. Ji Hoon had carved a Skull onto each of their cheeks, an infamous branding technique that he always employs to promote his gang. The move went against all the bylaws pertaining to our confidentiality, but it was effective enough to propel his position above mine."

His expression hardened at the mention of Ji Hoon and the predicament he found himself in.

"I couldn't have that and I knew how to blow him out of the water. There was a small gang, one that would overshadow any recruits he may have gotten from that publicity stunt."

He swallowed tightly.

"I had long tried to get Jae Won's gang under my wings. His gang was small, no harm to me if he never joined, but because he was *personally* trained by Soo Jin...because he was Soo Jin's right-hand man, he had skills that no other small-time gang leader possessed. Even in small numbers, the Dragons were respected and I knew I needed them by my side to supersede any recruits Ji Hoon may have gotten from Echo District's carnage. But I knew Jae Won's type. I knew even under the cloak of death, he wouldn't bow down to me...not unless I had someone by my side who commanded his respect—*his loyalty.*"

His eyes met hers. They were gentle and caring as they always were whenever they gazed at her. Yet as Yoori stared back into his eyes, she didn't feel any warmness. All she felt was immeasurable pain and betrayal.

"You were the key to all of that. I would've needed you by my side for a few short months until the merger settled. When I went back to the diner to get you, I had two of my men walk into the sea of people coming out of the subway to identify you once more to make sure that you actually resembled Soo Jin. One of them had bumped into you and sure enough, by how he was shaking in fear, you resembled her enough to make fearful cowards out of them. So I had them go ahead. I had them go find Jae Won first and told them that I would bring you later and I'd get the merger I wanted."

"You wore the hat because of the security cameras," she noted mindlessly, ignoring the throb of anger in her voice.

He nodded morosely. "I knew who worked there and I knew that there were security cameras there. In the timeframe that I had you, I knew I had to get you out of there fast so I did the only thing I knew would work quickly: I had to blackmail you and force you out of there."

"What did you do to the coffee pot?"

"Unscrewed it...very quickly before you came back so that it would be more than ready to shatter on to my hands when you lifted it up."

"What would you have done if I didn't leave that coffee pot there for you?"

"Something else," he answered faintly. "My end plan was to get you to leave with me. How I went about it wouldn't have mattered."

Yoori snorted resentfully before something crossed her bitter mind. "You said the plan was never to 'steal Ji Hoon's girl.' So why did you bring me to the warehouse to meet him?"

"Because I was angry when he left that voicemail of my sister," Tae Hyun answered at once, his voice touched with enduring anger. "I hate him more than anything and for him to leave such a disgusting voicemail for me, I couldn't think. All I saw was anger and all I saw was my revenge when I saw you sitting on the couch. My original plan was to bring you to the warehouse for him to see me with you—to kill him with jealousy that the love of his life was with me. But when the time drew near, I had a change of heart. I grew protective over you. Even then, I had already grown attached to you. That was why I had you wait for me in that limo...because I didn't want you to meet him and I didn't want to wrap you up in our mess."

He smirked bitterly. "Obviously that planned changed when you came running back for me. When despite my efforts to keep you away, you were there regardless, helping me—someone who pretty much blackmailed you into slavery."

Yoori heard the chaotic emotions in his voice and she knew that was the moment when she made her impact on him.

It was probably the moment where she found a place in his heart.

Ignoring the twinge of hope surging through her that perhaps they could look pass all of this, that Tae Hyun genuinely fell for her, she went on, her stubborn mind eager to find out everything before she allowed her emotions to erupt.

"Why have me as your assistant?"

"I didn't want to involve any emotions into it. I only needed you for a couple of months. I made you my assistant because I needed you by my side at all times. I needed you with me to continue to demand Jae Won's loyalty. It was just supposed to be for a couple of months. After things got settled, I figured I could just pay you and send you on your way."

Her hopes were again dashed after hearing this. *"...pay you and send you on your way..."* Pay her like she was a rental car used only for his personal amusement. The cruelty and selfishness of his plan offended her on all levels.

His face softened once he noticed the pain coursing through her expression. They knew each other long enough that Tae Hyun could read the emotions streaming throughout her entire body. He knew she felt that he only saw her as something worthless and he was determined to convince her that she had always meant more to him.

"It was *never* part of the plan to fall for you. I used all the power at my disposal to keep that from happening because even subconsciously, I knew you were going to be my downfall. I kept trying to distance myself from you, yet I could never go far because I always yearn to be around you. You were like a drug...an addiction I couldn't kick no matter how hard I tried."

He saw her shake her head, the anger boiling within her streaming out.

"Yoori, please don't look at me like that," he whispered, running his fingers through his hair in frustration. "I was a different person then. I've changed since then when it comes to you."

As if pained by the fact that she had already emotionally distanced herself from him, he tried to reach out to her.

"I trusted you from the beginning," Yoori instead seethed, jumping off the bed and backing away from Tae Hyun. Rage pumped in her blood. She couldn't let him touch her anymore, not after all that he had done to her.

"I had always believed that you would never hurt me. I had always believed that you were the good guy in this world. When others told me not to trust you, I blew them off because I didn't feel that they would know you better than me — because *I'm* the one around you constantly." She laughed self-mockingly. "Yet you've been using me since the beginning...you've *lied* to me since the beginning."

Wrath was rising through her and she wanted nothing more than to lash out at him.

She hated him.

She hated him so much.

"I had planned on telling you sooner, but something gets in the way of it every time." Confliction coursed in his voice. "I knew I had to tell you. I just wanted to find the right time for you when you were ready."

"When you were ready." Yoori wanted to laugh at those words. Who would've been ready for all this? Fury spiked within her, the first spark that would inevitably cause her to explode. She shook her head once she thought of all those times they spent together, all their silly moments. It was all tainted now. It was all tainted with his lies.

"You bastard..." Yoori finally hissed. The weight of everything falling apart in her little world spilled upon her.

"YOU FUCKING BASTARD!"

She lost it when her hands collided with his chest.

"You brought me into this world just because you wanted to get the fucking merger your gang needed?!"

She pushed against him, causing him to slam against the shelf where the soup once sat. It fell with a loud crash, the content of the soup and glass crashing on to their bare feet. She felt her feet bleed. She ignored it and continued to shove him. Anger overtook her.

"You're the reason for all of this!" she screamed at the top of her lungs. "You're the reason why my life is being put through hell! You're the reason why the Advisors are after me again!"

She continued to push him because he allowed her too, because even then, she saw in his eyes that he knew he deserved every abuse she wanted to give him. Yoori continuously shoved Tae Hyun against the shelf, all the contents above it crashing down in a million pieces. Their bare feet bled profusely at the millions of glass eating at their skins.

"You're the reason why Chae Young was raped—because people like Jin Ae are after me now! You're the reason why I'm here right now! EVERYTHING THAT HAS FUCKED UP IN MY LIFE WAS THE RESULT OF YOU! THE RESULT OF *YOU* AND YOUR GREED!"

She was falling apart, *exploding*. Her last shred of sanity was Tae Hyun. Her last shred of sanity was the one who stole her heart and now...having realized he was only using her...like an object all along...it pushed her...completely pushed her over the edge.

"HOW COULD YOU DO THIS TO ME?" Her was voice heavy with shrill as she stared at his pale face.

He was speechless, his expression completely broken while he stared at her in misery.

Her vision blurred, not because she was ready to faint, but because it was tears that were blurring her vision. She was crying. She was fucking crying again. She didn't even realize she was crying until she tasted the saltiness of her tears. She didn't realize she was crying until she saw the unfathomable pain in Tae Hyun's eyes, his distress that she had been pushed beyond all boundaries of emotions.

"Me? Of all people you did this to *me!*" The sobs spilled out of her chest and into her broken voice. "After all we've been through, how could you do this to me?"

"You don't think all of this kills me right now?" Tae Hyun finally shouted back, his expression torn apart from agony. "You don't think I know that every time you're in pain or every time you're crying now…it's because of that fucking decision I made in the beginning?"

He tried to reach out to her again, yet she escaped from his hold, causing him to breathe in pain while he stared at her longingly.

"I would do anything for you," he went on agonizingly. "And the sole fact that I can't stop you from hurting right now is killing me more than you'll ever know."

"Stop…just stop…" The tears wouldn't stop when she finally backed away from him. It wouldn't stop echoing from her chest as she pressed her fists against her stomach. It wouldn't stop. The pain…the betrayal…the anger…*none* of it stopped.

"It rips me apart every time I think back to the moment I brought you into this world." His soothing words were like knives to her. It tore at her soul. "It rips me apart every time to know that I'm the reason why your life is being put through hell right now. If I could go back in time and prevent that moment from happening, I would! If I knew what I know now, then I would've never placed you through all this pain because you're worth more to me than this world."

"Stop lying to me!" Yoori screamed, suddenly tossing the teapot in his direction. She didn't even realize that she had held on to it for leverage.

It scarcely missed and barreled into the wall behind him, spilling out water and broken glass that nipped the side of his neck before falling to the floor. He didn't even try to move out of the way. The surface wound on his neck started to bleed. He paid no mind to it and desperately tried to reach out to her.

"Stop it! JUST STOP IT!" Having enough, Yoori dodged out of his reach and was out of the bedroom before Tae Hyun could get a hold of her.

It didn't matter that they didn't know each other in the beginning. It didn't matter that he didn't know her. None of that mattered because for Yoori, his lies since the beginning tainted everything she had with him. All the wonderful memories…all the laughter…all the hope…everything was tainted now.

How was she supposed to look at him when he didn't have the decency to tell her all of this when she bared her soul to him the other night? There were so many chances for him to confess to her, plenty of chances for him to be honest with her. Yet he waited…waited until fate grew impatient and had her confront him instead.

She ran past the living room where unlit candles and icicle lights continued to adorn not only the room, but also the balcony outside. Yoori recalled the cakes they both forgot on the balcony, the Red Velvet cake she made him and the Oreo

Cookies and Cream ice cream cake he bought her. The memory pained her and was her catalyst for wanting to leave as soon as possible. She couldn't be with him anymore. She couldn't even look at him without feeling her chest tighten in anguish. It felt like it had been a lifetime ago since they promised each other that they'd find Paris together.

What a joke all that had been.

Yoori ran into the hall and made it onto the first landing of stairs when she felt Tae Hyun wrap his hand around her wrist, jerking her back into his arms.

"Yoori, please don't be like this."

She heard the desperation in his voice and felt the desperation in his hold. He was worried about her safety and he was worried about losing her. It was agonizing just to hear the care in his voice. It was a double-edged sword. It reminded her of the happiness she felt with him and reminded her of the fact that none of it was real. She had been the fool all along.

"Get away!" She fought against his grasp. "Get the fuck away from me!"

Yoori missed a step off the stairs and nearly lost her balance. She was able to catch herself with the railing before she tumbled out of sight and before Tae Hyun could reach down to grab her. Breathing heavily, she narrowed her eyes up to Tae Hyun. He was now standing five steps above hers, staring down at her helplessly.

"Get away from me," she ordered, backing down the stairs without looking back.

She kept her eyes on him. Even through her relentless anger, she saw the concern in his eyes. She knew he was worried about her, the state she was in, and how careless she was being with herself. They were still high up. If she fell, then it was likely she would break something.

He wouldn't allow that.

"Okay," Tae Hyun compromised, standing frozen on the stairs with his hands raised up in surrender. "I won't come any closer. Just walk down the stairs safely and I won't come any closer."

She knew he was lying to her—that he was just trying to make sure she was safe on solid ground before he chased after her again. She knew, but she didn't care. Without uttering another word, she turned around and sprinted off the stairs, running around every curve on the landing. She pushed the doors out into the lobby. As soon as her bloody feet touched the lobby tiles, she heard his descending footsteps and she knew he would catch up to her if she didn't pick up her pace.

So she ran, pushing people out of her way as she flew through the revolving door. Nothing mattered anymore. Her heart, her body, her soul...it didn't matter that all aspects of her essence were *begging* to be returned to Tae Hyun. The pain vibrating to the depths of her soul...the sobs threatening to escape from her chest...*nothing* mattered but getting away from him.

The weather was unforgiving when she ran out. Her bare feet instantly punctured holes into the snow beneath her heels. Her own bloody footprints followed her as the ice ate at her wounds.

Snow was raining down on the world beneath it, disturbing the hectic traffic on the street and blinding pedestrians who were walking around frantically, trying to get from point A to point B while holding on to their umbrellas. The wind was heavy, causing Yoori to tumble in her stance a couple of times.

Wearing nothing but a thin gray sweater and black pajama pants, Yoori felt all the cold, but it was bearable to her. Nothing could be as unforgiving as the betrayal and humiliation she felt.

"AHHH!" A group of people cried when she barreled past them, nearly knocking a couple of them off the curb and into oncoming traffic.

Desperate with nothing but the desire to escape, Yoori jumped off the sidewalk and into the hectic traffic. *Taxi, taxi, taxi*...She needed a taxi. There weren't a lot of cars due to the threatening weather, but there was enough driving through.

"Yoori!" Tae Hyun's voice suddenly called out from behind her.

At once, his strong arm wrapped around her, pulling her toward him just as a red truck squealed to a stop before her. It stood inches from running her over if Tae Hyun hadn't pulled her out of the way.

"You stupid bitch!" A chubby man with a green trucker hat honked and shouted at Yoori. "Get the fuck out of the way or I'll kick you out myself!"

He looked like he was actually ready to get out of his truck and do it.

Unfortunately for him, Tae Hyun would have none of it.

"If you even touch a single *strand* of her hair, I'll skin you alive, you piece of shit!" Tae Hyun roared at him, his eyes breeding nothing but fire.

Tae Hyun weighed less than the man, but because his shirt more than showed his muscles, it was clear that he could rip the man apart in an instant if he wanted to.

Flinching at the growl in Tae Hyun's intimidating stature, the man fearfully jerked his car to the right, nearly crashing into another car as he drove away from them.

"Get off me!" Yoori shouted after the truck drove away.

"Yoori, stop it!" he yelled, wrapping his arms around her waist, holding her body tightly against him. Cars, bicyclists, and violent snow continued to whiz past them. "You're going to get hit by a car if you keep doing this!"

"Good!" Yoori cried impulsively. In vain, she tried to pull out of his hold. His strength was unyielding. "Isn't that how people get their memories back? By getting hit by cars?"

She was hysterical and she knew it, but fuck being rational! Why did she even care anymore? She had been played for a fool. She couldn't give a fuck about trying to act sane for the people around her. She wanted nothing more than to get hit by a car.

Maybe if everything worked out her way, she would get hit by a car and forget everything. She would be able to forget Soo Jin *and* Tae Hyun—the two people she hated the most. She would be able to forget about all the pain they both caused her. Or worse yet, she would get her memories back as Soo Jin. With the incalculable pain she felt, recalling her memories again wouldn't be such a bad idea if she could just forget about Tae Hyun. At the moment, Kwon Tae Hyun was the one person she hated the most.

"Fucking hell, Yoori!" Tae Hyun growled in frustration. "I'm not going to let you get hit by a car!"

"Yet you *cared* enough to use me like a fucking puppet, you power hungry bastard!"

He had enough.

"Yoori, look at me! Look at me!" he commanded, cupping his hands over her cheeks.

They panted together and much to her own horror, she felt her nerves calm as their eyes held one another's.

"I'm sorry," he whispered, his genuine remorse enhancing those simple yet heartfelt words.

For the first time since the eruption of her emotions, she saw his pain.

It mirrored hers.

Yoori shook her head again. "Did you know what I thought of when I woke up this morning?" she finally asked, her heart still racing with rage and pain. She may have felt his pain, but she felt her pain even more.

He was quiet, awaiting her answer.

Her torn eyes held his. Her lips quivered uncontrollably while she spoke, the words spilling out of her like it were pieces of her heart.

"I didn't think about the fact that I was An Soo Jin, I didn't think about Chae Young being raped because of me, I didn't think about the horror I felt after murdering eleven men...I didn't think about any of that when I woke up."

Tears choked her throat, breaking her voice apart.

"I thought about *you*. I thought about how lucky I am to have met you. How blessed I am to have you in my life." She laughed self-mockingly, tears streaming her face and mixing with the snow frosting over her. "I've been such a fool. I actually believed that we've fallen for each other...that everything between us was real. All this time, I thought the emotions I felt from Soo Jin was her hatred for you. All this time, I thought I was hesitant to be with you because she despised you. Yet I know now that I was only hesitant because I knew you were going to do this to me one day. I knew I was going to end up like this one day – betrayed and humiliated by you."

She bit her lips, looking away. She couldn't even look at him now without wanting to hit him *and* cry for him.

"Yoori..." Tae Hyun whispered, his voice full of anguish.

Even in anger, Yoori felt herself soothed by his voice. Even in anger, she continued to adore him. This fact alone killed her.

He pressed his forehead against hers, his eyes pleading for her understanding. "What happened the other night between us was *real*. Everything that we spoke about, everything that we promised each other...it was all real."

Yoori wanted to believe him, but she had no more hope left inside her. All she had was the strength of her anger. She had to leave him and she knew just how to make him let go of her.

"This is why you're Dong Min and Ju Won's favorite, aren't you?" Yoori accused.

Her voice was cruel and taunting in a way that only An Soo Jin could drawl out. She wanted to hurt him. She wanted to hurt him so he could never have the strength to break her again.

"Because you're just as manipulative as they are...because you would give up anything for your precious Underworld."

Just as she had anticipated, ache splashed over his face as her words stabbed into him. She went on, knowing well that she had to keep hurting him until he couldn't breathe anymore.

"This is why Ji Hoon isn't the favorite," she persisted, noting that he had grown tenser. It was as if he knew where she was heading with all of this. "Because he sacrificed himself for Soo Jin—because he loved her unconditionally. I should've thought about it better when he offered himself to me...when he promised me the world. But I know better now. I know that he loved her and he placed her above his position of power. He loved her...more than you could ever hope to love me."

A bitter, knowing smile appeared on her lips. Yet secretly, her heart ached at her cruel words.

"Your soul had long deteriorated before you promised me the world. It had long deteriorated when you decided to use me like I was worth nothing and play me like I was a stupid twit."

She allowed no emotions to cross her gaze once she saw the immense pain take over his eyes. She went on, further drilling the malicious words into him.

"You could try to be human all you want Tae Hyun, but you're nothing but a scarred demon—a heartless monster. And if I could do it over again..."

And then, she whispered words she didn't mean and words she knew would kill Tae Hyun. It was the only way he would let her go. It was the only way she could move on without him chasing after her and breaking her heart further.

"...I would've chosen Ji Hoon over you."

She knew it worked.

She knew it worked when she saw the misery devour his eyes. She knew it worked when she saw the wretchedness cascade over his pale face. She knew it worked when she felt her heart wrenched as he gazed at her, his pained eyes looking for emotions within her to detect if she was lying.

She kept her expression cool, icy.

And that was enough for him to assume that everything she said was the truth of how she felt. It was enough for him to realize that they were done.

His hold on her slackened and Yoori used the opportunity to pull out of his hold. When she retreated further into the street, she saw a woman walk out of a silver taxicab. She moved toward it and gave Tae Hyun one last cold stare.

It was a stare that hid the tears she was ready to shed and the yearning she continued to foster for him. How was it possible that she loved and hated someone so much?

"Stay out of my life."

And with that, Yoori got into the cab and rode off. She rode off, never looking back as she *finally* shed her cool exterior and sobbed her broken heart into her hands. She never looked back to see Tae Hyun standing there, blood drained from his somber face as he watched her drive away from him – as he watched her drive out of his life.

With nothing but tears blurring her vision, Yoori pulled a hand away from her mouth and quietly pinched herself. The pain of the pinch was nothing compared to the agonizing ache of her heart, yet she felt it nonetheless.

It wasn't a dream.

None of this was a dream.

It was all real.

The scars that Tae Hyun left on her…the scars on what was once their blossoming relationship…the scars of his lies…the scars she left on him…all these scars…

It all existed and it was all *painfully* and heart-wrenchingly real.

Their end, as she knew it, was undeniably real.

"Our society isn't a world where love conquers all."

30: The Return of Gods

Unknown City, Japan

Huff...
Huff...
Huff...

"I need to see him!" a blonde, Asian man in his late twenties shouted, stopping in front of the secluded white mansion.

There were guards all over surveying the perimeters of the two-story mansion and two guards at the door, both of whom blocked the path of the man who was now panting for air.

"He just got back," one of them answered, staring at him strangely.

"No, this is urgent. I have to see boss, *now*," the man said vehemently, pushing past the two guards.

He didn't wait for their agreement. Whatever it was, it was important enough that he didn't care to go through the procedure of visiting his own boss.

"Wait! He said he didn't want to be disturbed!"

The other bulky guard tried to pull him back, but the blonde man was able to charge into the mansion like a bull. He veered to the left of the mansion, knowing exactly where his boss would reside after coming home from a trip.

He ran into the dim living room where he found his boss, who wore a white dress shirt and black pants, sitting on a black leather couch with his wife. She was wearing a beige dress and his hand was caressing her flat stomach.

"PC, you better have a good reason for disturbing me when I'm with my wife," his boss said severely.

There were suitcases on the floor. It was clear he had just gotten back from a long trip.

PC straightened his black suit and began. "Boss, I've been trying to reach you these past couple of days—"

"Reception isn't accessible for the places I went," he whispered coolly. He sighed, looking up at him. "What is it, PC?"

"Boss, this is urgent. I have news from Seoul."

His boss smirked, already bored with the conversation. "What is it this time? Has Ju Won finally chosen his heir?"

"No, not about that," PC said swiftly. "It's more serious than that. Right now, there are rumors circulating in the Underworld about a girl who has appeared by the King of Serpents' side. The rumors stated that this same girl was the one who killed a bunch of gang members in an alley..."

His boss sighed, leaning against the couch while he held his wife's hand. "Why should I care who Kwon Tae Hyun's girlfriend is?"

PC went on, eager to get to the point. "One of them was stabbed with a broken beer bottle. One side of his cheek was completely torn up like fabric."

His boss stiffened suddenly at this information.

PC hastened to continue. "The same bottle was pierced through the temple of his forehead. His throat was slit and his penis was cut off too."

A dawning light of realization not only filtered into his boss's eyes, but into the eyes of his boss's wife as well.

PC continued, basking in the same realization. "It is said that she resembles..."

"*My baby sister*," his boss whispered, astonishment filling his voice.

Silence flooded the room as the two guards behind PC, along with his boss's wife, widened their eyes in sheer disbelief. Their eyes rested on their boss, whose composure remained as cool as ever.

Then, without another word, he stood up from the couch, grabbed his black jacket from the armchair of the couch and then helped his wife up.

His eyes held emotions that were seemingly unreadable.

"Young Jae..." his wife whispered, her eyes already heeding what he was ready to do. "Are you sure you want to go back?"

His answer came in the command he gave to his men.

"Gather the rest of the Scorpions," An Young Jae ordered sternly. "We're heading back to Seoul."

ABOUT THE AUTHOR

Con Template currently resides in California. When she is not outside with her DSLR capturing reality, you can find her in between realities when she is writing about a "Queen," a "Source," a "Decoder," a "Gatekeeper," and a "Magister."

She is working on the third book of the Welcome to the Underworld novels.

You can follow her at *contemplate13.wordpress.com* or *twitter.com/contemplate13*.

Printed in Poland
by Amazon Fulfillment
Poland Sp. z o.o., Wrocław

65156555R00211